Anne Marsh writes sexy [romances—because the w] [alpha male. She started wr] [from her job as a technica] [happily-ever-after trumpe] [North Carolina with her tw]

Cara Lockwood is the *USA TODAY* bestselling author of more than twenty-five books, including *I Do (But I Don't)*, which was made into a Lifetime Original movie. She's written the Bard Academy series for young adults, and has had her work translated into several languages around the world. Born and raised in Dallas, Cara now lives near Chicago with her husband and their five children. Find out more about her at caralockwood.com, 'friend' her on Facebook, Facebook.com/authorcaralockwood, or follow her on Twitter, @caralockwood.

HER INTERN

ANNE MARSH

DOUBLE DARE YOU

CARA LOCKWOOD

MILLS & BOON

First Published in Great Britain 2019
by Mills & Boon, an imprint of HarperCollins*Publishers*
1 London Bridge Street, London, SE1 9GF

Her Intern © 2019 Anne Marsh

Double Dare You © 2019 Cara Lockwood

ISBN-13: 978-0-263-27392-2

MIX
Paper from
responsible sources
FSC
www.fsc.org   FSC™ C007454

This book is produced from independently certified FSC™ paper
to ensure responsible forest management.
For more information visit www.harpercollins.co.uk/green.

Printed and bound in Spain
by CPI, Barcelona

HER INTERN

ANNE MARSH

MILLS & BOON

CHAPTER ONE

Lola

HELL IS A party where the hosts expect you to mingle, asking random strangers for obscene amounts of money. It feels like a bad joke. Hi, my name is Lola. I'll do anything for a million bucks. I have very few boundaries left, although anal or sex slave for a year are still out. Around me, a crowd of beautifully dressed people chat about their newest business projects and sip champagne from crystal flutes. Waiters in black tie circulate, offering trays of delicious nibbles. I don't fit in here, a nerdy girl engineer in the thrift-store little black dress that's my go-to for social functions requiring heels.

This is the glamorous side of Silicon Valley, the part featured in glossy business magazines starring successful, extroverted dealmakers. It's also a pond stocked with fat, captive fish and I need to toss in my line and pluck one out. Tonight's mixer isn't even one of the now-legendary venture capital parties where the VC boys make disgusting come-ons and would-be girl bosses choose between start-up funding and ethics. This is a perfectly respectable party for grown-ups.

Instead of schmoozing, I watch from the sidelines, clutching my champagne flute. I don't "people" well. People are best in small doses. Plus, the VC guys judge relentlessly from the moment I start my pitch. It's like a beauty pageant but without the fun tiaras. While trying not to fall over in my heels, I'm expected to produce insightful, thirty-second sound-bite answers about how the company I founded is going to contribute to The Greater Good and make tons of money in the process. Coding is so much easier.

So I'm pathetically grateful when I spot a familiar face. Maple weaves through the glittering throng toward me. She recently launched an online yoga wear company building on her brand as a successful athleisure influencer. After six months of swimming in the start-up waters myself, I know she'll succeed. She doesn't take *no* for an answer and, thanks to years as a principal for the San Francisco Ballet, she's happy standing out while everyone looks at her. Tonight, she's a flamingo in a sea of penguins. In her neon yellow bandage dress, white blazer and chunky, tasseled heels she looks like the million bucks I need so badly.

She clicks to a halt by my side, heels together, toes out in a perfect first position. "Hit me with tonight's plan."

Lists are awesome, and without a checklist of things to accomplish tonight, I'd just walk from one side of

the room to the other and go home. I hold up my phone
so she can see tonight's list.

Hunt down two venture capital groups
Introduce self to reps
Trade business cards
Be charming (heh)

Maple borrows my champagne before delivering
the bad news. "The partners from J&H have already
come and gone."

Well, poop. VC firms pick a very few companies
to invest in each year and most look for unicorns—
privately held start-ups worth a billion dollars or more.
Invest in the next social media sensation and you can
buy your very own tropical island (and a yacht and a
private jet) when it goes public. Calla, my start-up, is
worth more like a thousand bucks, and that's just because I bought good office furniture.

Move on, I remind myself. Start-up funding is like
speed dating. "Bayview Capital."

"Four o'clock." She points helpfully as I'm currently
sans glasses and can't see more than two feet in front of
me. While I plot the shortest, least-peopled course toward the Bayview guys, Maple hums under her breath
and scans the room. Her party game is dividing its suit-
wearing occupants into hypothetical *keep* and *discard*
piles. Some people apply Marie Kondo's organizational
theories to their closets and kitchen cabinets; Maple
applies those principles to men. Since she's in a com-
mitted relationship and I'm adamantly not, I'm the one

who's supposed to rummage through the keepers and pick someone fun. She refuses to believe me when I say I simply don't have time for a relationship right now.

Ten minutes later, I've located Bayview Capital's representative (wearing a lovely Hugo Boss suit), made painful but effective small talk and exchanged business cards. The basic premise of the networking event is simple. Collect business cards and make introductions, hoping to score a request to come back and interview for the big money during working hours.

Mission accomplished, I return to Maple, scanning the room for the nearest exit.

As always, Maple cuts straight to the chase. "Are you going already?"

Uh, hello? The room is pushing the fire marshal's stated limits. Leaving would be civic-minded. "I've had a glass of champagne, handed my business card to twenty-seven random strangers who gave me their cards thus promoting us to *casual business acquaintances* and met the people I came to meet. Why would I stay?"

Maple gazes at me patiently. "To have fun?"

I get the sense Maple is serious and not making a joke. I love to laugh as much as the next person, but challenged in the humor department? Yes, yes, I am. Clarification is required. "You want to stay here?"

"Let me sum up—free champagne, free food." She tucks her arm in mine, ensuring I can't escape without towing her like a boat anchor. Thirty seconds later, we're tucked into prime real estate—a padded window seat with picture-perfect views of downtown San Francisco and the city night lights. When I first moved here, I visited the aquarium on the Wharf and strolled through a huge glass tunnel while a dozen species of sharks and rays swam up checking me out. This feels remarkably similar except the sharks in this room aren't particularly interested in me. I'm the tiniest fish.

"This is a party, Lola." Maple mimics scanning the room like a sailor checking out the horizon. Probably for pirates. "There are hot guys here."

"Really?" Successful people possess many fine qualities, including drive, discipline and intelligence, but when God handed out looks, they'd been too busy standing in the drive, discipline and intelligence lines to score hotness.

"Yes." Maple nods vigorously. I'm pathetically jealous that her sleek ballerina bun doesn't so much as wiggle on top of her head. "How about that one? Does he spark joy in you? Would you keep him?"

The blurry blond guy on the other end of Maple's pointing finger is perfectly fine. Emphasis on *perfect*—perfect blue suit, perfectly coordinated navy blue tie, perfectly groomed hair with just the right amount of styling products to keep everything perfectly in place. He's a total sand shark. Dating needs to be less work. From the data points of my most recent Friday night experiences, choosing a random stranger ends in disappointment. Imagining the possibilities is more fun and less work.

Maple smacks my arm when I share this conclusion with her. "Pick better, then. How about that one? I'll bet he has a huge penis."

Her new choice is tall, dark and handsome. He's absolutely yummy even if he seems like the MBA type. My ovaries vow on the spot that he's smart, dependable and the best baby daddy ever. Mentally I check off cow shark in the game of mental shark bingo I'm playing with myself.

Maple sighs and nudges me in the side. "When's the last time you went out on a date or had *me* time?"

"I don't have time for a relationship." She's only trying to be helpful, but as much as I appreciate her concern, it also makes me want to run and hide in my very nice bed. I'm thirty-one, I'm the baby sister who's failed to make good (so far) and I've just founded my first company. I have time for nothing but work.

"Sex," Maple announces in her outside voice, cupping my face in her hands. *"Hot sex.* The only ring you have to put on it is one of those vibrating cock rings. When's the last time you had fun?"

"Never with a cock ring. It's like plugging up the bath and running the water full bore. The poor guy's blood has nowhere to go, so he's totally focused on what's going on down there because it's distracting as hell, and he has no choice but to keep it up. It's like a corset for dicks."

The waiter leaning in to offer us a new round of appetizers beats a hasty retreat.

Used to my verbal diarrhea, Maple just waits for me to finish. "If cock rings aren't your thing, find some other toy that you do like."

"Have I ever struck you as a playful person?"

"Practice," Maple deadpans. "You just need practice."

"I could practice until I was eighty. It wouldn't make me *fun*. I'm an engineer. I'm a nerd. I'm a freaking entrepreneur. And I like all that. I might not be fun, but I'm happy."

Am I 100 percent happy? Details. I'm at least 51 percent happy, and that rounds up to 100 percent. It's basic math. In college I had Friday night study groups and lived in the computer lab. I wasn't a troll, but working on my social skills hadn't been a priority. After I dropped out due to a lack of funding and time management skills, I bounced from job to job. This was great for building my skill set, but not so good for peopling. I'd always moved on before I could build genuine friendships. Boyfriends had been the same song, different verse.

Maple, however, has no intention of giving up. "I bet you could be perfectly happy with someone in this room."

"Sex is a lot of work." I shrug, forcing Maple to make an emergency grab for my sleeve before I accidentally flash the entire networking event. Off-the-shoulder dresses are worse than corsets, requiring minimal movement and perfect posture. I should probably look for a new dress.

Slapping my sleeve back into place, she snorts. "Don't be such a giver, then. Be a *taker*. Let the guy do all the work."

"I'm not even sure I like sex all that much." Before Maple can tell me I need a good therapist, or to embark on a journey of self-discovery to find the right penis, I barrel on. "I mean, I don't hate it, but it's kind of like going to a spa for a massage. Do I really want to give up an hour of my life to tell someone where and how to touch me? Or do I want to keep on living the happily single life where I DIY and wear old sweatpants to bed and no one points out I haven't shaved my legs in days? Self-care is much more satisfying."

Maple groans. "Just promise me you'll get out there and sample a penis or two. DIY is for home repairs."

I polish off my champagne and squint, but I can't spot a waiter. "Maybe after Calla's launch."

"At least stay a little while longer."

"How long?"

"Twelve minutes." She beams beatifically at me.

Even though she's pulled that number out of her ass, I nod. Twelve minutes and then I'm out. I can kill at least six minutes in the bathroom if I play my cards right.

"Potty break." I stand up, twitching my dress back into place. Either it's gotten shorter, I've gotten taller, or parts of me have gotten larger.

Four minutes later, I'm procrastinating in front of

the bathroom mirror. My dress is definitely shorter
and tighter. The black jersey stops barely south of
my butt and far, far above my knees. The off-the-
shoulder sleeves seem to be squeezing my boobs in
a manner that's far too friendly. When Maple came
by my apartment earlier for a pre-party assessment,
she redid my hair into a high ponytail. She also ap-
plied my makeup, which means I'm wearing a ton
since Maple only does stage makeup. There's also a
whole lot of bare leg between the dress's hem and my
three-inch strappy heels.

Maple vetoed a wrap. She also ixnayed a bra. The
no-panties thing, however, is entirely my fault. I prefer to go commando, although I'm usually wearing
yoga pants and therefore not in danger of sharing my
beaver with the world. Still, I look good. Maybe I do
fit in after all.

My return trip through the throng of glittering
people takes much longer. I manage to score another
glass of champagne, but the event organizers dim
the lights before I reach Maple, and someone is holding forth in the center of the room in the sole pool
of light. I'm actually relieved to throw myself onto
our window seat—my feet are killing me. Instead of
hitting cushions, however, my left knee drills into a
hard, male thigh while my right lands on something
much softer. Off balance, I flail. Champagne sloshes
everywhere. I've crash-landed on the wrong seat—
and it's already occupied.

Hands catch me, probably more to halt my accidental assault than to help. *Fantasy hands,* my stunned brain supplies. Wow. I've definitely had too much champagne and not enough orgasms, because I swear I go supernova staring at the strong, capable fingers wrapped around my wrists. *Capable* is a judgment call on my part, but the fingers' owner is definitely strong—unlike ballet-honed Maple, I'm no light-weight. It's dark, but I'm close enough to tell he wears no rings. The most delicious black ink disappears beneath pristine white shirt cuffs. A dark tailored suit jacket stretches over his forearms.

Mesmerized, I lean closer. *Great white shark. Bingo.* This guy is the sleekest and deadliest shark of all. "I didn't think they let bad boys in."

Oops. That's my voice.

"Jesus." I try not to look up because his voice is every bit as amazing as his hands, a low, gritty rasp that makes me want to beg him to tell me more. About anything. This man *definitely* sparks joy in all the right parts of me. Looking up would spoil the fantasy.

Instead, I keep my eyes fixed on his wrists and those just-visible whorls of black ink. His skin is sun-bronzed, a downright lickable golden-brown against the impeccable white cuff of the dress shirt peeking out from beneath the dark sleeve of his suit jacket. He could have been a hand model or a mechanic, but whoever or whatever he is, I liked the way his hands caught me so firmly far too much. A guy like this shouldn't need instructions in bed.

My stranger's voice rumbles something. Words,

words, words. As always, I'm happier filling in the blanks myself. Maybe Maple is right and I need to settle for just sex because I'm on fire where my bare skin brushes my sexy stranger. He might even be worth giving directions to if it turned out he was a little less than capable in the bedroom department.

He reaches between us, cupping my bare knee, and goose bumps erupt where he touches me. I take a deep breath, fighting the urge to rub against him. His fingers feel better than any nonsolo sex act I've ever participated in.

"Move," he growls, sounding more than a little pissed off.

I look up.

And...just like that I fall in crush. Is that even a thing? It should be because with one upward glance, my overactive imagination goes crazy. The growler's face is the perfect cherry on a sextastic sundae. Dark blond hair pulled back in a ponytail reveals cheekbones a sculptor would kill to immortalize. He looks like the guy from *The Princess Bride* but a thousand times larger, harder and less nice. He stares at me, irritation painting his cranky, gorgeous face. When he shifts beneath me, I confirm he's all muscle. I take a hopefully discreet sniff. *Cologne, my best friend.* I'll have to go to Macy's and do my research because his scent will haunt my fantasies. God, if he could just never open his mouth, this would be perfect.

Maple teases me all the time about my crushes. I spot a guy and I fall in love or at least in like from a safe distance. Imagining the possibilities excites me. Once I get to know my crush, however, my feelings fade rapidly. Cinderella probably came to her senses, too, and realized that Prince Charming wasn't who she'd imagined him to be. Maybe he was better or –(more likely) he was worse, but once the distance between them was erased, things changed. I usually solve this problem by avoiding real-life dating and opting for an active fantasy life instead where there's zero disappointment as long as I've remembered to replace the batteries in my battery-operated boyfriend.

Over the years, I've enjoyed a number of memorable crushes. My first was the hot guy who played third trombone in high school competitive band. I spent more time staring at the impressive bulge in his shorts than at my sheet music. Next was a college literature professor for a required freshman seminar— I zoned out once imagining giving him a blow job and rejoined reality with the professor and the entire class staring at me because "I'd been making noises" (I'd dropped that class because there's no going back after relative strangers know your porn sounds). And then there were plenty of noncontact fantasies that started with sexy emailing and texting and ended abruptly when my correspondent announced *the ball is in your court* and waited for me to make good on my dirty promises. Actions aren't my thing—I ghosted those guys.

"Hello?" Tall, Dark and Cranky frowns at me. We're nose to nose thanks to my perch on his lap.

"I—" My heart does a delicious nosedive. Now is the perfect time to snap out something witty, but I've got nothing. I'll just have to make it up later.

"Never mind." He tips me off his lap and onto the seat as he gets to his feet in one fluid, panty-melting move, more barbarian than white knight. To be fair, I just crushed his balls with my knee. He straightens his jacket, revealing that my champagne has christened his right sleeve in addition to darkening his shirtfront.

I give him puppy dog eyes as he strides away. Fortunately, he can't see, so what's left of my dignity remains intact. I'm not sure he even looked at my face. He definitely didn't ask my name. Or tell me his. And there's nary a business card involved. He's *perfect* fantasy fodder.

Later tonight I'll relive these moments and remember the way he touched me. The heat of his fingers braceleting my wrists. His scent and the crisp rustle of expensive cotton. I'll touch myself when I'm alone, imagining what could have happened next.

Of how he might have kissed me with that sinful mouth.

Of how I might have bitten that full lower lip just to make him pay attention to me.

Of how I could have pushed my hands beneath his suit jacket and explored the hard, muscled chest he'd so thoughtlessly hidden from the world. The truth is, I *love* not knowing who he is. Tall, Dark and Cranky is a mystery. I know only that he's fit, horrifyingly attractive and—given his presence at this mixer—likely business-minded to a sharkish fault, but everything else about him is just a gorgeous possibility. He's the ultimate fill-in-the-blank problem where I can pencil in absolutely anything I want and he will never, ever disappoint me since I will never see him again.

CHAPTER TWO

Dev

MONDAY MORNING SHOULD not surprise me. After all, I wrote the agenda for my company's executive team meeting. When I stroll into King Me's San Francisco conference room, however, the mood is not jubilant. I closed a major e-commerce deal at the Friday mixer despite crazy chick's drenching, and that means more stock options, bigger bonuses and the hugest possible gold star. *Winner.*

I drop into my chair at the table and eyeball the room. People claim my surfer boy outside in no way matches my CEO insides. That I'm a cranky bastard who routinely demands near-impossible coding heroics from my people. I offer this truth: I make those people money and ergo there are no complaints. Something is up today, however.

"Explain." I point to the head of my engineering department. Simon Rand is an excellent software developer. He doesn't do the bullshit dance around unpleasant truths. This forthrightness saw him let go from two previous start-ups, where the CEO-owner-entrepreneurs preferred team members to blow expensive, happy smoke up their asses while the companies burned through VC capital and made rapid descents into bankruptcy. I prefer making money hand over fist, so I insist on truth-telling.

Simon makes a sour face. Rather than ask the logical question *explain what?*, he assumes I've acquired telepathy powers over the weekend and already know the *what*. He plunges into explanations.

I hold up a hand. "Stop."

Simon stops.

A tense pause follows as the team attempts and fails to get on the mind-reading train to figure out who I'll fire for this. It's tempting, because Simon's news (and it's news to me) falls into the no-good-very-bad-day bucket. It's also humiliating, frustrating and makes me see red.

I recap on the off chance I've misheard. I don't make mistakes but hell could freeze over. "Someone stole our brand-new e-commerce shopping cart code."

Simon nods.

"The exclusive code we've presold to twelve major online vendors."

Another nod.

"Exclusive code that is no longer *exclusive* unless Merriam-Webster has changed the definition of the word."

A veritable storm of head-bobbing around the table. We're all on the same page.

"Who is the cause of this really big fucking problem?"

No one moves because the first thing you learn in the corporate world is that moving makes you a target. Simon looks like he might be sick.

I try again. "How?"

This one should be easier to answer given the multiple levels of security I've instituted. Unfortunately, this question is also met with silence.

"So essentially we know nothing." The theft may now be a fact, but revenge remains an option. I build a back door and handy-dandy detonator into our apps. Steal my shit and poof—your e-commerce site sells rubber ducky dildos in fashion colors rather than whatever you've really got in your warehouse. And because industrial espionage is rampant and I trust no one outside my immediate circle of friends, I build in that safeguard from day one. I also build in a tracker that alerts when my software goes live on the internet, which must be how Simon knows.

"Yet," Simon clarifies. "We don't know anything *yet*."

Now it's my turn to nod. "Exactly. All we have to do is figure out the connection between the three seemingly unrelated businesses illegally using our code. We didn't sell it to them, but they've got it. Somehow. There's a pattern even if we don't see it yet."

Simon leaps to his feet, grabs a dry-erase marker and starts sketching on the whiteboard. While the rest

of the room pretends to listen intently to the stream of
engineering coming from his mouth, I brainstorm in-
ternally. The first business sells mail-order hemp can-
dles and I assume they'll likely get arrested on drug
distribution charges. The second business, an adult
pool float company, might not mind a deluge of rubber ducky dildos (I'll trigger the alternate version of
my destructo-code for them, the one that crashes your
site by playing endless loops of puppies and kittens).
The third company is a woman-owned, eco-friendly,
socially conscious feminine hygiene products start-up
that promises to donate a box of tampons for every
one you purchase in the ultimate two-for-one deal.
The only obvious connection between the three is
that none of these companies can possibly make any
money.

The marijuana maker inhabits office space three
hundred and forty miles north in Humboldt County
and an ocean separates me and the pool party, which
maintains offices in China. That leaves the girl boss
company. I check my phone. I can get there in forty
minutes, straighten out this Lola Jones who thinks
she can steal from me and still make my two o'clock.
I just need to *know*. I hate secrets. I've always sussed
out my Christmas presents early, I read the ends of
books first and I check for spoilers on my favorite
TV shows. Enjoying the ride is easier when you know
how the ride ends.

When Simon finally comes up for air, I stand up.
"Meeting adjourned."

CHAPTER THREE

Dev

THE HIPPIE CHICK at the receptionist's desk either doesn't recognize a heartless bastard when she meets one or she optimistically believes dating is the ultimate DIY project and she can fixer-upper me into happily-ever-after. From the slack-jawed way she's stared at me since I strode through the door and demanded to see the company founder, she may also be entertaining naked fantasies. My expensive suit is gift-wrapping on an amazing package and we both know it. Strip me down and, heartless or not, I'm gorgeous. I'm also not afraid to play dirty—in bed and out—and I'm confident.

Too confident?

Borderline asshole and all the way arrogant?

Noise.

I know my worth. In addition to my billions, I have surfer hair, sun-streaked and shoulder-length, salt-tousled and unruly. Ironically, given my chronic inability to sleep, I usually look as if I just rolled out of bed. Beast lord, billionaire bad boy, surfer, Conan the Barbarian, pirate king—I can star in any fantasy you jill off to and Hippie Chick has clearly zoned out to her personal favorite.

Her forehead wrinkles as she tries to bring her brain back online and do her job. "You want to see Lola?"

Pay attention to the fact that she doesn't ask why I'm here. She's made an assumption, an important and entirely incorrect assumption.

"That's why I came." She's wasting my time. I could have been in and out already, and that's no euphemism.

Hippie Chick beams at me. I could ask her out right now, but I'm not here to score a date. I have two rules: never bring a girl back to my place and never screw at work. It's too risky. Too drama inducing. Too boring. And while Calla Enterprises isn't technically my workplace, I'm here on business.

"Okay." Hippie Chick bounces to her feet. Literally. Instead of normal, ergonomic office chairs, this place has neon-colored yoga balls. As she flip-flops away, presumably to fetch Lola and not on a karmic journey of self-discovery, I admire the view even if I'm staying otherwise hands-off. *Business casual* has achieved a whole new level of undress, and the ripped jeans hugging her ass are spectacular—as is the white T-shirt over the jewel-green bra.

I used to be Mr. Impatient but surfing taught me to slow down (some) and pick the right moment to rush in full speed. Nothing beats chilling on the ocean, hanging on my favorite board until the right wave arrives and I ride it home. I put that same, patient plan into action at King Me, my software company. My IPO might have made me a billionaire, but my impeccable sense of timing has kept me riding the financial wave when so many of my competitors have crashed and burned—and I'm only in my midtwenties.

Calla Enterprises is ambitious. It's a fledgling start-up that promises women around the world easy, non-embarrassing access to tampons because tampon access is apparently an important first step toward gender equality. According to the website copy, tampons remove a critical barrier between women and important things like an education and a job. And while I'm all for vaginal self-care, this company will fail long before the grenade I planted in their e-commerce system ever detonates. In the company's brief life span of thirteen months and two days, it has yet to close a round of venture capital funding or bring its product to market. Cue the death march.

In addition to lacking both operating capital and actual product, the company naively assumes that its customers possess genuine humanitarian spirit. Calla promises to donate one box of tampons for every box purchased online. Think about that for a minute. If you were dating and scored two girls for the night, would you really want to hand one off to an unknown guy at the club? Nope. You'd keep them both for yourself and have a threesome. No one is as altruistic as Calla's founder hopes.

And hope is clearly said founder's strategy. Calla is located in a repurposed loft/warehouse deep in San Francisco's Mission District. The neighborhood reads like a Who's Who of busted start-ups. Despite constant tenant turnover, the building's great—a loft-style, three-story workspace with a big atrium, an open-space kitchen that reeks like lunch and an enormous disco ball. A handful of flip-flop-wearing, jeans-clad twentysomething women hunch over laptops on tables.

Oblivious to the impending financial doomsday, Hippie Chick flip-flops her way inside a conference room separated from the main space by a wall of glass. It's like a gigantic fishbowl, except it holds a lone woman and an odd collection of furniture instead of fish and fake mermen. The woman perches on yet another inflatable yoga ball. She's also head-down on her laptop—I'd have fired her on the spot.

When Hippie Chick bounces in, however, Sleeping Beauty somehow rolls off the ball and onto her feet without serious bodily harm. Seconds later, she marches toward me. *Hello.* The reason for my visit flies out of my head as the blood in my body heads south and stages a fiesta in my dick.

I think I know this woman. She's the one who crash-landed on me Friday. She drowned me with her champagne. She all but gave me a lap dance, and then I tipped her off and left. At the time all I could think was *what the fuck was that?* I scowl. It was dark and I didn't get a good look at her face—although just remembering the luscious peach of her ass wriggling against my dress pants… *This* woman is my thief?

I may need to revisit Friday night's rejection. Lola Jones is unexpectedly, seriously hot for an engineer turned CEO. Dressed even more casually than her receptionist, she wears black yoga pants and a tank top with skinny straps. The tank top is cute and pink, and even though I'd have bet my man card that she isn't wearing a bra, my thumbs itch to check. To nudge those thin strips of cotton down her shoulders. To mark every creamy inch of her with my mouth, my teeth and my body. I promptly start a Lola to-do list.

Lick her
Explore that sexy shoulder hollow
Nip
Suck. TBD what and where—or everything
Palm a sweet little tit hard
Catch her nipple between my teeth and—

Focus. The porn film in my head is simply reflex. See a pretty girl, think dirty thoughts. It's nothing I can't handle. Just as soon as I've finished here, I'll retreat to my Porsche and *handle* the problem she's created in my pants. Or I could be a gentleman about our *other* problem and let her make amends. On her knees, on her back, on top as she rides me like an enthusiastic cowgirl—I'm unexpectedly flexible about the terms.

She shrugs into an oversize, black-and-white flannel shirt, doing up the buttons as she gets closer. Dragging my eyes away from her now-covered tits doesn't help. Her hair is long and dark brown. She's twisted it up on top of her head in a spectacular feat of engineering. *Perfect for fisting. We should totally try it.* She wears tortoiseshell glasses that rest just above a spray of freckles on her right cheek (hello, dirty librarian fantasy). And since she wears no visible makeup, including no nail polish on her bare feet, my brain—both the big one and the smaller, temporarily in charge one below my Gucci belt—fixates on one thing. *She's wearing pajamas.*

And yet even half-dressed, she radiates confidence as if she knows this is her space and she completely owns it. I admire that assuredness, even though it's probably the reason she thinks she can get away with pirating my software. For those of you who've ever contemplated doing that: *don't*. Like many things in life, software is worth what you pay for it.

Despite my reputation as a bastard, I try to stay friends with karma. I buy flowers for my dates, I routinely spot the panhandler on the corner five bucks and I donate generously to animal charities. I can't and won't, however, let people steal from me. It's like sex and marriage. Why buy the cow if the milk is free? Why pay my premium subscription fees if you can just download what you want from a mirror site in Asia?

Oblivious, my sexy thief pads to a halt. She looks stunned, but only for a brief second. "You."

"Me," I agree.

"God," she groans. "This is so embarrassing."

Pink creeps up her chest and over her cheeks as she looks at me. She's staring, but I stare right back. I won every staring contest growing up.

Yes, you sat on my lap.

Yes, you felt me through your dress.

Yes, I know you weren't wearing any panties.

She has a heart-shaped face with high cheekbones and that distracting spray of freckles beneath a pair of melting brown eyes. A crinkle grows between those eyes as she frowns. I imagine kissing away that little look of confusion. She doesn't look impressed by who I am. Or scared. Or even, ever so slightly, wowed. It's more the embarrassed kind of look when you've just bitten into the last doughnut and realize you were expected to share. Perhaps Friday night's crash landing was an accident after all and she wasn't a founder hounder trying to meet and marry a tech billionaire.

She abruptly shoves a hand at me. "Perhaps we can start over? Lola Jones."

Ballsy but nice.

"Devlin King, but the jury's out on the second chance." I wrap my fingers around hers. Smooth and delicate, her hand would feel better wrapped around my dick. No polish, no rings, short nails, but that's okay. She can scream my name instead of digging her nails into my back.

She purses her lips as she reclaims her hand, skepticism written all over her pretty face. She rocks back on her heels. "You've never screwed up and needed a do-over?"

"I don't make mistakes." I lead off all my interviews this way, but my trademark quote doesn't appear to ring any bells.

Instead, she snorts. "Despite your unhuman good looks, I'm certain you're Homo sapiens. Ergo, mistakes happen. Crap." She slaps a hand over her mouth. "Let's pretend I never said that."

"It might be hard." Something about her makes me want to break my rules and flirt shamelessly. Her touch is electric, making my body burn, my hands itch to touch her more.

"Come with me." She's already turning, and anticipation hums through me.

Happily.

I follow her toward the fishbowl. I assumed she knew who I was on Friday night. Founder hounders are common on the Silicon Valley social scene, looking to strike it rich and score a start-up-wealthy mate. The demand is great; the supply is low; and I'm Grade A billionaire material. My company's grown to stratospheric levels and I have the cash and lack of a personal life to prove it. And although I've also got the racing cars, private jets and oceanfront property, the kicker is that I'm top five on the Billionaire Bachelors app.

Yes, there's an app for spotting tech billionaires. My best friend Max O'Reilly launched it three years ago and his dating algorithm made him a fortune when he IPO'd. Fork over your hard-earned cash and you unlock dozens of extra date-finding features, but the one that rakes in the biggest bucks is his signature Billionaire Bachelors List. For the price of a cup of coffee and a quick download of the Happily Ever After app, he'll push you a monthly hot list of Silicon Valley's top bachelors and bachelorettes—complete with rankings, pictures and favorite stomping grounds so that you, too, can hunt the elusive wealthy mate in native territory. I've topped the list for the last two years.

Lola drops onto a yellow yoga ball and waves a hand at me. "Sit."

Normal chairs of any type do not appear to be available. When in Rome, right? I choose a blue ball because I enjoy symbolism, roll it over and sit down. I don't rush into explanations or accusations. I just watch her. People rush to fill up silence. You learn a lot that way, plus it makes the other person nervous and confess misdeeds.

This time, the silence stretches on and on until the soft skin between Lola's eyes crinkles as if she's thinking about something tricky. The frown deepens, so probably not thoughts of me naked.

She darts a longing look—at the laptop on the table. "Give me a moment?"

Her fingers are flying over the keyboard before I can respond. Okay, then. Totally lost in thought, she rolls back and forth like a metronome on top of that stupid yoga ball. She must have amazing abs.

After thirty seconds, I get bored and set the stopwatch on my phone. After ten minutes, I tap the table in front of her. "Earth to Lola."

"Oh." She turns bright pink and promptly loses her balance. I catch her by the elbow. For the count of three, my mouth is by her ear. Her hair brushes my cheek and that's all it takes for me to learn that she smells like vanilla, like cookies and sugar. *Danger.*

I force myself to roll my ball away from hers. "We need to get going here."

"Right." She slides the laptop away with obvious reluctance. "So you start. Tell me about yourself."

I haven't decided how to play this. Threaten her with my lawyer? Present her with a hefty invoice for the software she stole? Or just inform her that her pirated e-commerce system will switch her product to rubber ducky dildos as soon as she goes live because of my anti-theft safeguards? As Inigo Montoya assured Miracle Max: *humiliations galore.* Making small talk, however, is not part of my revenge plot.

"You know all about me." The words come out more growl than nice. Whatever.

"Uh-huh." She fidgets with the edge of the laptop. Her gaze flicks to the screen. Back to me. "Well, Lev—"

"Dev," I correct.

She makes a face. "Sorry. I thought I read—"

"You can't believe everything you read." I glance at her laptop as I speak. It's just code—lines and lines of the stuff in the typical developer environment. Not my code. Not my problem. But the mess on the screen is all wrong. It's inefficient and poorly organized.

I nudge her yoga ball abruptly, scooting her out of the way so I can pull the laptop toward me. "This is so wrong. Jesus. Who taught you how to code?"

She sucks in a pissed-off breath, reaching for the laptop. "That's mine."

I shoot to my feet, balancing the laptop in one hand, typing like a fiend with the other. Delete. Delete. Delete. I scroll down, check a line, scroll back up. There aren't even any unit tests—does she really believe testing is optional? Lola yanks furiously on my arm, but not only am I much, much taller than her, I also spent a year commuting between San Francisco and Santa Cruz on the train. I'm a master at typing while the world around me sways, lurches and violates my personal space.

I hit Save at the same moment the laptop flies out of my hand. Lola glares at me from the top of the conference room table she's climbed so she can repo her hardware. Score one for her. She transfers the glare to her screen and anger morphs into visible outrage. Whatever. I drop back onto my blue ball and smirk up at her.

"You're welcome, sweetheart." Love me, hate me, or plan to bury my body in the alley behind Calla—

but I've just fixed a major showstopper of a bug in her code. She knows it, too.

Hippie Chick chooses this moment to stick her head in the conference room door. "Are you done?"

Not a chance.

But Lola jumps off the table, laptop clutched to her chest. As she lands, her hip not-so-accidentally checks my shoulder hard enough to rock my ball.

"You bet," she tells Hippie Chick.

"No," I snap at the same moment.

I'm supposed to discuss the reasons that brought me here. Read her the riot act. Make her life generally unpleasant and ensure that she never, ever touches anything of mine again without permission. Spank her for being a bad girl.

"He's hired," Lola announces as she strides out of the room. "He'll start tomorrow."

Wait.

What?

Hippie Chick fist pumps. "Welcome aboard, new summer intern."

CHAPTER FOUR

Lola

"Ass," I HISS under my breath. Exaggerated sibilance sounds way less cool than, say, when a wizard is speaking Parseltongue. Yes, I'm a nerd with a Harry Potter fixation (House Ravenclaw, naturally), and yes, some days it sucks being the girl boss. I've worked hard to get where I am, though, so I don't scream the truth to the rafters of Calla's amazing three-story loft space. If I did, that truth might deafen the departing ass.

My newly hired nemesis, Mr. Devlin King. *My intern.*

My Friday night crush.

I'd worked my clit feverishly remembering his muscled thighs and stern face. Even though I apologized for crash-landing on him and his magnificent lap (at least I think I did—the details are fuzzy), he's holding a grudge. He certainly doesn't seem to have spent his weekend fantasizing about the mystery woman who gave him a free lap dance.

He's still impossibly gorgeous, though. To preserve what remains of my sanity, I retreat to the kitchen and pretend to deep-dive into my code while what I really do is watch Dev walk away from me for the second time: tall, built and still in possession of the most amazing backside I've ever ogled. He totally owns his ridiculously expensive suit. He's also quite possibly the most brilliant programmer I've ever met, having solved in seconds what a team of Calla engineers has been wrestling with for a week. Unfortunately, a continental-sized ego and the suave manners of Attila the Hun accompany his stunning good looks and big brain. Working with him will be impossible, but there's no viable alternative. The man is a genius and he works for peanuts, almost literally. Naturally, I've already forgotten whatever was on his résumé—UC Santa Cruz?—but he's definitely a college student with a willingness to intern for almost nothing. Given Calla's financial state, personality is negotiable.

Nellie woofs, poking her square white head out from behind the trash can. Nellie is a scaredy-bear and she hides whenever she spots intruders. She resembles a miniature zeppelin on squat legs. Bringing her to work with me is the perk of being the boss.

I reach down to stroke the soft fur on top of her head. "The coast is clear."

Like me, Nellie prefers to people in small doses. Another surreptitious peek reveals I've been over-optimistic in my estimate of Devlin's leave-taking.

He's still on the premises, talking up Katie, Calla's receptionist.

As Nellie eases out to say hello to me, Devlin nods at Katie. Not a smile, nothing pleasant, just a brusque tip of his gorgeous head that makes parts of me long to grab him by that stupid tie and yank his head down to mine. I should look away but I can't. I blame the way his shoulders stretch his dark suit jacket, framing all those delicious muscles. It's too bad the man ever has to open his mouth. If he could just work and glower in silence, seen but not heard, he'd be perfect. If he could do that with a Scottish accent and a tartan, I'd come on the spot.

Katie clearly agrees with me about the pretty boy factor. She stares at Devlin King, her mouth working like a fish. I can practically hear the stunned pop, pop, pop from my hiding place as she drinks in our intern's brand of hotness. His voice rumbles, low, rough, way too sexy. I can't catch the words, but Katie beams as if he's actually, finally said something nice. Finally, our sexy troll steps out into the San Francisco sunshine and is gone.

No, thank you. No excitement. Definitely don't let the door hit your mighty fine ass on the way out.

That man is trouble, and not just because we're an all-girl team and he's the lone slice of chocolate cake. Diversity is good. A roomful of people who think the same way does not solve coding problems. But because Calla is on the edge, one nudge in the wrong direction will also send us careening to our doom.

After getting turned down by the last venture capital firm I approached for financial backing, we've burned through our remaining operating capital and yet electricity and flushing toilets remain nonnegotiable items for my team members. I not only need to launch soon, but I need the launch to be a success. It would be even better if someone left a sack of large-denomination bills on our doorstep. Wishful thinking. I'm a master.

A test version of Calla's website is up and operational in a sandbox, I remind myself. We've just finished integrating our new e-commerce platform. That platform is a thing of beauty, although I'm also secretly grateful I didn't have to tell anyone how I obtained it. My small budget inspired an equal measure of creativity and embarrassing desperation.

Nellie whines, alerting me to incoming humans. I mentally flush my thoughts of Dev—mooning over my much younger intern is crazy—and find myself face-to-face with Valerie. Valerie is our director of international marketing. At twenty-three, she has a degree from UC Berkeley, pink hair and glossy pink lips that match the hair. She was an "influencer" before we landed her, which means she posted carefully curated content to Instagram and other social media. Her brand, she'd informed me during our interview, was Start-Up Chic and she makes more money documenting the start-up lifestyle than she does from Calla's actual paychecks. I live in terror that she'll abandon us, but so far, so good.

She leans down to pat Nellie on the head. Nellie flinches. "Who was that and why are we hiding in the kitchen?"

"I'm caffeinating, not hiding." To back up my claim, I beeline toward the coffee bar, almost tripping over Nellie, who believes my energy level means we're hunting doggie treats. Ugh. All ten of Calla's team members are serious caffeine addicts, but none of us has a Martha Stewart–esque penchant for organizing or cleaning. The coffee bar is a sticky collection of used cups, spilled sugar and empty coffee pods. I made a note on my phone to Google proper intern responsibilities—maybe he can take over coffee duties.

Val points to the front door. "Our guest was gorgeous. Now tell me he's smart. And ours."

"He's definitely smart. He's got a huge brain. He has the personality of a troll." Darn it. Out of coffee pods. I sift through the cupboard, searching for instant coffee, and discover an empty box. "I'm naming him Director of All Things Coffee."

"Uh-huh." Val nudges me enthusiastically. She's a hugger, too, whereas my personal space requirements are more generous. "Bet he's got a huge something else, too."

I make the buzzer sound. "Inappropriate, Val. Would you want your future teammates discussing your body the minute you walked out the door?"

Pot. Kettle.

"Sorry." She pulls a face. "You're right. Not here."

I look at her apologetically, but I know she understands. Lusting after the summer intern falls into the category of Shit You Do Not Stir. Above all, it's wrong. Whether you're Team Vagina or Team Penis (or prefer not to state your allegiance), you should be able to come to work without your coworkers imagining you naked and performing sex acts. And second and more practically, not only is everyone working all out to launch Calla in two months, but we simply can't afford the drama and expense of a workplace harassment lawsuit.

I shut the cupboard door and toss the empty box into the recycling. "Come with me to the coffee shop?"

Val nods enthusiastically, which experience has shown is her default factory setting. She's enthusiastic about everything. When we step outside, my head starts swiveling. I tell myself I'm just soaking in the sunshine. It's a balmy seventy-two degrees and the morning fog has already burned off. Normally, I'd take a few centering breaths and appreciate being outside, but instead I scour my surroundings. For *him*.

Fortunately, Val doesn't notice. Instead, she enthusiastically launches into conversation. "Do you have weekend plans?"

Right. It's Friday, the day of the week normal people get excited about because they actually intend to leave the house. On *purpose*. I personally prefer hiding inside where there are fewer people. After I finish my monster to-do list, I have a hot date with a new book and takeout. And Nellie. Nellie and I are practically an old married couple. I tie her leash to the bench outside the coffee shop and plunge through the doors. There are thirty-two people here and the sound wave deafens me.

"No plans," I roar, stepping up to the counter and placing my order. *Don't feel sorry for the introvert, folks. That's how she likes it.*

"No hot date?" Val examines the muffins on offer. Smart. It's unlikely we have time for lunch and I've eaten my way through the box of tasteless granola bars stashed in my desk. I pull out my phone and make *order snacks* the two hundred and forty-seventh item on my to-do list. "When's the last time you went out?"

I tap my calendar. Dates are violet as pink feels clichéd—and violet is as rare on my calendar as unicorns are in my life. Which is A-okay with me. My crowded schedule has no room for hearts and true love.

Val snorts. "If you have to check your calendar, it's been too long."

"Three hundred sixty-one days." Precision is important.

Val digests my disturbingly long period of celibacy as the baristas bellow out names, the space-age coffee maker whoosh-whirs, and a dozen customers chat each other up and make business calls at the top of their lungs.

"You need to get out more," she says finally. "There are apps for that."

"Hello? Married to the firm?" I grab my chai latte

off the counter and head outside. Nellie barks enthusiastically. She loves coffee dates, even if she anxious-
pees if I take her inside. Popping the lid off my cup,
I pour her a taste. Uh-oh. Whatever's in this cup isn't
chai latte. Once again, I've stolen someone else's drink.

I debate slinking back inside and buying—I ro-
tate the cup until I spot the owner's name underneath
my pinkie—Ross a new drink. It's too much work,
though. Plus, if he really likes steamed coconut milk,
we'll never work out. I opt for fleeing back toward
Calla, Nellie trotting alongside me, licking her chops.

Val is right behind me. "Sex is like flossing. You
should do it once a day, twice a day is better, and if
you haven't done it, you lie and say you did anyhow."

I roll my eyes. "Who has time to do it twice a
day?"

My brain helpfully supplies an image of Dev. He
likely has both the time and the stamina to do it twice
a day. Probably twice an hour. *Bad brain.* Not only
is he much, much younger than me, but he's my intern. I meant what I said to Val about respecting our
team members. It shouldn't matter if Devlin is tall,
short, fat or supremely built. His outside package has
no bearing on his ability to do the job, and I won't
treat him any differently than I'd want to be treated.
My social skills might be lacking, but even I know
having your boss come on to you is at best horribly
awkward and at worst criminal.

Plus, I've already had naked fantasies about him,

and he's brought me to orgasm twice since Friday night even if he didn't know it.

Shit.

Hiring him is a bad idea. If anyone finds out I'm crushing on him, I'll look ridiculous. And then there will be the usual stupid, giddy delight at going to work, knowing that I'll see him for a few minutes. Or our shoulders will brush, our knees bump under the table when we work together. He'll lean in so I can point out something on my laptop screen, and his breath will rush over my arm, and then the kibbles of those brief contacts will turn me into a brainless babbler. It's happened before.

But how can I fire him now? Not only do I need his big brain to sort out the bugs in my software, but I have no legal ground to fire him for hotness. The grumpy asshole part gives me material to work with, but I need him. And not just in a naked-and-thrusting way. *Stop thinking about him.*

The ache between my thighs as I walk back into the office is totally wrong. And Devlin King has given me zero reason to believe he sees me as anything other than his new boss, so this is one-sided chemistry.

I'll just shut it down.

That's what I'll do.

CHAPTER FIVE

Dev

JACK LEVELS A look at me, an impressive feat since we're bobbing up and down on our boards a quarter mile off the Santa Cruz shore.

"I'm not sure if I should congratulate you on your new internship or knock you off your board," he says.

Jack is a big guy with the size to follow through on his threat, although we both know he won't. This is partly due to us having been best friends since our freshman year of college, where we shared an apartment and a major in computer science at the University of California at Santa Cruz. We spent most of our time hacking or surfing. Before I met Jack, however, I was the youngest brother in a family of four boys. I'm competitive about everything and Jack knows it.

Long-term friendship has pluses and minuses. On the plus side, Jack makes an amazing wingman and he really gets me. On the con side, he often knows what I'm thinking and acts as a self-appointed conscience and guardian angel whenever he decides I'm headed for the moral deep end without a life jacket.

His superpower is that, despite being the size of a professional hockey player (which is why I at least pretend to listen to him) and having the killer instincts of a shark, people like him. Unlike me, he's the amiable, happily married prince among men that ladies love to borrow as a loaner husband and confidant. Today, the shaggy hair that usually falls around his face is pulled back in a ponytail and his wet suit outlines his muscles. I squint. He looks sort of like the Hulk, but less green and way more smiley.

"You shouldn't have let that girl think you were her intern." But I have been, for a couple of weeks now. Jack eyeballs the ocean.

Today is the kind of day that comes to mind when you think of California. Bright blue sky, supernova-heated sand on the beach thanks to the sun, and ocean everywhere. Plus, the waves are perfect.

"She assumed. I capitalized on it." Jack plays by a very black-and-white set of rules, so in the Jack Rulebook, I've been a very, very bad boy. And while I know my new internship is questionable, I still feel I have a winning proposition.

"Why?"

"Because I need to find out who stole my software, Jack Ass."

Jack ignores his college nickname, stroking his fingers over the surface of his board as he tests the wax job. I've pointed out that the whole stroking thing makes it look as if he's jerking off an enormous dick. "You always build in a Trojan because you're paranoid."

True.

"So it's not like she can go live with it," he continues. "Plus, you have an awesome legal team, a big bank account for bankrolling a lawsuit and the social capital to burn her. Either pick the right fight or let it go and move on."

I grin. "The day after she launches, I'll pull the trigger on the Trojan and all her product will turn into rainbow-colored dildos and rubber duckies. Then I'll hit her e-commerce server with a million requests a minute."

"She'll be down within the hour, so why go out of your way now to infiltrate her office and give her any kind of leg to stand on?" Jack's familiarity with my game plan may have something to do with the number of times we pulled this stunt in our younger, more lawless days. Now that he's married, and owns a very successful VC firm with his best friend Hazel, he claims to be reformed.

"Who's Dev getting horizontal with now?" Max pops up behind me. Max O'Reilly is the third in our triumvirate and I blame him for the worst hacking offenses of our college careers. I may hate secrets, but Max has a vendetta against ignorance in any form. You know that stupid line about curiosity killing the cat but satisfaction brought him back? Just substitute *Max* for *cat*.

"He's upgraded his skill set to super ninja infiltration." Jack makes big eyes in my direction.

Max frowns. Literal at the best of times, Max takes a sledgehammer approach to most social situations—which makes the fact that he's the billionaire owner/creator of a successful dating app hilarious. Only Max would reduce human interaction to neat lines of code and end up with a fat bank account rather than an actual date.

Like us, Max wears a black wet suit. Even in June, the water off the California coast is cold enough to turn your balls into blue Popsicles.

"Remember the rule," Jack says.

"Which one?" Jack has too many. I bought him a copy of *Robert's Rules of Order* the same Christmas he gave me a label maker. Like the British royal family, we have a gag gifts–only rule for present-giving.

"*The* rule. No sex at work."

There's silence for a beat as we bob up and down on our boards. And while all three of us have flirted with the rule, none of us has ever broken it. The most we do is flirt, especially if the woman in question is a client. If she's an employee, we don't even look in her direction. It's asking for trouble. But…

"Does Lola's office count as work? Because technically I'm her employee. She's paying me."

"You need to keep your hands to yourself. Don't look at her, don't touch her."

Max nods solemnly. "Personal space bubbles are

important." Max has learned this in his capacity as uncle to his sister's twin demon spawn.

"What if she looks at me? And invites me into said bubble?"

Jack shakes his head. "Don't. I can have it tattooed on your dick if that helps."

Jack reaches over and slaps me on the back. "Does this mean your new boss is hot?"

"You bet."

"So what's it like having your first internship?"

Jack laughs so hard he almost falls off his board. None of us interned in college—we'd been too busy launching our first companies. We'd found the magic, winning chute in the Game of Life.

"Taking orders sucks. She wants coffee runs, photocopies, meeting minutes and code reviews. I'm not allowed to check in any code changes without written permission—it's like getting a field trip note from my parents. Then she points out every place I've done something different from how she would have done it—which is *everywhere*—and tells me to redo it."

"None of those are unreasonable requests," Jack points out.

"They're not *requests*. They're *orders*." Great. I sound like an unhappy five-year-old. Maybe I could whine *it's not fair* for my next trick. "I have no idea how normal twentysomethings handle this."

"They need the paycheck." Max sounds serious. I can't tell if he's pulling my leg or not. We all know interning isn't a lucrative proposition.

"But I'm right."

Jack, naturally, mock-wags his finger at me. "And she's the boss. What if she knows something you don't? Or her way of doing things is equally good?"

I consider the possibility before dismissing it with a middle finger in Jack's direction. "I'm the best at what I do."

"Think of it like sex," Jack says, checking the wave coming toward us.

"I do *not* want to think about sex and you." Max nods, in vigorous agreement with me. In college, we didn't hang neckties on doorknobs to indicate that the room was occupied; we'd just agreed that our triple was a bang-free zone and that we'd take girls anywhere else. The rooms at Santa Cruz were too small for sexcapades.

"Work with me here." Jack sighs, a long, dramatic, oh-woe-is-me sigh I blame on his one and only stint as a thespian. He'd signed up for UC Santa Cruz's summer production of *A Midsummer's Night Dream* because he'd wanted to bang Titania. Hazel had been the stage manager and she superglued the ass head to his hair because Titania—aka Molly—was her best friend, and she was too shy to tell Jack to bugger off. Jack married Molly four years later, and he and Hazel have been friends and partners in crime ever since. She's the prettier but no less cutthroat half of their VC company. Together they have their thumbs in some of the tastiest Silicon Valley pies.

Jack has suggested repeatedly that we grow up and

include Hazel in our Saturday surf dates rather than shut her out of our boys-only tree house. She's great, but I've shot him down every time—not because she'd prefer to discuss the hotness of the male of the species, but because she honest-to-God can't swim. Drowning Jack's business partner isn't a friendly move. The compromise is her sitting on the beach with a book and holding on to our wallets. Currently she's a bright pink dot wrapped in three blankets. In addition to not being a good swimmer, Hazel gets cold easily.

Jack continues, "You've got the moves, you're the foreplay master, you've got the whole night mapped out and it's going to the best orgasm she's ever had."

"So, a typical night."

Jack ignores that. "But your date knows what makes her come, so what if she wants to do something different? She's not wrong, right?"

Put that way, my actions might possibly seem a little immature.

Jack taps his heart. "What do you want to happen next?"

I blame Hazel for Jack's insane willingness to talk about feelings and relationship next steps. She's a terrible influence. Jack claims it's a side effect of being married, which just underscores what a dangerous idea the whole two-becoming-one state is—he's turned into a girl.

"Pretty certain misrepresenting yourself in the hiring process is illegal," Max says. "Plus, if she mistook you for the intern, there must be a real one out there somewhere. What if he shows up?"

"No problem. I'll be in and out."

"That's what *she* said." Max waggles his eyebrows and I knock him off his board.

CHAPTER SIX

Lola

MAPLE AND I are having sad desk salads for lunch. She's on some sort of mason jar salad kick this month, so she's brought us each a glass jar crammed with more fiber and vegetables than I usually face in a week. Nellie flops by my feet, disappointed that it's not bacon cheeseburger day.

Frankly, I'm voting with Nellie. When Maple hands me my jar, my first thought is *ooh, super pretty*. The greens and vegetables are layered inside like a healthy version of three-bean party dip. I unscrew the lid and poke my fork inside.

Maple aims hers at me. "How is Pretty Boy?"

She thinks it's hilarious that my summer intern is none other than Hot Lap Guy. She asked how he took finding out I'd be his boss for the summer, but I wasn't sure what to tell her. I tried to apologize, he announced he wasn't pro second chances, and then he stayed anyhow. I think that means he's decided we can work together. Yes, I've felt his penis up through his pants and he's had his hand on my knee, but no one has seen anyone naked and there's been no tongue (which is slightly disappointing, if I'm being honest).

I chew before confessing. "He's a grumpy bastard."

"A grumpy, gorgeous bastard?" Maple beams at me.

"He thinks I'm an idiot." I wrestle with a cherry tomato that's gotten wedged beneath a chunk of walnut.

"You're crushing on him." Maple doesn't bother making it a question. I'm always crushing on someone, probably because it's the safe kind of fun—I don't have to actually do anything besides lurk on the sidelines and watch. This makes me sound like a creepy voyeur, when it's more that if I ever actually had a real-life relationship, I'd want it to be a spectacular success. I hate failing.

"I'm not discussing my intern with you." I shovel far too much salad into my mouth just in case she wears me down. Anything I say now will be garbled by arugula.

"So there's something to discuss?"

"No!" I choke-swallow.

"But you wish there was." She daintily spears her own cherry tomato. "You've imagined it."

"It wouldn't be professional."

She sighs and screws the top back onto her mason jar. "You should go for it."

"I don't think we're compatible. He's gorgeous, but he insists on talking. Or barking orders. You'd think *he* was the company founder. I gave him a Burger King crown last week and he recycled it."

"So not Prince Charming?"

I make a face. "Think troll living under the bridge. He's cranky and he likes to jump out at people when they're least expecting it and make ridiculous demands."

"So shut him down." Maple waves her hand for emphasis. Unfortunately, it's the hand holding her fork and a piece of spinach crash-lands on my shirt.

"He's useful." I pick the spinach off my shirt, consider eating it, but opt for the mature route and instead deposit it in the trash can. "He organized the kitchen last week. He owns a label maker—do you think he qualifies as a psychopath?"

He'd tackled the kitchen because he was *bored*. Unfortunately, he had good reason to be. I'd code-checked the code he'd written for Calla and he could have sold it on the open market. He'd also finished in forty-three hours. When I'd questioned how he'd found the time, he'd yawned and said he had chronic insomnia and therefore more than enough spare time to knock out my stupid project. Then he'd proceeded to explain—in unnecessary detail—why my original request was flawed, which had led to yet another flaming row between us.

Maple groans. "Neither of you is crazy, okay? He's just super organized and you're—not."

"I could learn to be." My jaw is sending distress signals to my brain, demanding we go on chewing strike. I give up on the salad and make a mental note to hit the taco truck.

Maple snorts. "Or you could just keep driving him nuts."

I eye her doubtfully. "I either babble or go mute when he shows up. I don't think he's exactly struck dumb with lust by my sexy person."

Maple pats my shoulder. "Just sit on his lap again and it'll all work out."

Dev

Two weeks into my "internship," I have a workable morning routine. I get up at the crack of dawn and power through whatever King Me requires before heading over to Calla. I've been putting out feelers, doing the social engineering thing, but so far none of my new office mates seem aware that their e-commerce software is pirated. And since their network is lamentably unsecure, I've had a few opportunities to poke around in their files—and yet I've turned up nothing. No clues. No answers. I suspect I need to get my hands on Lola's laptop to uncover the truth.

Frankly, anyone who knows me as the billionaire boy genius would be horrified that I'm presently an administrative assistant and low-level code monkey, fetching coffee and contributing the odd line of entirely redundant code. Lola mumbled something about bikes and training wheels before darting off when I demanded better job opportunities, but she just doesn't want anyone else touching her code.

I get it.

I suck at sharing, too, but after five years running King Me, I've learned some important lessons. As much as I hate giving up control, I also can't do everything myself—and there are some tasks (accounting, payroll and cleaning the restrooms come to mind) that I refuse outright to do. I pay people well to do what I won't. Lola, however, is everywhere at Calla, doing everything. She's here constantly.

I sort of envy her her passion. I've considered selling King Me at the end of the year because I'm bored. Which probably explains why I'm here undercover at Calla rather than working in my posh office in downtown San Francisco. Yes, I named my company after the first game I ever won. I demolished my brothers at checkers and this way they can't ever forget. It was too easy after a while, rather like King Me. I'm still not sure what I'll do next. Sitting around on the beach and surfing all day isn't enough.

Today, I stick to what I've dubbed The Routine. I chat briefly with the receptionist because establishing goodwill with Cerberus is smart. You never know when you might need to escape hell quickly. After a minute of witty repartee, I hole up with my laptop and check email. Next, I fetch coffee. I've coded a coffee app that lets my temporary office mates weigh in and change their minds a half dozen times without my having to kill them.

Lola has yet to use the app since her phone is always buried at the bottom of the ginormous tote bag she hauls around. I've already suggested using a tile, a pocket, or her bra strap to keep track of her phone, but she shot me down on all three counts.

I step into Lola's office without knocking. Since her office has no doors and the wall between her and the main floor is glass, knocking is superfluous. Plus, her fat white dog makes a teakettle noise whenever I approach. She's sitting on top of her yoga ball, half staring off into space, half frowning at her screen. She puffs her cheeks out and exhales. In an instant, I'm imagining what that small breath would feel like skating over my skin. It's a stupid thought. It's not like she's even noticed that I'm here. Based on previous encounters, she'll ignore me unless she's decided to give me shit.

I saunter toward her, coffee tray expertly balanced in one hand. *Time to effect some changes.* This time when I slide her drink in front of her, I slide her laptop away at the same time. It's a well-timed move, rather like turning the TV off on one of Max's nephews. Her eyes widen in outrage, and like the nephews, she's seconds away from vocal protests unless I provide her with a better option or break out the voice of God.

I squat down beside her yoga ball, pop the top off the cup and make a show of wafting cardamom and cinnamon-scented fumes toward her. The dog materializes seemingly out of nowhere, waddling toward me. As the bearer of treats, I'm allowed temporary access to her domain.

"You know you want it."

Work inappropriate? Sure, but watch this. Lola just nods her head and grabs the cup. She's challenged in the dirty innuendo department. Pretty much everyone here at Calla has a Lola story about some spectacularly funny moment where our boss failed to grasp the subtext. But those same people really like her. Lola might be annoyingly vague and slow to get a joke, but she's painstakingly fair. She goes out of her way to be helpful, and where other people grant second chances, she's willing to go up to imaginary numbers. Last week Lola hired a random old lady from the Chinese market down the street to translate when the twenty-two-year-old director of shipping lost Calla's entire product inventory somewhere on the Chinese mainland.

Which makes it harder and harder to believe that Lola knowingly pirated my software.

After two weeks in her office, I've also learned that Lola needs more people time. While she might be introverted, she chats the ear off everyone she encounters, oversharing an unintentionally blunt stream of consciousness series of observations. Rideshare drivers are scared to come near our building. I appear to be the one exception to her nonstop talk fest because she promptly clams up whenever she sees me.

I wink at her. "Reporting for duty, sir."

After my "interview" at Calla, I haven't worn a suit again. I switched to jeans, a leather jacket, boots and a crisp button-up shirt. And a tie. I never forget the tie. A tie guarantees you attention.

Watch.

I adjust the knot, stroking my hand down the silky length, straightening it out. It's a 1920s-style brown-and-blue-checked tie.

My boss's hazel eyes zero in on my hands. It's like waving a string in front of a kitten.

"Nice tie." She drags her eyes back up to my face with remarkable willpower and I bite back a smile. *Still got it.*

A small frown crinkles her forehead. "Exactly how many ties do you own? You've been here two weeks and I've never seen the same one twice."

See? She notices me.

"Last Monday—plum with pink dots. Tuesday—yellow polka dots. Wednesday—gray silk. Thursday and Friday—skinny black tie, navy blue black tie. That's five ties in one week."

She ticks my tie wardrobe off on her fingers. Lola likes to count.

"Maybe I'm a tie model in my spare time and get paid in ties." I lean in. Her hair smells amazing.

Oblivious as always to my proximity, Lola sets her cup down and starts fixing her hair. The twisty-thing she does with it rarely lasts more than a few hours, necessitating repairs right about when I deliver her coffee. She wriggles and stretches, forcing her hair into an updo that looks like a double-scoop ice cream cone. Her arm brushes my shoulder. "You're what, twenty? What normal college guy owns an entire business wardrobe?"

Danger.

"Wait." She holds up a hand. She has a thinking pose like Rodin. "Don't answer that. I'm pretty sure it's an HR violation."

Saved by the rule book. "Are you sexually harassing me?"

"What?" Her face turns a fabulous shade of bright pink.

Has she thought about me in HR-inappropriate ways?

"Feel free to lie to me if it'll make me feel better." When the pink deepens, I help her out and change the topic. "I do have an awesome tie collection."

She frowns. "I'm not good with jokes. Is there an allusion hidden in there?"

"Do you want there to be?" I'm not ashamed to admit (to myself only and never to Jack or Max) that I've replayed our conversations in my head more than once over the last few weeks. I've also had more than one porn-worthy fantasy starring my boss, so I can't help noticing that she's staring at my mouth.

Does she…have a crush on me?

She sounds distracted, her eyes a little dreamy as she looks through me—*again*. I'm finding it hard to focus, too. I've never really noticed how pretty she is. We don't spend much time together like this—usually she drops by my desk, we fight over my interpretation of my most recent assignment and then she flits off to do whatever it is she does. I've looked at her ass, her tits and all my other favorite parts, but it's like I've never really seen the whole Lola.

I lean toward her without conscious thought, one hand resting on the side of her yoga ball. For balance. Not because it puts my fingers closer to her ass. Her leg brushes my hand.

She takes a hasty sip of her drink and chokes on it, spraying chai everywhere. I feel a small smile tug at my mouth, which I quickly hide as I whip out a handkerchief from my back pocket and start mopping up the mess.

Lola waves me off, producing a wad of paper towels from her bag. "Are you eighty? Who owns a handkerchief?"

"No, and this guy." I touch my handkerchief to the corner of her mouth. "You have a spot right here."

I don't miss the way her lips part.

I think she does like me.

Or parts of me.

She abruptly rolls her yoga ball backward, putting some space between us. "We need to discuss the rebrand of our packaging."

Right. She'd given me some dumb-ass to-do about researching "cute little pouches women can tuck a spare tampon in." I pull out my phone and look at her.

"You realize I'm a software engineer and not a graphic designer, right?"

She raises a brow. "Scared?"

I text her the list of options I've come up with. Hazel suggested I look on Pinterest for inspiration, and she's a genius.

Drawstring bag (pineapples, llamas, dogs)
Velvet pouch (crazy cats)
Anything with pom-poms
Bag with stupid inspiration quote
Anything Kate Spade

I also have a spreadsheet, product cost per piece and production times. I nailed it. Packaging isn't hard—it's mostly point, click, shop.

She sets her phone down. "Wow."

"Fuzzy bunnies, puppies, baby seals—cute sells to women. You can't help yourself. Big eyes, chubby cheeks and squishy bodies activate your mesocorticolimbic system and give you a major high. The more that high gets triggered, the more you seek it out."

"You think our tampon packaging should be addictive," she says dryly and then ostentatiously taps the trash can icon on her screen. "You need a do-over. The African artisans creating our pouches encountered technical issues ordering supplies. They have two thousand units of pink beads we have to incorporate."

"So now we have to redo the packaging to match. It's like making the drapes match the carpet."

Her face colors. "You're disgusting."

Okay, false alert.

My boss does pick up on some innuendos—and she doesn't like me.

At all.

CHAPTER SEVEN

Dev

AT SEVEN IN the morning on a Saturday, San Francisco's Mission District is torn between waking up and getting the day started and going back to bed to shake the Friday night hangover. When I park in front of Calla for some covert investigation, I spot two drunks passed out in nearby doorways. The snack vendors trundling their carts up the street bob and weave around them. Even the cinnamon scent of fresh churros can't erase the stink of days-old alcohol and piss.

Lola gave me the alarm codes for the door on my second day of work. This might have been a gesture of good faith, or it might have been insurance against a repeat of what happened after I accidentally set the alarms off when I arrived at 6:30 a.m. on my first day of work. I've never needed much sleep—a good thing given my chronic insomnia—and I like an early start.

Just in case I run into anyone, I'm wearing my usual work uniform of jeans, a button-up shirt and a tie. Today's neckwear selection is the horny prep school special—a big, bold, look-at-me-or-better-yet-look-down-and-admire-my-awesome-hugeness number with pink-and-maroon stripes. No one's around to appreciate it, however, when I enter.

The building is quiet, the lights off. Sunlight filters through the skylights and ricochets off the stupid disco ball hanging from the ceiling. It's immediately clear people have once again failed to clean up after themselves. In some start-ups, engineer ego and the bro-culture keeps trash lying around. Calla's engineers are simply oblivious, pushing code and driving toward launch while their dirty coffee cups overflow the kitchen sink, spawning mold and mutant germs.

I rearm the door and wage brief but effective war on the kitchen. The sink takes heavy casualties— a Hello Kitty mug that resembles a petri dish and various fossilized Tupperwares. Once I've got clean coffee cups lined up by size to dry, I place an online order for disposable coffee cups—the organic, compostable, made-by-some-worthy-charity cups that Lola prefers. *Order coffee cups* is probably on her to-do list, but her action items list is long and she refuses help.

OCD temporarily placated, I prowl my workplace, looking for magically delicious clues. It's really freaking quiet, despite the occasional siren or car horn burst from the outside world. Everyone seems to have dutifully taken her laptop home for the weekend. My spying plans were stupid anyhow and hanging around Calla is a colossal waste of time. I should turn the theft over to my lawyer, except I sort of like my ringside seat for the Lola show. I'm not sure what, if anything, is happening between us, but for the first time in a long time, I'm not bored.

Wait.

Maybe not *everyone* has taken her hardware home.

Light glows dimly from the far side of the workspace. I follow it straight to Lola's office.

And...wow.

Lola is truly hard core. Or dead. She's curled up underneath her desk in a ball. It must be more comfortable than it looks because when I check, she's not dead—just sound asleep on a yoga mat, head pillowed on her arm.

It feels like eternity while I watch her sleep, staring at the soft curve of her cheek. Her lips part ever so slightly, Sleeping Beauty waiting for a kiss, although I prefer Anne Rice's dirty version to the happy cartoon princess story. I itch to crawl under the desk with her, wrap my arms around her and kiss her awake.

Peel back the cardigan she's draped over herself like a blanket and taste her from those perfect lips to her bare toes. There are so many places I could start. All I have to do is reach out, to begin. I've thought about it more than I'll ever admit. What I don't know, though, is if she thinks about *me*. I *think* she might have a crush on my body, but I could be nothing more than her intern.

The strap of her tank top slips down one strong, toned arm when she shifts. Lola may not make time to go home, but she definitely makes time to work out. There are sculpted muscles beneath the soft skin. Somehow she feels almost naked, as if sleeping Lola is magically more vulnerable than awake, working Lola.

I don't need Jack to tell me this staring thing is wrong. You don't creep on a sleeping woman, and if you do, a restraining order and a long talk with Officer Not-So-Friendly are just a few of the well-deserved presents Santa Claus will deliver for Christmas.

So I force myself to walk away and pull out my phone. Not to take pictures—although I'm tempted—but to call for reinforcements. Ten minutes later, I'm armed with a chai latte courtesy of Uber Eats and ready to poke Sleeping Beauty.

In the sweeter versions of the fairy tale, the prince awakens Sleeping Beauty with a kiss. Anne Rice's prince gets straight to the screwing, crossing all dubious consent lines. My beauty is asleep, though, and that limits my options. As much as I'd like to kiss her awake, she hasn't told me yes. *Yet.* I thump the door frame with my free hand.

"Room service," I bark at her comatose figure.

Lola wakes in a rush, shooting upright and banging her head on the desk. Ouch. Fortunately, the enormous hair bun she rocks cushions the impact.

Patting the bun back into its orbit, she mutters something in Russian. Per office gossip, she spent a summer at a Moscow software start-up and learned more than curse words. The same gossip suggests we may be under intensive FBI scrutiny as a result. Color me skeptical. Tampons aren't terrorist weapons unless it's five minutes before midnight, the store is closing and you've forgotten which kind you were sent to fetch.

"What are you doing here?" She squints at me from her desk cave, pulling her cardigan around her.

I pluck her glasses off the top of her desk and extend them to her. With my other hand, I extend the coffee cup to her. "Getting a head start on my Monday to-do list."

She pops the glasses onto her nose and grabs the cup. She's remarkably composed for someone busted sleeping on the floor. "A for effort, Mr. King."

"Are you coming out?"

I shove my hand at her. It's reflex, a vestigial trace of gentlemanliness instilled by my mother, and honestly, I expect Lola to ignore me. It isn't easy being a girl boss and I hate that Silicon Valley so often put its women entrepreneurs through the wringer. Women have to play harder, fight dirtier and put up with stupid male shit because some of the most successful guys I know haven't progressed beyond dirty jokes and hoping to score. To my surprise, though, she places her fingers into mine.

It's the first time she's touched me intentionally. She crash-landed on me and we shook hands at my interview, but those don't count. We've also bumped shoulders, brushed arms. But this is different because she's chosen to put her hand in mine when touching isn't forced by gravity or dictated by good manners.

This is deliberate.

The heat from her fingers scorches my skin. Why do I want this woman? My brain yells that it's a very bad idea, that I should step back, walk away, walk *out* of this building and Lola's life and away from whatever it is I think I'm doing here.

Which is making a mistake. Making the worst possible, horribly awful, so-wrong-it's-good mistake.

I tighten my grip anyhow. She's my boss, or thinks she is. We're in the office, and offices are officially a sex-free zone. But the seconds tick away, my fingers holding hers, and she says nothing. Or maybe like me, she doesn't know what to say. Because my whole body's tight, on full alert and begging for more. She just breathes harder, or maybe that's my imagination.

I stroke my thumb against the palm of her hand as I pull her forward and up onto her knees. Her hand twitches in mine. She's waiting for me to do more, and I'm waiting for her to stop me. To drop my hand, to tell me to go away, to leave and to never come back. I'm bigger, larger and standing over her. She's shorter, smaller and kneeling in front of me. I take the decent half step back although I hate retreating. Sounds filter in from the outside world—the whir of pigeons sounding off and the Spanish bark of the snack vendors trundling their carts up and down the street. There's no air in here. Just heat and each of us waiting for the other to make a move because there's too much at stake to be the first.

"Sometime today, Mr. King." Her firm voice breaks our standoff. She looks up at me, and I have no idea what she sees.

Heart pounding, I pull her up slowly. Lola's on the tall side for a woman, maybe five feet seven inches, and she's got a few curves. She says nothing about the helping hand even though she's spent the last two weeks roasting my balls about not being a team player. Or maybe it's because she almost-not-quite brushes said balls in her upward trajectory. Or maybe I'm just an asshole. But whatever the reason, my dick makes like the Grinch's heart having a Christmas revelation and grows three sizes.

Lola's chest rises and falls rapidly and she stumbles as she comes to her feet. And then somehow she manages to lose her balance entirely and crash-lands on my chest. It's not my fault because I'm off balance, too, not expecting her to fall. But she does and my brain promptly goes off-line. If I had to pick a word, it would be *soft*. She's got great tits and she's not wearing a bra—just two layers of soft, fluffy fabric.

She barks something. It might be Russian or *back off, King*. I hesitate, however, to let go of her hand and her waist—somehow, yes, I'm groping the waistband of her leggings—because letting go means she definitely falls and her LZ will be me or the floor. And part of me wants to let her go, let her fall, and then I'll fall with her and take her right there on the floor.

"What are you doing?" She slaps her hands behind her, bracing herself against the desktop. There's too little space between us. Our thighs bump, our knees brush.

"Saving your ass."

I set my own hand beside her hip and my thumb brushes black cotton. I still want to fight with her, but now I want to strip her down, too. Make her admit that she wants me, too. My balls tighten. My finger traces her hip, finding the line of her hips but no panties beneath the cotton. Is she commando? Dirty, dirty girl.

She hasn't said no.

She hasn't said go.

Her eyes lock on to mine. "Do you have a white knight complex?"

I smirk. "Knights were supposed to be chaste, Ms. Jones."

Angry color flags her cheeks. "You suck."

"An interesting professional assessment. I'll give you mine. Your problem is that you *think* you like to be in charge. That you have to tell other people what to do or you won't like the results. Here's some free advice for you. Independence has teeth and it likes to bite people in the ass."

Her eyes narrow. "Really, Mr. King?"

"Why, yes, Ms. Jones." I snap my teeth at her.

"Because based on your work here, you very much prefer to work alone."

"I've finished both of my projects."

"They were *group* projects," she hisses, pulling off her glasses. "You were supposed to be collaborating with other members of the Calla team. Instead, you just went ahead and did them yourself."

"They're done." Point. Made.

Her pretty mouth tightens. "Perhaps your coworkers would have had valuable insights."

"I knew exactly how to handle those projects," I tell her. "You know it. I know it. You should be grateful to get that kind of work for twenty bucks an hour."

"You are an intern." She glares at me, trying to set my hair on fire with her eyes. "You are supposed to be learning."

"And I am." In the past two weeks, I've learned that fetching coffee sucks, that I dislike taking orders even more than I thought I would (which is a lot) and that working two jobs is exhausting (so my hat's off to all of you who are doing it). Oh, and that I can program circles around anyone here at Calla.

She leans forward. "Name one thing that you've learned."

I wink at her. "That I'm the best programmer you have. You should promote me now."

Her eyebrows practically marry her hairline. "Are you serious?"

I smile innocently. "One thousand percent."

"One thousand percent is impossible," she scoffs. "Plus, you've only been here two weeks!"

"I move fast and I'm great." This is like the fortune cookie game, where everyone breaks open his or her cookies and reads the fortune out loud before adding *in bed* to the end of it.

She just shakes her head. "You have to learn to work in a team."

"Why?"

"Because it's important. Because life is not an individual event." And then she pulls out the big guns. "Because I said so."

"You are the boss from hell."

"How?" She actually throws her hands up in the air. "There is not one thing wrong with your internship except for you."

"Because *you* don't let *anyone* help you."

And then *it* happens. Lola launches herself off the desk, her knees slamming into mine. "I'm in charge here. I'm the boss."

"Really?" I drop onto her stupid, asinine yoga ball seat, tugging her down until she straddles my knees, her legs hugging mine. "We should definitely discuss that."

"Yes." The word explodes out of her mouth, a harsh, sharp burst of sound that I feel on my own.

My hands dig into her hair as my mouth slams into hers. Or meets hers halfway because she's reaching for me, too, as if she could devour me with her lips and her teeth. Her tongue pushes into my mouth, taking the space it needs, and I bite back a groan and lean into her. She tastes so good. We kiss harder, deeper, a noisy, wet, perfectly messy kiss that makes me forget all the ways we hate each other and wonder only how she could surprise me next.

At first we kiss with our eyes open, both of us refusing to break eye contact. This is a game I've played before and I press myself against her, moving in a hard rhythm against her thighs and ass. I watch her lashes flutter down, as if she doesn't want to watch what happens next and is raising the white flag.

"Please," she whispers, eyes still closed.

"No," I growl. "You have to use your words, Lola."

I could touch her clit. I could rub until I find the perfect rhythm for her body, the pressure, the beat, the tease that makes her scream for me. Or I could come over her now, strip her down and ride her until we're both shaking from our orgasms. I could bare her, kiss her, teach her to ride my fingers and my tongue, but I don't. I don't feel like playing nicely, so I slide my tie free and use it to tie her hands behind her back.

Her eyes fly open. "Do I need a safe word?" She's laughing at me, her expression a little unsure, a whole lot amused.

"It's the magic word *no*. Tell me *stop* and I stop." I rock against her, teasing her.

Our second kiss is longer, slower, less mean. It's as if the first kiss was two people bumping into each other, both angry but trying to hide it. This second one, however, we've discovered that maybe we're not strangers after all, even if we don't quite know each other. Yet.

"Is that *it*?" she demands when we finally break apart.

"So impatient, Ms. Jones."

She growls, lunging for my mouth. Yoga balls make poor office furniture. Lola bounces off my lap, I roll to catch her and we both end up headed for the floor while the yoga ball streaks in the opposite direction. I twist so she lands on top of me. Lola holds her breath, as if she's afraid someone else might have heard us. As if she can't believe she's reacting this way.

"Tell me," I say quietly. "Tell me *exactly* what you want me to do to you. How you want me to touch you. What makes you come the hardest. If you're going to order me around in the office, you have to use your words here, too."

The blush staining her cheeks is the hottest, brightest pink, but her eyes stare into mine.

"Slow," she orders. "Today I want it slow."

"Like this?" I cup the side of her face, running my fingers down her cheek. I skim the line of her throat, learning what she feels like.

She's so warm and soft, the best weight pressing me down. Is she wearing panties? I plan on finding out. Why does this girl make me so crazy?

"Do you want to be naked?"

She thinks about it. "Not in the office."

Part of me is disappointed. No, not *that* part. I've seen the outside parts and Lola's gorgeous, but I'm a greedy bastard with a great imagination. I've been *imagining* what her tits look like underneath those cotton tank tops, how her ass curves like the perfect pear, if she waxes or shaves or just does whatever *she* likes.

I have to kiss her, so I reach up and shove my hand into her hair. She comes willingly, her face finding mine, her mouth open and seeking. We kiss, tasting, exploring, testing each other. I can't stop thinking about other places I could put my mouth and what she'd taste like *there*. Her breasts press into my chest, her legs hug my hips and she grinds against me in a slow, hot roll.

"This is sweet." She leans into me, catching my bottom lip sharply between her teeth, and nips. The sweet sting blossoms through me. Like she just rang the doorbell on my dick or something. I've never been into biting, but this I love.

"But I'm not in the mood anymore," she continues. She must see my disappointment because she laughs. Somehow, smiling up at her beautiful, happy, take-charge face, I have the strangest thought. *I like her.* Don't tell anyone. I'm not headed to Harry Winston to buy the biggest, most ethically sourced diamond available. It's just that she's more person than boss or business rival now. She's Lola and that means she's funny, sometimes vague, always game and quirky.

"I can make you be in the mood." I slide against her where we're pressed together.

She's flushed, nibbling on her lower lip with her

teeth. Her eyes sparkle with humor. "But did I ask you to do that?"

Point to Lola. "Tell me what you want."

She manages to get her hands on the top button of my jeans. "Binary or infinite? How many options?"

"Do you want a list? Now?" I can't stop looking at where we touch, can't stop wondering how much better it would be if we were naked.

"Send me the list later. Boobs or mouth?"

"What?"

"Do you want to fuck my boobs or my mouth?"

Holy shit.

"Is it Christmas? Can Santa come twice?"

She grins at me. "Unless you're really, really ana-tomically gifted, you have to choose, intern boy. You can't be in both places at once."

"Then boobs—although we may need to revisit that decision."

She gets busy, sliding her tank top down with a sexy little wriggle. By the time I've got my brain working again, the shirt's near her waist. I should either lean back and enjoy my show or I should be showing my appreciation. With my tongue.

She frowns down at her boobs. "I like them and they feel great, but Cleavage-R-Us I'm not."

Small, medium, large or supersize, I've never seen a boob I didn't appreciate, but I've spent too much time these last two weeks imagining what these particular boobs would look like. Now the only thing between me and dreams coming true is the cotton bralette skimming the top of her nipples. White has never seemed so sexy. She wriggles off me and I groan.

"Up."

I can do *up*. I stand up and wait. It's weird, letting someone else call the shots. It's also the hottest thing I've ever heard. Maybe it's because Lola's really telling me what she likes, sharing her fantasies with me and letting me in. Or maybe it's just dirty and, just this once, I'm willing to try something new.

"Lose the jeans," she orders.

Her wish is my command. I shove the jeans and boxer briefs down. I watch her looking at me and get harder. "Can I touch you?"

"Only what you can reach," she orders—and then she drops to her knees in front of me. God bless yoga because Lola turns out to be very, very limber. Her hair brushes the inside of my thighs as she reaches for me and I bite back a groan.

The disadvantage to tying her hands is that she can't work me with her palms. My balls also regret that decision. The rest of me, however, thinks it's fantastic. I work my fingers through her hair and discover it's a ponytail tucked inside itself like that alchemy symbol of a snake eating itself. The long brown length comes apart in my hands and I wrap the thick length around my palm and pull her closer.

She looks up at me, mouth parted, my dick resting on her bottom lip, all impish eyes. This is *Lola*, my annoying, spacey, grouchy boss. Her tongue slips out to wet her lip, grazing me. *Fuck. Me.*

Her lips part wider and I slip inside an inch. She hums something and I push inside her mouth. Screw waiting. Everything about her turns me on. If I'm not careful, I won't last long. She pulls harder, taking me deeper. Shit. Her mouth is sweet, wet heat. My balls tighten, ready to shoot my load.

"Tell me to come," I growl.

I'm not sure how she's supposed to answer when her mouth's full, but Lola's creative. She nods her head and groans something. Good enough—or maybe that's the wicked edge of her teeth skimming my sensitive head. Girl boss is still trying to take control. Unfortunately, I don't care because she's sucking me off with a skill and speed I didn't expect. I tunnel my fingers into her hair and fuck her mouth hard. Harder than is strictly nice, but she lets me. Nothing has ever felt so good and that makes this whole banging-my-boss thing an even *worse* idea.

I should pull out.

I should ask if she's okay with this.

Instead I lose myself in the soft wetness and blow up in her mouth.

She rocks back on her heels as I pop free. Then she wipes her mouth on her shoulder as I put myself back together.

"My turn," she says.

I shove her pants down her long, toned legs. She's not wearing panties. She's completely naked from the waist down, and it's not enough. She leans back against the desk, off balance because her hands are still tied, and I lift her up until she's seated on it before stepping between her legs. I can smell her, so wet and slick.

"Sucking me off turned you on."

"I'm selfish." She crosses her legs behind my back, her heels resting on my ass. "If it didn't turn me on, I wouldn't do it. Did you think I was faking it?"

I reach between us, sliding my fingers down, until they rest against her where she's so wet. I lean into her, pressing her back against the desk until she's flat beneath me and our mouths are so close that I feel her breathe.

"You're wet."

"Do something about it," she challenges.

"Do you want my mouth between your legs? Or do you have other fantasies?" I pull my fingers free and paint her lips. "Tell me how to do it."

Her breath hitches, her eyes drifting closed. She's thinking about it. Lola loves fantasies. This is her favorite thing, imagining the possibilities. When her eyes open, I know she's picked a favorite, her expression changing from slightly awkward awareness to 100 percent sensual.

Hazel eyes are hard to pin down. Are they goldenish or brownish green or do they change when you least expect it? This close, Lola's eyes are almost amber today, and I fight the urge to keep tipping forward, to fall into her eyes. Falling would waste the time we have.

She levers herself up on her elbows. "Run your

hands down my body. I love your hands. They're big and a little rough."

I do as she narrates, dragging my hands down her body and over her hips. My fingers press against her skin, traveling over her curves and digging in. She's soft, her skin pebbling beneath my touch.

"Are you cold?" I slide my hands beneath her ass.

"Your mouth follows your hands so I'm not cold." Her eyes darken. She's watching me, waiting for me to do as I'm told.

I kiss my way down her body, learning what she tastes like. When I reach the soft curve of her belly, I turn my head, resting my cheek against her. "And then what do I do?"

She thinks for a moment. Or maybe she rehearses what's coming next in her head because the sweet, salty scent of her arousal grows stronger. It's as if she feels everything twice as intensely, once in her imagination and then once more with me.

"I might be shy, so you brush one cheek over me, and then the other. You haven't shaved recently and I love the way your stubble feels."

"Like this?"

"Yes." She exhales, eyes still closed. "Do it again."

"Perhaps I blow on you, teasing you," I suggest. "Since you like it slow."

"I like it slow today," she says. "Maybe."

Her breathing grows faster when I send my next breath skimming over her. And then the next. And the next after that. Her heels rub against my shoulders in a gentle, dreamy rhythm and I wish I could see inside her head. Her eyes are closed again.

"But you're impatient, so you push my legs over your shoulder so you can see me. You love looking at me."

"I do," I answer. "I could look at you all day. You're fucking gorgeous here."

"That feels good," she says. "But it feels even better when you taste me."

She's so right. She tastes unbelievable, sweet and juicy. I hold her open with my thumbs and I kiss her, breathing her in, licking up her wet. All the usual words tumble through my mind—*peaches, sugar, cream*—but those are fantasy words and the reality of Lola is even better. I wish I could tell her how good she feels, but instead I show her.

"Do I push a finger inside you?"

Another pause.

"No," she says dreamily. "You lick me deeper, over and over."

I do it. I drag my tongue through her slick folds, learning which spots make her moan and which make her squeal. She opens wider, her heels digging harder into my shoulders, because it feels good. Sweat dampens her body and I kiss her harder, rougher, surer. She's told me her secrets and I know how to please her.

"You—" Her voice catches as her thighs tense.

I dig my fingers into her ass, controlling her movement and how she rolls against my mouth. "You want this."

"Yes," she whispers. "I do."

"But you want to be the one in charge." I suck lightly at her clit and she makes a noise I haven't heard before, a rougher, greedier sound. She's so close.

I give her clit another kiss. "You think your way is best."

And she breaks character, forgets the rules of our game. "Make me come now."

"So bossy." I give her pussy the smallest of smacks and she moans. "Always certain your way is the best. But what if you're missing out on something better?"

Another tiny tap. Another moan.

"Too bad for you, princess. I'm not in the mood to play your games today. Naughty bosses don't get orgasms."

I could sink into her.

I *should* finish her.

Instead I step back.

She glares at me, dazed. It's a bitch trying to lever yourself up with your arms tied. This is why I don't let my lovers tie me up. Or take control. You end up *out* of control.

"See you Monday."

I saunter out the door. I have to hand it to her, though. She doesn't beg or plead. She pulls it together enough to yell after me.

"You're the world's worst intern."

I'm not fired, though.

Not yet.

CHAPTER EIGHT

Dev

I DRIVE TOO fast down the coast to Santa Cruz. I need to get out of The City and put substantial distance between me and what just happened. Or more accurately, what didn't happen. Scenic Highway 1 is gorgeous, the classic California experience with enormous redwoods that seem older than God. Late afternoon sun flashes through the branches. The road twists, knifing back on itself with zero tolerance for stupid mistakes, and the curve up ahead claims lives every year.

I did my boss.

No. You cock-blocked her to prove your point. I pick up speed, hurtling through the next bend. I have a problem with arguments. And with power plays. And with feeling out of control. So instead of doing Lola right, I blew up in her mouth and then left her high and dry. It's funny in a practical-joke-gone-wrong way, but it's also painfully stupid. I could have done her tonight, but instead I've likely not-screwed my way out of discovering who stole from me.

Fair enough.

I'm an employee with zero follow-through. I'd fire me.

I shoot out of the last, tree-lined curve and into the straightaway fronting the ocean. The Pacific stretches away on my right, dotted with oil refineries. Closer to shore, where some truly spectacular waves break, surfers ride their boards. A smallish strip of beach houses and surf shacks cling to the sand between the highway and the water. The break is close—a short paddle, and boom. I'm tempted to stop, but I don't have my gear and I hate rentals.

Plus, as Santa Cruz has twenty-nine miles of beaches, I haven't surfed this particular spot, which makes a good ride less likely. I'm not familiar with how the waves break, or with what lies underneath the ocean's surface. Predictable is good. Like my well-organized life, my surfing habits are a finely honed balance of discipline and routine. I've practiced the same surf breaks for years, polishing my skills, growing better until I'm the absolute *best*. I won the last two surf competitions I entered, wiping the floor with my competition.

I keep moving and make it to Santa Cruz without getting pulled over or wrecking my car. There's no one-size-fits-all label for Santa Cruz. Parts stink like cheap beer (college town), while other parts reek of hemp oil (the outdoorsy types), money (check the real-estate listings and you'll know what I mean) and suntan oil. There are beaches, cliffs, awesome surf and sixty-five thousand residents shoehorned into less than sixteen square miles of living space alongside surf bums and cruise ship visitors. All types of people pass through, but living here year-round is a different game. Real estate is pricey, building up is necessary and there's always at least one house under construction in my neighborhood.

The neighborhood itself is a warren of one-way, twisting streets jammed with cars. Getting a parking permit may require screwing the city council, and I've heard two permits necessitates an outright orgy. My house is the queen bee of the block, perched at the very end of a cul-de-sac (score!) and so close to the ocean that spray hits my bedroom windows on a windy day. Three thousand square feet of Spanish mission style, it fronts an amazing stretch of ocean.

I slam into the house, pissed at everything and the world. Despite the miles between Lola and me, she's still right here in my head, taunting me. I ignore the uncomfortable feeling in my stomach. It might be guilt or discomfort. Whatever. It's unfamiliar and I don't do feelings. *Fuck.* I almost never make mistakes.

Lola's scent still clings to my fingers, a little fainter each time I bring them to my nose. Usually I hit the shower fast after hookups, but she smells amazing. I expected to be over her now that we've played our game, yet I have a bad feeling there's no forgetting this afternoon. She twists me up inside somehow.

Giving up on the shower, I head outside. A steep, private staircase leads to the beach, a quarter-mile stretch of sand bookended by some serious rocks. The tide's been out for hours and the few waves are flat; it's the worst possible time for surfing, but still a good time for clearing my head.

I flop on my board, staring at the sky. It's peaceful, my board rocking gently with each baby wave. After a while, the noise level picks up. Music pounds from Max's house, a house distinctly resembling a pink cupcake with turrets. Max, Jack and I are neighbors. There wasn't much on the market when we bought, so three houses in a row required the flexibility of a yogini. Max drew the short straw and had to settle for Casa de Pinkie.

My board bumps sand—and kneecaps. I open my eyes.

Max frowns down at me. "Did someone piss in your cornflakes?"

In no mood to discuss my epic screwup, I flash him the bird. "Did you raid my kitchen again?"

"Not in the last two weeks. And there was definitely no golden shower action, although I may have stolen a beer."

A beer sounds great, but Max is empty-handed, the tease. He also isn't dressed for surfing. Instead of a wet suit, he wears knee-length black swim trunks, a white T-shirt with a pink bow tie bedazzled at the throat, and a two-thousand-dollar tuxedo jacket that's slowly absorbing salt spray. Crap. Tonight is the launch party for Max's newest dating app.

The party is the love child of his publicist and

PR person. Max himself is adamantly antisocial, but he's been promised loads of D-list celebrities and paparazzi, so it's party time. Speaking from experience, many guests will regret the open bar when they check their social media in the morning. I promised weeks ago to make an appearance, although I drew the line at participating in a bachelor auction featuring the best of Billionaire Bachelors.

"Party time," Max announces.

I stand up, haul my board out of the water, peel off my wet suit and follow Max to his staircase. Max will loan me a shirt to go with my board shorts, and the party's likely to be clothing-optional anyhow.

Because I'm pathetic, I check my phone. After the third time I went swimming with it, I realized that I either had to take up skinny-dipping or take preventative measures. I opted for a waterproof phone condom. There are no messages from Lola.

Max's pool contains more women than water and appears to be swimsuit-optional. A bar with blow-up palm trees, pink flamingos and a tiki man with a gigantic dick round out the decor. Music pounds because Max hates silence. He codes to earsplitting music—it's a miracle he retains any hearing.

"Classy." Coming up behind us, Jack slings an arm around our shoulders.

My phone dings and I look down. Two-for-one pizza offer. *Delete*.

The arm around my shoulder digs into my armpit. "You didn't surf today."

I make a show of checking my phone. "I went in to work. I may also have made a tactical mistake."

Neither Max nor Jack seem surprised, although it's Max who correctly interprets *tactical mistake* and asks the obvious question. "Did you bang her?"

"Technically? No."

Jack shakes his head. "I told you being her intern wouldn't have a happy ending."

"Yeah, well, Lola definitely didn't get her happy ending," I overshare.

"Gonna need a few more words about that."

Max snags three longneck beers from a passing waiter while I try to find the words to explain. His pool is now filled with foam and the photographers are going nuts. This might have something to do with the behavior of Max's VIP guests. It's raining bikini tops on our private beach.

I finally settle on a strictly factual account. "I got her consent. We fooled around. I tied her up—which was *also* consensual—I came and then I left her."

"Tied up." Jack pops the top on his bottle.

"Yes."

"High and dry."

I shrug. "I'm certain she took care of business later, but yes."

"You have any idea how much trouble you're in?" Jack keeps his voice low, an effort that I appreciate. I don't need to find today's episode of stupidity plastered across a gossip website.

"Depends on whether Lola has a sense of humor or not."

Shit.

I'm in so much trouble.

Jack, of course, presses his point. He's the responsible one, which is one of many reasons why he's also the only one of us who has actually managed monogamy, marriage and genuine friendship with not one but two girls. "You think there's anything funny about tying a girl up and leaving her like that? What if someone else comes in while she's *tied up*? What if that someone takes advantage or takes pictures or just sees that mental image in his or her head every single time they see Lola after this?"

"I used a tie," I point out. "Not cables or plastic handcuffs."

Max cuffs my shoulder. "Even I know that this is not about the delivery mechanism for your kinky fantasies."

Maybe we could have had sex. Maybe we could have had something really great or even something that was just nice. But now I've likely made her feel frustrated and stupid—plus, I've probably screwed up my chances of busting my software pirate. It's a clusterfuck of epic proportions.

"Should I text her and apologize?"

Jack smacks my other shoulder hard enough that I almost land in the pool. "You want to put your stupidity in writing?"

No, I want to put it behind me, but that doesn't seem to be an option.

I point my bottle at Jack. "I don't have her phone number." Which is an oversight I can remedy with a laptop.

"No," Jack says. "You don't get to do that."

Max just grins. "What aren't we doing?"

"No hacking," Jack tells him. "You've reformed."

There's an eighties movie about a kid who hacks into the Department of Defense computer system and plays games with the artificial intelligence brain controlling the country's nuclear arsenal. The kid isn't thinking about nuclear winter or accidentally wiping out the world; he's just a curious smart-ass who thinks it would be fun and wants to see if he can pull it off. That kid could have been Max's mini-me. Or his doppelgänger. Max loves hacking and he's really, really good at it.

I slide a sidelong glance at Max. "Does she have a Happily Ever After account?"

Max pulls a pained face. "Privacy laws, man. I can't disclose that kind of stuff."

"People post dick pics and beaver shots!"

Max just shrugs. "If Lola wants to post her phone number, she can. She can draw it on her tits in black Sharpie and take a picture. I don't care as long as *she's* the one initiating, but you can't look without her permission."

"You suck," I tell him, and he takes a bow.

For the next couple of hours, I put on my happy

face and concentrate on having Max's back even if I don't want to be here. I turn down multiple phone numbers and fend off several drunk girls who would like to show their personal appreciation for my software. I can't stop thinking about Lola, however. What she looks like when she's about to come, the tiny sounds she makes, the way her legs tighten as if she's holding on to the sensation with everything she has.

Promptly at ten minutes to ten, Max literally pulls the plug on the music. Snatches of overloud conversation fill the sudden silence.

And then he said "nice panties."

I can't believe he's cheating on me.

She has really nice tits and I—

"Party's over," Max roars. "Gift bags are by the front door."

A stampede ensues as the party guests head for said door. Max's generosity is legendary, plus word has leaked about the sponsors.

Jack looks at me. "Are you hitting the bar? Molly's traveling for business, so I'm free."

During the daylight hours, we borrow Jack from his wife and surf until our balls are Smurf-colored. Afterward, we head to T&T for tacos and tequila (the two *T*s, naturally) when it gets dark. But instead of surfing today, I almost-banged Lola. I'm off-kilter. Tequila and company seems like a bad idea.

"Not tonight," I tell him.

Max mimes astonishment. Being Max, he's none too subtle about it. He likes making a point as much as I do. "Are you sick? Unexpectedly married? Self-flagellating after today's earlier sexual misfire?"

"It's nothing," I say. "I'm just tired."

And the funny thing is, the tired part isn't actually a lie. I am tired. Not with the flu or even with something that can be fixed with a visit to the doctor, or I would fix it. I have a reputation as a player, a reputation I've earned. Practice makes perfect, and I've put in my hours in the bedroom. I've always loved sex, but lately? Well, lately, it's all seemed a little too routine, a little too predictable, so tonight I'm taking my toy and going home.

CHAPTER NINE

Dev

TWO DAYS AFTER I stripped my boss naked, put my mouth on her pussy and ate her until she not-quite-came, I try out various apologetic combinations of words in my head. Nothing feels right, and that's all wrong, too. Since when do I have *feelings*? And what do I think happened? My usual insomnia was worse than ever, giving me plenty of time to relive each moment and pick my favorite. Contender number one: Lola dropping to her knees and taking me into her mouth. Contender number two? She let me blow up in her mouth and then she swallowed. Contender number three…the whole goddamned handful of minutes, if I'm being honest, because I can't forget any of them. She's under my skin and I don't like it.

Still, I'm officially one up in our game, so Monday morning I saunter in to Calla, playing things nice and easy. You can't tell I'm evaluating the chances I get fired or sued. A casual glance toward Lola's office doesn't turn up my boss, although it reacquaints me with her desk. I promptly get hard remembering what she looked like, spread out before me.

Figure your shit out, Sherlock.

With a ticking clock, I need to prioritize. Plus, there's always the risk that someone at Calla recognizes me. As far as I can tell, I've gotten away with the masquerade only because Lola is too new to the industry and her team members are equally young. Eventually, though, someone is going to connect the dots, read an online piece or just use Max's stupid Billionaire Bachelors app—and I'll be busted. Pretending to be the intern was stupid, my "employment" most definitely has an expiration date, and I need to make the most of the time I have. Ergo, I take advantage of the morning coffee run to swing by the IT gal's desk. She hasn't placed an order, but I know what she likes, and I slide it in front of her.

"Wow." IT Tech Babe stares at me. "I did not see that coming."

"Just being helpful. Trying to learn. Working up to world domination." I've brought her an iced triple-shot espresso with four artificial sugars, but the pièce de résistance is the can of Mountain Dew I wave in front of her.

"You are so evil." Cara fixates on the can in my hand. She's been on the South Beach Diet since Friday, so she's got to be ready to crack.

I open the can and take a sip. The sugar rush is instantaneous. "I figured we could chat. You can tell me all about what your job entails. What you like about it." Look at me, Mr. Butter-Won't-Melt-In-His-Mouth. "What sucks."

"Why?" Her flip-flop smacks against the floor. Bwap-wap-wap-wap.

"Self-improvement." I wink at her and hand over the soda can.

"Bless you," she breathes. Before I can even roll up a yoga ball, she's mixed the espresso and the soda together in the world's biggest stainless-steel coffee mug. Soooo gross.

We make chitchat about her job for a minute and then I go for the kill. "So how did you pick our e-commerce platform? I mean, it's not one of the usual suspects. Did you roll it yourself?"

Cara snorts. "Do I look like a sadist? Not a chance. Lola gave it to me and had me integrate it into our site."

I take a casual sip of my own coffee. *Reel her in.* "You got it shrink-wrapped in a box?"

She outright laughs. "Not even close. Lola put it on our file server and I grabbed it from there."

Okay. So it makes me wonder if Lola has told anyone where she got the software. It doesn't look good. It shouldn't be such a secret and I'm sort of tempted to stand up and announce who I am. That they're using *my* software without my permission and that it's all rather felonious from where I sit, sprawled on top of their freaking yoga ball. In other words: *Boo.*

"Cheers." Cara taps her cup to mine.

I flash her a smile, kiss her mug with mine and

then thank the universe that I've got to my feet already because my phone goes off in my back pocket.

The *Jaws* theme song fills the air. Duh-duh, duh-duh, duh-duh. Followed by tiny guppy pops because you really can't take life too seriously and Lola is only slightly scary. The scary parts include her big brain and the way she puts two and two together at lightning speed. She could be an apex predator in the programming world if she wasn't so nice. She gives a genuine shit about the people who work for her and she has morally upright social justice missions that have her investing her time and talents into revolutionizing feminine hygiene rather than making a mountain of cash.

That's the guppy part, the part that genuinely believes everyone swimming along in the Silicon Valley fishbowl has equally great intentions and will do the right thing. It makes Lola vulnerable, a fact I plan on taking full advantage of.

I look down at my phone. My office. Now.

Go. Don't go. I don't know who has the upper hand now. She came on to the summer intern, but I'm the one here under false pretenses and who had my hand in her panties. Followed by my mouth in places my mouth had no business going in the office.

My phone dings again.

You don't get to make me wait twice.

Good to know where we stand.

I saunter toward Lola's office.

CHAPTER TEN

Lola

I'M EITHER HAVING a panic attack. Or maybe an honest-to-God heart attack. My chest tightens until my breath whistles through my teeth. I've tried downward dogging to release the tension, I've petted Nellie until she hides under the table, I've mainlined chocolate, but there's no magic fix: my intern has up-close-and-personal knowledge of my beaver. Worse, I sort of really want to do it again.

Do *him*.

I spent the weekend imagining possibilities. He obviously has a whole life outside Calla that I know nothing about. The only way to learn is to ask, but that's suspiciously date-like when he's a complete and total ass who badly needs to be taught a lesson. Plus, *intern*.

Not for the first time, I curse Calla's open floor plan. There's nowhere to hide and the memories hit as soon as I sat down. Dev angry-kissing me. Me on my knees. The *tie*. Does he honestly think I'll let him get away with leaving me hanging? We can't just continue to work together—I have to address what not-quite-happened between us. I've seen his penis. I've had him in my mouth. And truthfully, I enjoyed every bossy, arrogant, take-charge moment right up until he decided my orgasm was a power move in the head game he was playing and took his toy and went home.

I'm not ashamed to say that I went home and jilled off like a madwoman. Coming makes everything seem clearer and I spent Sunday thinking things over. At first, my primary emotion was embarrassment. Devlin King completely, utterly played me. Panic had quickly succeeded embarrassment, however. Unless the man was a sadist or a narcissistic asshole, he'd had a reason for denying me my happy ending. Unfortunately, I still don't know what it is. What I do know is that I have to establish who's in charge here and establish it *fast*. Devlin doesn't run this company. He doesn't own this office. He isn't the boss. *I* am.

I wait until he returns from his coffee run to put my plan into motion. He hates orders, so I text him to report to my office. He's sitting with Cara, the two of them chatting away over cups of coffee like life-long best friends, and he visibly pokers up when he gets my text.

But he gets up and saunters toward my office. The full frontal view is as amazing, and even his surly attitude does nothing to make my panties less wet. It just reminds me that I'm in charge and he's supposed to do as I say.

When he raps on the door frame, I pretend to ignore him because riling him up is fun.

Dev isn't patient. He lasts three seconds before growling at me. "Tell me what you want."

The words fly out of my mouth before I can stop them. "You're such an ass."

He smirks as he closes the door. "That's very unprofessional."

"Come in and shut the door." I slam the lid down on my laptop. "Sit."

"I'm not a dog—"

I jump to my feet, march over to him and point at the bright blue yoga ball on the other side of my desk. "Sit there."

He doesn't sit. Nope. He stands there, arms over his chest, looking down at me like a big, angry, uptight rock. That I want to climb said rock is a personal problem.

"Someone's cranky and uptight today. Perhaps you'd like to tell me about your problem?"

I'm sure my disbelief is written all over my face. "Are you always this rude?"

"You know what you need?" The bastard actually smirks, which makes it clear that any suggestion he's about to make will be X-rated.

"Nothing from you," I snap.

And since we've already crossed the line of office-appropriate behavior—have, in fact, plunged into the Grand Canyon of career-ending mistakes—I have no reason to hold back. I kick the yoga ball behind him and push down on his shoulder. For once, he's listening to me. For once, he's doing *exactly* as he's told.

A harsh noise escapes him, cut off quickly.

"Really?" He recovers quickly. "You sure seemed to *want* something on Saturday. Do you tutor all your interns so thoroughly on the company's needs?"

The gasp that escapes me is genuine. He is *such* an ass and he does *not* get to have the last word. I won't apologize and I won't swallow my annoyance with him.

"No, Mr. King. My intern couldn't get the job done, so I took care of it."

Dev

There's a bitter, twisting feeling in my gut. Bad tacos? Too much Sunday night tequila? It takes me a moment to realize the twisting sensation is an honest-to-God—and most unwelcome—emotion. I'm…jealous. Of whoever or whatever got her off. My nemesis just smiles and scoots her sweet little ass onto the desk.

The desk where I almost but not quite brought her to screaming orgasm. I actually consider finishing the job right now because being alone with her here is driving me crazy. I need to know what her O face looks like, if she gets louder or quieter when she comes, if she's the type of woman who pulls her man closer, digging in with her heels and her nails, or if she pushes him away because it's too much in those final seconds when her body splinters, coming apart. I've been hard since she texted me.

She stands there, watching me with a cat-in-the-cream smile. Fortunately, she keeps her eyes on my face and not on what's happening lower down, in my jeans. Parts of me like her attitude just fine, even if other parts of me are fantasizing about pulling her over my knee and spanking her ass cherry red. Marking her until every time she sits or squirms, she thinks of me.

I lean forward, arms on my knees. Her tits are literally right in my face, her body mere inches from mine. It's been mere hours since I touched her and I remember every detail. *Push.* "Is this a performance review?"

She raises a brow and pushes right back. "I'd be happy to review your performance. You're too quick, too forceful and you think small."

"Small."

She smirks at me. "Very small. But that's not why I called you in here."

She leans over the desk, reaching for a bag I hadn't spotted before (probably because I can't stop staring at Lola and remembering her naked). It's a gift bag, with colored handles and curly ribbon. Pastel llamas cover the sides. Or maybe they're alpacas. Fuck if I know.

"This is yours." Her hostile gaze bores holes into me. Likely she's aiming for my ego but the attitude just makes my dick sit up and take notice. She dumps the bag in my lap and then strolls toward the door.

Stops.

"I need the newsletter plug-in completed by the end of the day." She's moving again, the words tossed over her shoulder as if I'm really that unimportant. "Get on that, okay?"

I glare at the bag. There's no way it contains anything good. I should get up, walk out, call time on our game. But I don't. Instead, I open the bag. Inside, wrapped in green-and-white polka-dot tissue, is my tie from Saturday. Sharpied drawings of a penis cover the pink stripes in neat, methodical lines. A really small, sad salad of a penis.

Game on.

CHAPTER ELEVEN

Lola

WHEN LUNCHTIME ROLLS AROUND, I hide in my office. The morning's been a bust and the lines of code dance on my laptop screen, taunting me. I've written exactly nothing since this morning, so I welcome the quick rap on the door.

"Come in." My response is automatic, leaving my mouth before I remember to check who my visitor is.

"Ask nicely."

I look up, startled. Not the Easter Bunny or the Tooth Fairy. *Ah, my old nemesis the summer intern. We meet again!*

"Let me know if you need me to define *nicely*," Dev growls.

As if I can't guess that *ask nicely* really means *beg me*. "Have you finished your assignment?"

"Already done. Now tell me you're impressed."

"Only if it gets the job done," I say sweetly right as he comes up behind me, his legs bracing my back, his arms slamming down on either side of me. I'm trapped, caged between him and my desk, and my body goes up in flames.

"I'm the best at my job." His mouth brushes my ear and I panic. I work in a fishbowl, for crying out loud. People can *see*. But when I gaze frantically out my stupid glass walls, there's no one watching us. It's lunchtime and everyone's either gone out already or is busy in the kitchen.

Dev reaches inside his jacket—he must be headed out for lunch, too—and pulls out a small, tissue-wrapped rectangle decorated with a pink satin bow. He drops it in front of me, on top of my keyboard. My head brushes his chest, he's so close.

"Since we're exchanging gifts," he says, "I thought you could use these. Since you seem to have lost yours."

I open my mouth—although I have no idea what to say—but he's already leaving, moving for the front door at a ground-eating stride. That's probably good. I don't think anything that I said now would be work appropriate. Or quiet. Without realizing it, I tug at the pink bow. It's stupid to play his game, but now I'm curious. I undo the package gingerly, as if it were a bomb that required careful handling.

You seem to have lost yours.

He's given me a pair of pale pink La Perla panties. Delicate bows hold the sides together. They're feminine, absolutely delicious and probably cost as much as my electric bill—and he's *defaced* them with a pink marker. It's like drawing a mustache on the *Mona*

Lisa. Or—I turn the panties around, trying to deci-
pher the lines—a winding road sign? Knowing Dev,
it's probably a penis and a vagina, but it's a good thing
I didn't hire him for his drawing skills. His artwork
might be a battering ram storming a castle. Or just
a whole lot of Freudian squiggles. The only thing I
know for certain is that the man just gave me panties.

At the *office.*

I storm after him and find him in the alley between
Calla and the neighboring building. He's straddling
a big black beast of a motorcycle. Funny. I'd have
thought he rode hellhounds or something. That he
looks sexy as hell just makes me angrier.

I toss the panties in his face. He catches them easily, holding the tiny scrap up for the whole world to
see. Lovely. Pretty sure my face flames. Fine. So he
gets to me. So he knows it. I want to scream at him,
to slap the smirk off his beautiful face, to reach down
and grab his balls hard. He makes me *crazy.*

Instead, I use my words. "You don't get to storm
off in a snit."

He turns the bike on with a casual flick of his
hand. It's one of those superexpensive, high-tech
numbers that has no key—he just does some kind of
voodoo with his fingers and the engine turns over.
Like I did.

I came to the conclusion weeks ago that he comes
from money. The clothes, now the bike—someone
in his family hit the ball out of the financial park.

"According to California labor laws, I'm entitled to

a lunch break, Ms. Jones. Surely you don't want me to faint at your feet. You wouldn't get your money's worth then."

"I'm *entitled* to your respect." I glare back at him. I never yell but he just has to prove that I have zero control around him. "Do you have any idea how long it took to untie my wrists?"

I don't know who moves first. I'd like to blame him, but my fingers are definitely wrapped around his stupid, sexy tie, yanking him toward me even as his hands find my hips and pull me closer to his big, heated body. It isn't as if I came out here planning to manhandle him. Or kiss him. But both are definitely happening.

His mouth closes over mine and I'm too hot, too impatient. He's made me wait for this, and now, touching him, I'm giddy and on fire. I need this man in so many ways, even if he's dangerous. I lose focus around him, falling under the spell he weaves so effortlessly. We still fight when we're kissing, but it's different. His tongue tangles with mine, his mouth seeking an advantage.

He eases back, his mouth leaving mine. "Have sex with me."

His lips are still close enough that I can feel his smirk against my own mouth. His tongue teases my lower lip, his teeth grazing the sensitive skin.

"We shouldn't."

"But we will. Say yes." He trails his mouth over my throat, and I moan, relaxing into his hold.

"Dev—"

"Say *yes*," he repeats. His big hands skim up my sides beneath my tank top, cupping my bare breasts. Of all the days to skip the evil bra, I had to pick this one. Confident fingers tease my nipples. "Let me make you come."

"We're outside. Anyone could walk by." My objections don't come out as forcefully as they should, or maybe that's because my hands are pulling at his belt. I feel wicked, more daring, completely ready to strip down and bare myself to Dev.

"No one will see." He does something to my nipple that makes me moan like a porn star. "I promise."

"Alright." Fighting is so overrated—fucking is infinitely better.

He kills the bike and lifts me until I'm straddling his lap facing him. My legs fall open shamelessly as I brace my hands on his shoulders and lean in so I can kiss him. I'm so wet that I ache. As if he already knows my dirty secret, he slides his hand into my pants, hand resting just above my mound.

"Watch," he orders.

I hold his gaze. I feel different when he touches me, a freer, wilder Lola 2.0 who has a chance to do in real life what she's only fantasized about before. Part of me just wants him to *do* it already. Honestly, the whole day's been foreplay. I'm ready for him to shove inside me and yet at the same time I feel far too naked, more naked than if I truly had no clothes on. His gaze slides over my face, down my body, a fierce mix of heat and need.

"Touch me now?" My fingers dig into his rock-hard thighs.

"Yes." He slides his hand lower, his fingers stroking gently over my slick folds.

The erotic ache builds as he parts me and then pushes a finger inside me. I've never cared much for this kind of foreplay. It's too intimate, too intrusive. In some ways, it still is. I'm intensely aware of his finger moving my body. He pushes in slowly, inexorably, stopping just long enough for me to adjust to his invasion and even then there's a slight sting as my body gives. But along with the embarrassment and the uncomfortable intimacy comes heat, a bright spark of dark pleasure that grows until I'm panting and burying my face against his throat.

Dev groans. "Fuck, I love being inside you."

"That makes two of us." I wrap my legs around his waist, letting him all the way in. His finger burns now. I'm not quite wet enough, but I'm getting there fast. He finger-fucks me like he does everything, intently, with a sure confidence and skill. If I don't think, if I shut down my brain and just feel…the orgasm hovers so close.

"You have no idea what I want to do to you," he whispers against my ear. "I've thought about it all weekend. Eating you out, spanking you, taking you here."

Another finger pushes gently but firmly against

my back opening. Stars explode behind my closed eyes. He likes fantasies, too.

"Tell me what to do first. Tell me what you like best. Or tell me to choose for you, Lola, and I'll do it."

"Yes," I whisper back, riding his hand but needing more. "Do that."

"Which?" His voice teases.

"Choose," I whisper back. He knows I'm close and he gives it to me. He finds my clit, rubbing and pinching gently, and that blend of sweet and pain has me tightening, holding my breath as I push myself against him and I come. He holds me steady as I shatter, his eyes on the spot where he touches me so perfectly, his arms steady around me. He's got me and it's safe to let go.

For a moment, I just breathe him in, waiting for his answer, for the next hard beat of his pulse. Noise filters in from the street—cars passing, people chatting, a dog barking. It only feels like we're alone together. We're still a dirty secret, a broken rule, a screwed-up game we play with each other. I'm not sure what we're doing together, but he's more than a crush.

Dev shifts, unbuckling, unzipping. His penis springs free and it's thick and long, a greedy, heated weight in my palm. A fire truck tears by and our alley echoes with the deafening sound. *This is crazy.* I don't think I care. I fist his dick, squeezing my hand up, and he groans, shoving himself against my palm.

"Rougher," he demands. "Make it hurt good."

I do it, closing my palm around him and dragging my hand down. Back up. He's so hard beneath the velvety skin. Pre-cum slicks the fat head, but it's not enough for this. I reach between my legs where I'm wet and cover my fingers.

I think about taking him into my mouth, but I'm not getting down on my knees in an alley for him. Instead, I work him with both hands, one on top of the other, squeezing him tight. I already know what his face looks like when he comes, but I want to see it again. I want him to let go, to surrender to me like I did to him.

It's his expression that makes me stop and think. The way he watches my hand working him, his face fierce, needy, *certain*. He wants to have sex with me, so that's what we'll do. Never mind that this is my job, my career, my only chance to get this start-up off the ground and I've bet everything on success. He just wants, so he'll take because that also puts him ahead in this screwed-up game he's playing.

I let go and swing my leg over the bike. Straightening my clothes, I wish I could put myself back together as easily.

"Bitch," he whispers.

I meet his gorgeous eyes.

"Bastard," I counter, tugging his tie free. "This game I could play all night."

A hint of a smile plays around the corners of his gorgeous, filthy mouth.

I pocket his tie, lean in and press a chaste kiss against his cheek. "Have a nice lunch."

I make it into Calla without looking back.

CHAPTER TWELVE

Dev

HAVE A NICE LUNCH.

I sit there on my bike in the alley, pants open, dick doing a flagpole impression, while my nemesis saunters away. She's got her happy ending and she's left me wrecked.

What the ever-LOVING fuck.

She's just scored a triple-word play in this game we're playing.

I pull myself together, stuff Mr. Not-So-Happy back in my jeans and weigh my options. Did I just finger Lola until she came? And then she pantsed me and left me high and dry? Since my unsatisfied state would make riding my bike right now torture, I swing my leg over the bike, shove my hands in my pockets and get the hell out of the alley. Clearly neither of us is normal.

Which is only brought further home by the way I sniff my fingers. She's marked my skin, let me bring her to orgasm and then walked away as if she needs nothing more from me. She also—damn it—has my tie.

Again.

I get looks and two thumbs-up on my way to the taco truck that's three blocks away. San Francisco is a colorful place, so I must look like I've been ridden hard. This is driven home when the woman in the taco truck can't stop breaking out into spontaneous giggles as she takes my order and bags up my tacos. Whatever. I'm not starving just because Lola won our last match.

I slink back into Calla and make a beeline for the bathroom. It's all old-world glamour with dark purple wallpaper and gold curlicues. The ladies have stocked it with the essentials—a flat iron, a round curling iron and something that looks like a brush, a hedgehog and an electrical cord had a ménage à trois and produced a kinky baby. Naturally, there's a branded basket of feminine hygiene supplies. I throw the lock on the door and brave a look in the bathroom mirror. Wow. It's worse than I imagined. I look like I just escaped from Christian Grey's private pleasure party.

My hair's a mess. My hair tie's gone. Daily battle against the curls and waves? Lost with epic casualties. Not a hint of smooth, cool, in-control remains. A dozen harpies finger-combing couldn't have created a bigger mess—except for my shirt. Not only have I lost my tie, I've lost the topmost buttons. My comic book T-shirt peeks out, shouting KA-POW! for all to see. Apparently Ms. Jones likes undoing things. I'll have to present a bigger challenge next time.

Abort. No.

She's right about one thing. We shouldn't do this. It's rash, stupid, insane, career suicide and destined to fail—pick your favorite description.

My clothes and my ego aren't the only things that sustained damage. I didn't even notice when she bit my lip. It's slightly puffy from her attention. And…I have a hickey on my throat. The only soap is a violet-scented foaming number, but I strip to the waist, lather up and shove my head under the icy tap.

I'm fucked. Or rather, not fucked. Cold water doesn't make anything clearer, so I turn the water off, grab a handful of paper towels and concentrate on scrubbing away the visible evidence of our dirty lunchtime encounter. I scowl. I have no idea what we're doing, although I'm now perfectly clear on what we're *not* doing. I'd had a plan. I was going to find out who'd pirated my software, exact appropriate vengeance and walk away. But then my boss bounded in, all clingy yoga pants and sexy little tank tops, and I've somehow gotten lost between her spectacular ass and those big hazel eyes that both look through me and yet *see* me at the same time. She's annoying as fuck, vague and way too hippie for her own good. I mean, she still believes that hard work and good intentions can make the world a better place when I know it takes cold, hard cash and the threat of serious consequences.

Noise filters in from the other side of the door, a

wave of chatter that sounds like a horde of seagulls. My coworkers are returning from lunch. What do I do about Lola? I've had my fingers in her pussy. She's had her hands on me. We've seen and touched parts of each other that are never, ever supposed to be visible at work unless your place of business is a strip club and I can't unsee her.

I could walk away, but that means admitting she's won. She won't know it, but the final score will be in her favor. Plus, if I leave, whoever stole from King Me will be free to do it again, and next time the thief might score something even more valuable. Vigilantes-R-Us, that's me. Nobody touches my shit. I need to understand how someone got her hands on my private code and shared it with someone else. Imagine you took naked selfies for your lover and then found out random strangers were getting off to your dick or your tits on a revenge porn site. It's like that.

Worst case, if Calla launches with my software, there's the Trojan option. It would rain dildos on her site. I still have a problem with my own clients, the ones I've promised an exclusive new e-commerce suite to, but I can code them something new. Something bigger and better, slicker and with more bells and whistles. Four weeks is enough time to develop it since I rarely sleep more than a few hours a night. Nevertheless, pulling the plug on Calla is the smarter decision, a business-oriented call—not an asshole one.

Why can't I keep my hands off her? I pull my T-shirt

on and then shrug into my shirt, doing up the buttons. I'm still running scenarios in my head when someone bangs on the door.

"Are you dead? Trapped? Reading *War and Peace*?"

"Reviewing your convoluted-ass code," I yell back. "Come back tomorrow."

Someone mutters "Gross" on the other side of the door. As if I care.

I can do this.

Or *not* do this.

This being Lola Jones. It would be just like high school. I was a late bloomer and super skinny. With three older brothers, I hadn't worried about getting teased to my face or beaten up, but I hadn't been a social butterfly, either. I'd gotten on with the business of getting out of school (valedictorian, naturally) and into college and on my way to financial success. Sure, I loved sex as much as the next guy, but I hadn't felt the need to woo every girl I met, and they'd found it easy enough to resist me until I'd had a growth spurt and a come-to-Jesus moment in the gym my freshman year of college.

So this should be easy.

Just concentrate on the million and one ways Lola annoys me.

I'm at my desk, working, when Lola wanders by. A familiar flash of blue and white catches my eye. She has my tie wrapped around her waist like some kind of trendy trophy.

She wants to play.

A few minutes later, I saunter up to her desk.

"What?" She's already lost in her code, not looking up. I don't even think it's on purpose. She's just that into her work.

I drop her new panties on her keyboard.

"Oh my God." She slams the laptop closed, sandwiching her panties between the keyboard and the screen. Nice save.

I smirk at her. "You lost those. You're welcome."

CHAPTER THIRTEEN

Dev

THE DOOR TO the conference room is shut when I return from my Wednesday morning coffee run and three suit-wearing strangers are facing down my darling Ms. Jones. Her back is to me, preventing me from seeing her face, but the suits wear an expression I'm very familiar with. It's a combination of *no fucks to give* and a sadistic pleasure in knowing that they've screwed you, at an exorbitant cost to you, and you haven't enjoyed the experience, the business world equivalent of anticipating the world's biggest banana split with whipped cream but instead getting an iceberg salad.

"What's up with the suits?" I drop off Cara's triple espresso, waving off her offer to pay.

She makes a face. "Production issues. Those guys are management from the factory that's manufacturing our tampons. There's some delay and they can't start shipping until August, so buh-bye July launch."

I'm headed toward the conference room before I

realize it. No product means a delayed launch, and Calla has an expiration date that's fast approaching.

Lola slams into me as she barrels out. My fingers curl around her arms, steadying her. Damn it. I'm touching her again.

"What did you tell them?" I jab a finger toward the departing suits. "Did you give them a pass on their deadline? A pat on the head and a *try harder, guys*?"

"Let me guess. You'd have done it all differently." She growls the last word, clearly itching for a fight. I can certainly help her with that. She hasn't spoken so much as a word to me since our Monday lunch encounter.

I'm delighted to get in her face. "You're too god-damned nice."

"And you're a *goddamned* grumpy bastard. I'm building a team here. I don't have to be a bitch *or* a bastard to win at life. Believe it or not, my way is effective." Her eyes narrow.

"Mine is better."

"Really?" Her hand slashes the air. "Because as far as I can tell, everything is a game to you and your brain is one big score card."

"Believe me, I take shit seriously."

"Not that kind of game." She sounds frustrated. "*Nothing's* fun and easy with you. Instead, everything is about winning. It's one big competition with you keeping score."

"While you want everyone to hold hands and sing church hymns."

She heads up the stairs to Calla's unused second floor. "I believe I can learn something from other people and that they're worth listening to."

Uh-huh. I tag along.

The view as she bounces up the stairs in front of me is rewarding—her yoga pants hug her ass with each step—but I'm still not sure why we need to make the second-story trek.

"Are you just in the mood for a change of scenery? Feeling the need to burn off the morning muffin? Why are we up here?"

She heads toward the far corner. "I'm up here because I'm putting our new test box in the server rack. You're up here because you can't take direction."

"This is what you have Cara for."

"Cara has an appointment and I *like* doing this."

There is something fundamentally satisfying about bringing a new server online. Given the small size of the team here, everyone sits downstairs. This floor is mostly storage—and the server closet in the back corner. When Lola opens the door, cool air hits us first, followed by the steady hum of the hardware stacked inside.

The new server waits on the floor. Lola gets to work immediately, unscrewing bolts in the rails and tightening screws. I help where I can, holding bits of hardware and tools. The rack has been loaded with textbook precision from the bottom up and the empty slot is at the top, so when it's time to lift the server into place, she starts issuing directions.

"Take the front end." She points to the server. "I'll do the back."

I lift, she lifts, and together we slide the server into the rack. It's a small space and we end up stuck together, legs touching, hands brushing as Lola finishes the install. It also starts to sink in that we're alone. I keep my eyes fixed on the blinking lights of the nearest server because this keeps me from looking at Lola. She has a freckle in the shell of her ear, a soft, velvety spot of brown that I've never noticed.

Lola shuffles, I shift in response, and we do the age-old dance of two people in close quarters who are trying very hard not to touch each other's good parts. Except we fail. Her hand brushes my hip and my own curls around her shoulder. And our mouths—well, our mouths are so close we might as well be kissing.

Guilt flashes through her eyes. "We can't do this."

Lola's honesty is one of the things I like about her. She won't pretend that she's not attracted to me. She's completely up-front about what she wants, even if she dislikes wanting those things. I know I'm not good for her, for so many reasons, but I also don't want to move.

My mouth brushes hers. "Bad, bad idea."

"Help me out here. Give me the list." She's staring down at my dick—who is enjoying the attention—so I can't be blamed for not understanding her.

"The list?"

She gestures impatiently. "The list. You have one for every situation, so tell me why we can't have sex.

Why hooking up with my intern is a horrible, awful, no good, very bad idea."

Oh. *That* list.

"Alphabetical or rank order?"

She grabs my tie. "You drive me nuts."

"Right back at you." I take a step forward. Since the closet's small, my advance means her back hits the wall. I reach between us and loosen the knot of my tie and hold it out. *Play with me.*

She hesitates, and I count off the seconds in my head. *One one thousand. Two one thousand.* Her fingers close around the tie, tugging it through my fingers in a silken rush. Her upper teeth worry the cute pout of her lower lip. She's thinking again, so I distract her with the list.

"Item 1: You're my boss, but I don't take orders in bed."

I add a kiss. Kisses are punctuation.

"Item 2: I don't do relationships, but we work together, so we already kind of have a relationship."

Another kiss. This one steals the little, greedy gasp she makes.

"Item 3: I think I could screw this up."

Kiss, kiss. If I was a better person, I'd add the last item, the one I'm thinking but that I'll never, ever say out loud. *Item 4: I'm not who you think I am.*

"Let's hear yours," I say instead.

"Mine?" She sounds dazed, her mouth reaching for mine.

"Your list."

"It's short." She presses her fingertips against my mouth. "You're my intern. This is our workplace."

She thinks for a moment, tracing her fingertip over my lower lip, back and forth. Then she adds, "And you're younger than me. I don't think we're in cougar territory, but it bothers me. I won't take advantage of you."

"I won't let you take advantage," I promise her. "Everything else is just noise. Get naked."

Lola

We've never done this, not all the way, not completely naked and not pissed off. This isn't the right time, the right place or even the right people—but neither of us wants to stop.

I press my fingertips against his mouth one last time. "Always with the orders."

"You like my orders."

I push gently past him, reaching for the edge of the door. I know he thinks I'm leaving. I should. Smart Lola mocks me, pointing out the ways this can—probably will—go wrong. I was honest when I gave him my list. He's too young, too brash, too much of a player for there to be room for him in my everyday life. In my imagination, however, there's all the room in the world. That's how my crushes always work. I dream big, writing a thousand different endings for those not-stories, and in doing so, I realize that I've accidentally chosen not to live my life.

The lock clicks shut and I turn to face him. He really is beautiful. Without conscious thought, my hand is already reaching for him, trying to pull him closer. My fingers brush his chest. He's always so buttoned up, so confident, so I reach for the first button on his crisp dress shirt and slip it free.

And then I do it again.

Slowly, as if we have all the time in the world rather than stolen seconds in the hardware closet. He watches me, lips parted. Another button. One more. He stands there so casually, as if he truly is the king of his world. Part of me doesn't mind that arrogance— that's the part of me that's fantasized about this moment a million times. Dev, however, doesn't need to fantasize. If I ask, he'll tell me he's done this before and I'm the only workplace virgin here. He's such a bastard, a beautiful asshole I intend to make mine for a few minutes. Almost angrily, I shove the shirt down his arms, yanking the cuffs over his hands and letting the expensive fabric fall carelessly on the floor.

The T-shirt underneath is unexpected. I expected white cotton or an old university shirt, not a manga hero. I sort of hate him for being quirky and surprising. He's supposed to stay in the box where I've put him, the box labeled *workplace hookup*.

"Nice." I trace the horned skull of the hero wizard on his chest. "The ancient and inhuman magus who buys a magically talented human slave girl. Are you imagining parallels between her career path and yours?"

"What's not to like about magic?" He winks at me. "House Slytherin for the win."

I've seen this man's penis. I've had him in my mouth and I've watched him come. And yet I suddenly feel like only now is he a real person. Or maybe it's that—finally—he's more than just my work crush.

He abruptly yanks the shirt over his head. "Taking too long."

His words break the strange spell between us. He shucks his clothes and I do the same, arms brushing, legs bumping. It's funny, more than a little cute and awkward, and I wonder if it's okay to laugh during the hookup. And if I ever get the chance to do this again, I'll do it somewhere with a bed. And room service. My stomach growls, reminding me I skipped lunch.

I look at him, keeping my eyes on his face. I'm probably supposed to praise his penis or write a poem to its mighty manliness, but screw it. He gets me. "I don't know how this is supposed to work. This is my first time doing it in the closet, so you'll have to tell me the rules."

He'll have them because he always does. His eyes darken and he steps into me. My heart pounds, and not just because I'm listening for sounds of unwelcome company on the other side of the door.

His hands push into my hair, cradling my head. "First rule. You have to be quiet."

I can do quiet. I've never been a screamer or even a dirty talker. It spoils my concentration. His mouth covers mine, and somewhere in his kiss, I forget how awkward this all is. I forget I'm naked in front of a not-quite-stranger, about to have sex at work. It just feels…good.

I arch against him, nothing separating us. I'm hardly a virgin. I've read books, done things, made fantasies into wish lists when I stumbled across something that made me think *yes, do* that *with me*. But nothing I imagined has prepared me for the reality of Dev. I whimper, leaning into his touch, hating myself for this weakness.

"Tell me *yes*, Lola."

Because that weakness makes me mad, I tease him back, taking my time to answer, running my fingers over my own skin because it feels good. Finding the hollow of my collarbone, skating down and over my ribs until I shiver. And until I find his thick, hot penis and wrap my fingers hard around him. We both like it a little rough.

"Yes," I whisper finally, going up on tiptoe to kiss his ear.

"Bite me," he groans.

I press my teeth against the smooth, hard flesh of his shoulder. No give. I move lower, catching the flat brown circle of his nipple between my teeth and biting down. He jerks, a harsh sound hissing between his teeth. Devlin King definitely likes it rough.

That's okay, so do I sometimes, at least in my head. And it turns out that I like it IRL, as well. Plus, Dev really, really knows what he's doing. He hardly needs directions at all. He picks me up and sets my back against the wall, his big hands cupping my butt. He's thrusting against me, his penis hitting my favorite spots, and I wrap my legs around his waist. Then I wrap my arms around his neck and bury my face in his throat where he smells so good.

"Don't drop me," I order against his skin.

He says something, but I don't really care what. I'm almost certain it's a promise, and I know he wouldn't hurt me, not that way, so it's all good. Or bad. Bad, bad, bad because that's almost the last conscious thought I have before he rolls on a condom and drives inside me. I take him, gasping and trembling and stretching to hold him.

"You're huge." I may bite his ear as retaliation because he should sting the way I sting.

He groans and then he starts to move. He doesn't hold back, working me on his penis, his hips slamming into mine. It shouldn't be enough, but it is. Or maybe it's just that I've been thinking about this, about sex with Dev, for weeks, and now that I'm seconds away from coming—

I can't hold my orgasm in any longer. I ride him hard and wild, digging my nails into his shoulder as he slams into me. There are stars and comets—maybe supernovas, too, or even a black hole and a whole new universe—exploding behind my eyes. I come harder than I've ever come with anyone else in my life, and I feel him shatter inside me as I do. I need to remember each second, each step that brought us here, so I can re-create it, dream it later because—

He's ruined me for anyone else.

CHAPTER FOURTEEN

Dev

"WE NEED TO get back to work." Lola eases herself as efficiently off my dick as she put herself there in the first place. The woman is a wonder. I'm still debating what to do—compliment her? Go for an awkward, naked snuggle?—but she's already grabbing her clothes and pulling them on. Even I don't usually bolt this fast.

A noise penetrates from the outside world—yet another fire truck tearing past Calla's building. From the frequency with which they go by, sirens blaring, all of San Francisco should have burned down by now. But the sound panics Lola. She scoops my abandoned clothes up and tosses them at me.

"Jesus, Dev. Get *dressed*."

I straighten and pull on my boxer briefs. The hardware closet smells like sex, like Lola and me. Anyone walking in here today will know exactly what's happened. I file it under Shit That Can't Be Fixed and focus on what can be changed.

"I want to do this again." I step into my jeans. How do people have these conversations anyhow? I've never worried before about whether or not my hookup wants to see me again—I've always been too busy running out the door.

"This?" Lola's voice is muffled by the hoodie she's pulling on. It's navy blue with little bows at the wrists and gold beads that click furiously as she tugs everything into place. I add it to my new list: Things I've Taken Off Lola.

"This. Us. Whatever this is."

Her head pops out and she stares at me. Thank God she seems riveted by my abs and the dark slice of cotton where I haven't buttoned my jeans because I'm not sure what my face says. I never go back for seconds.

"It's just sex," she says. "Just one day at a time. Nothing more. You're a hot boy."

"You have a beef with hot boys? Is there anyone who *wants* to date an ugly boy?"

"Do you want a list?" She flings her arms wide. "Of course I have a beef with hot boys. I'm a nerd. It's practically obligatory."

I'm pretty sure that someone hurt her once. Or maybe more than once. I wait, but she doesn't expand on her statement, and now isn't the time to ask. Not that I'd know how to ask. I mean, do I even really want to know those sorts of details about Lola? *You might*, the little voice in my head whisper-roars. *She's pretty amazing. Sex with her in an actual bed might be amazing, too.*

"You know," she says, "this was great. Thanks. But now I'm going to head back downstairs. If you could wait a few minutes before you follow, that would be great, too, because I'd really rather no one knew about us. It would be—"

I can fill in that blank.

It would be awkward.

Messy.

People wouldn't look at Lola the same way and that's not fair, but it's also the way our world works right now. If I were a better person, I'd try to change that, too.

"Gotcha." A pause. I should say something else.

"See you later," she says and runs out the door.

The day after we have hot server closet sex (which was a first for me), it's business as usual. Lola demands to code review my latest project, and before I know it, we're in a heated debate about thread-locking and whether or not I've violated every tenet of good software development (I haven't—she's just crazy). Ten minutes into our "discussion," I'm not even sure what we're arguing about anymore, if I'm being honest.

We retreat to our corners. For a few minutes, silence reigns. Then I catch her staring at me through that stupid glass wall. She smirks, and then she mouths *I win*.

Not a chance, I mouth back. I finish making my changes (she has no idea what a deal she's getting on my services), commit *without* checking with her first and then text her my next move:

Are you free for lunch?

I hear her phone ding. She slaps a hand around her, looking for it, but no go. Aargh. She tossed it in her bag earlier but seems to have zero recollection of where she put it now. Eventually I text again: Cold. We play that game for an unbelievable fifty-seven seconds while she looks for her phone. Colder, warmer, warmer, colder, LOOK IN YOUR PURSE, hot, hotter, THANK FUCK YOU FOUND IT.

She looks down at the screen. She looks over at me. I wave. She yanks her gaze away from me and glares at her phone. She puffs out her cheeks and exhales. Then she taps out a message: Are you crazy? Lunch? One of us would poison the other.

As if. I snort and text back: I'll play nice if you play nice. Or we can take turns taste-testing. Just tell me what you want me to eat.

Lola's lips move as she reads and then she stands up and heads my way.

"What game are you playing?" She frowns down at me, foot tapping anxiously.

"I'd like to take you to lunch. Here." I show her my phone. I've made a reservation at a cute little boutique hotel that's five blocks away. Jack took his wife there for a staycation for their third anniversary, so it's both classy and girl-approved.

She thumps down on my "visitor" yoga ball. "You want to have room service so badly that you booked a room?"

"Jesus, Lola." For a beat, I believe her, and then I spot the twinkle in her eye. She's playing me.

"We don't know each other," she says.

"Is this the *don't get in a car with a stranger* thing?"

She shrugs. "Sort of?"

"So it's okay to see me naked but not to go somewhere with me?"

She hums for a second. "I didn't actually get to see you naked. It was dark and we were rushed. We don't know each other."

"But we could," I argue.

Her mouth curves in a smile. "You want to fight about this, too?"

"You send me a list. I'll send you one. Okay?"

She fumbles slightly with her phone. I wait until my phone dings and look down: Name the last three Yahoo! news articles you read.

Easy. I text back: Weather report sidebar, drone shots that revealed hidden secrets, movie spoilers. Now you.

Lola: Now tell me why.

Me: I surf, I always wanted to fly and I hate secrets. I like knowing how things end.

Lola: Wow. Royal baby (love me some Prince Harry), top ten tropical vacations and a woman who poisoned her nurse husband so she could hook up with a convict.

I slide my phone back into my pocket. "Are you trying to tell me something? Like I only have a chance if I'm royalty or you only do it on islands? Because I can buy an island but it'll take a couple of days."

She stands up. "You're weird."

"Hello? Pot, kettle." I fall into step beside her.

She stops long enough to grab her bag and then we head out. Then she stops and looks at me. This is my game, my show. I'm in the driver's seat.

We agree to take my bike to the hotel. It's only about ten blocks, but we don't have much time since we're officially on a lunch break. I insist she wears the helmet—she's the boss and her brain is more important. Her eyes laugh at me as she gets on my bike. Then we're whipping through the San Francisco streets.

The lobby's ceiling arches above us like a Victorian greenhouse, the gold and stained glass drawing attention as the afternoon sunlight pours through it, bouncing off rows of crystal chandeliers.

"Wow." She stops and turns in a full circle in the lobby. "Can't you just imagine who's been here? Movie stars or royal princesses or some aging, still glamorous former model with millions of dollars?"

Hotels are places to sleep and sometimes hook up, more of a way station in my life while I hurry and get to the good stuff. I've never thought about who might have been here before me. If I had, I'd have wondered how well the hotel cleaned the room or something equally not fabulous. I pull Lola to my side and for a

moment we stand there together, heads back, gawk-
ing at the ceiling like a couple of tourists or people
having fun.

"I love hotels," she admits after I've checked us
in a few minutes later. "They're full of possibilities."

I guide her over to the elevator bank and into the
first free car. "How do you feel about elevators? And
kissing in said elevators?"

Naturally, she thinks about it. It takes her three
floors to come up with an answer, which is time I
could have spent kissing her. I'm not sure I mind,
though. Watching her is even more fun than checking
out the lobby like tourists. She chews on her bottom
lip, looking up and to the left as she turns *elevator*
over in her head, and I wonder what's going through
her head and if she'll tell me.

"Kissing's good." Her voice is husky, as if her elevator thoughts were a slideshow of people doing it
rather than words. "But I have issues with the walls.
If this hotel has two hundred rooms and an average
occupancy rate of 80 percent, that's at least a hundred and sixty people a day. Maybe sixty thousand
people touch some part of the elevator getting on
and off, right? So then if you're kissing and you have
your back to the wall, it's kind of gross. And there
must be cameras. In books, they just pop a Post-
it note over the camera lens, but that seems like a
big security hole to me, so I'll bet there are hidden
cameras, too."

"You're thinking too hard," I tease. Not that I

mind. It's kind of nice hanging out with someone who insists on thinking for herself. She's not worried about my money or my firing her. She's just Lola doing Lola. "What kind of books are you reading? I might need some tips."

She leans against me, resting her hands on my shoulders, to press a quick kiss on my mouth. "Romance novels, Mr. King. The mother lode of all things fun."

The door slides open and I reach for her, grinning.

She must interpret my expression correctly because she dances away, laughing. I'm fast, though, and much, much bigger, so I catch her before she's more than a few steps down the hallway and swing her over my shoulder in a fireman's hold.

She smacks my ass. "Not romantic."

"Send me your favorite book," I suggest, tickling her side gently. "Or better yet, text me a list of your favorite scenes. Stop wriggling. You're going to make me drop the card key."

A minute later, we're inside our suite. Three minutes after that, I'm inside her. It feels like we've been waiting for days for this, cataloging each fight, each brush of our bodies against each other, each casual touch. Neither of us holds back when the door clicks shut behind us.

I shove my hand into her hair, pulling her face to mine for a kiss, angling her head so I can kiss her harder. Her tongue drives into my mouth when I fist her hair. "Yes?"

"Now." She's already shrugging out of her shirt.

As soon as her hands are free, she grabs my head again, holding *me* still for *her* kiss.

Not to be outdone, I run my hands down her sides, grasp the bottom of her tank top and yank it over her head, barely pausing our kiss. Her hands work the front of my shirt, unbuttoning and pulling until we're both bare from the waist up.

I draw my fingers over the satiny skin of her ribs and trace the curve of her stomach. She giggles, then moans. When my hands reach the waistband of her yoga pants, I shove them down and she kicks them off.

Her hands find the buckle on my belt. There's nothing sweet and gentle about how we touch each other, and I love it.

"Look." I fist her ponytail and turn her head. We're reflected in the enormous vintage wall mirror. "Look how fucking gorgeous you are."

This is the first time I've seen her naked in the daylight. Her body is long and toned, but still curvy. The dark ribbon of her ponytail spills halfway down her back above the generous, peach-shaped ass. I turn us around so we're kneeling on the bed, Lola in front of me facing the mirror.

"Take a picture," she demands.

I reach for my pants and pull out my phone and a condom, holding the phone up to capture the two of us. My hand is on the soft curve of her belly beneath her breasts. Her head rests against my shoulder. I text it to Lola and then toss the phone onto the pile of our discarded clothing. I roll the condom into place.

She rolls her ass against me, shifting on the bed so her knees are farther apart. "I want to do it like this. Do you want that?"

I move my hand down, cupping her. Yes, I want that. I sort of hate that I want it that badly because this is casual hookup sex and yet it's not. What I thought was a sprint and quick race to the finish line might be a long-distance race. I bite her ear as I part her with my fingers, and she moans. She likes it rough and fast, I remind myself. This is okay.

I grab my dick with my other hand and line it up, pulling her back into me. I push into her until I'm fully seated. My eyes meet hers in the mirror.

I move, hands on her hips, working her against me as I pound into her from behind. I pull back and then slam forward, riding her harder and faster with each thrust as we find a rhythm together. I'm not going to last long. Fortunately, she breaks first, her eyes drifting shut, her hands closing around mine as she comes. I let myself go, driving into her once, twice more, before I bury my face in her throat and come apart inside her.

After I take care of the condom, we sprawl on the bed, holding each other. Lola's breathing evens out and she rolls so she can rest her cheek against my chest as her fingers toy with my nipple.

"Wow," she says eventually. Her voice sounds a little dazed and I want to preen. "Now I see why older women go for younger men."

"I'm not that young." I gently pinch her ass.

"How old are you?" she challenges. "I bet you're just a baby."

I roll, lowering myself on top of her. My arms cage her head. "Naughty girls have to stand in the corner naked. They may get their asses spanked."

She grins up at me. "You're not motivating me to behave, Mr. King."

Her smile's amazing. It's so fucking happy and in the moment. Part glee, part devil, all Lola. She'll have laugh lines and happy crinkles at the edges of her eyes when she smiles in another twenty years and she'll be even more beautiful. I drop a quick, hard kiss on her laughing mouth.

"But you *are* paying attention," I say.

"Mmm." She slides her hands around my neck and wriggles with downright predictable effect. "Ooh. Are you going to smack me with your big ruler if I don't?" Then she frowns, clearly off on a tangent again. "How old are you, really?"

I know it bothers her that I'm younger than she is, so I've avoided the question so far. "Promise you won't get all funny if I tell you?"

She shrugs. "No idea. I can't promise until I hear the number."

Lola, it seems, is always honest, sometimes painfully so. Not the kind of blunt truth-telling shit that people like to pull under the guise of being holier-than-thou honest when what they really like is making others feel bad, but the kind of conscious decision that she won't lie. I'm not like that.

"Twenty-six."

She makes a face. "And I'm thirty-one."

"You could have been my high school crush, the hot older woman."

She sneaks a quick glance at the bedside clock, checking. We still have time. "Did you have many crushes?"

"Thankfully, just one. I was a skinny, nerdy teenage boy. I didn't shoot up until my senior year." I begin moving while I talk, stroking up and down. I've been inside her once today and it isn't nearly enough. "Tell me about yours?"

"Trombonist in our state's competitive band," she says promptly. "He was first chair, I was third, so I sat right in front of him. He was a manspreader and every time I turned around, I got an eyeful of this enormous bulge in his jeans. Competitive band lasted a week and I turned around so much that my neck was sore. It was so much fun."

"Did you ask him out?"

She shakes her head. "Of course not."

As if it was that simple. As if she'd been happy to look and to daydream but anything else was a *no*. Or a *pass*. I banged my high school fantasy chick, but Lola fantasized. Her eyes, looking through me, are warm and unfocused—she's doing it right now, when I want her here, with me.

"Why not? He would have been yours in a heartbeat." I don't know the trombonist, but I know high school boys.

Her mouth reaches for mine. "Because the fantasy was more fun. I didn't really want to have sex with him, Dev. I just loved the idea of him. Of imagining the possibilities. If I'd asked him out, things would have changed, probably not for the better. I mean, how many people find their one and only in high school?"

I don't want to think about that, about whether Lola might want to find a guy she can settle down with in happy, boring monogamy.

"Did you touch yourself thinking about him?"

"Oh yes."

"Give me the list."

And then she does, and one thing leads to another, and it turns out that our second time isn't that much slower or gentler than the first. After she comes, she flies off the bed and starts grabbing clothes. Normally I'd find this convenient, but today I sort of like the idea of holding on to her a little longer. Probably because she's naked.

"Dibs on the shower," she bellows, already through the door.

"Someone needs to work on her sharing skills."

I prowl after her. That *someone* is going to be late back to work today.

Friday I'm in Nordstrom's, buying more ties. I eye the selection on the counter, debating which to choose. Shopping isn't something I generally do voluntarily, but Lola's hard on my wardrobe and she seems to love stealing my ties, and yes, I'm hoping she pillages me again. I know I'm overthinking this, but I can't help wondering which one she would like best. Would she be a fan of the elegant, understated Hermès tie? The green-and-blue-striped one? Navy blue with bright orange cameras?

I'll just text her and ask. Most likely, she won't even answer—or she'll demand a project status update.

"I need to ask the boss," I tell the hovering sales guy, who does a not-so-discreet check of my ring finger. I ignore him.

Me: Which tie?

I stare at my phone but there are no bouncing dots. Huh. It's as if she's not waiting around for me to text her personal questions. I check the time—it's 7:00 p.m. It's Friday. I doubt she's gone home yet—wherever that is—so maybe she has her phone turned off? Or the battery died. It would be simpler to buy all three ties.

My phone dings with Lola's answer:

I've rank ordered—you're welcome.
Orange cameras!
Do they have pineapples? Polka dots are boring.
Hermès?! You could buy a sofa for the price of that tie!

I slide the camera tie around my neck and take a selfie that I send to Lola while the salesclerk swipes my black AmEx.

Lola: Where are u?

Me: Why? Are u up for a bathroom quickie?

Lola: Ewww. No sex where people poop. Ever.

Me: Would you say no to sex on the beach?

Lola: Sand.

Me: Ocean waves, moonlight, stars.

Lola: Maybe, but not in Cali—too cold.

She has a point, but I go for the win.

Me: Birds poop on beaches. Crabs, dogs and people poop on beaches. So bathroom sex is okay by your criteria. It's a Venn diagram.

Lola: Are you really texting me for wardrobe advice?

Me: Nice diversionary tactic. Communication skills are important. My boss says I need to practice them.

Lola: Your boss is a wise woman ;)

Me: So tell me something about yourself.

Lola: ???!!

Me: Are you refusing to communicate with me?

Lola: I'm busy, Dev.

Me: Then make a list. Lists are short.

Lola: You think an ordered collection of objects is communication? You definitely need help.

Me: Rule #1—our lists should have at least three bullets.

Lola: This is crazy but I agree with you. Otherwise it merits a semicolon and looks lonely.

Me: See? We have common ground after all. But no more than six bullets. After that, it's an appendix.

The email app on my phone alerts me that I have mail. When I check, I discover Lola's sent me a gift card.

Lola: I owe you a tie.

I'm trying to process how I feel about that when she sends me a picture. She's wearing just a blue-and-white-striped men's oxford shirt. Unbuttoned to her waist, it's held together with the tie she stole from me yesterday and her long, bare legs are on full display. The picture starts at her throat—I can't see her face. I'm not sure if that's because she hates having her picture taken or if she's still worried about our personal exchanges going public.

I save the picture to my Lola gallery.

Me: See you Monday?

Lola: ☺

CHAPTER FIFTEEN

Dev

I'VE SPENT SO much time with Lola that I see her everywhere, like the sunspots that light up the inside of your eyelids when you close your eyes after staring too long at the sun. The woman wandering along the shoreline is simply the right height and build, with the same ridiculous ice-cream twist hairdo and unfathomable love for yoga wear and pink. Fuck, she even squints the way Lola does when she misplaces her glasses and the world is a blur mere feet from her face. Whoever she is, she can't see me. I'm too far out.

I arrived at the beach almost before the sun was up. It's not the prettiest or most remarkable stretch of sand in Santa Cruz, but something about it calls to me. It also has parking—a miracle—and is inexplicably never crowded, even on weekends. I ride my last wave, watching the beach glide up to meet me as the wave peaks and propels me forward. Lola can't be here. The odds are better that the California lottery will draw my six numbers on Tuesday.

But she totally is. She wanders down the beach toward me, leggings shoved above her knees, feet in the surf. Nellie's padding along beside her, paws firmly on dry sand. The dog's smart. Lola's toes must be Popsicles; even during the summer, I wear a full wet suit. As always, her brown hair is twisted and looped above her sun-pinkened face in full defiance of gravity even as stray bits escape in the breeze. At some point, she's shoved her sunglasses on top of the mess. She's shed her usual flannel, although it's tied around her waist within easy reach, the edges wet from the surf. She holds up her phone, snapping a picture of the ocean.

Her face lights up when she spots me. Since she has no glasses on, this means she's all of four feet away. "Hey."

Is she stalking me? We aren't at the office—this beach is *my* space. My private world. "Why are you here?"

She looks around, clearly startled. "It's a beach?"

"Why *this* beach?" I'm being an asshole, but too bad. She shouldn't have crashed my beach and my space. Isn't it enough that we see each other on weekdays?

"Because it's a *public* beach?" She crosses her arms over her chest and levels The Glare at me. Nellie barks once, clearly agreeing with Lola. "Unless you're some kind of secret billionaire hot boy and you bought it off the fine state of California when nobody was looking? In which case, you need to hire bouncers. Or put up a sign."

"Jesus," I growl. "Look, I just want to know why you're here."

"Because you're the beach police now?"

"Answer the question."

She narrows her eyes. "Answer mine first."

"I realize we have a thing going at work, and it's hot, but we don't have a relationship. You don't get to stalk me on the weekends and ask what I'm doing or why."

"Wow." She does *not* look happy. "I'm glad you clarified that for me. I might have mistaken our up-close-and-personal knowledge of each other's bodies as an indicator of some kind of intimacy. Which it *is*—and the fact that you don't know that or don't want to recognize it or just have some massive stick up your gorgeous ass about letting anyone get close to you? That explains why you don't have any relationships."

"*Excuse* me?" I toss my board on the sand.

She smacks my chest. "I know you're awesome and you've got your cranky on, but I actually didn't come here to ogle you. My life does *not* revolve around you. I didn't get up this morning thinking, *Ooh, I wonder how I can insert myself into my intern's life today!*"

Okay. I may—just possibly—have overreacted.

"Lola?"

"Get lost." She strides away from me, bare feet

sinking into the sand. Equally indignant, Nellie prances along beside her person. I let them go. Short of groveling, there's nothing to say. I was an ass. Lola called me on it. End of story. I peel my wet suit down to my waist while I assess the situation. I still kind of really want to know why she's here.

My phone plays the *Jaws* theme song. Automatically, I pull it out. Lola has texted me a list of San Francisco/Bay Area attractions:

Presidio—check.
Golden Gate Park—check.
Line too long for cable car so rainchecking that.
Heads-up.
Checking out Santa Cruz next in case u need evac to higher ground or something.

She's also attached a picture. It's snapped from a guidebook, touting the "wonderful views" and "ample parking" of my beach. My assholery drills me worse than my last wipeout. I fire a test shot.

Me: Lola?

A phone dings somewhere on the other side of the enormous sand dune I face. I try again.

Me: I may have overreacted.

Another ding and a brief pause.

Lola: Delete two words from that sentence.

Okay. So I'm an ass. A colossal, jumbo, Trojan-horse-sized ass. There's only one surefire way to atone. Ten minutes later, I'm back on the beach after a pit stop at the snack shack.

Me: Marco.

Ding.

Me: Hint: you say POLO.

Another ding. I hike over the dune and slide carefully down beside Lola. She's curled up, face turned toward the sun, eyes closed. I hold an ice cream cone in front of her face.

"Peace offering."

Her eyes flicker open. The chocolate-and-vanilla twist is great—although the cone tastes like cardboard—and always reminds me of the beach. Lola takes my peace offering and transfers her attention to her phone. I pat Nellie on the head and she barks once before returning to her nap. I debated bringing ice cream for the dog, but Google said that was a no go.

I stopped by my car to strip and drop off my board; I also grabbed a towel and my favorite UCSC sweatshirt. The sweatshirt is officially on life support, the cuffs threatening to part company permanently from the rest of the sweatshirt.

I tap Send on my phone. Lola's phone brays. Awesome. I've graduated from being a vanilla ding to full-on ass. She lets it hee-haw on purpose while she chases a drip of ice cream with her tongue. *Lick me like that*, I want to say. Instead, I text.

Apology Options (please rank order):
Flowers
The grovel
Skywriter with apology highlights
Diamonds
E: All of the above

I try to watch the waves while she reads my message, but the way she works her cone is indecent. Her tongue licks and curls, exploring the ice cream with short, teasing strokes. From the way her eyes laugh at me, she knows exactly what watching her eat does to me.

Eventually, I cave and concede this round. "Am I forgiven?"

"You think ice cream can be substituted for these other options?" She makes a raspberry sound. "Dream on because now I'm dreaming big."

"Well, you'd have to come with me if you want diamonds." I make a show of patting my swim trunks. "There are only two priceless jewels I keep on me and neither of *them* are diamonds. I'd be happy to show you, though, so you could check them out. See if you see anything you like."

"Hmm." She sucks on the last inch of her cone.

That's the best part, the place where the ice cream melts into the tiny cone squares at the bottom and the whole thing becomes a sweet, gooey mess. I reach over and snatch it. "Hey!"

"There's a business lesson in there for you." I bite down and devour half the cone stub before offering her the last bite. She eats it from my fingers, sucking on one, and I file the memory away for future appreciation. Right now, given the quantity of clouds and seagulls overheard, I'll be lucky if Karma doesn't rain or shit on me.

When I look back at Lola, she's pinched my cone. She winks. "I learned from the best."

"Do you have a status update for me on my apology?"

"You were an ass." She sounds tired.

"I was."

"The world doesn't revolve around you."

"Not always."

She huffs out a breath. "So modest. Can you even do any of that stuff? Like flowers?"

Ha. She's challenged a master. I whip the handful of verbena and dune primroses I picked by the parking lot out of my hoodie pocket.

"Impressive, Mr. King."

"I'm sorry."

There's silence for a heartbeat, broken only by the ocean and Nellie's snores. Finally, I take a chance, reaching out an arm. I'm oddly disappointed of games.

Somehow, winning our argument no longer matters—
but Lola does. So I wait.

Another heartbeat, this one harder, faster.

Thud-thud.

Thud-*thud*.

"Do you mean it?" She asks her question so quietly
I almost don't hear her over the sound of the waves
breaking on the beach.

I think about it, arm out, feeling like an idiot. A
hopeful idiot. "I want to mean it?"

She nods and scoots away, reaching for her bag.
My stomach wipes out. But then she shifts again, and
I feel her slide into the curve of my arm and tuck her
body against my side. I pull her closer still, lifting
her onto my lap.

We sit like this for a long time. I breathe her in.
Exhale and find her again. Like a swing that goes up,
comes down and somehow finds the perfect rhythm.
Or maybe gravity and falling explains it, too.

"I almost didn't recognize you without a tie," she
says a long time later.

I angle my head so I can see her face. She's smiling. "You've seen me without a tie plenty of times."

"Nine times," she says. "And you were naked. It
was distracting."

I could make a joke, tease her for not looking at
my face because she focused lower. But this peace between us feels fragile and we both understand we've
crossed another line. Flowers, diamonds, a skywrit-

ten apology—those things aren't enough. Not even getting lost in her skin, her scent, the wet, slick welcome of her body is enough anymore. I have to let her in, at least a little, or I'll lose her.

"Did you bring a swimsuit?" I ask. "I'm hoping for an itty-bitty polka-dot bikini, although I'm also partial to red. And stripes. Ruffles. Pretty much anything minimalist works for me, too."

"Did you mistake Santa Cruz for a Caribbean island?"

"Naked surfing is an option." I shrug. "But you'll fall off the board and flail about, and if you're not wearing a suit, I can't guarantee my good behavior."

"You want to go *surfing*?" She leans away from me, incredulous. "Are you nuts?"

"Have you been? Because if you're ticking off the tourist to-do list, surfing lessons are definitely a must."

The corner of her mouth lifts. "Yes, I have a swimsuit."

Changing is a logistical challenge. There's no dressing room. The snack shack's the only building and it's actually a food cart the owner tows with his truck. If you need to pee, you use the ocean or pick out a sand dune. Or, in Lola's case, the back seat of her car while I humor her and stand guard. My reward is Lola in a blue-and-white-striped bikini. It's going to be hard to keep my mind on surfing lessons.

In the next hour, I almost get her up on my board.

She falls off much more than she stays on, and her sense of balance is for shit. Still, there are lots of opportunities to get my hands all over her and I'm a business-minded guy—I convert my opportunities.

She's laughing when we paddle out to the surf break (okay, I paddle, she rides) and ride back in. Not standing up because she's afraid of falling off (and also of sharks, rocks and riptides), but sitting down like total rooks. I keep my arms wrapped around her, guiding us through the wave, and she laugh-shrieks the whole way, her nails digging into my forearms as if that's enough to keep her from falling. As if I'd *let* her fall.

Anyway, eventually we have to head in. Not only is the sun going down, but Nellie needs company and Lola's stomach is growling loud enough to be heard the next state over in Nevada. Or possibly in Japan. She topples me off the board, however, when I point it out, and then we spend a fun few minutes rolling around in the shallows as the waves break over us and we argue about who gets to be on top.

And somehow it turns in a little more. Lola's on top, so I blame her. She leans down and cups my head with her hands and then her mouth follows and the rest of her and we're kissing. It's tricky not drowning, but I thrust up against her, undeterred by the cold water, and she giggles. I'm reaching for her bikini top when someone clears his throat. Lola freezes and I tilt my head back to see who I have to kill.

Upside-down Max grins at me, Nellie wagging her tail by his side. "I see you already have plans for tonight."

CHAPTER SIXTEEN

Dev

IT TAKES SOME sweet-talking to convince Lola to join the guys and me at T&T. She *doesn't want to intrude* she tells me. And then she whispers to Max—in a voice they can hear at the other end of the beach— that Dev *likes his space*. She may also mention that I *don't take kindly to intruders on the beach* and something else about *having to storm the castle*. I'm pretty sure Max is half in love with her before we ever reach the beach bar.

We convoy to T&T, sandwiching Lola between our cars as she hasn't been there. I sneak a look at her when we reach the cars, wondering how she'll react. She makes a face but says nothing. Lola's smart. The only reason she hasn't pegged me is that she's far too trusting. She drives an ancient Jeep covered in dog hair that can barely stay ahead of Max's Porsche although she seems to have no problem crowding my bumper even putting along at a grandmotherly pace of twenty-five miles an hour.

T&T is exactly what a beach bar should be, a rambling, open-air wooden palapa with a thatched roof, brightly painted wooden furniture and no pretensions. Tacos and tequila are served, with tequila available in two forms: the margarita or the Corona with a chaser. The outdoor tables mean Nellie can come, too, even if I suspect she'd rather hang out in the Porsche.

Jack's waiting for us, along with Hazel. Jack's wife is apparently out of town again. Lately, she seems to spend more time away than at home, but Jack's life is his business. When I introduce Lola to Jack and Hazel, she hesitates briefly but then clearly decides to roll with it. Even with just a first-name introduction, it's clear she knows who they are—and that she won't bring it up unless they do. It makes it even funnier, though, that she's clueless about Max and me. She's so heads-down seeking venture capital and building her company that she doesn't recognize Silicon Valley royalty.

It's surprisingly easy, adding Lola to our group. We order tacos, margaritas and beers, while my friends fill her in on our college hijinks. Lola contributes, too. As she drains the remainder of her margarita, she waves her hands, describing yet another job that she's held. For someone who's only thirty-one, she's worked her way through (or possibly out of) a long list of jobs. She and Hazel one-up each other, vying to see whose job was the dirtiest and most ill-paid. Jack checks his phone while Hazel leans against his arm. If we had one more girl, we'd look like we were on a date.

* * *

Jack goes with me to collect our next round of margaritas from the bar. He rattles off the impressive list of orders without hesitating; I suspect I'm only here to play waiter. Hazel is particularly challenging. Not only does she want her lime margarita with no salt, but she's allergic to most food colorings, so Jack quizzes the bartender and then actually insists on reading the labels on the mixer bottles.

He checks his phone while the bartender gets busy, but he must have no new messages because he puts it away and looks at me. "You don't have to screw this up."

"What?"

"This thing with Lola—you don't have to screw it up. It's okay to let her in."

I give him a side-eye stare. "Are you Mr. Sensitive now?"

Jack snags the bowl of tortilla chips the bartender slides our way. "Just more experienced."

"Not all of us want to get married." I stuff a chip in my mouth, but Jack makes a good point. Exhibit A? The impressive collection of margaritas the bartender is making. I'd have just ordered two of everything so that everyone could find something, but Jack notices details about people. Maybe that's why he's married and the rest of us are not.

Jack tosses me a menu. "Pick one."

"What?" I sound like a goddamned parrot.

"Pick the drink you think Lola would like most."

Is he nuts? "We just ordered her a drink."

"You can pick a drink out for your girl, Dev. Just think about what she likes, and then read the nice words."

"She's not my girl."

Jack tosses a chip at me. "Just because you've always refused to have a relationship with anyone of the opposite sex doesn't mean you *can't*. It means you *won't*." My face must convey the WTF-ery I'm feeling because he elaborates. "Lola seems great. You seem happy."

"So it *seems* like we should have a relationship?"

"You already do."

"But—"

He grabs another, larger handful of chips. Jack's appetite is legendary. "Make it a good one. Make it not just about sex."

"But I like having sex with Lola."

"Noted," Jack says dryly. "But ask yourself this— is that all you like doing with Lola? It's naked times and nothing else?"

"I'm not sure I should take relationship advice from a man who uses the phrase *naked times*."

"Yeah." Something flickers in his eyes and then it's gone. Probably too much salt. He points a chip at himself. "I'm going out on a limb here. Which of us is not relationship-challenged?"

It is true that Jack got married a week after our college graduation. Molly doesn't hang out with us often because first she was finishing a PhD in gender studies and now she's got her academic career to think about. Max thinks we'd give her a lot of material to work with, but she clearly prefers her space. But since she and Jack are coming up on their fifth anniversary, he's right about one thing. He's Dr. Relationship here.

"So you're saying I'm about to totally screw this up."

He smacks me on the back. "I'm saying *don't*. *Don't* screw up. *Don't* run screaming into that good night because you have a pattern of noncommittal dickitude."

"Now you're just making words up."

"Lola seems great." He passes his credit card to the bartender. "But I'm concerned about how the two of you met. I'm concerned that she's smart but she's gonna feel stupid when eventually you come clean about who you really are. Sex is great and the two of you should do whatever consensual shit you want. As long as you're honest with each other and you're both happy."

I look back at our table. Hazel's narrating a story, hands waving over her head. She looks like an octopus having a seizure. Lola is laughing so hard that she has tears in her eyes. She's sunburned, her hair salt-tangled and down for once. She looks quirky and gorgeous, free-spirited and downright amazing—and that's just the outside packaging. I don't need Jack to tell me I'm a lucky bastard and that I'd be a first-class idiot to let her go.

I exhale and go there. "I don't know what I want."
But the possibilities are scary.

Maybe I do want more.

More Lola.

More nights *and* days.

More lists, more laughter, more being there when life takes a bad turn and she needs someone to hold her while she cries or (since this is Lola) to piss her off and give her an outlet.

"Pick a drink," Jack repeats.

I grab the menu and sort through possibilities. In addition to the usual beer and cocktail suspects, the bar offers a number of house specialties. They're out of the ordinary, rather like Lola—so check. Spicy tamarind margarita? Lola doesn't like hot food although she won't admit it. Plus, I don't think either of us knows what a tamarind is. There's a margarita with limes and passion fruit but that will be on the sour end and Lola likes sweet. I finally settle on the ginger rosemary margarita. I also order tacos al pastor because Lola loves food even though she never cooks or makes time to grocery shop. *Bon Appétit* is her food porn. The tacos have mango pineapple salsa, so they count as a serving of fruit, too.

Winner.

When we return to the table, Hazel is expounding on the dangers of hot boys. She makes the *I'm watching you* sign, drawing her fingers away from her eyes in a V and pointing them at Jack and I. Somehow Max gets off scot-free. She's also grossly overestimating Jack's ability to be bad, if we're being totally honest. He's a happily married man who lives for his wife. It would be disgusting if he wasn't thrilled about it.

I set the frosty green margarita in front of Lola. It smells amazing, even if it's the color of a garden hose. "Here."

She points to her other glass. "I'm good."

"I wanted you to have this one."

"Oh." She fiddles with the stem of the glass for a moment, while the conversation washes over us. I expected her to be more curious.

"You don't like margaritas?"

"No! Yes! I totally do." She blushes. She colors up over the strangest things.

"Drink." I inch the glass closer to her with my finger.

She squints and I hand her her glasses. "Did you put something in it?"

"Christ." I snatch the glass back and take a gulp. Maybe rosemary wasn't the best idea. Or maybe it needs more tequila? It tastes like one of those super healthy green drinks except that there is no way more alcohol is good for us. "Poison tested. I swallowed. Your turn."

"That's what she said," Max deadpans. Fucker. But Lola giggles and grabs the glass back from me.

"I thought you would like it."

Although apparently it tastes like shit.

So… I suck at this.

She takes the world's smallest sip. It's more of a lick than anything.

"Well?" I demand.

Jack face-palms from his end of the table. I'm cocking this up.

She fiddles with the glass stem. "It's great."

"So drink up."

Now she frowns. "I can't. I have to drive home. The size of the shot is the variable, but I'm a hundred and forty pounds pretending to be a hundred and thirty. If I finish both drinks, I'll be at .048 if the bartender poured a standard shot. I shouldn't drive at that point, but if he poured on the generous side, I'm over the legal limit."

"Wow." Max sets his own margarita down and stares at her. "Marry me?"

I roll my eyes. "So crash at my place. It's a ten-minute walk from here and we can come back tomorrow to pick up the cars."

It's surprisingly easy to toss The Rule out the window and invite Lola back to my house. Jack flashes me a thumbs-up—apparently, I've redeemed myself. Ten minutes later, Lola and I are walking back along the beach, Nellie bouncing ahead of us. I stole a to-go cup from the restaurant so we could take the rosemary-whatever margarita with us, and we take turns swigging from it. Lola hums under her breath, giggling to herself. My chest pinches. She's really a lightweight. And fun. She's so many things.

We stop to stand on the beach for a moment. The

sky looks amazing tonight, the stars scattered across the ink-black emptiness like a sparse, lean piece of code. The surfers have gone home and it's just us and the lights of the houses lining the cliff. We have to pick our way through the rocks and then go up and down more than one set of stairs because this isn't the Caribbean. California makes you work for the beach.

To take my mind off the way Lola's leggings showcase her ass, I ask the question that's been bothering me. "So what's up with the hot boy vendetta?"

Her forehead wrinkles adorably. "What?"

"Back there? At the Mexican place? You and Hazel were bonding over a shared dislike of hot boys. Is there something in particular you dislike?"

"Mmm." She flops down at the top of the last set of stairs. Not because she's out of breath but so she can look up. When I lie down next to her, the sky is amazing. It's still pretty cool even when Nellie sandwiches me on my free side.

"How can you not enjoy the occasional hot boy? It's like giving up candy bars or never having deepfried Twinkies at the fair. You might as well go on one of those horrible no-sugar diets."

She turns her head, so she stares at me instead of the night sky. "Are you the deep-fried Twinkie in this analogy?"

I shrug. "If you want me to be."

Her expression shifts. "I dated in college—the two years I went before I dropped out. Then I backpacked around Europe and hit Africa. I met guys, really fun guys, and sometimes we traveled together. Sometimes they stayed awhile."

"So they broke your heart." I bet I can find them and kick their asses. There are advantages to having a computer programmer boyfri—

I shouldn't go there.

She laughs quietly. "No, Dev, they didn't. They were just crushes. I didn't know who they were, not really. They might have been fabulous or awesome, but I never got to know them because I was having so much fun enjoying the fantasy of it all."

"Do you think about them?"

"Not really." It's her turn to shrug. Tired of the disturbance in the nap force, Nellie moves to an empty step, curls up and goes back to sleep. "Do you think about the women you've slept with?"

"Not really."

I may be just a bit of a manwhore. The truth is, I almost regret it. Just for a nanosecond. A nanosecond, for those of you without access to Google, is a billionth of a second. In that brief fraction of time, electricity can travel eleven point eight inches. So let's just say that my regret is really fleeting. I've filled my plate up at the dessert bar in an all-you-can-eat buffet and only now learned that the chef will make crêpes suzette just for me. Lola's gorgeous. Spectacular. An understated, elegant sweetheart of a beauty (poor wardrobe choices aside) who makes my mouth water. I in no way deserve her.

We listen to the waves for a moment. Her hand reaches for mine.

"We suck," I announce.

"I did." She lets go of my hand, rolls over and straddles me, her legs hugging my sides. "But I've gotten my shit together finally. After I dropped out, I did that traveling. Then when I came back to the US, I was years behind all my college classmates. They'd stuck it out and graduated, but I was broke and degree-less. I didn't know what I wanted to do, so I held a series of minimum wage jobs as I worked my way across the country. Car wash attendant, the girl at Costco who passes out the free cheese, library assistant, proofreader for a card catalog conversion project." She ticks these off on her fingers. "I've done a lot of things. And then I discovered coding and that I liked it and was good at it."

"But no keeper guys?"

"No." She shakes her head. "No keepers."

It sounds like we're both relationship virgins (although she sounds more like the sacrificial virgin than a virgin-by-choice).

"So you don't want anything more right now?"

Her expression shifts and she pulls her phone out of her bag. I watch her fingers picking out letters on the tiny screen. When my own phone dings, I shift just enough to pull it out and read.

I have a company to launch.
I have the world to conquer.

I have no time.
I always get it wrong anyhow.

She gets to her feet. "There's no room in my life for a real relationship."

She stands over me, frowning, silhouetted by the night sky as she says all the things *I've* said to my lovers before. Not now, not here, not you. It doesn't feel good.

Whatever. It shouldn't matter. I get halfway to my feet and then pat my back. "Your noble steed awaits, princess."

"Even better than holding out for a ride in Max's Porsche," she says solemnly.

She leans against my back, sliding her arms around my throat. When I stand all the way up, she tucks her legs around my waist and buries her face in my neck. She only does that when we're having sex, which means I'm getting horny and run-walk into my house.

CHAPTER SEVENTEEN

Dev

I FEEL MY face heat when I shove my key in the lock. I don't bring girls back to my place—see the aforementioned Rule—so this lightning burst of panic is a new and unwelcome sensation. *Did I pick up? Are the sheets clean?* And *Do I even* have *condoms here?* Condoms aren't the sort of thing you order up from Uber Eats. But it's too late to plan now, so I open the door and lead the way inside. Lola's close on my heels, probably because she's been groping my ass the last hundred yards of her piggyback ride and not because she knows I'm panicking and need the distraction. Damn it. I have to stop thinking about Lola. And sex. And Lola.

"Wow." Lola halts just inside the door. She may say something else but I miss it, too busy messing with the alarm and pretending I'm not painfully hard.

"Your house is amazing." She scoots into the main living space, twirling in a slo-mo circle. Nellie follows her, barking happily. "And it's *huge*. You could fit my entire apartment in here."

The living room runs the length of the house with floor-to-ceiling windows overlooking the ocean. The ocean's now an inky expanse of black pricked with starlight and tiny whitecaps. Cruise ship lights hurry stage right. I'd had a decorator pick out the furniture after Hazel suggested Frat Boy 101 wasn't a good look for a twenty-six-year-old boy genius, so I'm the proud owner of matching leather sofas in a creamy, milk chocolate brown. There's also a generous helping of white linen, some faux fur stuff (no Mongolian lambs were sacrificed to decorate my man cave) and lots of spindly gold crap. It's a compromise I can both live with and drink a beer on. Nellie seems to agree because she hops up on my designer sofa and passes out.

Slightly drunk Lola moves around touching things and making cooing noises that remind me of a happy pigeon at the 16th Street BART station in San Francisco.

She strokes a white vase shaped like a seashell. Or a gouty snail. "Where did you find this?"

"Here?" I gave the decorator a key; she moved shit in.

Lola points toward a watercolor and raises an eyebrow.

"Still no clue," I admit. Now that I look more closely, however, I kind of like it. It's streaky, dreamy blues and yellows. It might have cost me thousands of dollars or might be something the decorator's kids finger-painted.

She waves her hand around the room. "Did you pick any of this stuff out?"

"It matters?"

"You have no memories." She toes off her flip-flops and throws herself on the empty sofa. Her T-shirt rides up, exposing a sun-browned expanse of stomach, soft and curvy and perfect for kissing. I drop down beside her, brushing my fingers over her skin. She has a freckle to the right of her belly button. How have I not noticed the freckle before? What else have I missed?

"I have plenty of memories," I argue, lying down beside her. "Scoot over."

"You didn't choose anything here. It's just stuff—no stories, no souvenirs." She pats my chest. "It's sad."

Her hazel eyes roam the room, examining everything. I try to see it through her eyes but give up. Stuff matches, it's paid for and everything looks relatively tidy even though the cleaner won't come again until Monday. Looking at Lola is far more interesting than debating the provenance of my knickknacks.

Our margaritas have definitely gone to her head. Her eyes are warm and happy. Bedroom eyes. Her hair is tangled around her face and she's sort of coming apart, her T-shirt rucked up and the strings of her bikini top peeking out. I tug on one and it comes untied in my hand. Of course I appreciate the possibilities.

Her big brain is also clearly on slo-mo because her eyes suddenly widen as she realizes that if these are my things, then I haven't rented the place furnished. "Is this *your* house? Like, you own it?"

Deflect. "Does it matter?"

She waves toward the inky expanse of ocean. "How does a low-paid summer intern afford a place like this?"

"State secret." I lean over her, capturing her bottom lip between mine, and suck. She makes the sweetest sound, her breath growing faster as her eyes flutter closed.

"Can you afford hot water?" she whispers when I let go.

I roll off her, offer her a hand and pull her to her feet. "Let's find out."

Lola

Margaritas and I were best friends during my college days and I periodically renewed my acquaintance with them on a Mexican beach. Now that I'm a newly minted thirtysomething, however, tequila has clearly decided to renegotiate our relationship. My head swims, the world swinging slowly around me like an ornament on a Christmas tree. It's pretty but dizzying, which ups the odds that I throw up. After setting up Nellie for the night with water and the spare can of dog food I carry in my purse, I've spent the last twenty minutes in Dev's master bathroom working on getting my head screwed on right. Eventually, a shower seemed like the best answer, so I dropped my clothes on the bathroom floor and shut myself into his massive tiled shower stall.

The house's previous owner transplanted Morocco to California. Dark blue tiles surround an enormous copper soaking tub beneath teak shutters overlooking the ocean. More patterned tiles are set into the red stone floor—and they're *heated.* Lying down and napping merits serious consideration. The fluffy white towels rolled up in baskets beneath the vanity would make excellent blankets.

"What are you thinking about?" That's Dev's voice, just outside the shower.

Don't tell him the truth.

Hot water pours down around me as if I'm in some kind of exotic, heated rain forest. I half expect birds to sing or the sun to magically come up and turn the drops to rainbows. Frankly, it's hard to believe I have any higher brain function, but apparently I do—and it's all focused on one man. *Devlin.*

"Can I come in?"

The devilish grin painting his gorgeous face warns me there's a dirty joke hiding in his words, but all I manage to squeak out is a yes.

That's Dev's fault because Dev naked is something to see. For starters, there's so much of him. His penis probably has its own page in the record books. Or its own zip code. I giggle-snort because when I do tear my eyes away, his dick points up toward an equally phenomenal set of abs. Talk about your abundance of riches.

"If the whole business entrepreneur thing fails to work out, you should totally consider underwear modeling."

"Lola?" Laughter fills his voice. Not at me but with me. Dev always invites me to share the joke.

"Hmm?" My gaze is stuck on his nipples when I should be making eye contact. I force myself to look up. Ooh, brown eyes. That's good, too. That's—

"I think your magnificent good looks fried my brain," I admit.

"Christ." I think I've stunned him, which is weird. I'm sure plenty of women have admired him, so I have no idea what his problem is. He opens the shower door and steps inside. The stall's big enough for half a dozen people. "I think you should absolutely tell me what you were thinking."

He lifts me up effortlessly, as if I haven't just devoured my weight in chips and margaritas. Since drunk me is feeling helpful, I wrap my legs around his waist. The tip of his amazing penis brushes against me in a very sensitive, happy spot.

"Show or tell?" His mouth is so close to mine that I feel the words on my skin.

"Definitely show." I nod agreeably and the world spins slowly around me.

He cups my face with his big hands, angling my

mouth for his kiss. He kisses the corner of my mouth, my lips, the line of my jaw. So many kisses. I close my eyes, a whole lot in lust and there's—*no*. No thinking beyond this moment.

Beneath me he's hard and needy. *I think I love this man.* The thought whirls away, lost in the world's spin, and the growly sound he makes as his kiss grows deeper and fiercer. I love that Neanderthal sound. It shouts *mine* and *right now*. It makes me feel sexy and beautiful, as if I'm exactly, perfectly what he needs.

"Is this okay?" he whispers. His fingers slick over my soapy skin, setting me on fire.

"Let's play house," I whisper back as I open for him. "Welcome home and come on in."

"I missed you today," he says as his penis nudges against me, slipping that first delicious half inch inside me. I squeeze him tight and he rewards me with another, rougher sound. No condom, I register dimly, but it's okay. I'm on both the Pill and the celibacy train. I think I must say that out loud because he says something that sounds like *Christ, Lola, you're killing me* but all I can think is *Oh* as he slides in farther.

The walls of the shower stall have fogged over, cocooning us in our own, small world. I lean back in his grip, taking him another inch, and trace my finger over the steamy glass. *I could make a list.* The letters flow beneath my fingertip, appearing before slowly filling in with steam and vanishing.

"What are you doing?"

"Making a list." I trace new words on the glass.

"Now?" His hands grip my hips, easing me down-ward.

"It's a very important list. It's all the ways I want you to kiss me and me to kiss you."

Kiss my hand as if I were your princess
Kiss my cheek as if we were friends and happy
to see each other
Kiss my forehead because you feel close to me
Kiss my neck
Kiss my shoulder
Don't not kiss me

My list can't last. The words dissolve as fast as I finish them. Right now, I don't care. Instead, I write and rewrite my list on slick, wet skin. *Kiss me. Touch me like* that. *Play with me. Don't rush to the end. I think I could love you.*

We kiss and kiss. There are so many things I could pretend. That we're lovers in the rain is a favorite. That we're standing here, entwined while the skies open up and the water rains down on us and washes away the regrets and the fears, leaving everything else new and fresh.

When the dreamy, slow pace of his thrusts starts to pick up a faster rhythm, he walks me out of the shower, wraps a towel around me and carries me to the bed. We spray water droplets everywhere as we sink into the white duvet, but I don't want to be practical. Tonight I don't want the foreplay or the games. I just want him.

"Is this okay?" He pushes deeper inside me.

Shit. Did I say all that out loud? I need a rewind button on life. The silence stretches out between us. I can hear the waves hitting the shore close by.

"Lola?" He says my name against my mouth, his lips brushing mine. Tears prick my eyes, so I close them. We don't do tears or feelings, so he can't see.

"Never better," I whisper back. "Show me, okay?"

His hands dig into my hair, smoothing, holding me closer. Whenever we have sex, I smell of him for hours afterward. When our summer is over, I'll miss that.

His new kiss is sweeter, slower. This is different from the way we've kissed before. It feels good, too, the way all of his kisses feel good.

Gently, he peels back the towel, patting, rubbing, running the luxurious cotton over every bare inch of my skin. He tells me how beautiful I am, how badly he wants me, how dirty and perfect I am.

"You're beautiful. I'm not one of them, okay?" He presses the words into my throat, punctuating his question with kisses. *Not one of who?* I want to ask. But I know. Not a hot boy, not my hot boy, not mine.

When he finally reaches between my legs, I whimper. Waiting is a painful anticipation. I've never craved anyone's touch like this, holding my breath, imagining what might come next and then willing it to happen because my imagination isn't enough, isn't Dev. His first touch is soft, almost tentative.

I tell him how he makes me feel. How he makes me wet and achy. How hearing his voice teases me and makes me feel good. I cover his hand with mine and together we touch me.

He tells me how beautiful I am there, too, how fucking beautiful all over, and that I make him feel so many things. He craves me, he says, and I think he steals my words.

I come before I mean to, my body tightening, bearing down on our fingers even as I reach for him, not wanting to be alone. Somewhere he's found a condom anyhow because he brushes my fingers gently away and rolls it on before pushing slowly inside me. I'm wet, but between the ocean, the latex of the condom and far too much sex, I'm tight. He has to nudge his way in, coaxing my body to open for him, and it's perfect. Slow has its own magic.

I hang on to his broad shoulders, legs tight around his hips, as he rides me toward his own happy ending. It feels so good, even just the little, accidental touching bits, like when I run my fingers up his shoulders and draw little circles in the hollow of his collarbones. Nobody feels as perfect as he does.

He comes quickly, as if now that I'm done, he thinks he should be done, too. I wouldn't mind if it took him longer. I love the soft, sleepy feeling of him working himself inside me while I just relax in my happy place. Then I can just feel him and pay attention to the thousand and one Dev details that I lost sight of when I'm coming. Like how he smells, the perfect blend of man and sweat and salt. Or the sounds he makes. And definitely how his eyes always drift shut right before he comes. I wish I could take a picture of his O face because I'd look at it when we're apart. He collapses against me briefly and I run my hands up and down his back while he mentally puts himself back together and zips up all the pieces that he keeps so tightly under control.

His arms around me afterward are even better than the sex, although I'll never admit it. This is why I've always chosen to live and love in my head. He's so painfully real. I'd think about it more but I'm drifting off now into the arms of my best friend Margarita. I feel his palm stroke over my head, followed by a rough chuckle. I don't mind amusing him, though. I mind even less when he slips out of the bed and comes back with a comb so he can painstakingly detangle my hair. I don't have to do a thing but lie there, basking in the delicious scratch of the comb against my scalp. He talks, though, a soft flow of words. I'm too tired, too drunk, too…something to pay much attention, but all the talking is strangely comfortable. Maybe he needs to fill the silence as much I need to hear his voice.

"Lola?" He whispers my name by my ear.

"Yes?" I think I'm smiling, although I might be smiling in my sleep.

"I'll take you around San Francisco and show you the sights, okay?" His voice is husky.

"Okay," I say quietly. "It's a date."

CHAPTER EIGHTEEN

Dev

MY APP SHOWS no coffee orders. Zero. Zilch. A quick visual inventory of Calla confirms bodies are present. The Wi-Fi works, too, so we haven't gone abruptly bankrupt. I know people who have come back from lunch and find themselves locked out of the office because the business went belly-up with no notice. I take myself and my questions over to Cara. "Are you dead?"

She eyes me. "Not unless I've died and gone to heaven. Nice suit."

I have an evening meeting I can't get out of, so I've traded my jeans for suit pants. My car is parked in forty-dollar-an-hour parking a few blocks away for a quick getaway.

"Why no coffee?"

Cara pats me on the shoulder. "Boss girl said you had a meeting downtown and she hereby relieved you of the fetch-and-carry portion of your job description."

Something has shifted in my relationship with Lola in the last couple of weeks, and the change is bigger than my no longer believing she could've had anything to do with my stolen software. It's even bigger than just where we have sex. There's talking involved now. And overnights. And yes, I'm terrified that this woman I've met by accident will march out of my life when she discovers the truth about me. I'm not ready to give her up yet.

I don't need Jack to know that Lola won't react well to learning that she hired me under false pretenses. Right now, though, all I can think about is sex—sex and getting inside Lola as fast as possible. I do a quick run-through of the best hotels in downtown San Francisco, mentally starring the ones we haven't visited yet. There's one right on Market Street that Lola would love. They have the most amazing suite bathrooms.

I rap on the door to her office. "You need me?"

She's bent over her desk, fiddling with something on her laptop, and she's wearing a *skirt*. My brain turns off and my dick takes over. The skirt is vintage, a gray pinstripe with ass-hugging fabric. She's wearing a discreet button-up white blouse beneath a rather sassy suit jacket. The best part, though, are her heels—slim stilettos with delicate straps that wrap around her ankles. We need to have sex while she's wearing those heels.

Lola straightens.

"Oh, good. You came."

Not yet.

I grin. She's wearing my tie threaded through the loops of her skirt and tied in a jaunty bow.

"Follow me." She grabs her phone and a messenger bag and heads for the door. It's not until we're in the Uber that my brain works enough to ask where we're going.

"Since you've kidnapped me," I say. "I really think you should tell me where we're headed."

She laughs and pats my shoulder. "I thought I'd give my intern an opportunity."

"Specifics, Lola."

"I'm pitching to a VC firm. I thought you'd like to come along. You can meet some useful people and see how a pitch works firsthand." She beams at me like she's just offered me the choice of having her blow me for an hour or allowing me to lick crème brûlée off her gorgeous, naked, tied-up body.

I panic. I know all the tech VC guys worth knowing; Jack's the king of VC and his backyard barbecues are a prime networking spot (plus he serves awesome beer). There's no way I'm not going to know these people—and that they're not going to know me. *Brazen it out.* This is just a pitch event.

Pitching to VC firms isn't like the TV shows. You can't go in cold and expect to walk away with a million bucks. Lola's already proved she has skin in the game by investing heavily in Calla, but she's exhausted the crowdfunding angle. She needs to secure additional capital and this is the only feasible way to do so.

Sure enough, as soon as I follow Lola into the bland office suite where we're pitching, I spot familiar faces. Trey and Ben are savvy investors with an eye for spotting new companies that need additional seed money. They're not unicorn chasers—they're not looking for a billion-dollar payout—but they get results. Their companies make money.

They nod at me, clearly curious. Lola is already introducing herself and then she gestures to me. "This is—"

"Devlin King." I cut her off. "I'm sitting in."

I'll pay for that interruption later, but it buys me some time. Trey and Ben settle back in their seats while Lola runs through her pitch deck, making the case for Calla. She covers management talent, the financial forecast and Calla's product. Yes, she's showing pictures of tampons to three guys. VC isn't a loan scenario; Lola won't be paying them back with interest. Typically, the VC guys get their return on investment when you either IPO or sell the company.

I'm reluctantly impressed. She's done her homework. Still, if she were pitching to me, I'd tell her she was too early. She hasn't gone to market yet, so even though she has a warehouse of product, she also has no customer traction despite promises from fifty thousand starry-eyed do-gooders claiming they'll beat down her doors to purchase ethically manufactured feminine hygiene products. It's interesting, but not something you can bank on, at least not yet.

There's certainly not enough in it for Trey and Ben, and the three of us know it. In dating terms, she's offering a cup of coffee and a chance to chat when they're looking for a hot hookup and huge immediate gratification. So I interject and point out it's not just about tampon access. It's also about the underlying order and delivery mechanism—developing a working software prototype that can be repackaged and resold for other products. *That* makes Trey and Ben start thinking.

When we're done, Lola hightails it out of the conference room like her gorgeous ass is on fire.

"Are you—" Trey stops me on the way out. He's actually a decent guy.

Sleeping with Lola? Yes.

In way over my head? Hell, yes.

"Working with Lola Jones? Yes, I am. I think it's important to give back to the community and her software design is top-notch."

Trey nods. I have to hand it to him—he keeps a straight face when I suggest my motivation is charitable. My reputation is the perfect red herring to distract from my feelings about Lola. "If you're backing her, I think we can get on board. I'll review her deck and have my assistant send her an invitation to pitch to our management team."

I nod, thanking God when the elevator doors slide open. I've avoided lying outright, but Trey clearly assumes that I'm mentoring Lola and have given her the King seal of approval. He probably *also* thinks we're sleeping together and that's why I'm taking an interest. For a shot at my network, he'll take a small chance on Lola. It sucks that's how Silicon Valley works because she's got a great product vision. It's just her timing that's off.

Lola isn't in the lobby; I find her standing outside our pitch venue, foot tapping impatiently while she waits on the curb and glares at her phone. She doesn't glance up when I look over her shoulder. Our Uber is just around the corner, but with San Francisco traffic, that means minutes at best. Her phone dings; Trey has sent a request for a follow-up.

I glance at her. "Congratulations."

"What were you doing in there?"

"Our meeting?"

She nods. *Tread carefully.*

"Pitching?"

She gives me the bird. "Let's try again, Mr. King. That was *my* meeting and *I* was pitching. *You* were observing and learning."

"You're unhappy I stepped in."

"You didn't step in," she hisses. "You took *over*. You decided that you had a better plan and so you just went ahead and executed it—like you always do."

"And it worked," I growl, waving off the Uber when it pulls up. "You got your follow-up. Trey's going to fund you unless you burp the alphabet at your next meeting. I was *helping*."

"You took over. And you just did it again." She gestures at the departing Uber. "This is my life, my business, my choices. You are my intern. I am your boss. You don't get to tell me what to do."

"You like it when I tell you what to do in bed."

She rolls her eyes. "That's the oldest line in the book. It doesn't work."

The oldest line was *want a bite of my apple?* And it *definitely* worked. I lean over her. "You. Like. It."

She's not the same woman who chattered my ear off on the way to the pitch session, or even the same woman I held in my arms last night. That Lola was playful, geeky, thoughtful. She was also interested in me, in who I was and what I thought. This Lola has dismissed me as a subordinate, as someone who doesn't matter.

I see red. Anger isn't productive, but right now I don't care. "Let's go."

I set a hand at the small of her back. She told me once that the gesture is sexist and outdated—and still makes her panties wet. She shook her head while she confessed, as if she couldn't believe herself, so my touching her like this will be fuel on the fire.

"I didn't need your help in there." She just won't let it go.

"You got it anyhow. And you really should work on your manners and say fucking thank you because I pulled your ass out of the fire *in there*, baby."

We're yelling at each other on the sidewalk. People are looking. The only reason security hasn't interfered is because we're both wearing suits.

"Fuck you," she says sweetly and whirls to march up Market Street.

I have no idea what her plan is, but she doesn't walk away from me. I pull her to me and I angry-kiss her. When we pull apart, we're both panting, but I still have a point to make.

"Say *please* and I'll fuck you."

CHAPTER NINETEEN

Dev

LOLA GLARES AT ME, her breath tearing from her in
harsh, panting gasps. "Are you insane?"

Yes, I'm crazy for you.

"Tell me to fuck you again, and I'll do it."

The hate coursing through me is real, as is the
rage. There might be pain and some other emotions
in there, too, but I'm ignoring those. My dick tents
the front of my dress pants.

"Have you ever fantasized about a hate fuck?" I
step into her, crowding her with my body. She won't
back down, so now we're thigh to thigh, so close we
might be embracing or jammed into a crowded com-
muter car together. "There are no excuses for wanting it. You just do. You do because you want to mark
that other person. You want to get deep inside them
and make it impossible for them to ignore you or shut
you down. You do because there's nothing better than
the post-fight adrenaline and taking it out on the person who caused it."

I pause and let silence fill in the space between us. We're standing on the busiest street in San Francisco, the lunchtime crowd pouring around us, giving us sidelong glances, muttering curses because we're in their way, and no, we're not moving. Not yet.

I pull out my phone and book a room in the hotel where she just pitched. Lola watches me, but it's not as if I'm trying to hide what I'm doing. I'm only hiding who I am.

"Yes or no, Lola?"

"Fuck you," she says quietly, her eyes on my face. Then she takes my phone and drops it into her bag.

I'm not sure how we get into the hotel. There's nothing but white noise and red rage and this desperate, stupid, *fucking* need I have for this woman. As soon as we're in the elevator, she shoves me against the mirrored wall, the decorative brass rail that runs around it stabbing into my ass, and then she throws herself at me, angry-kissing the ever-loving daylights out of me.

Her mouth is hard and hungry, her tongue chasing mine when I gasp and let her in. We kiss with our eyes open because neither of us wants to give the other that edge, to be vulnerable. Her hands cup my head, pulling my head toward hers. Her eyes have gold in them. I'm not sure if I've just never noticed or it's just that we're really, really close.

She bites my lower lip hard and yanks her head back. "I hate you."

The sound of our harsh breathing fills the elevator.

"Fine by me."

It's clear what we're doing here. I've booked a room so we can have angry sex and then we'll go back to work as if nothing has happened. She'll have my jizz dripping down her thigh, though, especially if she's not wearing panties. Lola never wears panties and I fucking love the idea of her dripping wet with my cum. She won't be able to ignore me then.

I curve my hands around her ass. "You wearing panties today?"

"Check." She's fierce, the way she won't back down. Even when she's scared or unsure—which I think is more often than she lets on—she just jumps in with an *oh screw it*. I like that about her.

Right now I'm all over her and she won't give. She tilts her head, her gaze holding mine. The smooth bun-thing perched on top of her head isn't looking so perfect anymore. That's my fault for having my hands in her hair, but it makes me think about undoing her more. I drag my fingers over the soft curves that are accentuated by the well-tailored suit skirt. I find the zipper that starts at the small of her back and tug.

The sound of the zipper going down is overloud in the elevator. Lola's panting, her breath coming in short, harsh gasps. She wants this as much as she hates me, but this isn't a surrender. I haven't won this battle we're fighting. I slide my hand inside her skirt. Her skin is so soft. It always surprises me, how someone so driven can have this tender, hidden side once I get past the walls she puts between us.

She is wearing panties, but there's not much to them—a creamy satin thong that splits the gorgeous cheeks of her ass. She was on her best behavior for the VC guys. Which is probably wise because I've heard enough hinky shit about what some of the less ethical guys expect in return for their checks.

I pull her harder against me until she's riding my thigh. Her hands work the buttons of my dress shirt. She likes it when we're both equally naked. But not yet. I have a point to make.

When she tries to pull my shirt apart, I capture her hands behind her back in one of mine. She makes a rough sound, almost feral. I cast a quick glance at the panel of floor numbers above the door. I don't have much time. She grinds down on my thigh, and I work my free hand between us until I'm between her thighs. She freezes for a moment. Lola likes fantasies and scenes. She needs a lot of foreplay and not just with my fingers or tongue—she has to feel the mood. Today, though, she's already soaking wet.

"Tell me yes."

She glares at me. "Yes, damn you."

That works for me.

"You want to tell me what you want today? Or do you want me to choose?"

I tuck her thong to the side and push a finger inside her. She's wet and her body yields before the steady pressure of mine. I don't touch her clit or kiss her. There's nothing smooth about me—I just need to touch her, to somehow make myself a part of her.

The sound of my finger-fucking her is almost covered up when she speaks.

"Dev," she whispers.

I wait for more, my finger tunneling carefully in and then almost back out, but she's silent. She just watches me as I penetrate her. The elevator whines as it starts to slow. She's so fucking tight, slick heat squeezing me, that I'm tempted to dry-fuck against the elevator wall I know she hates because I've never needed to come more badly.

"Give me an answer."

Naturally, she makes me wait another second, silently death-glares me—and then she squeezes my finger tight. "Let's do it your way."

Elevator dings and the doors start to slide open. Right. We're in the hotel. It's a public place. I have no idea what either of us is thinking, but this is dangerously crazy. Lola steps back and my finger pops out of its snug nest. I ram my other hand against the door open button.

She smirks at me as she shoves her skirt back into place. "I should leave you here."

"But you won't. You want this as much as I do."

I stride out of the elevator, not waiting for her to catch up. It's not as if I can't see her. The hotel has these ornate, decorative mirrors every few feet, so my vision fills with Lolas. She sucks in a breath, and for a moment I almost think she'll do it. That she'll let the doors close and that she'll go back downstairs and walk out of my life. That she doesn't really want to steal an hour with me. That she doesn't want me anymore. But then she strides out of the elevator, pulling the hair tie out of her messed-up hair so that long brown hair falls around her face in big waves. She doesn't look so put together now.

We walk to the room like that, shoulder to shoulder. I sort of want to thread my fingers through hers but I'm also pissed off. Hell, *she's* pissed off. Her chest heaves and pink flushes her cheeks. I can't stop remembering all the other times I've stripped her down, how she looks out of that fuck-me suit.

As soon as we get inside the room, she's already stepping out of her shoes. "Leave them," I order.

She gives me a look—the one that says I'm a crazy bastard—but she does it.

I take a quick survey of the room, mostly because I'm inventorying the available surfaces to take Lola on. Writing desk, armchair, enormous king-size bed and, just in case we haven't worked off our voyeuristic fantasies enough, a window seat beneath an enormous mullioned window overlooking a busy city street. Some hotels install one-way glass, but I have no idea what the situation is here. There's a massive marble bathroom through a half-open door. From the bit I can see, it looks like Versailles mated with a bathroom showroom, all gold and shiny crap.

Normally Lola would explore. She loves hotel rooms with a passion others reserve for sports teams or museum exhibits. She always snaps a few quick photos and then steals all the complimentary toiletries. I've traveled enough for business and pleasure, however, that the novelty's worn off and I can't help but wonder who's done what in that big-ass bed. Or in the elevator we just rode.

I scoop her up and toss her on the bed. Lola's not a small girl and I love that. There's nothing sexier than a woman who owns her curves. This time when her fingers go to the buttons on her blouse, I grab her hands with my own. She doesn't get to take control. Not yet, not when it's my turn.

I pull away ignoring her squawk of protest. My tie slides off easily and then I'm gift wrapping her wrists. The bow's a little floppy—unlike me—but she can slip free anytime she wants. I've already got at least six inches and sixty pounds on her, so I don't want her feeling trapped. She can push me away if she feels the need.

I finish what she started in the blouse department. I pop the remaining buttons free one at a time, working steadily down. The striped cotton falls apart, revealing a satin push-up bra that matches her thong. She doesn't have huge tits, but they're nicely showcased.

"Tell me to stop if you want to stop."

She nods. "I'm okay."

"Then I'm not asking again. Use your words if there's a problem."

She leans up, aiming for my mouth, and I'm almost tempted to let her catch me, but I have plans. I drop down her body, searching for the hem of her skirt. She squeals as my fingertips graze her bare thighs, her hips rolling. We both know what's coming. I shove the skirt up.

And because she's invited Barbarian Dev over for a playdate, I don't bother sliding her panties down her legs. I just tear them off and shove them in the pocket of my suit jacket. I deserve a trophy for today, even if it's just the participation prize for showing up. Plus, she keeps taking my ties, so maybe I'll start a panty collection. Her fingers reach for me, trying to drag my head up toward hers. But I have a lesson I want to teach her, starting with who's in charge here.

It's not her.

I drop down, slide my hands under her ass and put my face between her thighs. I get my tongue in her slick, wet heat. She tastes deceptively sweet. I lick a path from top to bottom, fucking her with my tongue until she moans and starts moving against me. I explore each tender fold, storing away new memories of which touches make her louder and which make her whisper "More." Lola's not a screamer—she talks with her body. Her thighs grip my head so tightly that I'm concerned for a moment I can't breathe. Her hands pull silently at my hair, the sting of her grip building my pleasure. When she's with me, she feels. There's no way she doesn't feel *us*.

I look up at her, sprawled on the bed, hair messed up, clothes half on, half off. She's my beautiful mess and she doesn't stand a chance. I won't lose this game we're playing.

I know what she looks like when she's coming now. Her whole body tightens and freezes up, as if now she's found that one, perfect sensation, she's holding on to it in case she loses it. Today she fights it for a second. Then she's over the edge, falling and coming.

I shove my dress pants and boxer briefs down far enough to free myself. I'm so hard it's painful, and even though she hasn't even touched me yet, it gets me going that she's let *me* touch *her*. She reaches for me, clearly intent on showing me the same sort of love I've shown her. Her fingers curl almost roughly around me, stroking and pulling. I think my eyes may roll back in my head.

"I need to get in you." I almost don't recognize my own voice. *Hoarse* doesn't begin to cover it. I sound needy and desperate, two things I never do.

"Come on, baby." She rocks against me, a teasing, mocking smile lighting up her face. Her bound hands slide down my chest, find a nipple and pinch. A groan tears out of my mouth before I can hold it in. We're not hurting each other—*much*—but it's intense.

I shove her legs wide, position myself at her opening and thrust. Fuck. *Condom.* She's on the Pill, but we can't take chances. I pull out, dick bobbing inelegantly against my stomach, and rummage in my pants pocket until I come up with my wallet and a condom. I ram it on and then I'm back, pushing into her with a pained sigh.

God, she's amazing. There aren't words for the

sensations tearing through me. I can feel myself pushing deeper, making space inside her body for me, but
she's there, too, her body gripping me. Our hips move
together, the slap of skin on skin, our bodies slick
where we touch. She's chanting something but I'm not
silent, either. To my horror, I realize I'm whispering
things like "You're gorgeous," "Please," "I'm sorry"
into her shoulder. And as I drive into her body, pull
back, return, the words pile up in my head.

I'm sorry I took control of your meeting.

I'm sorry I'm such a dick.

I'm sorry you don't know who I am.

I'm sorry I didn't tell you.

I'm not sure who comes first or if it's a tie, both of
us reaching the finish line together, but I let myself
collapse on top of her for just a moment. My hands are
tangled in her hair, my face pressed against her neck.
Christ, she smells good. I think I kiss her throat but
it's hard to think. She sprawls beneath me, loose and
relaxed, breathing heavily. Her eyes drift closed. My
whole body's still shaking, my lungs working double-
time. When I get to ten in my head, I force myself to
let go and roll to the side.

"Are you okay?" *Are* we *okay?*

"Yes." She doesn't open her eyes as she slides her
skirt back down. At some point, my tie's come undone. It's half under the pillow. She's still wearing
those sexy heels and her shirt's all undone. Part of me
wants her to look at me, except I'm not certain what
I'd see in her eyes. Suspicion, anger—or something

worse. Maybe I'd find nothing there because we're each other's dirty secret and nothing more.

I reach for her, intending to shift her so I can pull back the expensive duvet we've just had sex on, but Lola swings her legs over the side of the bed, already doing up her buttons. I wish we could lie here and sleep the afternoon away. Instead, she pulls herself together and hotfoots it into the bathroom. I've missed my chance.

I get dressed, mentally rerunning what just happened between us. We fought, I fingered her in an elevator, possibly in front of security cameras, and then we had hot, rough hotel room sex. My dick stirs, jonesing for a repeat, but I ignore it. Something's not right.

For the first time in forever, the sex feels all wrong. And it's not that I've had sex with my boss or hate sex or even lunchtime quickie sex, but that I've done it with Lola. I'll see her at work tomorrow. And then the day after that and the day after that until summer ends and things change. I feel a stab of something that feels like regret, but then the bathroom door opens and Lola marches out.

I want to say something, but I don't know what. Sex I'm good at, but I don't know how to do anything else. So I run away.

"Be right back," I say and duck into the bathroom.

I stare into the mirror, trying to make sense of what just happened. Of how badly I've screwed things up between us. My hair's on end, my face flushed, but otherwise I look the same as I always do. The bathroom, when I look, is equally untouched, all the little bottles and boxes on the countertop standing in orderly, unpillaged rows. Lola always steals those and takes them home with her. Wherever that is. I should know that—but I don't.

My phone plays *Jaws*. I have a text from Lola.

No more hotel rooms.

When I go out, she's gone.

CHAPTER TWENTY

Lola

AFTER WE HAVE angry sex, I expect that we won't see each other for a day or two. At the very least, I expect the weekend to give us space and time to think things through. I'm not stupid. I'm fairly certain my intern is no start-up virgin. He lives in an expensive house, he knows people, and he's far too adept at pitching. At taking control of a room. At making people sit up and pay attention to him. Maybe it's a family network or maybe he's had prior experience—but he hasn't shared that with me. And yet I don't pick that fight. I don't insist on the truth. I don't know why he makes me feel so many things, but he does. I also think this is more than just a crush, at least on my part.

I worked from home the rest of the day after Angry Sex Day, but he texts me good-night and then good morning at a ridiculously early hour. He texts me lists, too, ridiculous lists.

Dev: Quick. List 3 things you'd try if you knew they'd be amazing.

Lola: And I have the gift of immortality?

Dev: We're not thinking about the same things.

Lola: Hot air ballooning, cage shark diving, owning daylily farm.

Dev: Huh.

Lola: What were you thinking?

Dev: The crazy pages in the Kama Sutra, boning in Golden Gate Park, clam chowder in those stupid, carby bread bowls tonight together?

We don't do hotel rooms anymore, although we do make out in Golden Gate Park. Instead, I either spend the night at his palatial palace in Santa Cruz or he spends the night at mine. Honestly, I admire him for not bringing up his wealth and for wanting to achieve a career on his own merits. I suspect he could have landed a cushier internship but instead he chose Calla. I get a stupid little glow thinking about that.

My apartment is in the Mission District. Unlike his house, my place is studio-sized. It turns out it's impossible to fit two people in my shower (even if one person is technically inside the other), my bed

squeaks louder than a bad porn movie but you can't
hear it over the crazy street noise and Dev is fasci-
nated by my collection of romance novels. He keeps
marking scenes for us to try. We go on what feel suspiciously like dates, even though we're careful never
to label what we're doing.

Now we have just two weeks left. I try not to think
about it but the countdown timer in my head won't
turn off. The Tuesday that's just slipped by? One less
day I have with Dev. I've tried talking to him about
his post-summer plans, when he returns to UC Santa
Cruz to finish his degree, but he just kisses me. He
does that a lot, kisses me when I ask for words.

I shouldn't overthink things. We're not a couple,
no matter how many nights we've spent now in each
other's arms. He's slowly pulling away from me and
I have to let him go. It's time to put on my big girl
panties and be the best boss and mentor possible. I
can't tie him down now, when he has a career to establish. After he's had a chance to explore and build
that career, he'll either come back to me or he won't.
But he needs the chance to go.

Today's networking lunch in downtown San Francisco is a step in that direction. It's a mixer for software professionals and their summer interns, drawing
start-ups as well as midstage and well-established
companies, according to the marketing email. As an
added bonus, there's a no-host sandwich bar with a
choice of turkey or tofu chicken salad. Maple laughed
hysterically at the thought of me peopling voluntarily.

She'd have laughed harder still if she'd known that I forgot to give Dev a heads-up about where our lunch-time destination is.

I'm used to his take-charge attitude and confidence; in the office, we've established a precarious but workable relationship. It's our out-of-office time that confuses me. I don't know what he wants from me and it might be nothing.

Still, things have shifted since he first walked through Calla's doors and into my life. I'm not sure if it's for the better or not. We still can't keep our hands off each other, even though we both agree workplace relationships are a bad idea. It could still come out that we're lovers and people might believe I've used my position to talk him into doing something he didn't want to do. Most of all, I'm scared I'll miss him so much that I'll beg him to come back to me and let the whole world know that we're a couple. I don't want to be the punch line in a news story about yet another boss who took advantage of a subordinate. Somehow, there has to be a way for us to be partners.

Today's networking luncheon is in a swank hotel fronting Market Street. I love the energy of San Francisco. It's perpetually cold and foggy before noon and the cost of living makes Bora Bora seem like a viable option, but it's also a place where you can't not feel alive. Crowds of people move purposefully through the crosswalks and up and down the streets, going to work, launching companies, imagining software that could change the world against the romantic backdrop of the Golden Gate Bridge. I like to think I smell the ocean in the air.

I took the BART from Calla's office and after exiting the station it was a right and two lefts to our meeting. I expect Dev to be waiting out front, given his penchant for early arrivals, but he's nowhere in sight. Instead, I hang with the panhandler on the corner, dropping a couple of ones into his empty coffee cup. His sign reads *Friendship always free but tips appreciated.*

He reaches up to shake my hand when I finally give up and turn to go. "You have a blessed day now."

"I hope so." I flash him a smile and try not to panic as I make my way inside the hotel. The hotel smells of expensive floral arrangements and money. If this was the game where you find the thing that doesn't belong, everyone would point at me.

Don't panic. Inviting Dev to join me was a token gesture on my part anyhow because I'm the company founder and his boss. Despite feeling like an impostor in the tech world, I'm fully qualified to be here. Having Dev at my back just makes me feel safer, bolder about leaping out of my comfort zone—but I can do this mixer without him. He's just late. Dev texted earlier that he had an interview, and I suggested he meet me here when he expressed timing concerns. So it's fine. He's just finding work for the school year. He'll be here.

Pacing around the hotel lobby, I try to marshal my thoughts into some semblance of order.

When my phone pings, I'm relieved. He's texted: Just pulling up.

I grin. Somehow I doubt *pulling up* means an Uber or even the BART. The man loves his toys. Given the speed at which he prefers to drive them, the perpetual San Francisco gridlock must drive him nuts. I scan the lobby, looking for him and pretending the twinges in my stomach are just peopling nerves. *There.*

Dev strides through revolving doors, barely slowing. He wears another dark, posh suit with a rose-colored tie. It's terrifying how much my heart jumps at the sight of him. My first thought is to forget the mentor luncheon. I want to jump him on the spot, throw my arms around his neck and pull his face down to mine.

My second thought is that he totally belongs here. The price tag on his suit must be phenomenal. He's the kind of tall and broad-shouldered guy that dominates a lobby filled with suit-wearing entrepreneurs. His blond hair is tousled about his face as if he's run his fingers through it repeatedly while he thinks through a coding issue. The moment he steps foot inside, he's scanning, looking for *me*. All those other eyes on him, watching him, smiling for him, and he homes in on me.

There's a moment of awkwardness when I rush to meet him halfway. We both sort of come to a halt and look at each other. Do we shake hands? Kiss each other's cheek Euro-style? Go for the passion-filled clinch?

A smile crinkles the corners of his eyes, as if he senses my dilemma. "So what are we doing today? How's the plan to take over the world doing?"

"How was your interview?" I ask at the same moment, the words exploding out of my mouth. *Way to get in his business, Lola.*

"Ladies first."

"Securing Series A funding has made a huge difference. World domination is still iffy, but bankruptcy is now in the rearview mirror. I think you're my lucky charm," I say. "I probably shouldn't have said that, right?"

He shrugs. "It's okay, Lola."

I decide to take his words at face value and move us toward the ballroom. As we fall in with a stream of suit-wearing people, most of the suits are noticeably older than their companions. I may have a few years on Dev, but I generally try not to think about it. Older boss, younger man—it has the makings of a Lauren Weisberger book. I intercept more than a few interested glances aimed in our direction, which I attribute to Dev being hard to overlook.

I sort of wish we could go back in time, that he would make another pointed, asshole comment about my code or my work practices so that I could go back to hating him rather than remembering what he looks like as he comes.

"You look good," he says casually as he glances over the shoulder of the people in front of us.

"It's my one and only suit," I point out.

He winks. "But I prefer how it looks on my floor."

"No." I fight the urge to poke him in the ribs with my index finger. Injuring the intern isn't acceptable professional behavior. *Neither is sleeping with him.*

"We could leave," he suggests casually. "Skip this event."

Part of me perks right up with a *yes, please*, but that part of me doesn't get to be in charge.

"I'm trying to help you," I say with a smile. "But I can go bitch boss on your ass if you prefer."

A wicked smile lights up his face. "Are you going to *mentor* me?"

I snort even though I shouldn't. At some point, we really do have to talk about our future. Now, however, is not the time. We step into the ballroom. It's nice, but a trifle bland. A large plastic banner stretched across one wall announces Software Mentors Do It Best! Subtle.

Dev tilts his head back, taking in the massive signage. "Jesus."

"Surprise," I say awkwardly. Shoot, we're blocking traffic. "Hopefully, your interview this morning went well, but I figured it wouldn't hurt to make some new connections."

I hand him a leather card case. I had business cards made up for him because I don't know if he has his own. He didn't give me one at our interview, so probably not. They read Devlin King, Software Engineer. He stares down at them, his brow furrowing.

A woman wearing a marigold-yellow pantsuit and

an organizer's tag rushes up to us; she shoves a glossy
folder into Dev's hands and then proceeds to twitter on and on (and on) about how thrilled they are to
welcome *Mr. King.* As if Dev's the boss and I'm the
newly hatched intern.

I nudge him in the side as the Gusher reluctantly
retreats. "Are you the Pope? Bill Gates in disguise?"

"Damn it." He scrubs a hand over his head. "This
wasn't a good idea, Lola."

I consider asking for a list, but a sleek, well-groomed
woman in a black power suit strolls up to us. She's the
kind of lean that requires an amazing trainer and her
white blouse has been unbuttoned to show the tanned
hollow between her breasts. I'd bet the remainder of
Calla's operating budget that suit is designer. Like Dev,
she fits in here.

"Devlin King," she announces. He hasn't donned
his badge yet, but she knows who he is. "What a surprise to see you here. I didn't realize you were in the
business of mentoring newbies."

Tasteful Cleavage Girl smolders at Dev, clearly torn
between jumping him and killing him. And while I
understand her dilemma, having faced it myself on
numerous occasions, I sense some serious under-
currents. Plus, I'm not happy watching anyone eye-
fuck my intern.

"So." I give excellent loud, cheerful voice. "How
do you two know each other?"

"Alicia." She doesn't bother with a last name—or

a business card. "You must be familiar with the Billionaire Bachelors app."

Dev sort of freezes beside me. I really need to download that app for my phone. Everyone keeps talking about it. *Except I sort of thought I already had a boyfriend.*

Alice steamrolls ahead. "Dev here hooked up with me. And then, true to form, he didn't call again."

The stab of hurt I feel is ridiculous. We're a not-couple and any relationship we have is definitely on the down low.

"You knew I wasn't looking for more," Dev begins. *Funny, that's exactly what you told me.*

Alicia pulls a face. "You never are. If you'd bothered to call or text just once, however, maybe you wouldn't be missing a key piece of your business portfolio."

I've never seen this look on Dev's face. It's beyond angry. I've seen it on Shark Week, though, right as the great white lunges out of the water and chews some poor sea lion in half. Whoever she is, Alicia just made a very big mistake.

"Excuse me?" His voice is icy polite.

Alicia, on the other hand, looks gleeful. "A certain e-commerce suite that you're about to launch exclusive access to? So sad that it's already gotten out into the wild." She flicks her gaze over my laminated badge. "It just might possibly have been ever so briefly available on Fiverr—where I believe Calla's founder bought it. How cute."

This is like one of those horrible stress dreams where you're an entire semester late for class and the final exam is today and somehow you have to pass it, naked, completely unprepared and running slo-mo through molasses.

I look at Dev. "You wrote Calla's e-commerce suite?"

I need to understand this, to figure out why his gorgeous face is suddenly so remote and hard. To reach up and touch him until the tension fades away and he's just my Dev again. I've never seen him so furious before.

"Yes," he says tersely. "I did. What I did *not* do was put it on Fiverr."

Panic sprints through my brain. I bought pirated software? I'm two weeks from launch—not only do I not have the operating budget to replace it, but I simply don't have the time. Calla's minuscule amount of operating capital, after all, is why I went the Fiverr route in the first place.

Alicia winks at me. "Dev made the classic mistake of leaving his laptop unlocked while he used the bathroom. Anyone could have done anything."

My gaze ping-pongs between the two of them. "You worked together?"

Alicia is staring avidly at Dev. He's not the only sharkish creature in the room. "We hooked up. He has a reputation for being a one-and-done guy and I deserve more than that."

"So you took his software project hostage?" Something here isn't adding up.

Alicia shakes her head playfully. "Let's just say I exacted a penalty for his rudeness. If he'd called or texted, you'd have saved five bucks and he'd still have his exclusive software."

Dev just looks at her. "You'll be hearing from my lawyers."

"They'd have to prove it, darling."

"They will." His gaze flickers over her name badge, taking in her company affiliation. "I'm in the mood to acquire. You won't work in Silicon Valley again."

Do I know you?

Something is very, very not right here.

Alicia gives me a quick, dismissive glance. "Is he as much of a bastard as a boss?"

"He makes an excellent intern."

"Intern?" She laughs. "God. He's a billionaire and the CEO of King Me. Devlin King hasn't interned a day in his life."

She holds her smartphone up so I can see the screen. Dev's face stares back at me from the Billionaire Bachelors app. The list underneath his picture promises me that he's single, worth a billion dollars and owns King Me.

I'm not sure what I'm supposed to do now, so I walk away. Were we even really dating? What was he doing at Calla? It's not as if there weren't clues. He drives a Porsche, for crying out loud. He owns a luxury beach house. Humiliation spirals through me. He must think I'm stupid. Possibly, it's another move in his never-ending games. The entire summer has been one lie after another.

I make it as far as the lobby when I feel Dev's hand on my arm. Fine. We can argue here as well as anywhere.

I laugh, shaking off his hand. "You're a billionaire."

He actually freaking hesitates. "It depends on the market, Lola."

"Let's stick to yes or no answers." My face is flaming with embarrassment and anger now. No *wonder* everyone rushed to greet him when we arrived. He's a rock star and a king, and I'm the little girl who was too naive to recognize him.

"Yes," he says.

"You obviously didn't come to Calla looking for an internship."

He shakes his head. "I didn't, no."

"Then why did you come?"

"Not a yes or no question, Lola."

"Don't make me kill you, okay? San Quentin's only picturesque from the outside."

"Calla deployed my software," he says quietly. "I build in alerts so I can pinpoint pirates. I came to shut you down. You mistook me for your interview candidate."

"Where is my real intern?"

"My team tells me he's currently holidaying in Australia. My best guess is that he ghosted you."

"I'll pull the software." I look away. "But you could have told me up front about it. Some of us feel pretty strongly about doing the right thing. Instead, you've demonstrated clearly that you have no respect for me. You lied to me, and quite honestly, right now I'm torn between feeling stupid and feeling dirty. I'd like to tell you that I'd love to hear your reasons why, but I honestly don't give a rat's ass."

"Lola—" Something brushes my hair.

I don't know what he's about to say, but there's no fixing this. Plus, if I blink now, I'll cry. There's only one thing to do.

"You're fired," I say.

CHAPTER TWENTY-ONE

Dev

LEAVE.

> *Do not pass Go.*
> *Do not collect two hundred bucks.*
> *Do not see Lola again.*

I tell myself it doesn't matter, but it does.

I tell myself she's just another hookup, but she's not. She's not a one-night, onetime deal—she's a once-in-a-lifetime deal. Lola is different and I love different. So I need to figure out how to be different, too.

I make a list. And then another list. Dozens of lists. *Ten Things I'd Like to Do with Lola. Ten Things I Wish I'd Said to Lola (When I Had the Chance). Ten Ways to Win Lola.* I send her instructions on how to remove my Trojan horse from her code. I tuck the step-by-steps and the magic password into a box of that horrible, too sweet Turkish delight she stress eats. I could hack in, but I'm working on respecting her boundaries. But she sends the box back to me and tells me she's already implemented new shopping cart software. And as much as I know she's got this, that she will rock the world, I still wish I was there. Beside her. Part of her world. But she doesn't want me and I don't need Max and the others to tell me that I've lost someone important.

Still, I send a happy birthday card (singing, of course) when Calla launches and I badger everyone I know into buying a lifetime supply of tampons. Four weeks after Lola left me standing in the lobby, I give up and call for reinforcements.

"I need the nearest bookstore with a romance section." I've just busted into Max's house. The breaking-in part is easy as I know the door code (the course number for our first computer science class), but the begging part will be trickier.

Max sits there for a few seconds, trying to dissect my face. Or my plea. Perhaps he's just enjoying his big-ass leather couch and doesn't feel like moving, even if it is just his tongue. We're wasting time and I fight the urge to hop from foot to foot. I'll look like a toddler who has to pee and I've already sacrificed all my dignity.

Finally, Max deigns to speak. "Do I look like Google Maps to you? And maybe you could try knocking before entering? What if I was naked?"

"Or with a girl," Jack suggests helpfully, popping his head up from the other side of the couch. He has bedhead. "Because then you'd have to choose between making revenge porn and forever having the image of your friend's naked, thrusting ass stuck in your head."

Max waves his arms expansively. "She could be on top. He could be looking at my girlfriend's ass."

"Can we focus on me here?" I snap my fingers. "I have a problem and I need to fix it."

"If it involves your dick, you need the self-help section." Max sounds as if he's trying not to laugh.

Clocking my best friends won't help—even if it temporarily makes me feel better.

"Yes, tell us, Dev, what you'd be looking for in said romance section." Jack grins expectantly at me.

"I fucked things up with Lola, okay?" I stride over to the window and stare outside. The waves aren't great today.

"Walk us through it," Jack prompts. "Give us the use case."

"She found out I wasn't an intern. I found out who stole my code. The person who shared this information with us was a hookup I met through your app." I glare at Max. "And that former hookup outed me to Lola at a very public intern networking lunch."

"So Lola now feels stupid, humiliated and angry." Jack ticks his talking points off on his fingers.

"Yes. I need to fix that."

"Why?"

"Because I made a mistake. Because I miss her. Because—"

The ocean outside the window is no help, the selfish bastard.

"She fired me," I admit to the window. "She's pissed off and humiliated and she's not talking to me or responding to my texts. I have to get her back but I've ruined everything."

Max groans. "Then you either want the communication section or the travel section—the right gift can erase bad memories."

I turn and meet Max's eyes. "I need romance."

Max frowns. I can practically see the input/output error occurring. "Why?"

"Because I love her but I don't know how to tell her that. I don't blame her for walking away from me, but there has to be a way to convince her to come back, right? So I just have to figure out the best way to grovel until she forgives me."

Max's frown deepens. "Why romance books?"

"Have you read those things?" Seriously, this is a genius plan—all I have to do is find the one Lola will like best. "They're like recipes for how to grovel and be romantic and sweep a lady off her feet. They're perfect."

Jack looks doubtful. "They're fantasies."

"Exactly." I point at him triumphantly. "They're the best ever cheat codes to getting inside a woman's head. Plus, Lola loves fantasies. And romance novels. You wouldn't believe the shit she thinks up."

Jack coughs into his fist. "TMI."

"Whatever. I just need to get her attention so she'll listen to me."

"Which you plan on doing by cribbing from a

bunch of romance novel heroes." Max sounds skeptical but he wrote an algorithm that picks your best sexual match. He's hardly a believer in true love.

"You own a houseful of books. I know you're feeding your addiction. Just tell me where to find a good bookstore."

Max always knows exactly where every bookstore—new, used or otherwise—is. He always has a book stashed somewhere close by. Plus, he reads *anything*. Package inserts, instruction manuals, in-flight magazines—he's happy if it has words.

"Bookstore. Now." I snap my fingers.

"Bossy, isn't he?"

I don't have time for this. I'm mad at myself. I screwed up my relationship with Lola, and I have to fix this. *Now.* Or yesterday. Even better, if I could roll back time to the night we first met, I'd play it smarter. I had a chance to seal the deal and I blew it. But if I can't win her back, what's the point?

"Eleven point two miles," Max volunteers.

Jack rolls his eyes. "Or raid Hazel's stash."

We end up at Hazel's place after all. The local bigbox bookstore has slashed its romance section and pickings are slim. According to Max, there's an all-romance indie bookstore in Los Angeles with the best name ever that sounds perfect, but Max calculates it would take us five hours and eighteen minutes to drive the three hundred thirty-nine miles.

Hazel lives halfway up a mountain, so it's almost forty-five minutes before I'm pounding on her door.

Jack texted her to give her a heads-up that we were coming as Hazel dislikes unannounced drop-ins. He also strongly suggested that we come bearing dough-nuts, which is why the trip took forty-five minutes rather than thirty-eight.

I shove the box of doughnuts at Hazel when she opens her front door. "Take me to your books."

"You screwed up. Big-time." Jack has clearly shared my unhappy news with her.

"I did."

"And now Lola isn't talking to you. I don't blame her. I can't fix this for you, even if I wanted to. I *liked* her."

"Me, too," I admit.

"Okay." She waves for us to follow her. "So how far are you prepared to go? What have you tried so far?"

"Flowers, gifts, all the usual stuff. I went to Hall-mark and they have *cards* for this. I bought one."

"For future reference, handmade is better. Hand-made and it sucks? *Gold.*"

"You think I should do that?" I'm sure there's a YouTube video on handmade cards that say *I know I was a dick, but I'd like to be* your *dick.*

"I think you have to figure out what Lola really wants and give her that." She pads down the hall. "Step into my lair. You definitely need expert help."

Apparently Hazel keeps her romance novels in her bedroom, which I try not to think about. Everything is gray, silver and fluffy—except for the three large black bookcases with glass doors and tiny crystal knobs. Those shelves are bursting with books.

She gestures toward the bookcases. "Dukes and lords on the left. Werewolves and vampires in the middle. Rock stars, small-town heroes and dirty billionaires on the right."

I might be out of my league, but somehow I need to become Mr. Romance. I press Jack and Max into service as my reading wingmen, although I'm not sure how much help they're going to be since Max promptly gets sucked into a copy of *Fifty Shades of Grey* and Jack takes a nap on Hazel's bed.

I could buy a Scottish castle, if that's what would make Lola happy. And I could definitely pull a *Fifty Shades* number, although from what Max shares, the hero seems to need a good therapist. I know these are fiction, not fact. But they're also fantasies and dreams—and Lola deserves all the dreams.

But it's not enough.

The castles and titles are fun but they're just a really good security system. It's about how the hero makes the heroine feel safe, safe enough to be herself with him, safe enough to trust herself with him. It's not about winning Lola—because she's not a game. She doesn't come with rules and she's not a playing piece I can move around the board of life until I score. Winning is fun, but playing together is even better.

I do some more thinking as I wander out back with my phone. The reception sucks up here since Hazel's surrounded by the world's biggest, densest trees. I have just enough signal to send a text. I drop into one of the cherry-red Adirondack chairs ringing a firepit, take a deep breath and start typing. The First Ten Reasons I Love Lola. Because ten isn't enough and I can't pick and choose my reasons.

I love that you punctuate all your texts like Merriam-Webster. Or a granny.

I love that you own fifteen pairs of yoga pants but never do yoga.

I love that you have a freckle in your right ear.

I love that you always have a million questions and can never just say *yes*.

I love that you believe there's a book for everything. Or an explanatory YouTube video. FWIW, I've learned you're right.

I love that you believe in sniffing books.

I love that you laugh even when you don't get the joke.

I love that you count everything.

I love that when I'm with you all my plans go out the window.

I love that I want to be a better person when I'm with you, but that it's okay if I fail.

I love that you're counting my reasons.

And they're not ten.

Or enough.

But I love you.

And then I hit Send.

CHAPTER TWENTY-TWO

Lola

THE GOOD THING about being the founder of a start-up is that there's no time to feel sorry for myself, not if I don't want to fail epically. I can't take time off work and hide out in bed, drowning my sorrows with pecan bourbon ice cream and retail therapy. I have work to do. And as much as I resent the fact that our Series A funding is entirely due to Dev, I won't put my pride over Calla's future. I take the money because bootstrapping isn't feasible anymore. I've already maxed out my own credit limits and emptied my bank account.

I know I need to make some life changes, though. It's not enough to throw myself into Calla, so I make a list of the things I've always fantasized about doing. No, not *that* kind of fantasy (although no one in her right mind would say no if a royal prince came knocking). Maple helps me write it. I start with a list of the places *I* want to see rather than boxes to check on my tourist bingo card. The Farallon Islands for whales and great white sharks. Snorkeling at Monterey Bay. Definitely, the saltwater taffy at Monterey Bay (probably twice). A beach that's nothing but miles and miles of sand dunes. Driftwood collecting. It turns out that getting out of the office and out of San Francisco helps me clear my head.

Dev won't go quietly into that good night, however— he comes by my studio apartment and by Calla. He's respectful—I'll give him that—and goes away when I refuse to answer the door or to see him. Still, I watch him through the window because even though he's not who I thought he was, it still hurts. I'm like that stupid, heartbroken girl in all the music videos who presses her fingers against the glass as the dream boy walks away. I could call him back, but I'm not sure I'm strong enough not to fall into his arms. And I can't do the just-sex thing anymore, or live on the scraps of a relationship. If I can't have all of Dev, then I need to let him go. For my own sake.

So I do. One memory, one day at a time. Beach walks, wharf walks, ice cream runs—I do them again, by myself, as if I'm testing for sore spots. Does this hurt? What about here? I do hang on to the ties, however. They're souvenirs I'm not ready to let go of yet. I should get drunk and burn them all, or hand them over to Goodwill, or just toss them in the nearest dumpster. But I don't. And honestly, perhaps my first clue that we didn't have a genuine relationship should have been the lack of stuff. Dev didn't leave things at my place; he didn't need the drawer in the bathroom, we didn't acquire couple crap, we didn't do presents. It seems like it should be so easy to erase him since he left so few marks, but it's hard.

"You should date." Maple announces this one night as if it's a novel conclusion and it's never occurred to me to try. "Someone better. An upgrade."

She whips out her phone and starts swiping through pictures. "Or girls. Perhaps you should switch things up and try batting for the home team?"

I'm not sure she's got that metaphor exactly right, but I snort. "I'm good."

"Too good." She nods with mock solemnity. "Maybe you should try a bad boy?"

Bad boys are certainly Maple's area of expertise. Her current boyfriend, Madd (yes, he claims that's his real name), is undoubtedly hot, and is either the best or worst of the bad boy breed. He's been able to slide through life with a wink, a smile and a judicious use of charm. I've managed to avoid actively bad-mouthing him, but as far as I can tell, his appeal is entirely visual.

After Maple leaves, I poke through the Billionaire Bachelors app, trying to imagine Max creating this. He's a good-looking guy with a great body, but he's also a bit of a nerd. I have no idea how he's managed to reduce dating to math, but I suspect he may have overlooked something.

A scratching noise catches my attention. God, I hope it's not rats. Or mice. Or whatever vermin my landlord claimed absolutely could not be in our building—but was. When I get up to check, however, there's a piece of fancy paper half stuck under my front door.

Come out to the fire escape.

The handwriting's bold, a dark, impatient scrawl on the blue paper. And I stupidly tear up because now I realize that I've never actually seen Dev's handwriting. Which is fortunately followed by indignation. People don't go sitting around on fire escapes in San Francisco. For starters, the fire marshal would have something to say. Second, those are fire *escapes*. Not fire *choices* or fire *really-plush-places-to-hang-out*. They're basically metal Tinkertoys and only an honest-to-God actual fire would send me down one.

Another piece of paper materializes under the door.

Please.

A third piece of paper promptly follows that one.

I'll make it up to you.

Okay. That one I can't let go. I scribble *indeterminate referent* on the note and slide it back.

I look out the peephole. Just to make sure it's Dev and not some weird stalker who just wants to pass notes to me. And totally not because I sort of want to see him. No one is supposed to be able to get inside the building unless that person is a resident, but Dev is a smart guy. I'm sure he's found more than one loophole. Or hacked the security code.

Dev is sitting in the middle of my hallway. He looks tired, his hair ruffled, and he's not wearing a tie. He's sitting there on the floor as if he owns the world, but something in his eyes makes me think he's not happy.

"Open the door," he says.

How stupid does he think I am? I've never been a screamer, but I'm tempted now. Maybe if I yell the words, they'll actually penetrate his big, amazing, completely stupid brain.

I look down at Nellie. "We should move. I bet we could totally run Calla from Antarctica."

Instead, I go over to the window and look out. At the fire escape. It's full of books. Stacks and stacks of books bristling with rainbow-colored sticky notes. I have to hand it to Dev—this wasn't what I was expecting.

But I'm not interested.

At all.

I check the peephole, but he's gone. A few minutes later, while I'm still dithering, there's a knock on the window that looks onto the fire escape. Of course there is.

I go back over to the window. "I'm not letting you in."

Dev flattens a palm against the window. He's

wearing a short-sleeved T-shirt that shows off his ink. I realize I've never asked him the story behind his tattoos, how he got them or when. Or why. From the look on his face, he might even tell me.

"Open the window," he demands.

"Can't." I think I'm smiling. "It's broken."

His eyes narrow, assessing the window. "Unlock it."

Whatever. I've tried multiple times to unstick that window and failed. I flip the lock.

Forty seconds later, the damned thing slides open and Dev swings his legs over the sill. He sits there, big hands on his thighs, looking at me.

"Are you waiting for an invitation to come in?"

"Yes." He gives me a look I can't interpret. "I'm waiting for you."

He reaches behind him and grabs a stack of books that he hands to me. And then another and another. Werewolves and Scottish lairds, firemen and small-town heroes. Dirty businessmen, dukes and a dragon shifter.

"I marked my favorite scenes," Dev says.

"The ones where the hero grovels? And admits he was wrong?"

"I was wrong," he says. "I should have set you straight the minute I realized who you thought I was. I was wrong to let you think you were just a hookup. I was wrong about a lot of things."

I set the books down and pluck the topmost one off the stack. My chest burns. "So you brought me a duke?"

Dev looks at the book in my hand and frowns. He steps toward me, reaching for me, pulling me into his arms. "I brought you me."

I open the book. He's marked the last chapter, the one where everything finally works out and the hero and the heroine get their happy ending. He's done the same in the next book and the next book after that.

"Why the books?"

"I was going to borrow from them." He frowns. "Pick the biggest, best, most effective grand gesture of them all."

I flip through the pages of the book I'm holding. "You were going to crash a ballroom and realize you were in love with me but you weren't worthy while I'm wearing a Cinderella-worthy dress and millions of pounds of diamonds?"

"That's the problem," he says. "Those were someone else's stories. They're not us and I like our story. I like us."

His arms tighten around me as if he's thinking about never letting go, but it's hard to forget the past few weeks. Or the summer. I knew because I'd tried.

"You lied to me. How do we just start over?"

"We take a chance," he says quietly. "I am sorry. I'm sorry I hurt you. I'm sorry I spoiled what we had. I'm angry at myself for pushing you away when I started to fall for you and then didn't tell you the truth. I should have done a lot of things differently, but what I need right now is a chance. Let me make it up to you."

I stare down at the cover of the book. I want to ask him if he really means it, if I can trust him, how I can trust him. But the truth is, I already opened the window. I let him in. All the way in.

"I love you," he says. "And so these books weren't going to work anyhow. Those aren't our story."

"We have a story?" I pull back enough to see his face. "Because I hate to break it to you, but a handful of texts don't constitute a *story*. That's more of an outline."

He wraps an arm around me tightly while he pulls out his phone with the other. "That's why I wrote this."

My phone dings. He's sent me a file.

"I'm hoping we can write the next chapter together and then the next chapter after that."

I open the file. It's written in code.

```
Chapter One
class TrueLove
{
public static void main(String[] args)
{
System.out.println("I love Lola");
}
}
```

"Chapter one?"

He cups my face. "I thought we could work on the next chapter together. And then the next one after that. I love you and I want to make this work. Tell me yes?"

"I may have a few ideas for chapter two." My hand finds his face.

"Is that a yes?"

I press a kiss against the hand cupping my face. "Yes."

Another kiss against his jaw. "Yes."

A kiss against the corner of his mouth. "Still yes."

"I'd be happy to make suggestions if you need a list of places to kiss next," he whispers.

"I'm crazy for you," I admit. "I love you, too. And this is more than a chapter. It's a book. Definitely a book."

* * * * *

DOUBLE DARE YOU

YOU

CARA LOCKWOOD

MILLS & BOON

For PJ, the stars and moon in my sky.

PROLOGUE

HIS LIPS CLAIMED hers and, in that moment, her entire body came alive. The rumors about this sex god were true, beyond true, she realized as he pulled her into his arms, flat against his muscled chest, and the world outside faded away. Nothing existed but their bodies before the woodstove in this small lodge on the top of a remote peak in the Rocky Mountains. He tasted like pure animal magnetism, pure white-hot desire, everything she'd ever wanted and more she hadn't dreamed of. Her clothes came off. Before she knew it, she was naked, and then it was electric skin against skin. She could almost feel the pulse of his need against her belly. She didn't know where her heat began and his ended, and she didn't care to draw boundaries. She wanted them all gone. God, how she'd fantasized about this moment, with this man, and how she'd never believed it could ever happen, not in a million years. He had his pick of women in Aspen, but now, finally—and at long last—it would be her turn.

The blizzard howled outside the wood lodge, a

mournful call she felt in her chest, mirroring her own desperate need. She'd wanted him since she first laid eyes on him but had been so long denied. She'd pined in silence for months, even years. She'd yearned for this since she first fell in love with him, only she'd been in hell ever since. She'd been slowly chipping away at that friendship line, and now, finally, she'd gotten him to cross. She knew she was risking everything, his very friendship, and yet she didn't care. Her need for him was just too great, her want burned in her hotter than the crackling wood in the stove. She couldn't have stopped herself any more than she could stop the snow battering the windows outside. This might be her only chance, and she'd take it, her head buzzing with wine. She understood the dangers here, knew she was playing with fire. He didn't do relationships, didn't do love. He'd break her heart if she let him. This man wouldn't settle down with anyone, wouldn't be tamed, but that was why she wanted him so badly, she realized. She wanted to stand in the wind and howl, she wanted to consume some of his wildness and feel it run riot inside her. She wanted to be obliterated, completely, and then put back together again. She wanted him, the chaos he brought, and she wanted to ride it until she couldn't ride anymore.

He laid her down on the bearskin rug, its fur surprisingly soft against her bare back. She soaked in all the details, because she'd want to remember this, now and always. She didn't care about tomorrow. She

only cared about right now, this man she'd stupidly
fallen in love with. The man who might never love her
back, but she didn't care. She'd have his body even if
she couldn't have his heart.

CHAPTER ONE

Two months later

WHAT WAS *HE* doing here?

Allie Connor froze at the bar, her ruby-red cran-
berry vodka in the martini glass stopped halfway to
her mouth. Liam Beck, looking too damn fine for
words, eased through the crowd at the Aspen lodge,
seeming like he already owned it in his ruffled-blond,
leather-jacket glory, with more than a hint of stubble that said he only marginally cared what anyone
thought about his shaving habits. He looked just as
cocky as ever, and ridiculously fit, chiseled from free
rock climbing, river rafting, snowboarding or whatever *extreme* thing he could think of to do to his body
lately. What crazy-ass thing was he doing now? Bungee jumping without a bungee cord? Free-climbing
up cliffs? Jumping into ponds of alligators?

When it came to Liam Beck, anything was possible. And whatever crazy risk he was taking suited
him. He looked good enough to eat.

Not that Allie was falling for it. Not this time.

Stay in your lane, she told herself. *This all happened because you didn't stay in your lane.* She needed a straitlaced nice guy who regularly contributed to his 401(k). Not somebody who liked to hurl his body off snow-covered cliffs with nothing but a snowboard and his wits to save him.

"Trouble, two o'clock," Allie murmured, pushing up her round, nearly clear-framed glasses, careful not to gaze directly in Liam's direction again, lest he see her. She half turned, keeping him in her peripheral sights. Some upbeat, too-bright Christmas song floated through the crowd. Behind her sat a roaring fire in a stone fireplace, circled with small pub tables, and to her left a giant bar made of reclaimed wood, old antique iron fixtures hanging from the ceiling giving the pub a modern take on the gold rush times. Allie tried not to think that two months ago she'd had the misfortune of tumbling into Beck's bed. Or, actually, the tremendous fortune. He'd been—bar none— the best sex she'd ever had in her life.

And then he'd not called her after that weekend. Or texted. Or acknowledged her at all. She might have thought he'd had a horrible skiing accident, except for the pictures of him plastered across social media smiling with a parade of pretty tourists. She'd expected more from the man who'd claimed to be her friend before they'd taken their clothes off. But deep down, she knew she had only herself to blame. She tangled with something wild. Was it a wonder it came back to bite her?

"What the hell?" Allie's best friend, Mira, frowned as she first saw Beck clap a friend on the back. Beck was six-three and impossible to miss in a crowd, his tawny blond hair and perpetual tan from practically living outside in summer *and* winter standing out like a beacon. Somehow, he was moving *closer*. She felt that familiar pull in her chest, as if he'd buried a beacon for himself there, one that lit up only in his presence. Why couldn't she even stay mad at him? It hardly seemed fair.

"I definitely did *not* invite him. You know I didn't."

"Someone did." Allie suspected that someone might be Channing, Mira's roommate, who happened to be secretly hoping for a hookup with one of Aspen's most famous bachelors. *Good luck with that*, she thought, as she saw the sleek blonde light up from across the room and squeal Beck's name. Then again, since when did Beck ever need an invitation anywhere? He was used to showing up to adoration wherever he went. Allie did not have time for this. She sucked another deep drink of her nearly full cocktail and thought about bolting. Was sticking around for a round of free holiday drinks at the resort worth it?

"Maybe I should go." The minute the words were out of her mouth, she felt like a coward. She should be able to be in the same room with him, after all. She'd known what she was getting into that weekend, but she hadn't cared. That was her mistake.

"Do *not* let that X Games junkie scare you away from *my* party." Mira's dark eyes flashed with fire.

Technically, it was Mira's boss's party, the man who owned the upscale Aspen resort, Enclave, where Mira worked as an events coordinator. But Mira had planned and organized the party for Enclave's various employees. She was running the show tonight. Mira had made sure to add Allie as her plus-one, to take advantage of the holiday party and the free drinks. Allie self-consciously patted her loose bun, finding an errant strand of auburn hair had fallen loose at her temple. She tucked it behind her ear and wondered if Beck would notice the new bright red highlights in her auburn hair, and then hated herself for wondering. *I don't care what he thinks.* "You are *not* moving to Denver because of him, okay?"

Allie was considering a job offer in Denver, one that would take her three hours away by car. An old college friend had reached out on LinkedIn, and the accounting firm had a new position opening in the New Year. She would've turned the job down flat two months ago, but since then, she'd started to think maybe a change of scenery would do her good. Maybe getting away from Beck's gravitational pull would help her heal.

"I haven't decided about that job yet. I've got time. They don't need the position filled until after the New Year."

"Don't let him scare you off," Mira added.

"I'm not scared," she hedged. She wasn't frightened of Beck, exactly. It was more the case that she was scared of herself around him. Of what she might do. Of how she might feel. She hated that, even now, her body responded to the fact that he was in the same room, breathing the same air. As she watched his big shoulders part the crowd, her stomach instantly wound itself into a Gordian knot. Despite the fact that a throng of people blocked him from her, she could still track almost every movement he made, no matter how small. She hated that her whole body seemed tuned to his frequency, a channel she couldn't seem to change no matter how hard she tried.

Remember what it was like, she told herself, waiting for him to call the morning after. And then the week after, and then the month after. Remember the stupid messages she left, the rambling ones, trying to be cool, but failing miserably. Remember how she spent hours combing over every delicious position she'd shared with him in bed, and then worried that, somehow, she'd come up lacking. And then pretending none of it mattered at all, when, truly, she was horribly heartbroken. Knowing it was all her fault. She knew what Beck was. Local ski and sex god. Gods didn't wind up with mere mortals like her.

"I just don't want the hassle." Allie wished she could be one of those immensely mature adults, the ones who could stay friends with hookups or exes, but Liam wasn't the kind of man any woman could just be friends with. He exuded pure sexual energy. There literally *was* no friend zone with him and that was his whole problem. Even when they were "just" friends, she'd harbored a secret crush on the man.

She saw, from the corner of her eye, that he'd been cornered by Channing. Good. Let Channing realize she was playing a dangerous game with a man who lived his life with no rules at all. Despite Allie's better instincts, curiosity got the better of her and she found herself turning toward the couple, and staring directly into Liam's ice-blue eyes.

Dammit.

Now he'd seen her.

A slow smile crossed his face, amused and almost a little…dangerous. The man knew his own power, and he wasn't afraid to use it.

Look away, Allie, for God's sake. But then she glanced away too quickly, like a rabbit who'd locked eyes with a wolf. Now he'd know he rattled her. She fiddled with the frames of her new glasses, self-conscious.

"Brace yourself. He's coming over here," Mira warned as she sipped at her glass of white wine.

"God, no." The last person on earth she wanted to talk to was Liam Beck. Yet her body vibrated with the excitement of doing just that. Her body, ever her mind's betrayer. They had never been on the same page as far as Beck was concerned, and might never be.

"Al?" he said, and she felt his baritone in the pit of her stomach, a vibration that tingled all the way down to the crease between her legs. She almost flinched a bit at the sound of her nickname. He'd called her that warmly when they'd been friends, but it took on a new meaning when he'd whispered it in her ear that weekend they'd spent together, naked on the floor of his wood lodge, tangled up on the bearskin rug, the thick wool throw on top of them. The memory of his taut skin against hers, his strong hands on her body, made heat flush her cheeks.

"Get lost, Beck." Mira narrowed her eyes at him, flicking her black hair over her shoulder. "She doesn't want to talk to you."

Allie cringed. Mira's full-throated defense made her sound like she *cared*. She didn't. Not in the least. Her body might, but she told herself that was just pure animal instinct. Lust, really. What straight woman didn't lust after Liam Beck? But human beings were made of higher stuff than just base instinct, thankfully. Allie shot her friend a glance, but Mira was focused on Beck, her head tilted up, her shoulders squared. Not that the five-foot-three, part-Asian former marathon runner could do much against him, but the warning look in her eyes told Allie she'd try if she needed to.

"Is that so?" A grin split Beck's face, as if he was mulling over a joke at her expense. He probably was. Could he see the blush? Would he know he caused it? Of course he would. He thought everything was about him. She glanced upward at his perfectly chiseled features, reminded again that he was one of the few men so much taller than her. At five-ten, she never felt tiny. Except around Beck.

"I don't really care, actually." Allie congratulated herself on sounding pretty even-keeled. Bored, even.

She sipped her drink and deliberately looked away from Beck, using all of her willpower to drag her attention away from those powerful blue eyes. She could still feel him studying her, the attention feeling like the heat of the summer sun on her face. What did he think of her hair? Worn up in a loose, messy bun? Or her new glasses? Did he notice that she'd lost ten pounds since that ominous weekend? She knew it was silly to be so affected by two days at a lodge, but there it was. After Beck cut her from his life, Allie had trouble choking down food. She had trouble sleeping. She had trouble doing everything. But day by day, week by week, she'd gotten better.

"New glasses?" he asked her. He'd noticed. That was something.

"Yeah," she said and nodded.

"I like them." She beamed in the compliment and then mentally berated herself. Why did she care if he liked her glasses? His gaze flicked downward, slowly, taking in her tight cashmere sweater and skinny jeans, paired with a sky-high pair of stiletto boots. Impractical for the Aspen weather, but necessary for navigating the single scene. "You look…thin, Al."

She heard the note of concern in his voice. As if he had a right to be concerned. Aspen was a small place, and so avoiding her for the last two months took some doing. He'd been almost surgical in his precision. So it was clear that he'd done it on purpose. So why did he care how she was now? She glanced up at him and wished she hadn't. A little worry line etched his forehead, marring his otherwise perfect skin. He almost looked as if he truly cared. That, she knew, would be her undoing. "You doing okay?"

The air felt suddenly thin then, and she knew it had nothing to do with the altitude, even though they were perched probably somewhere around 8,000 feet high in the Rocky Mountains. She'd lived in Aspen for years, and the altitude never got to her. Her sudden light-headedness had everything to do with Beck.

"Al?" he prodded, and Allie realized she'd not answered his question. She was busy just staring at him like a fool. Her baser instincts had taken over, clearly, her body in control. But her brain wasn't going to tolerate it for long. It hummed the truth: it was none of his damn business how she was doing. He hadn't cared two months ago, so why should he now? He was the one who'd run away. She wanted to ask why, but she wasn't sure she wanted to know the answer.

"I'm fine." There was an edge to her voice, one she hadn't intended. Unable to handle the weight of his gaze any longer, she looked away. She tried to find something—someone—more interesting at the bar but failed. Even the moderately cute-ish bartender with the floppy brown hair and the lopsided grin who kept sending looks her way suddenly paled in comparison to Beck. His massive shoulders, the easy way he held the beer he was drinking, the bottle looking small in his huge hands, like a doll's plaything. She looked at the bartender, even though all of her other senses were completely focused on Beck, standing less than two feet from her. She could almost feel his body heat through the T-shirt he wore beneath his worn leather bomber jacket. His defined pecs begging to be stroked beneath the thin cotton fabric. Why did he have to look so damn...delectable? She suddenly hated Beck and his stupid muscles and the caring look on his face. His just-rolled-out-of-some-model's-bed sex appeal. *Remember, he probably did.* That musky, manly scent coming from him was probably just stale sex.

The thought jolted her to the present. He was a walking rabbit hole. One step too close and she'd fall in again.

"Beck!" squealed Channing, as the tiny blonde bounced up to the three of them and locked her arm inside his. She was wearing a ridiculous Santa hat and a red corset top that she was practically spilling out of and too-thick false eyelashes that made it look like spiders were crawling across her eyelids. Trying too hard, Allie thought. She knew Beck well enough to know he hated that. One of his biggest turnoffs. Channing didn't even acknowledge Allie or Mira, choosing instead to tug her prize away from them. "You *have* to meet my boss. She's right over there. She's the one I told you about. The one who books tours."

At the sound of possible new business, Beck's interest diverted from Allie to Channing. Not that he needed new business. His extreme mountain tours and heli-skiing excursions were the best in Aspen. Everyone knew that. At the height of tourist season, he had to turn away customers. Everybody wanted to go on a ski expedition with the two-time silver medal Olympic champion. Few people seemed to care if he had a death wish, always pushing things a bit harder, a bit farther than he should. Channing glanced at Allie. "Don't waste time here. Come on." Before she left, she turned and murmured "Greenie" beneath her breath. Allie wasn't even sure she'd heard right. *Greenie?* What the hell did that mean?

Channing pulled Beck through the crowd, and he went, casting one more look over his shoulder. Concern once more on his face. *Don't fall for it*, she told herself. *He's not really worried. It's all just part of the game.*

"Good riddance," Mira almost spit, glaring at his retreating figure.

"What does 'Greenie' mean?" Allie asked Mira, who glanced at her, suddenly looking guilty.

"Nothing," Mira said, but she bit her lip, a telltale sign she was lying. Allie had known Mira for years, and she was one of the first people she'd met in Aspen.

"You *know* what it means."

Mira hesitated. "Well…"

"Spit it out." Now Allie was beginning to be frustrated. It had to be bad, because Mira was stalling. The strand of hair popped loose from Allie's ear, and she twirled it around her finger. Suddenly, she felt anxious.

"Well…look, I saw somebody's Snap about you. It

was one of Beck's...*friends*." She said it with disdain, so Allie knew she meant one of the many women rotating through his bedroom. "I guess...well, I guess someone—I don't even know who, actually—gave you a nickname." Mira took a deep breath. "Greenie, as in a green run."

"What does a bunny hill have to do with me? I'm a decent skier." She wasn't an Olympic champion, but she was a black-diamond skier. She'd been skiing for years and thought she was pretty good.

"It doesn't have anything to do with skiing," Mira said. "They mean that you play it safe."

She was an accountant born in a family of non-risk-taking accountants. Of course she played it safe. The only risky thing her parents ever did was occasionally go about two miles over the speed limit. Her parents had raised her to be afraid of almost everything: strangers, trampolines, drugs, driving too fast in the rain, and the list went on and on.

"And what's wrong with that?" Allie challenged.

"Well, nothing—except when you're in bed."

"Wait... You mean..."

Mira gave her a knowing look and the full realization hit Allie. Beck thought she was boring in life *and* in bed. Plain Jane. Greenie? The unfairness of it felt like a slap. She was *not* boring in bed, at least she didn't think she was with Beck. In that damn lodge, she'd done things with him that she'd never done with anyone else. But maybe Beck's pulse had barely ticked up a notch. Oh, God. Maybe that was why she'd never heard from him again. Maybe…she'd bored him so much he ran away.

She felt a deep, stinging embarrassment, and heat rushed through her from her nose to the roots of her hair. Had he measured her against the dozens and dozens of other women he'd taken to his bed and found her wanting? Had the best sex in her life… turned out to be the worst for him? She felt a hard, slick pit at the bottom of her stomach, an oily nauseating mess. She suddenly badly wanted the floor of the bar to open up and swallow her whole.

"But you're not. You know that, right? You are *not* boring." Mira was babbling now, trying to comfort Allie in a rush. "You're badass awesome, and if he can't see that, then screw him. Who cares what he thinks or anybody else thinks? I know you're amazing and fun, and if he doesn't, that's his loss. You are one of the most exciting and dynamic people I know. If he can't see that, then he's blind."

"I can't believe he thinks I'm boring." She felt… crushed. Completely and utterly crushed. She wanted to run home—immediately. Or she needed to drink. Literally everything in this bar. She grabbed her cocktail and took a huge gulp.

"On the bright side, do you know how many women in Aspen would *kill* to get a nickname from Liam Beck? Even a bad one?" Mira was just grasping at desperate jokes, trying to make her feel better, but Allie felt like she'd had the wind knocked out of her. At the very least, she'd thought Beck had been…

her friend. Friends didn't treat friends like this. It felt like one more betrayal. "Oh, geez. I'm making this worse." Mira shook her head. "Look, do *not* let him into your head like this. This is why I didn't want to tell you. Who cares what he or any of his loser groupies say?"

Allie did. She wished she didn't, but she did. It was that simple. The worst part was that, deep down, she didn't believe it was true. She'd seen Beck's face when he'd come; she'd looked right into the man's eyes. He didn't look bored. He looked…electric, enthralled, completely and utterly focused on her. And would a bored man have gone back for seconds…thirds…*and* fourths? It seemed like his frantic want had matched hers, that he'd needed it as much as she had.

But maybe she'd read him all wrong.

After all, he hadn't called her. On the contrary, he'd deliberately avoided her. And now…that damn nickname. Greenie. She wasn't timid or boring or any of those things. She might be an accountant raised by helicopter parents, but she wasn't a mouse. She glanced over at Beck and saw him throw back his head and laugh, his teeth almost too white against his tanned face. Maybe he and Channing were laughing at her right now.

"I think I should go." Allie didn't want to run scared, but she also didn't want to be in a room anymore with Liam Beck.

"Stop that right now," Mira commanded and snapped her fingers near Allie's face. Once more, her attention was on her best friend. "Don't let him ruin your night. You hear me?"

"He can't ruin my night," Allie said. "Not if I don't let him."

"That's my girl," Mira said, her dark eyes fierce. She glanced over at the bartender, and her face lit up. "Why not get your mind off Liam Beck. I know!"

"What?"

"Go kiss that bartender." Mira nodded over at the floppy-haired server who had a silver martini shaker high above his head. He was no Beck, but he was cute. Kind of. In a slightly-out-of-shape, cuddly way. But, on the bright side, he probably wasn't the type to go free-climbing up one of the highest peaks in the Rockies, without even the thought of a harness. The bartender was one hundred percent nonthreatening. Not like Beck, whose flick of a single eyebrow offered a whole menu of dangerous options. The bartender did have kind eyes, and Allie liked the flannel shirt he wore. He seemed nice. Maybe after Beck, *nice* was what she needed. Though, her body rebelled at the thought. Her body didn't want nice.

"I couldn't," she said, laughing self-consciously.

"Why not? I bet *he* won't think you're boring. Because you're not. You will knock his socks off."

"No, I won't!" Allie laughed.

"I *dare* you." Mira's red lips slipped into a devious grin. "I *double* dare you."

"Mira. Come on. We're not in third grade." She didn't need to prove anything. She knew who she was.

But she also knew that the one weekend she'd spent with Beck had kept her head spinning for two months straight. Nothing quite seemed normal.

"No, and hold that thought—my boss wants something." Mira nodded over to a dark-haired man in his forties who was signaling her. "Probably wants to make sure we have extra bottles of his favorite champagne. I'll be right back. Meantime… Get *on* that bartender, would you?"

Allie was tempted. She glanced over at Channing, who was practically rubbing herself on Beck like a cat.

Why the hell not? How did she even know if she didn't like "nice" until she tried it? Maybe the cure for Beck was to hop into bed with his exact opposite. And she was no coward. She wasn't going to let Beck run her out of the bar. That would mean he won.

"Well, then." Allie took a deep breath and slipped off her new glasses, putting them in her pocket. "Looks like I'm going to do this."

"Atta girl," Mira called over her shoulder.

CHAPTER TWO

BECK SAW ALLIE move from the corner of his eye. He was only half listening to Channing. She loved talking about herself, and while she found the subject endlessly fascinating, Beck most certainly did not. He wanted to head right back to Allie. She looked tired. Worn down. Had he done this? Guilt pricked the back of his neck, feeling like the scratchy edge of a clothing tag he'd forgotten to cut out. If he didn't know better, Allie looked heartsick and he hated himself. He *knew* she couldn't handle casual, but he'd gone in anyway. It was just that…he couldn't resist her. That was the problem.

If he were truly honest with himself, those two days with Allie in that snowbound lodge had blown his mind. He couldn't even say that if he had to do it all over again, that he'd do anything differently. Afterward, he'd spent weeks dreaming about her petal-soft skin, and the fact that he'd never in his whole life had a woman so attuned to him, so willing, so completely focused on the moment. Plus, he practically sneezed and she came. Once, twice…and again, and again and again. And none of them faked. That was the amazing part. They were one hundred percent real, just like Allie herself. Most of the women he took to his bed seemed to be only there to star in their own personal porn, acutely aware of which angle looked best for them, as if performing the whole thing for some imaginary audience, but Allie wasn't like that. Allie was carefree, completely authentic. Because of that, she was the sexiest woman he'd ever met.

But he'd crossed a line he'd promised he'd never cross with her. She'd been one of the few women he'd managed to be friends with and he'd gone and let a little wine and a blizzard get in the way of his good judgment. All he'd been trying to do was minimize the damage afterward. He thought if he made himself scarce it would somehow be easier. Sure, for him, but also for her. She could recover and they could both pretend those two days never happened. Maybe, even, after a little time, they could be friends again. Because what was he going to do? Settle down? Ask her to marry him? Have two kids?

Marriage, kids, a picket fence—those were never going to be in his future. He had too much Beck blood in him. Becks didn't do families. Or when they did, they did them all wrong.

He'd disappeared for her own good, but it looked like she'd done a lousy job of recovering. And it was all his fault. It didn't look like she was thriving. Sure, she was as gorgeous as ever, especially with the new hair—yellow and red like a single flame—and those sexy AF librarian glasses. God, they made her look razor sharp and…so delectable. But the faint circles under her eyes told him she wasn't sleeping, and her too-slim hips told him she wasn't eating enough. Beck knew that when she was stressed, she didn't eat. Like during her busy time at work last year when he'd have to practically force-feed her dinner, because she fretted so much about her deadlines that she forgot she needed food to fuel her. Who was making sure she ate now? Her cheekbones were sharper, her waist thinner than usual. She needed to eat, that much he knew. He wanted to scoop her into his arms and take her to the nearest burger joint and watch her gobble down a large order of fries. The instinct to take care of her burned in him.

That was why they'd made such good friends. He wanted to take care of her. But now they'd slipped into bed together and everything had changed. He'd known it would, but he'd crossed the line anyway. He was a fool.

She moved like the model she should've been: tall, elegant, lean. Just watching the bar light catch those fire-engine red highlights of hers made him want to put his hands in that messy bun and tug it down, unraveling the silky strands with his fingers. He remembered the feel of her waves in his fingers, soft but strong, and the feel of her thick lips on his. He recalled, too, her sheer lace underwear—and garter belts. She might be a buttoned-up accountant on the outside, but peel off that first layer, and any man was

in for a surprise. Her lingerie had matched perfectly—
a shock since the blizzard had taken them both by
surprise, and they'd ended up stuck at the same lodge
by sheer accident. He had wanted to study it and rip
it off at the same time. He wondered what she might
be wearing beneath that tight cashmere sweater. Red
lace? God, he hoped it was red.

His groin tightened at the mere thought.

Stop it, he told himself. He wasn't crossing that line
again. It was best for her. He knew that even if she
didn't yet. He'd plowed through a couple of rebound
trysts since then, but he'd had to choke them down,
force himself. Liam Beck had never been the kind
of guy who had to force himself to oblige a willing
woman, and yet, lately, sex had become a chore. In
fact, he hadn't even touched another woman in a full
month. Because the more women he took to his bed,
the more he realized they were nothing like Allie.
He'd been through enough plain cotton thongs and
mismatched sports bras and fumbling awkwardness
to last a lifetime. They all seemed immature somehow, even though none was more than a couple of
years younger than him. Even Channing, with her
corset and plunging cleavage, seemed just like a girl
playing dress-up.

Allie, on the other hand, was a woman. Complex,
grown-up, sexier and infinitely more dangerous. He
watched her glide through the crowd, the men and
women parting to let her to the bar. She was tall, lithe
and graceful as she leaned in to get the bartender's

attention. Not that he needed a signal. He dropped everything and scurried over to get her order, his eyes lighting up at the sight of her. Of course. She was gorgeous, that auburn hair and delicate pale neck. She was a knockout, not that she knew it. Her power over men always came as a surprise to her. Not to Beck.

He frowned as he watched the bartender's eyes light up as he bathed in her attention. He remembered the feel of being the focus of those clear green eyes, and the feeling, too, of truly being *seen*. He noticed their conversation dragged on longer than should be right for a quick order of drinks. The man laughed, too, at one of her jokes, he assumed, and then Beck wondered with a shock if she were *flirting* with him. The dad-bod bartender? The one with the patchy beard? Looked like he couldn't grow any in on the middle part of his chin. Was she serious? He was maybe a three, and she was most definitely a nine. Was she doing this to get his attention?

If so, goal achieved.

A muscle in his jaw twitched. Why was she leaning so far over the bar? The bartender's eyes drifted down to the V-neck of her sweater, which barely contained her. And he suddenly wanted to fly across the bar and remind the man about good old-fashioned manners. The jingly, upbeat Christmas music drifting out through the speakers suddenly grated, as his mood turned dark. This wasn't the happiest season of all. He hated Christmas. It reminded him of the day he watched his dad being led out of their house in handcuffs. He hadn't come from the kind of family who baked cookies and sang carols.

The whole season got him into a defensive mood, and it didn't help watching the bartender fall all over himself to serve Allie right now. He had a goofy grin plastered on his face as if he couldn't believe his luck. Well, of course. He'd just won the lottery with the sexiest woman in the bar whispering something directly into his ear. Whatever she said, she seemed to make his night. And then he realized with a shock that maybe she *knew* him. Was she dating this guy? Were they a...thing?

Then, in a flash, she was kissing the guy, *on the mouth*, in front of everyone in this damn bar. That answered his question then. What the holy hell? If he hadn't seen it with his own eyes, he wouldn't have believed it. What was Al doing sticking her tongue down that guy's throat? Then he had to remind himself that he'd set her free *for this very reason*. He clutched his beer harder. Didn't make the reality of her using that freedom any easier to take. Whoops and hollers of approval went up from the bar, as the nearest revelers seemed to enjoy the show. The attention didn't bother Allie at all, which confounded Beck. How could this be? She hated the idea of people watching her. Then the bartender reached up and *put his hands in her auburn hair*, threatening to bring the whole messy bun down.

He couldn't watch anymore. He turned away then, chugging a big swig of beer.

None of your fucking business, Beck.

He set her free, and it was for her own damn good.
If this was how she used her freedom, then that was
her choice. He'd had this stupid notion that he'd nobly
let her go and she'd find the man of her dreams, a
boring lawyer type who'd deliver all the things she
wanted: an engagement ring, a white picket fence and
kids—the life he'd sworn he'd never have. He wasn't
the kind of man to be domesticated. He had serious
issues with his father, but the one thing he'd learned
from the drug addict was that it was best not to put
someone in a cage who didn't want to be there. Otherwise, he'd hurt everyone around him trying to escape.

He took another drink of his beer. Then a cry went
up from the bar—Allie's cry. He whirled in time to
see some other patron at the bar deciding to get in on
the action. He had an arm around her and was dragging her to him against her will, asking for a kiss as
well, though the look on Allie's face told him she was
in no mood to oblige him. The bartender was gestur-
ing and yelling at the man, but whatever the threat
from her new boyfriend, it wasn't enough. Before he
could stop himself, he'd stashed his beer on a ledge
near Channing and was on the move, every muscle in
his body telling him that he had to intervene. He felt
a sense of possessiveness he had no business feeling
rising up in him, a ridiculous primal instinct he knew
was wrong but couldn't fight. Nobody touched Allie
without her permission. Ever. Period.

He made it to the bar just in time to see Allie give

the patron a good stomp with her stiletto ankle boot on the inside of his foot, and he leaped back, cursing. Allie's frown and the wagging finger in the man's face told Beck she had the situation handled. But then, she always did. He felt a fierce swell of pride in his chest. That was his Al, all right. Lord help the man who underestimated her. God, he missed her. She swiped past him, glancing up for a split second, her green eyes ablaze. He watched her head to the ladies' room, and without thinking, he followed her into the small corridor. He found her outside the locked door, leaning against the corner and fiddling with her heel. He watched as the heel fell off the sole of her shoe. She'd broken it against the man's foot! He couldn't help himself—a sly grin wiggled across his face.

"Well, that's one way to make sure he understands the value of consent," he managed, folding his forearms across his chest. "You okay?"

Her head snapped up then, her green eyes fixed on him, fury still flickering there. She'd stashed her librarian glasses somewhere, and now he could see her green eyes clearly, large and burning. The fire in them didn't cool when she saw him, either.

"I'm fine," she said as she tried unsuccessfully to reattach the heel. Whatever had held it there was useless now.

"I might have superglue in my truck," he offered. The idea of her wobbling about on lopsided shoes for the evening wouldn't do.

"I don't need your help." She ground out the words

as she glared at him. There was a series of novels in that one little sentence, added meaning behind every word. Frustrated with her heel, she let out a sigh and stopped trying to affix it to her boot, as she sagged against the wall one legged, like a depressed flamingo. He almost laughed but thought better of it. Laughing would make her only more furious and he didn't want to chance her breaking her good heel on *his* foot. She wobbled a little, biting her lip in frustration. She ducked down and tried to unzip the broken-heeled boot, but balancing on one stiletto in a small corridor with no good handholds made her less like a flamingo and more like an amateur athlete stuck on the end of a pole midvault.

"Al…" He leaned in now, close enough to get a whiff of her amazing perfume, the signature floral scent that always used to drive him mad. She smelled like the Rockies in springtime, all in bloom beneath the Colorado sunshine. "Please," he said with deliberate deference. He reached out and touched her elbow. Instantly, her wobble steadied. "Let me help."

She glanced up at him, an unanswered question in her emerald green eyes. He knew he wouldn't be able to strong-arm her any more than he could tell daffodils where to grow.

"Please, Al."

She softened a bit. Fairly confident she wouldn't try to stick her good stiletto in his eye, he knelt before her and helped her unzip the broken boot, her delicate foot slipping out, revealing sheer lace socks. His eyebrows rose in appreciation. Only Al could make socks sexy. He saw the bright green polish on her toes and thought of her eyes. Still kneeling, he held her tiny foot on his knee, giving her a steady base, and tried not to think about the warmth of her toes against his jeans. He studied the shoe, and the heel that she wordlessly handed to him. He wasn't sure if glue would work after all. Beck studied the slope of the boot's sole, surprised to find it more like suede than leather, more pliable.

"Can I see the other one?" He reached for the good boot. She hesitated, but then let him, slipping her socked foot on the mat near the bathroom doors and raising her other foot. He slowly worked the zipper down the side, trying not to think about how he'd taken off her boots just this way...that night at the lodge. Boots...then jeans...then the delicate lace beneath. She stood very still, eyes watching his every move. He freed her from the second boot, and now she was standing in her lacy socks, her freshly painted green toes a beacon. He wanted to kiss them and stroke her calf all the way up to her knee. He watched as she shifted uncomfortably from one foot to the other.

"Floor cold?" he asked her, and she gave him a swift nod. He glanced around, seeing a stack of kitchen towels stashed in the shelves near the bathrooms. He grabbed a thick one and dropped it down near her feet. She tiptoed on the terry cloth delicately and stood there on the balls of her feet. He managed to divert his attention back to her boot in his hand. The good one. He'd put the broken one down on the floor. He straightened, as he studied the black suede boot, an idea coming to him. An idea she wouldn't like, but that would help prevent her feet from freezing for the rest of the night.

He took the boot, which seemed so delicate and small in his hands, and quickly snapped the other heel off.

"What the hell!" cried Allie, her face beet red with anger. "Beck!"

"You can walk in these now and your feet won't get cold," he said, even as she gave his chest a shove. He tried to defend himself against her blows. "And calm down. I'll buy you a new pair."

She angrily swiped the boot out of his hand and jammed her foot in it. "I don't need you to buy me anything."

"I know," he said. Allie could take care of herself, but that didn't mean that he wouldn't want to if she'd ever let him. Her head bounced up, a tendril of auburn hair falling across her forehead.

"I just want to make sure you're okay, that's all."

"So you break my shoe?"

"I *evened* the pair," he managed. Now her ire was fully focused on him, the jerk at the bar long forgotten. Suddenly, the heel fiasco was all his fault, instead of the handsy SOB who'd started all this—or the wimpy bartender who couldn't defend her even in his own place. "I didn't want your feet freezing, or for you to fall and break your knee hobbling around like a pirate."

She stuffed her other foot in the other boot and zipped it. They both glanced down at the flattened boots and saw her toes pointing oddly in the air. The once sexy ankle boots looked a bit like something that one of Santa's elves might wear. Now Beck really did want to laugh. Hard. But he had to swallow his chuckle as she glared at her feet, exasperated.

"I look ridiculous now."

Beck said nothing. She did, kind of, look ridiculous in her elf shoes. Not that any of the guys at this bar, or any other bar, would care. No man would be looking at her feet. She could wear a pair of stuffed bear paw slippers and still get hit on by every straight guy in the place.

Allie frowned, more tendrils of loose hair falling forward in her face, her bun all but coming undone. He wanted to put his hands in her hair and finish the job. He longed to see her face framed by the silken auburn streaked with red, wanted to feel that silky hair once more on his bare chest. He mentally shook himself. More thoughts like these and he'd have a hard-on in the bar, right there. And he'd promised himself: hands off Allie. Period.

"I don't think your new boyfriend will care about the shoes, if that's what you're worried about," Beck offered.

"Boyfriend?" Confusion crossed Allie's face.

"The bartender?" Beck reluctantly nodded toward

the bar, still not quite believing that the solidly below-average man was Allie's choice to replace him.

"Him?" Allie laughed, confusing Beck. "He's not my boyfriend. Any more than you are."

The sting of the comment was surprisingly sharp. Beck blinked fast. "Sure seemed like you guys were friendly."

Allie's gaze focused on him with the intensity of a lion looking for the weak member of a pack.

"Were you watching me?" she asked, a note of accusation in her voice.

"Of course I was." If she were in the room, then that was where his attention would be. Plain and simple. That hadn't changed, might never change. "So you're not dating him?"

Allie laughed. "The bartender? No."

Relief flooded Beck. "Good." That bartender couldn't handle a woman like Allie. She was way out of his league.

"I don't even know his name," she added.

This felt like a punch in the gut. "You *kissed* a guy and you didn't even know his name?" Beck felt like an alien had come down and taken over his friend's body. She was not the make-out-with-strangers-in-a-bar type. Allie picked her lingerie with care, and her men with more deliberation. It was one of the things that made Allie...Allie. They'd spent enough time at enough happy hours to know how the other operated, enough time together lamenting the Aspen dating scene to know what made the other tick. It had been why they'd been such great friends. Until the blizzard that had snowed them in on top of the mountain and everything changed.

"Why?"

Allie shrugged. "Because Mira dared me to."

"Dared you?" None of this made sense. "What the hell is that?"

Allie laughed. "I'm playing a game of double dare you. So why do you care? Don't you have some mark to make tonight? Is it Channing?"

Beck flinched. They were back in Allie and Beck mode, friends mode, where she'd be his wingman at the bar and he'd reveal the real truth about what it was like being Aspen's most-talked-about bachelor. It was comfortable. Dangerously comfortable.

"No, I can't stand Channing."

"She sure likes you." The words seemed to have some weight to them. Beck tried not to think about what that meant. Despite the fact they were acting like good old friends, something was off. Beck knew exactly what. It was because he'd tasted every inch of her body and he'd liked it. Liked it so much, he craved another round. And another. "Well, I'm sure you'll have your pick of the bar. Anyway, I've got to go. The bartender told me he's off in fifteen minutes."

Now Beck felt like he'd been hit with a ton of bricks. She was going to take that lame guy *home* after that pathetic show at the bar when he let that patron slobber all over her? She was going to show him her red lace? His brain felt short-circuited. The world he lived in no longer made sense.

"You're going to fuck him?" He stared at Allie as if seeing her for the first time. "You don't even know his name."

"That never stopped you before."

"Yeah, but, Al. You're not me." He thought this was obvious. Al didn't do casual. She'd never done anything casual in her whole life. She was all in or nothing. There wasn't an in-between with her.

"I'm not?" The challenge in her voice was unmistakable. "Maybe I've been going about my life all wrong. Maybe I've been *boring*."

What was she even talking about? "You're not boring." She was anything but. And taking after him was the last thing she ought to do. If only she knew how little he'd enjoyed anything or anyone since the weekend they'd spent together, how he drifted aimlessly through nights with strangers like a robot. He could go through the motions, but he felt numb inside, as if he was stuck in a performance trying to convince himself that sex could be half as good with anyone else. He already knew it would never be as good with anyone as with Allie.

"Al…" He sighed. He knew all he had to do was pull out his phone right now, and in seconds he'd probably have a Tinder hookup waiting in the parking lot. There was no way she'd believe that was the last thing he wanted with her standing in front of him. "If you take that guy home, it'll be a mistake." Then she'd feel the emptiness he felt, the uselessness of it all. "You'll regret it."

He was speaking only the truth, but she immediately took offense.

"I'll be the judge of that," she said. He recognized Allie's stubbornness, but not this newfound determination to sleep around. She didn't avoid her problems by having sex with strangers. That was Beck's coping mechanism, as ill-advised as it was.

She cared too much, that was Allie's problem, and she wasn't built for casual sex. It was why it had been a colossal mistake for him to go there. He wasn't a relationship guy. Allie deserved the guy who bought her flowers and wrote his own sappy poems in Valentine's Day cards. Not the guy who didn't plan his life more than a week in advance. "Please don't take him home." Beck realized he had no sway anymore. As much as he wanted to protect her and keep her safe from scruffy-bearded bartenders, he actually didn't have a say in her life.

"Why do you care?"

"Because…" He never stopped caring—that was the whole problem. Because he was jealous, even though he had no right to be. "Because I don't want you to get hurt."

"I think it's a little late for that." She blinked, and he worried for a second she might cry. If she cried, he'd be undone; he wouldn't be able to keep his resolve. He'd pull her into his arms and beg her for forgiveness. And that wouldn't help either of them.

How could he tell her that he'd just find a way to disappoint her? Later, five or even ten years down the line, the Beck genes would come roaring to the surface. They always did.

"I'm…" He almost said "sorry" but stopped himself. Sorry wasn't enough. "Just…please don't do this."

She took a step closer to him and he felt his own heart tick up, the thought of pain and heartbreak slipping away. Her perfume was in his nose, and all he wanted to do was inhale. She was so close he could dip down and kiss her now, show her what it meant to be properly kissed, not slathered on. He could kiss her in the way he knew she liked. Every bit of him wanted to. Wanted to feel her lips once more against his. Make her sigh into his mouth.

"You can't tell me what to do anymore," Allie said, voice low.

Beck couldn't help it. He chuckled and shook his head slowly. "Al, I never could tell you what to do." And he wasn't dumb enough to start now. "I just don't think the bartender is the answer to your problems," he said. "Trust me, I know." He couldn't even remember the names of the women he'd been with but he knew that they'd only made him feel lonelier.

"Maybe the bartender is just what I need." Her green eyes were ablaze with defiance. "Maybe I'll just accept any crazy dare that Mira or anyone else throws my way. Not because I'm scared of what Mira or anyone else thinks, but maybe I'll do it *just be-cause I can.*"

Allie stabbed a finger in his chest, and Beck felt laughter bubble up in his throat, which he promptly squashed. There was no way he'd tell her that her anger coupled with her elf shoes made her off-the-charts adorable.

"Look, you don't have anything to prove to me, okay?" he managed. If this was about trying to make him jealous, he needed to stop this right here and now. She needed to get past him if she was ever going to truly be happy with someone else.

"Why do you think it's about you? None of this is about you." Allie's right eyebrow twitched, her tell. She was lying.

"This isn't about me?" Beck knew he shouldn't poke the bear. Knew he should just let her leave the little alcove feeling like she'd won this fight. But Beck couldn't let it go. She needed to face her feelings, or they'd always have control over her. She'd never get over him, if she was always trying to prove she was over him. The ultimate irony.

Not that he'd done much better. He'd faced his feelings for Allie every day since that weekend, and it hadn't helped him one bit. He had no idea how forty-eight hours had upended his life, but they had.

"You think it's about that weekend? It's not." Again, her eyebrow twitched. "I don't even *think* about that weekend."

Now he knew for sure she was lying.

"You don't?"

"No. I don't." She glared at him. He'd made her come more times than she could count, and she'd shouted his name in a hoarse ecstasy that he'd never heard before. She absolutely remembered. He would bet money on it. Hell, he'd bet all his money on it. "You think I won't take that bartender home? Just dare me. I will." He almost wanted to catch her up in his arms right then, show her who she should be taking home tonight.

"If you need me to dare you, then maybe you're not all that into the idea," he said dryly.

She flipped her hair from her eyes and looked as if she might breathe fire, burn him to ash if she could. *That's it*, he thought. *Get angry.* Angry was much better than sad. Anger could help her get stronger. Sadness would eat her alive, but anger would help her fight. Help her recover. "You're impossible. I'll take him home anyway."

"You'll take him home and you'll think of me."

Shock bloomed on her face as her mouth fell open. He'd rendered her speechless—for once. He grinned. He knew she needed to get angry, for her sake, but he was also enjoying pushing her buttons. He'd forgotten how easy she was to bait and how much he loved her temper. He was drawn to that heat, that fire, in her.

"I *will* not," she managed, once she found her voice again. "How dare you even think that I'm somehow hung up on you…"

"Because you are."

"I'm not." Now the teasing was going too far. Annoyance bubbled in Beck. Why wouldn't she just admit it? He knew it was about pride, but if she just admitted it, she could move on.

"Okay," Beck said, his mind feeling like it was crawling with ants. Allie was getting under his skin. He took a step closer and almost felt like he wanted to drown in those green eyes. So defiant, so full of ire and so stubbornly unwilling to admit that she still had feelings for him, which she clearly did. He was going to do something rash, something that broke his own rules, but he had such a hard time toeing the line. Hell, he didn't even see the line with her right in front of him. "If you are over me, and I don't mean anything to you, then prove it." She blinked fast. He grinned, slowly, letting the tension build. He was going to enjoy this. "I dare you to kiss me."

CHAPTER THREE

ALLIE FELT THE entire world on the other side of their little nook fade away into nothing. For a second, she forgot to breathe and there was just her and Beck, the only two people on earth. Because it all seemed more than absurd, she laughed. A brittle, bitter laugh.

The man must be joking. That was the only way she could think to explain it. How else was it that Beck, who'd been happily sleeping with the tourists of Aspen for the last two months, wanted to kiss her? He was the one who'd made it clear to her that they had no future, and yet now he wanted to come back for more?

"Why are you laughing?" His steady, serious gaze told her she'd miscalculated. He was deadly serious.

"Because you have to be joking."

"I'm not." He was so close now, she could see the darker flecks in his blond stubble. The man seemed as if he belonged in the middle of a snowboarding commercial beneath the bright mountain sun. She wanted to put her hands in his hair. Touch it, see if it was as soft as she remembered. She had to shake herself. That was not an option. Not now. Not ever. "If you don't care for me at all, then kiss me. I'll be able to tell, and then I won't bother you anymore, and you can take that scruffy bartender home."

"This is ridiculous." She shifted her feet in her broken boots, the soles feeling oddly angled against the bar floor. She felt exposed.

What was the man's game? He could have anyone in the bar, and in fact, Channing was already in a pout across the room because she'd lost her prize.

There was only one reason why she could think that he'd be interested in her again.

Was the adventuring ski god of Aspen...jealous? He didn't want her for himself, but didn't want anyone else to have her?

"So? What about that dare?" His blue eyes never left hers. They were steady, serious.

She laughed again, but this time it came out sounding thin and a little nervous. "No," she said and folded her arms across her chest.

"Why not?" Now he moved a beat closer. She could almost feel his body heat, and she'd forgotten how broad he was, and the nook they were in barely contained them. He was all muscle, and if he wanted that kiss, he could get it whether she wanted it or not. But that wasn't Beck's way. She knew it as well as he did. Besides, women in Aspen would line up for a chance to kiss Liam Beck, for a chance to do much more than that.

The worst part was that even though he'd discarded

her just two months ago, her body didn't seem to care. Right in that moment, all she wanted to do was reach on her tippy toes and kiss that man right here. After all, he was a phenomenal kisser. A man with that much practice couldn't help but be.

"You know why," she said, voice low. *Because we had amazing sex and then you dropped off the face of the earth. Then I hear you think I'm boring.* But Allie couldn't get herself to say those things out loud.

"If you take that bartender home, but you're still hung up on me, it's not going to be good for you."

White-hot anger rushed through her, warming her right through her toes. "It's my mistake to make, then." She could not believe this man. He ghosted her, then spread rumors she was a dud in bed, and now he was micromanaging her dating life?

"You don't get to pick who I sleep with, Beck."

"I know." Beck glanced away, almost looking guilty. "I know that."

The vulnerability he showed in that moment sliced through her. He seemed so lost...so untethered. For a second, she wondered if the breakup had hit him hard. Harder than she'd imagined. Here she thought he'd just resumed his life, no worse for wear, but the look of pain across his face told her a different story. Could it be that he had suffered, like she suffered?

It almost made her want to kiss him, just to make him feel better. She nearly laughed. She wanted to make *him* feel better? What was she thinking? She wasn't. She never did when it came to Beck.

"Go ahead, then," Beck said, sounding resigned. "Go back to him."

She hated that in that moment of him dismissing her, it made her only want to stay. Why, she didn't know. The more Beck pushed her away, the more she wanted to be with him. She hated that weakness in herself. She glanced over Beck's shoulder and saw the bartender eyeing them from the bar. He'd come to her rescue if she signaled him, she thought. But part of her didn't want to be rescued. She wanted to stay just where she was and that was what worried her.

"Maybe I will."

Beck stared at her for a beat. "You're not moving."

No, she wasn't. It felt like she was caught in Beck's gravitational field, fixed like a moon in orbit.

"I don't think you want to go," Beck said at last. Damn him for reading her mind. She scooted a bit against the wall, but her elf boot hit the edge of a nearby mat, and she stumbled. He caught her, steadying her. His strong hands on her elbows made her remember how talented they were in exploring other parts of her body. How she felt so delicate, so little, in his arms. Allie froze then, the moment turning serious suddenly. He ran a finger down the outside of her upper arm. His touch felt hot. She watched his finger trail the seam of her sleeve, remembering how well his hands already knew her body. Despite all her logical misgivings, some part of her still burned for him. "I think you want to kiss me. I think you haven't gotten enough of me."

There was no boast in the words. It was true, after all. How could he read her so well?

She blinked fast. Her heart ticked up a notch. She wanted to kiss him, but she was scared. One kiss and she might be a slave to him again, a slave to her own passions, all logic and will gone. Beck moved forward, and she was in the dark corner of the alcove now, away from the bar, out of the line of vision of anyone there. The bartender wouldn't be able to help her now, but she didn't want anyone's help.

She decided then and there, she wasn't going to be afraid of Liam Beck. She could kiss him and not feel anything. She could do this and prove to him and herself that she was beyond him.

"I'll kiss you, just to prove that weekend meant nothing," she said. "I don't feel anything for you, Liam Beck."

Beck nodded, once. "Good. If that's true, then I'll leave you alone."

She needed Liam Beck out of her life. And if kissing him one last time was the way to do it, then she'd do it. *It's just a kiss*, she told herself. It would mean nothing. And then she'd be free of him.

"Fine." She tilted her head up, lips ready. Beck wasted no time. His big palm sneaked behind her back, and he pulled her to him. In seconds, she was pressed flat against the massive muscles in his chest. He was so big, she felt tiny. She held a breath, her heart fighting like a rabbit trying to get out of its cage. Beck took his time. His eyes studying hers and then moving ever so slowly down her face to her lips. They parted on their own accord, already tingling in anticipation. *It won't mean anything. I won't feel anything,* she told herself.

He pressed his full lips against hers, tentatively at first. Gently. She kept her lips still. *If I don't move, then everything will be fine.* But she knew already this wasn't going to be a quick peck on the lips. Beck had something else in mind. The second his lips moved on hers, the entire last two months disappeared. It was as if they'd never spent a second apart and they were right back in that lodge.

His mouth, warm and determined, found hers in just the way she liked. Instantly, all her senses lit up, like blinking lights on a massive Christmas tree, and she felt the surge of electricity down to her fingertips. She didn't know whose tongue sought the other's first, only that soon the kiss turned deeper, more dangerous. He anticipated every move she made and countered it, in a way that made her feel like they were partners in the world's oldest dance. There was something about the way the man tasted, something so irresistible that she didn't want to stop. In seconds, her hands, with a will of their own, had crawled up the back of his neck and into his hair. Yes, that thick, soft shock of blond, and his neck thick with muscle. His hands kept firm on the small of her back and she was reminded how big his hands were, how they seemed to span most of her waist.

And then Beck's hands snaked up the back of her

sweater, and she felt his palms on her skin. The heat from his hands traveled all the way through her. Want, powerful and raw, came to life in her belly, and she realized how she'd stuffed down her own desires for weeks, how she'd denied herself, how she'd tried so hard to forget how Beck felt. Now here he was, mouth on hers, and all she could think was *more. I want more. I want his lips. I want his hands. I want everything.* She felt as if she'd only just woken up to the fact that she had been starving for this.

His hands roamed downward, outside the fabric of her jeans, and he cupped her possessively, pushing her flat against him, and then she felt the hardness bulging in the front of his jeans. He wanted her, too. Badly. The discovery made her kiss him even harder; she wanted to devour him. Stand in that chaos once more that was loving Beck, cling to him in the ferocious whirlwind that was him. Kissing the bartender was now a distant, faint memory. Here, right here, this was what passion was meant to be. His hands roamed freely now, as did hers, neither seeming to be able to stop groping. She realized the stark truth: it wasn't that she *couldn't* stop kissing Beck. She didn't want to stop.

Distantly, she heard someone come out of the locked bathroom behind them, and in a second, Beck was steering her inside. She went willingly, unable to believe how fast things were moving, but then, that was what Beck did. He tackled everything fast: slopes, cars, women. Beck himself was like a thrilling roller coaster ride, one without a safety harness. She pushed him against the bathroom wall, running her hands up his thick, fit chest. And then she realized that she could have him, right there in the bathroom of this bar. No one would have to know.

She pressed her hand to the front of his jeans and found him hard and ready. All she'd have to do was free him, a single zipper standing between her and him. That was all she wanted. One more time. One more and she'd be done with him.

Or would she? She wondered if she'd ever, truly, be over Liam Beck, or if he'd stay in her blood forever, like a dormant virus, ready to come to life at the first touch. She pulled away from Beck first, breaking the spell. She saw surprise on his face, as he panted, out of breath. The extreme snowboarding athlete that never met a mountain he couldn't climb or ski seemed winded and disoriented. God, she wondered what she looked like. Hell, probably, her lipstick smudged, her hair a mess. She felt as surprised as Beck looked. Well, guess he wasn't expecting that, either. He'd forgotten, just as she had, how electric they'd been. How much like gasoline on flames. It was why he was so addictive, so hard to quit. That kind of fire didn't come along every day. Or, hell, every lifetime.

"Al…" Beck's voice was a guttural growl. His blue eyes nearly black, his pupils were so big with desire. His hair was ruffled, too, she noticed. That was where her hands had been two seconds ago. "Al, oh, but I missed you."

The words sliced through her. She wanted to tell him she'd missed him, too. She wanted to take him home to her bed and show him just how much she'd missed him. But she couldn't. Things were different now. They'd never be the same.

She slid her hands down the front of his pants and he groaned. A flicker of mischief ran through her. She glanced downward, at her hand covering his fly, and then she slowly worked his zipper down, a centimeter at a time. She expected him to…what? Stop her? Tell her they weren't right together? That this was all some kind of mistake. Would he warn her about tomorrow or the next day when he wouldn't call?

But the want in his eyes was like flame, and she knew he wasn't going to stop her. She reached into his pants and wrapped her hands around his thick shaft, and he sucked in a breath. Smooth, hard and thick, just as she remembered. Absolutely, blindingly perfect. Then, just as quickly, she released him.

She smiled, slowly.

"Looks like *you're* the one who's not over me, Beck."

And then she turned, leaving him leaning against the wall, face frozen in shock. She left him there, and he let her go, the look in his eyes telling her that whatever it was between them was far, far from done. Why did she have a sudden and definite feeling that she'd kicked a hornet's nest?

CHAPTER FOUR

"YOU DID *NOT* seriously do that! Left him, dick literally in his hands!" squealed Mira the next day, as she jabbed a piece of spinach salad and forked it into her mouth. They sat in the retro-styled café near the slopes, which seemed both quaint and modern at the same time, with sleek stainless-steel tables and leather-bound booths. More Christmas music blared happily from the speakers and the restaurant was decorated floor to ceiling in freshly harvested garlands and wreaths. The whole restaurant smelled like pine trees. Allie was busy explaining why she'd made a hasty exit the night before, leaving well before the party was over. Mira had to stay until the end—it was the party she'd helped organize, after all. "Serves him right. That'll teach him to ghost you. And here I thought you were in hot water with Beck. I knew he'd gone after you, but I didn't think… Well, damn, girl. I didn't think you had it in you."

"Why? Think he'd kiss me and I'd beg for more?"

Mira glanced at her friend, wary. "Well, yes. The man is a sex god. *Look* at him." Her friend sent her a sympathetic look. "And you did say he was amazing."

"Whose side are you on?"

"Yours—obviously." Mira leaned closer. "You sure you didn't feel anything when he kissed you?"

"Nope." Technically, she didn't feel anything. She felt everything. Every possible nerve ending in her body lighting up, like a power grid that only Beck could ignite. But she couldn't let that derail her. She knew Beck, knew that he could never truly be serious about anyone.

"Good. I thought you might be sucked into his web again. He's not the kind of man who's ever going to settle down. Or if he does, he'll be sixty and opt for a twenty-year-old."

"I know. I should never have thought about him as relationship material. That was my mistake. He was a good time, nothing more." The more she said it, the more she hoped it would be true. The problem was she'd had feelings for Beck for a long time before they rolled into bed together. Again, her fault. She'd always prided herself on being the girl who wasn't sucked in by the guy every girl wanted. Then again, she'd always been bookish, so it wasn't like the hottest guy in school was after the honors society president, either. Still, she told herself it was mutual as she'd steered well clear of the popular and gorgeous egomaniacs who devoured her friends' self-esteem and left them used and mangled. But then came Beck. She thought being friends with him was a safe bet, but it turned out to be anything but. She'd fallen for him hard. Just like most of the women in Aspen. She was almost disappointed in herself for stumbling into the same trap, for being so ordinary. She thought she'd had better sense than every other woman in town.

"Not to mention, who wants to be his girlfriend anyway? Waiting for him to come home after one of his skiing trips in avalanche country?"

Mira nodded. "He's an adrenaline junkie. It's like he's addicted to it."

There was something in Beck that seemed hell-bent on self-destruction. Some people did it with drugs or alcohol. Beck did it with crazy stunts on the mountains. Allie always wanted to show him things could be different, but he didn't seem willing to see that. And now she wouldn't really get the chance.

"He'll probably be dead by forty."

"Don't say that." Allie's voice was sharper than she intended. They might not be a couple, or hell, even friends anymore, but Allie couldn't bear the thought of an accident taking Beck's life. She realized she'd just shown Mira that she still cared, and she hated that. She wondered when there would ever be a time she truly could care less about Liam Beck.

"Sorry." Mira backed away quickly, her dark eyes full of apology. "I didn't mean it."

"I know you didn't." She sighed. Allie fiddled with her spoon. Suddenly, the steaming hot bowl of cheesy onion soup in front of her didn't seem so appetizing anymore. The upbeat jangly holiday music grated, and all she wanted to do was skip over the cheery holiday mood and land in bleak late January. Allie pushed around some of the melted cheese in the bowl in front of her.

"It's just that if he really cared about you, he would've called."

"I know."

"And not just that." Mira searched for the right words. "If he cared, he would've made room for you in his life. He seems like a man who puts everyone in a box. As long as you were in the friend box, that was okay. But then, when you hopped on out of there and wanted a bigger box, a girlfriend box, he freaked out."

Allie nodded. "Well, that's the nice way of looking at it. He freaked out because he cared too much about me, instead of the fact that sex with me bored him to tears."

"Look, you're no *Greenie*. I may never have slept with you…" Mira raised her eyebrows. "And as your *straight* best friend, never will, but I am willing to bet you are great in bed. You are like the hardest worker *I know*, so I can't imagine you're lazy in bed."

Allie laughed a little. "Thanks, Mira." Allie felt a little bit better. "I do think I have some skills."

"Of course you do!" Mira chirped. "I do have a question for you, though. So, all that time you were friends with Beck before *the weekend*…did he ever invite you on one of those crazy tours of his? The heli-skiing?"

Allie shook her head. "Me?"

"You're a kick-ass skier," Mira said. "You eat black diamonds for breakfast."

"Yeah." Allie glanced downward. She was a pretty good skier. It was the one thing she'd split with her conservative parents on—she'd learned to ski and kept skiing, despite the risks. Of course, she wore one of the best helmets money could buy—at her parents' insistence. "But even if he'd invited me on one of those tours, I would've probably said no, anyway."

"Bullshit. If Beck had invited you, you would've bought a new skintight ski suit, gotten a full-body wax and *then* you would've gone. Girl, please." Mira spoke the truth. Even Allie had to admit it. "But he never asked you. Even though you guys were friends who hung out almost every week."

"Yeah."

Mira jammed another bite of salad in her mouth, chewing fiercely. "It's all because you didn't fit into that extreme sport box. It's that he likes to keep his life arranged in neat little boxes: his one-night stands in one, his friends in another, adrenaline junkie stuff in yet another. He reminds me exactly of a guy I used to date in college." Mira waved her now-empty fork in the air. "Even *if* you dated him, or hell, even if you could get him to marry you, he'd probably just put that in another box. Along with each kid you had. Never the two or three or four or five boxes shall meet."

"I don't think he'd do that." Why was she defending Beck? Mira was probably more on target about Beck than even Allie wanted to admit.

"Really? Is that why when you tried to climb out of that friend box and get into that sex box he decided he was better off without your friend box than having someone who wouldn't stay in it?"

Allie felt the punch of truth. She wasn't going to finish her lunch for sure now.

"Ugh. I'm sorry." Mira reached across the table and clutched at Allie's hand. "Your face looks like I kicked your puppy. God, I need to shut my mouth and mind my own business."

"No." Allie gave her friend a weak smile. "I know you want what's best for me."

"And I'm proud of you for not trailing after him like some stray cat, like half of Aspen." She squeezed Allie's hand one last time and let it go. "I want you to see that you can do better than Liam Beck. He's never going to rearrange those boxes for you in his mind. He'll always be trying to put you in one."

Allie let out a frustrated breath. She knew logically that might be true, but in her heart, she simply wanted to believe he could change. And part of her wasn't so sure she could do better than Beck. She could feel his lips on hers, how he'd made her whole body come alive with a single touch. What other man could do that? He'd been as good as she imagined— no, even better.

"It's probably just Christmas. Between Thanksgiving and Christmas, more ghosting and breakups happen than any other time. Too much pressure with the holidays."

"Is that true?"

"I saw it in a meme somewhere, so probably not." Mira laughed to herself as she dabbed her mouth with a napkin.

"Probably is true with Beck. He hates the holidays."

"Did he ever tell you why?"

"Not exactly, but it has to do with his family." It was one of the many secrets Beck kept. She knew the broad outlines of his childhood: addict dad, absent mom, and the fact that Beck spent his childhood in and out of foster care before he turned eighteen and set about taking care of himself. It was the same story that had made him such a favorite in the Olympic Games. Kid from a broken home makes good with two silver medals. But none of that explained exactly why he hated Christmas so much. Allie had just assumed Christmases had been hard for him, growing up. But he refused to talk about them, or pretty much any of his childhood.

"You're sure he didn't rattle you?" Mira asked, looking suddenly concerned.

Allie let out a false laugh, which sounded a little too forced. "No, of course not. I'm the one who left him in the bathroom."

"But you also kissed him."

"Right, to prove that there was nothing between us," she said. "Which there's not." Now, that was definitely a lie. But Allie told herself she'd keep on telling it until it was true. *Fake it till you make it*, she told herself.

Mira stared at her friend a beat. "Okay," she said after a while. Allie was glad her friend didn't push it. Suddenly, she didn't want to talk about Beck anymore. Allie took a gulp of ice water from her glass.

Mira's face softened, and she reached out and clutched Allie's hand on the table.

"I didn't mean to doubt you," she said. "I just care about you, and Beck is trouble."

"I don't want to be hurt again, either." Allie sighed, dunking her spoon once more in her soup. She pushed it away from her, frustrated. "Look, don't worry. I can handle myself. It's not like he's…" She glanced at the waiter who strode by carrying a tray filled with two decadent chocolate desserts. "He's not double-fudge brownies with extra chocolate sauce and whipped cream."

"Don't even talk to me about chocolate right now." Mira munched another bite of her salad and glared at the desserts. "I couldn't even zip up my jeans yesterday. I've already gained the holiday ten pounds and *it's not even the holidays yet.*"

Allie laughed at her friend's exaggerated expression of disgust. "You look your adorable little self as always."

"No, I don't. And if this keeps up, Dockett will fire me just because I don't look the 'hospitality part' anymore." Allie frowned at the mention of her boss, Bill Dockett, who owned Enclave. Dockett subtly pressured his employees to stay trim, put together and trendy. Allie thought it absurd and likely illegal, but Mira was paid well, and she was doing what she loved, and the only downside was working for a dinosaur of a boss who'd never heard of #MeToo. Mira looked at her friend. "You're lucky you're tall. You've got more places to stash the weight." Mira cocked an eyebrow. "Not that you need to worry about that. *You're* the one who needs another brownie. You're literally wasting away."

"I am not," Allie protested.

"The heartbreak diet has done its job, but now you need to eat, my friend." Mira pushed the bowl of onion soup toward Allie. "You need to at least have three more bites." She dipped the spoon in and lifted up a bite, as if she planned to feed Allie herself.

"What am I? A toddler?"

"I'll make the airplane noises for you if you want," Mira joked. Allie made a face at Mira, the woman who'd answered her post for a roommate back when she first moved to Aspen. The two had hit it off immediately since they'd both been from Nevada. What were the odds she'd find someone else who learned to ski in the Sierra Nevadas and then moved to Aspen to get more snow? Allie dutifully took the spoon and had a bite of now-lukewarm soup. "Seriously, though. Come out with me tonight. You need a do-over from yesterday. No Beck this time."

"I don't know." It wasn't that work had been busy at

her small accounting office, but Allie wasn't usually a hit-the-bars-two-nights-in-a-row kind of woman.

"Don't flake out on me!" Mira scolded. "I double dog dare you," Mira teased.

"Don't start that again!" Allie cradled her head in her hands in defeat. "Pretty soon, I'll be jumping off a cliff because someone asked me to. You know I can think for myself, right?"

"I know," Mira said. "But maybe you're too much in control. Maybe you need to give it up a little bit. Shake things up. Come on, admit it. Last night was fun. The bartender?" Mira banged the table with her open palm, making the silverware jump.

It wasn't the bartender Allie was thinking about, as she remembered Beck's strong hands at the small of her back, the feel of his hands in her hair.

"It was fun," she admitted. Not the fun she planned to repeat, if Beck was involved.

"But seriously. It's fun to shut your brain off now and again. Let someone else do the steering."

Allie couldn't help but feel that her friend spoke the truth. She'd always held on to things in her life so tightly: her job, her friends and even Beck. But look at where that had gotten her. She thought the tighter she held on to Beck, the more he'd be hers, and yet the opposite had happened. He'd walked out of her life anyway. Maybe the way to happiness wasn't keeping a tight rein on everything in her life. Maybe it was all about letting go. Letting chance take the wheel.

"Come on," Mira said. "Let's play this game to-night. See if we can't get more people involved."

"More people?"

"Let's ask *our* friends to give you a few decent dares just for fun. See where it leads. Come on. You need some fun. *This* will be fun."

Beck spent the night and following day thinking about Allie. Her soft lips, her delicate voice, how that vixen had grabbed him literally by the balls and then left him wanting. She was the only woman who could do that, wrap him around her finger, make him do what she wished and then leave him panting for more. He should be mad, but instead, all he could do was admit to himself that he deserved it. He never should've kissed her like that. He'd crossed a line *again*. He was always doing that with Allie and it was getting to be a problem. Not that he'd planned it. The woman lit a passion in him that burned white-hot, woke desires in him he didn't know he had, his basest primal instincts.

He knew there was a kind of darkness in him, one that invited in the chaos, but when Allie was around it boiled in him, almost impossible to control. Even now, thinking of her delicate cool fingers around his cock made his heart pound. The fact that she'd left him with a nasty case of blue balls just had made her hotter. No woman toyed with him like she did, no woman left him wanting more. That bombshell au-burn hair with the highlights of fire. That electrifying kiss that had all but made him come right there. And part of him wanted to have her ride him until she was spent, but another part also wanted to just curl up with her naked and cuddling in bed, her snug in his arms. That was what made Allie so dangerous. It wasn't just the sex; it was how he wanted to take care of her after.

"Uh, hello? Anybody in there?" Willis waved his hand in front of Beck's face, and he realized his business partner had been talking for quite a while and Beck hadn't been listening. He straightened, taking his feet off his messy desk in the small office of Aspen Adventure Tours, the business the two old friends owned together.

"Sorry, man. I zoned out." Beck gave Willis a sheepish grin. He'd known Willis since the Olympic Village in 2006. Willis invented some of the tricks that were now staples on the half-pipe.

"Mmm-hmm." Willis studied him. "Doesn't have anything to do with Allie Connor, does it?"

"Why would you say that?" Beck's voice was sharp, defensive, even to his own ears.

"Because I know she was at the party last night, and rumor has it...well, that you two had a reunion of sorts."

"It's not like that." He didn't like the idea of anybody spreading rumors about Allie. The muscles in his neck tensed. There it was, that rise of protectiveness in him.

Willis leaned back in his seat, dark eyes focused

on Beck. Judging him. Willis had never much liked Allie, though Beck was not certain why. Part of him thought Willis was jealous of the attention she sucked away from the business, and the way she was always trying to get him to scale back on some of the more dangerous tours.

Willis, however, thought people paid more for danger, and that was what they were in business to deliver. The two friends couldn't be more different. Beck was blond and blue-eyed. Willis, dark haired and wiry, was almost all beard, which went all the way down to the third button on his shirt.

"Look, it's none of my business, man, but she's your polar opposite. Yet that girl has you *wrapped*."

Beck knew this was true, remembered how he'd stood frozen in that bathroom while she'd walked away from him. Still, he could think of worse things than to be in love with a woman as amazing as Allie Connor.

"So?"

"So, didn't she try to change you? Try to get you to sit home and knit or something? All those accountant types are the same."

"That's not exactly it."

"You're going to retire, then? Give the business over to me? I wouldn't mind." Willis grinned.

"I'm not retiring." Beck glanced at Willis, feeling heat at the back of his neck.

"Okay, then, maybe you should do some work instead of stalking your ex on Instagram." Willis nodded at the smartphone lying faceup on his desk, Allie's profile up on it. He quickly swiped the screen away on his phone.

"I just wanted to see if she's okay."

Willis shook his head slowly and absently smoothed his beard. "Right. Sure. Hey, it's your life, man. I'm just glad you didn't give all the accounting over to her."

Beck had been tempted. Allie had offered numerous times to do their accounting work. As of now, she just calculated their taxes at the end of the year. Beck was not a numbers guy, but Willis seemed to be happy to pay their bills and do the payroll and Willis didn't see why they should pay an outsider to do it.

"Have you thought more about my suggestion of expanding to Vail and Breckenridge? Maybe Keystone?" Willis's eyes lit up at the prospect.

Beck might take risks on the mountain, but when it came to finances, he made only deliberate, safe decisions.

"They already have adventure tours. The competition is thick there."

"With your name? We could blow them all away." Beck hated playing off his fame. He hadn't gone to the Olympics for fame. He'd done it to prove he could.

"But I live here. I'd hardly ever be on those tours."

"So what? Your name is what sells, man. Go for the opening, stay a week, then come back here. You'll have people lining up in droves just to say they skied the same backcountry trails Liam Beck did." Willis was pushing this hard. Beck didn't know why. They both had enough to get by. More than get by: thrive.

"Aren't we already making enough?" Beck asked.

"Is it ever enough?" Willis countered.

Beck didn't think much about money. He had enough in his bank account and his bills were paid. He didn't worry about much more beyond that. They were doing well and he didn't see the point in risking overextending for a few extra bucks.

"What if the new venture failed?"

"I'd run it for the first year. It won't," Willis promised.

"How could you run both Vail and Breckenridge?"

"I'd figure it out," Willis said.

"I don't know." Beck shook his head. "Why do we need to expand so fast? We've got a good thing going here. And if we save up for another year or two, then maybe."

"By the time we do that, it'll be even more competitive. And somebody else will have a name they can use, too. You know there are a ton of other punks out there, fresh off the last Olympics, probably planning their own gigs right now. We've got to get out there, make our mark, first. We could *own* Colorado."

Beck still didn't like the idea of spreading himself so thin.

"You're asking me to take on all the risk," he said.

Willis paused a moment, seeming to contemplate what he planned to say next.

"I'm asking you to open your eyes to the possibilities, that's all. I'd like my paycheck to be as fat as yours one of these days." This was Willis's way of reminding Beck that he didn't think their deal was fair. Beck knew Willis hated the sixty-forty partnership split, but what could Beck do? He'd already laid down most of the capital—all the money he'd made from snowboarding endorsement deals after the first Olympics—and had taken on all of the risk of losing it all. Willis had come later, bought in after Beck had laid the groundwork. Sure, Willis worked more hours on the mountain than Beck did these days, but that had been the deal from the start. "Listen, just read this, okay?"

Willis held out the folder stuffed with paperwork he'd put together, numbers for what it would cost to open two new locations. Reluctantly, Beck took the folder. He owed it to Willis to at least read the stuff.

"It would be a nice Christmas present if you said yes," Willis said as he nodded toward the folder, his eyes full of expectation.

"You don't watch it, you're just going to get coal," Beck joked, and his old friend's face broke into a smile, not that he could see most of it, covered as it was by his mountain beard. He glanced at the folder, which was brimming with numbers and spreadsheets. God, how he hated spreadsheets. "I guess I can take a look."

"That's all I'm asking you to do." Willis's mood

seemed lighter, happier. "Want to grab a few beers tonight?"

It had been a while since Willis had asked him out for a beer. The two kept monstrously busy schedules, but also, Beck had felt his friend grow a bit more distant lately. He knew he should say yes, but, frankly, he didn't quite feel like it. He wanted to sit and brood about Allie. Maybe scroll through her social media accounts once more. Willis would definitely not approve.

"I think I'm gonna call it an early night," Beck said. Willis shrugged one shoulder.

"Sure, man," he said and stood. "See you tomorrow, then." Willis grabbed his big silver puffer jacket from the coatrack and headed out the door. He shot one parting glance over his shoulder at Beck, but Beck couldn't read his partner's expression. He wondered if he'd made a mistake not taking his friend up on that drink. What was he doing sitting at his desk and cyber-stalking Allie? But he knew why. He couldn't get the woman out of his head. Or his heart. Or his life. The harder he tried, the more she dug in, somehow.

Beck's phone dinged then, an alert that Allie had posted something new to her account. He turned his phone over and checked, seeing a new photo of Allie at the bar, holding up her own phone and a list of new contacts she'd entered into her phone—all men's names. Beneath it read the caption *Dared to get five men's numbers in fifteen minutes. Dare complete.*

Beck sat up. What the hell was this? Five numbers in fifteen minutes?

He read backward and quickly surmised the game: Mira had sent out a post asking all their friends for suggestions on dares to help Allie "get out of her shell."

Beck's back teeth ground together. He liked Allie just fine in her shell. There was no need for her to come out of it. He also took note of the several shots she'd already downed that night and it wasn't even six yet. What was the woman doing? She had the tolerance of a mouse—and that was before she'd dropped ten pounds. Now she was out there getting men's numbers and probably kissing more bartenders and doing who knew what else. He looked at the last picture and recognized the miner's big telltale copper bell at the end of the bar. That was the North Star.

North Star was one of the oldest bars in Aspen. It was where silver miners used to go to celebrate their finds or drown their sorrows, and the big bronze bell still stood at the end of the bar—the bell miners rang when they had found a big lode of silver and planned to buy their fellow miners a drink. Beck loved the feel of the place. It was what Colorado was all about: adventuring souls who shared their good fortune. And now the bar catered to locals looking for cheap pitchers of beer and several big screens of whatever game might be on. If Allie was going to North Star, that meant she might be hitting on people he knew. Why didn't she just go to one of the nice resorts that he knew she preferred? Sleep with tourists he wouldn't know and would never see again?

Just leave it alone, Beck. She probably doesn't want you crashing her big get over Beck *night*. It was a mistake, though. Aspen might be a major ski resort, but in the end it was really just a small town. About ten thousand residents lived in the area all year round, but tourists doubled that population on average every day. So the locals ran in tight circles and mostly kept to themselves. And they gossiped. So much. It was why Beck tended to keep to the tourists. He could have his fun and then not worry about the consequences. If Allie took a local home, there'd be rumors swirling around them for weeks. Even months. Locals got bored, especially around the holidays, and they loved nothing more than to talk about each other.

Another photo came up, a new one, and this time Allie was standing next to a rough, tattooed dude with a beanie cap on and a loop through his nose. He looked like one of the many pipe rats that littered the slopes these days—kids thinking they'd invent the next big trick that would land them on the podium at the Games. Beck took a closer look. Wait a second. He wasn't just any pipe rat. That was Taylor Johnson and he was nothing but trouble. First off, the man was married. He'd gotten hitched two weekends before in a hasty ceremony since his girlfriend was eight months pregnant. So Beck had no idea what he was doing out at the bar, posing for pictures with Allie and *not* wearing his wedding ring. Beck wondered if Allie knew any of that.

There was one way to find out. Looked like he was headed to the North Star.

CHAPTER FIVE

ALLIE WAS HAVING the time of her life. At least, that was what she told herself, and the more she drank, the more she believed it. In the last hour, she'd gotten five strangers' numbers, bought another man a drink and had exchanged her scarf with Taylor's checkered scarf, which she now wore draped around her neck like a trophy. Beside her, her new friend Taylor was showing more than a little interest, and his frame was enough like Beck's that she kind of liked it. He was tall and blond, though he had streaks of bright green in his hair, a look that normally she'd say was trying too hard to broadcast that he liked to risk life and limb trying a double backflip, or double cork, in the half-pipe. She hadn't met him before tonight, but he was actually quite nice, and eager to buy her drinks and feed her compliments, and for once she wasn't thinking of Beck.

"Have I told you that you're the sexiest woman in this room?" Taylor leaned in, his brown eyes earnest as he slid another beer her way on the ornate but old-fashioned bar. Beneath her feet lay the sticky floor and mismatched tiles. This was a far cry from the trendy, upscale places she usually preferred—the tourist hangouts with the trendy drinks, where she and Beck would so often run into each other. But that was the whole point. She was hoping *not* to run into Liam Beck.

The bar was small and standing room only since they were running a locals' happy hour, with beer on tap half-price. Mira and Allie claimed a small corner of the bar by the wall, and Taylor maneuvered himself between Allie and Mira, and now almost had Allie pinned against the wall. Normally, Allie hated guys who were so instantly territorial, but given how much kissing Beck had rattled her the day before, she was eager to put that in her rearview. That meant Taylor would get a pass.

"You're so sweet," she said and took another drag of her beer.

"You've got another dare!" Mira chimed in, beside her, as she sipped at her vodka soda and glanced at her phone. "Ooh, this one is good. Kiss the first bearded man you see."

Mira glanced up and looked around the crowded bar, and Allie did, too. Usually, beards were a dime a dozen in Aspen, the longer the better, but tonight the place seemed all stubble and no beard.

"Seriously?" Mira asked no one in particular. "*No* beards?"

"How about I go grow a beard and you kiss me?" Taylor suggested, and he moved closer to Allie, and now her back lay flat against the wall. Allie felt a little uncomfortable with his hemming her in, so she laughed a little and wiggled to the side.

"I don't think that would count."

Taylor leaned in and whispered low in her ear, "Why don't we get out of here and go to your place?"

Allie couldn't believe his boldness. It was barely nine, she'd known him all of fifteen minutes and Mira was standing right there. Not that she'd heard.

"That's not part of the game," Allie said, deflecting him.

"Ooh! Here's another dare," Mira said, pulling up her phone. She read it, squinted and read it again. "Uh…"

"What is it?"

"It's Beck," she said, frowning at the screen. "He's asking if he can play, too."

Beck? What the…? Allie turned then and locked eyes with Beck, who was already moving through the crowd, parting the patrons easily as they shifted to make room for him. His eyes were focused on her and she hated how she felt a little flame of excitement tickle the back of her neck, how her body reacted instantly, how she was already leaning into him, even though he was still across the room.

"Well, this is going to be interesting," Mira said in the understatement of the year.

Allie looked amazing, even if she was wearing that ridiculous scarf around her neck. That was Beck's first thought. His second was that he wondered why every time he saw her his breath caught a little as if, somehow, all the way across the room, she was managing to squeeze him from the inside. She wore dark shadow around her eyes that made them pop and told him tonight she planned to take no prisoners. Good. Neither did he. Allie was silently sending him about a dozen messages across the bar, most of which he could tell started and ended with *WTF*. Well, he'd explain himself later. And she probably wouldn't be grateful, but he wasn't going to let her hang with a man who was clearly deceiving her. All he wanted to do was get to Allie. He was there in a few long strides and clapped the man—hard—on the shoulder. Taylor whirled, a frown on his face, and then it lit with recognition.

"Liam Beck." He said the name as if it left a foul taste in his mouth.

"Taylor. You don't sound happy to see me." Beck kept his hand on the man's shoulder a beat too long. He could smell the beer wafting up from him. He'd had a lot to drink already, which could make what came next messy.

"I thought you'd be too busy losing gold medals to come out drinking." Taylor sneered at Beck, as he usually did. The punk thought that silver was a loss, that he could do better in the next Olympics. Beck welcomed him to try. The sport only got more competitive every year, harder and more dangerous.

"At least I have Olympic medals," he muttered

beneath his breath. "So, Taylor. Where's your wife? Melanie?"

Taylor turned as white as the beer coaster on the bar. "Home," he said.

"Wait. You're married?" Allie clearly had no idea.

"Has she had the baby yet?" Beck had to admit he was enjoying this just a little bit. Taylor and Allie both looked like a light wind would blow them over.

"Baby?" Allie echoed, horrified.

But Taylor didn't even bother to answer. He had defeat written all over his face as he finished his beer, set it on the counter with a thump and then put his back to them all and left without so much as a word.

"Did he just leave?" Mira cried, staring after him.

"He's married, though?" Allie said. "But he was trying to kiss me."

"That's what you get for playing with amateurs." Beck leaned into the spot Taylor had left.

"I cannot believe the nerve of that man. I'm going to out him," Mira said, and she began furiously typing on her phone, probably posting something not so nice about Taylor.

Beck kept his attention solely focused on Allie. "So I'm here. I'm ready to play double dare."

"Beck, you can't play," Mira said, not looking up from her phone.

"Why not?"

"Fine. I *dare* you to leave, then," Mira suggested.

Beck shook his finger slowly back and forth. "I'll only take dares from Allie. This is the game we started last night, and I just wanted to finish it." He stared at her long and hard, and almost thought she was imagining the same things he was: her lips pressed against his, his hands running up the tender skin of her back. She was the most beautiful woman in this bar—hell, in this state. Could she feel that current running between them? The invisible tether that connected them? He wondered if the whole bar could feel it.

Mira glanced back and forth between Beck and Allie. Clearly, she'd noticed the connection.

"Can you give us a second?" Allie asked Mira at last.

"You sure about this?" Mira eyed Beck like he might be a poisonous snake. He couldn't blame Mira for looking after her friend. He would've done the same in her position.

"Mira, it's okay," Allie said. "We have some things to settle."

"You sure that's a good idea?" Mira asked, but Allie gave her a long look, and she swallowed her protest. "I was going to go get another drink anyway. And I think I see some people from work I know over there." Mira nodded to the corner. "If you need me, that's where I'll be."

Allie stared at Beck the entire time Mira moved away. Mira sent worried glances back at her friend, but Allie never looked in her direction.

"What are you doing here?"

"I'm here to finish our game," Beck said and grinned. "You didn't let me finish last night."

"That was on purpose." She tapped her foot angrily against the floor. "That was for…breaking my boots."

He laughed and shook his head. "I was only trying to help."

"Right. Like you're only trying to *help* me now."

"I am," Beck said. He leaned in and got a whiff of Colorado wildflowers. God, he loved her smell. "Or was one of your dares sleeping with a married man?" He cocked an eyebrow.

Allie let out a frustrated sigh. "No, that was *not* one of the dares. I can't believe he was pretending to be single. He wanted to go to my place!" Allie smacked her forehead. "What would've happened if we'd gone? I feel like an idiot."

"You're not the idiot." Beck blamed Taylor. "He's the idiot. For thinking you'd fall for it. Even if I hadn't come along, you would've figured it out. I was just trying to spare you the trouble."

"You think?"

"I know." Beck nodded once, swiftly. "Come on. You see through all my bullshit."

"True," she said and gave him a playful nudge with her elbow, her eyes suddenly grateful. He saw how hard she was trying to be on her own, how much she wanted this all to work. He knew she wanted to believe there was nothing between them, when even Beck could feel it there, like a living thing between them, this bond, this connection. The lodge mattered, no matter how either of them tried to deny it to themselves. He hadn't been the same since, and he knew she'd felt the aftershocks in her life, too. Why else would she be acting out like this?

He just wanted to pull her into his arms, tell her to stop trying to fight against it so hard. But then again, wasn't that what he was doing?

"Al," he began. And he was going to tell her... what? They were going to live happily ever after? He was never going to break her heart, when that was all he seemed to know how to do with the women in his life? That was all Becks were ever taught.

"Yes?" She seemed so hopeful in that moment, that part of him broke.

"How about tonight, just take a break," he said.

Confusion flickered in her eyes. "From what?"

"From trying to be me." The best way to get out of this emotional quagmire was a good distraction. And Beck was the king of distractions. Divert, tease, make light of any situation. Whenever any conversation got a little too close to the heart, he'd pivot. He'd been doing it his whole life.

"I'm not *trying* to be you."

"You are," he teased. "Double dare you is like my favorite game."

"Not true. Strip poker is," she deadpanned, and Beck barked a laugh.

"Okay, *second* favorite game. Come on, Al. Let me play. Please?" Beck could see Allie weigh her options. He could also see her physically trying to fight his charm. But he should tell her it was a losing battle. She'd give in eventually. "I promise not to get in the way of anything. And, upside, I make an excellent wingman."

"You? You want to be *my* wingman?" Allie coughed in disbelief. "You want to sabotage me."

"I do not. Look, you set the rules of the game. Anytime you want me to leave, I'm gone."

"How about now?" she joked.

"Not yet." He grinned. "We have to play first."

A playful spark lit in her, and Beck could tell she was warming to the idea. "Okay, so we dare each other to do things."

"Fine."

"And if you don't complete a dare, then…" Allie thought for a moment. "Then *you* have to personally apologize to every woman you've slept with this last year."

"What?" Beck was taken aback.

"You have to personally apologize for loving and leaving them."

Beck shook his head. "The women I sleep with know what they're getting into. I don't pretend otherwise."

Hurt flickered for a second across Allie's face before her brave mask came back up, and Beck mentally gave himself a swift kick in the ass. What was he doing? He knew Allie was the exception to this rule. He knew it. Yet there was something about Allie that was like walking truth serum. He couldn't *not* tell her the truth. It was unnerving, especially for a man who'd spent his whole life carefully boxing away all the things he didn't like to unpack.

"I mean, yes. Fine. I will."

"You'll apologize publicly. Social media, wherever, and promise to do one thing to make it up to them." Beck knew Allie was talking about herself. Okay, then.

"Fine. I'm not worried about losing." Beck had never faced a dare in his life that he hadn't easily taken on. There was very, very little that scared him in this world.

"And if *you* renege, then you stop this game. Once and for all," he said.

"Deal," Allie said and held her hand out for a shake. He took it, and the second her small palm pressed against his, he felt a small bolt of electricity that went straight to his brain. There it was again, the feeling of connection, that there was a bond between them, something both delicate and strong at the same time.

"Okay, I'll go first. I dare you to…" Allie considered this. "Order a frozen piña colada, with extra umbrellas."

Beck groaned. He was a strict beer or whiskey guy. But he had promised to play the game, so play the game he would. "So that's how it's going to be, huh? Fine." He signaled the bartender. "But I dare you to drink a single shot of jalapeño tequila."

"Ew." Allie made a face and stuck out her tongue in disgust.

"You started this," Beck said. "Ready to quit yet?"

"Hell, no," she said and slapped the bar next to them with enthusiasm.

Beck ordered their drinks and in seconds was staring at the frilliest drink he'd ever seen: four umbrellas, two cherries, complete with a tourist's take-home pink-rimmed glass, and somehow, against all odds, the drink was bright blue. He hoped nobody in this bar took a picture of him drinking the monstrosity. Allie, for her part, stared at her shot glass with disdain. She hated tequila. It was the one alcohol that always got her into trouble. Beck knew this all too well from last year's Cinco de Mayo.

"You're seriously going to make me drink this?" Allie said, sniffing the cup and making a gagging noise.

"I could ask you the same thing," he said, nodding at his umbrella monster drink. She laughed.

"Oh, you're going to drink that. And I'm going to take a picture." She whipped out her phone and snapped a quick shot. "And I am going to post it everywhere."

"Of course you are." Beck shook his head.

The two of them drank: Allie a tiny sip of the fiery tequila and Beck a big gulp of much-too-sugary blech. It was more like a slushie than an actual drink. In the standing-room-only bar, a high table opened, and Beck nodded to it. "Shall we?"

On their way, a college-aged kid brushed past Beck. "Hey…aren't you…?" Recognition dawned on the college boy's face. Recognition and reverence. "Aren't you Liam Beck?"

Beck glanced at the kid who looked suddenly star-struck.

"Two-time silver medalist at men's snowboarding cross? *That* Liam Beck?" The boy glanced at the fruity drink in Beck's hand and looked momentarily baffled.

"Nah, that's not me," he lied.

Allie flashed him a brief look of pity. Beck shrugged. The Olympics were a long, long time ago. He'd long since had his fifteen minutes of fame.

"No, you're definitely Beck, man. I'd know your face anywhere."

This time, Beck didn't argue. But he wished the kid would stop gushing. It always made him uncomfortable.

"You're my hero, dude. The way you shredded that course! Like…amaze-ing. I—I mean I *learned* to snowboard *because* of you!"

Nothing like a young punk to make him feel ancient.

Beck and Allie settled into the high top. "We'd like to finish our drinks, okay?"

"Oh, yeah, man. Sorry… Just… I mean, you're my hero!" He held up his hand for a high five and Beck reluctantly slapped it. As the boy slid away, Beck shook his head.

"Still don't like fans?"

"It's not that." Beck shrugged. How could he tell

her it all felt undeserved? "I didn't do it for the fame. I did it to prove something to myself. The fame is just kind of an annoying side effect."

"The same fame that helped you launch your business, though," Allie pointed out.

"Yeah," Beck said. "And Willis wants to use my name to open a few more adventure tours in other cities."

"Can you afford it?" Allie asked, concern wrinkling her brow.

"Not sure." Beck needed to look over those papers.

Allie studied him a minute. "Okay, next dare, then. I dare you to…tell me something you've never told me about the Olympics."

"What?" Now Beck felt on high alert. This game was supposed to be about putting Allie on the spot, not him. "I thought this was a game of double dare you, not truth or dare."

"A dare's a dare." Allie took another sip of her tiny shot of tequila and then coughed, patting her chest.

"You're supposed to slug that."

"You didn't say that in the dare," Allie pointed out. "So I'm going to sip this one. It tastes awful." She wrinkled her nose. "So? Go on. The Olympics. Tell me about it."

What was there to tell? His father had promised to go, and Beck had even sent him a ticket, but he'd gotten too high and missed his flight. By the time he arrived in Turin, Beck's event was over. His mother had just had another baby with the new family she'd created far from him in Florida and didn't feel like she could make the trip. By the time Vancouver rolled around, he hadn't bothered to invite anyone. It had been better that way.

"Not much to tell," he said. "I didn't do it for the fame. I did it to prove I could because everyone told me I couldn't. Just went there and skied hard. And wished I'd gotten gold both times." That was the short answer, the textbook answer, and she knew it. She knew all that already.

"Was your family there?" she asked him.

"No."

"Why not?"

Beck stared at her. "Why all the questions all of a sudden? And how many questions do you get to ask with one dare?"

"As many as I want," she countered. "This is my game. And you haven't told me anything I don't already know about the Olympics. Tell me one thing I don't know."

Beck sighed. "I don't like talking about it because I wanted to win gold and didn't, and now I won't have another chance." Beck shrugged. "I don't want to think that my best accomplishment is in the past, but it might be."

Allie studied him a beat. "Being a medalist doesn't define you."

"Doesn't it, though?" Wasn't that why people flocked to his adventure tours. Or looked at him twice when he went into a bar?

"Only if you let it." God, he missed her so much. Missed how she managed to cut through all the noise and make him feel seen. Few people had that skill and even fewer people could snap him out of a pity party. "And, by the way, thank you. For warning me about Taylor."

The gratitude took him by surprise. "You're welcome."

A woman walked past their table then on the way to the bathroom. She eyed Allie with some disdain and then sent a long, knowing look to Beck, who realized he knew her, vaguely. They'd had a night together maybe two or three years ago. Her name started with a *K*. Kayla. Kaylee. Something like that. "Hey, you," she murmured in a much-too-familiar way as she passed him. Then she leaned over as if to whisper something in his ear. "Why don't you drop by my place later?"

The petite blonde in the too-tight leggings and too-low-cut sweater glanced over her shoulder as she passed, seeming not to care that he was sitting across from Allie.

"What did she say?" Allie's voice sounded hard. Jealous.

"She wants me to come over."

"Will you?" Allie bit her lip.

"No." Beck shook his head. What he remembered was that she'd taken a selfie of herself *in his bed*. He didn't want to know what she'd done with it.

"She was one of your marks, though."

"More like, I was *her* mark." Beck shuddered a

bit. No way was he remotely interested in taking her home again. He felt like she'd probably steal things from his condo for souvenirs, or take selfies in his closet next to his medals and his Olympic jackets.

"Mmm-hmm." Allie looked at him, that old disapproval on her face. Before the weekend at the lodge, she'd teased him relentlessly about the women who rotated through his bedroom. Only she could make him feel moderately ashamed and more than a little bit shallow for simply doing what came naturally.

"Look, as much as you love talking about what a dick I am, can we just focus here? I dare you to…" He looked at Allie's big green eyes, attentive and watchful, and suddenly just wanted her to come back to his condo, so that it could just be the two of them, where he could hold her. She broke his gaze and he realized she was staring at Kayla/Kaylee's back. The girl had on a too-short tight sweater and her lower back was completely bare. There was a tattoo there, Olympic rings. Of course there would be.

Allie held up a finger. "Wait a second," she said, and then she downed the entire shot of tequila. He hadn't expected that. Then she grabbed a passing waiter and ordered another.

"You sure that's wise? Tequila doesn't agree with you."

"I'm sure I'm going to need it to get through this next dare."

"I dare you to…"

Meanwhile, from the corner of Beck's eye, he saw

the starstruck kid come back, carrying shots of tequila and slices of lime.

"Hey, man, just wanted to buy you these," he said, beaming like a little boy who'd managed to tie his shoelaces for the first time. "It's an honor to share a drink with you, *Liam Beck*, and you, uh…" He glanced at Allie, unsure.

"Allie Connor," she said and happily grabbed the shot glass. She took it a bit too quickly and it sloshed on the table.

"Allie, careful," Beck cautioned, but it was too late—she was already glugging it down. Since when did Allie shotgun tequila? She had the tolerance of a fly. Two drinks and she was buzzed. Three and she was on her way to hammered. And tequila took her there twice as fast.

The boy held up his shot glass, and she took that, too.

"Allie, give that back," Beck said, but she was in no mood to oblige him. She held on to it.

"Here, take mine," Beck offered the kid. He took it and drank.

"You're just the coolest ever, man. I'll go buy you another," he offered. Before Beck could argue, he was hurrying back to the bar. Beck refocused his attention on Allie.

"What the hell are you doing? Tequila makes you sick. Remember Cinco de Mayo? I only dared you to drink *one* shot."

"Well, this is the *new* Allie." Her eyes had already

taken on a glassy sheen. Not a good sign. She pushed back her chair. "I'm going to the bathroom."

Her mood had soured, and it had everything to do with Kayla/Kaylee and tequila. Beck knew it. This was why he was no good for her. He just brought a bundle of drama to her life that she simply didn't need. He couldn't help it if women approached him, but she seemed to take every single woman he'd ever slept with as a personal affront. How could they ever really have a go at a relationship if she let every woman who glanced at him twice get into her head? This was why Allie was better off without him.

She stumbled a bit getting off her chair. The tequila was working its black magic and fast. He steadied her, but she was determined to get away. What had caused this? Was it Kayla/Kaylee?

"So, I'm taking you home now."

"I don't need your shelp," she slurred. The shots took hold fast.

"You do need me. Or you'd fall down."

"Is that a dare? You daring me to fall down?" Allie asked, unsteady on her feet as she reached for the women's restroom door. Her eyes were having the slightest bit of trouble focusing on him. She'd had way too much to drink in a short amount of time.

"That would hardly be a dare. You're going to do that all by yourself," he said.

"Well, then, what are you going to dare me to do?" Allie asked, blinking fast.

"I..." But before he could get another word out, she'd grabbed him by the shirt.

"Too slow. My turn." Before he knew what happened, she'd arched on her tiptoes and planted her lips against his.

CHAPTER SIX

ALLIE HAD NO idea what she was doing. Her body was on autopilot, and she had her tongue in Beck's mouth before it even registered that she was kissing him. *Again. For the second night in a row.* Her brain was awash in tequila, and the room had already begun to spin a little. Was that the tequila buzz or Beck's mouth? She wasn't sure, but what she did know was that her body, even dulled with alcohol, felt the pulse of heat between them and the promise of more pleasure to come. It took her a moment to notice that Beck remained entirely still. For a heartrending second, she thought Beck might not kiss her back, but then his lips were on hers once more, his hands at the small of her back. *Yes, kiss me. I want you. I've missed you.*

The thoughts ran unheeded through her brain, and she suddenly forgot why she'd decided to kiss him in the first place. She was proving what exactly? That she was better than that blonde with the tattoo? That she could somehow compete? That she even *wanted* to compete? Why did she even care who Beck slept with? He wasn't hers, would never be hers.

Her head spun, literally spun, as their lips met. She felt they were both twirling in a fast circle.

Then, as abruptly as the kiss began, it ended. Beck pulled away first, chest heaving, his big strong hands on her arms.

"You're drunk," he said, his eyes telling her it took more than a little willpower for him to keep her at arm's length.

"Yes, I am," she conceded and hiccuped. Not that it mattered. She'd feel the same about Beck if she were sober. She felt wild, impulsive, and realized that being with Beck made her feel out of control, reckless. And she liked it. That was the problem.

"I'm going to take you home," Beck said. She wondered if he planned to stay the night in her bed. In her current state, she wouldn't tell him no.

"I don't need your help," she said, defiant. The room took another spin then, and she knew it had nothing to do with Beck's hands on her and everything to do with the tequila she'd hastily downed. Her stomach roiled, suddenly in revolt. She realized she was about to lose the last tequila shot she'd drunk and more, as she spun and ran into the bathroom, barely making it to the first stall before she lost the contents of her stomach. Beck must've heard the commotion outside because he rushed in, steadying her by the toilet as another wave of nausea hit her.

"What was that about not needing my help?" he asked her, holding her hair back, as she retched again.

* * *

Allie woke the next morning feeling like her head was a delicate soft-boiled egg, its shell cracked in a dozen places. Her hands flew to her temples as she groaned, the bright light on the other side of her closed eyelids like daggers to her brain. She didn't even want to open her eyes, afraid the sunlight would send more shards of pain pulsing through her head. What on earth had happened last night? She groaned as bits of the night came back to her...too many shots, the dares...that blonde at the bar and the way she was eyeing Beck, and then...how Allie had reacted like a scorned girlfriend and drowned her sorrows in tequila. What was wrong with her?

Then she remembered that she'd been sick. She remembered throwing up at the bar and...the game of dare. With Beck. What had happened? She couldn't remember. She moaned and pulled the covers up over her head, shielding herself from the memories of the night before and the morning's sunlight. Her head throbbed and all she wanted to do was stay in this warm, snuggly goodness forever. It was only then that she realized the blankets over her were heavier than her own. They had the feel of weighty down instead of the loftier, lighter cotton fill of her own comforter beneath her white eyelet duvet cover. The realization slowly came: these weren't her sheets. If they weren't hers, then whose were they?

She pushed her head out of the covers and opened one eye. The first thing she saw was the blue-and-white-checkered scarf she'd traded with Taylor the night before. One of her first dares. Oh, no. Did she go home with...Taylor? No. She didn't like him. He was married, the jerk. She remembered. And then Beck had arrived and... She sat up then and glanced around, realizing quickly this was not a stranger's room. It was far worse than that. She knew this bedroom.

Allie was in the middle of Beck's king-sized bed, the thick goose-down comforter with the navy blue cover tucked around her soundly. She knew the room from the dozens of times he'd invited her to parties at his place, big sprawling affairs with dozens of locals. In a panic, she glanced down and saw she wasn't wearing her clothes from the night before. They'd been replaced with one of Beck's long-sleeved T-shirts with his adventure tour logo emblazoned on the front. She reached down and was mortified to discover she had no pants on.

What had happened? She racked her brain trying to remember, but no more memories came. She was at the bar, she got sick, Beck was there and...what? Well, clearly he brought her home. Had they...? Good Lord, did they...? Allie pressed her hands against her body and was glad to find that she still had her bra and low-cut bikini on, her pink-laced ones. Okay, if they'd...gone there, then she probably would be completely naked beneath Beck's shirt. The worst part was that she couldn't figure out if she was relieved... or disappointed. What the hell was wrong with her?

Falling into bed with Beck would be the worst thing she could do.

She scanned the room. More important, where *was* Beck? That was when she heard rattling in the kitchen. She heard the sound of a pan coming out of the cabinet, and the high-pitched squeal of hot water through coffee grounds in his single-serve coffee maker. The aroma of freshly brewed dark roast drifted into the bedroom and she suddenly badly wanted some. Her uneasy stomach cried for coffee. The sizzle of freshly cracked eggs on a buttered pan hit her ears as she swung her bare legs over the side of Beck's massive bed. Her head revolted, almost sending her back to the sheets, but she knew coffee and food were her best ways out of this hangover. Her stomach felt dangerously empty, and she needed to fill it with grease and fast.

She glanced at the bedside table and saw her phone and her glasses there. Beck had left them in reach, which seemed sweet. She put on her glasses and headed to the door. The fact that she'd have to face Beck didn't occur to her until she'd cracked open his bedroom door and saw the man—shirtless—frying up eggs at his stovetop. He turned and saw her, grinning from ear to ear.

"Well, she's alive," he said and shook his head slowly, the crook of his lopsided grin telling her he was going to enjoy having fun at her expense. "It was touch and go for a while."

Embarrassment burned her face and she wished

she'd checked her reflection in his bedroom mirror
before coming out. Too late now. "Was it that bad?"

Beck cocked a blond eyebrow. She tried very hard
not to look at his smooth bare chest, the ripples of
his muscles beneath his rib cage. The man was the
only one she knew who actually carried a real six-
pack. She remembered running her finger along those
ridges that weekend at the lodge. How he would laugh
and tell her he was ticklish. "You don't remember?"

Allie glanced at her bare toes, the green nail polish beginning to flake off. "Uh, no. Last thing I remember was being at the bar with you. Even that is
spotty, but I think I…" She swallowed, recalling the
humiliating trip to the bathroom. "Uh, I think I got
sick in the bathroom."

She glanced up once more but found all that bare
skin of his distracting. The man ought to put on a shirt,
but she didn't want him to think his half nakedness
was bothering her at all. He wore only a pair of mesh
gym shorts, the ridges of a V pointing down beneath
his waistband. She looked away, to his stark apartment,
noticing that there weren't any Christmas decorations.
He never decorated for Christmas. Not even a tree, for
as long as she'd known him. Not even when he'd had a
Christmas party here for half of Aspen two years ago.

He laughed and then flipped the fried egg in the
small pan, and it sizzled in the butter.

"You did indeed. Is that all you remember? Nothing else?" He sent her a sly glance. Oh, no. Did she
sleep with him? She woke up in his bed, after all.

She glanced at his pronounced chest muscles. Did she run her hands along that bare skin last night? She wasn't sure what bothered her more: the idea that she'd done it, or the fact that she couldn't remember it if she had.

"N-no." Now she was getting worried. He was enjoying this far too much. She was almost afraid to ask anything about the night before, but she had a feeling he would tell her anyway.

Her head still pounded from her hangover headache. She reluctantly moved to the breakfast bar, which at least obscured some of Beck's bare skin. He handed her a cup of coffee.

"With nonfat milk, just like you like it."

"You remembered," she murmured, surprised, wrapping her hand around the mug's handle and taking a long sip of the warm liquid. She didn't think a little detail like that merited a place in Beck's memory.

"I remember everything about you, Allison Connor."

He sent her a long, deliberate look. How did he manage to do that? Make her feel like she was the only woman in the world who mattered? She glanced away from him, not sure if prolonged eye contact with him shirtless, and her without pants, was all that good of an idea. Her headache might be going strong, but even it might fall to Beck's humming charisma.

She hugged the mug of coffee with her hands as

she watched Beck dole out a fried egg onto a piece of toast. He slipped the plate over to her with a grin.

"Thanks," she said, suddenly so grateful for the food she wanted to cry. Her stomach growled, and despite having clearly not fared so well last night, it was ready to consume. He cracked another egg into the pan and waited, studying her.

"Go on and eat," he said. "You need your strength." He grinned. "Don't wait for me."

She took a bite of breakfast goodness. It was just what she needed, and she moaned in gratitude. When she opened her eyes, she saw Beck watching her. The expression on his face had grown serious. He seemed intent on watching her eat. She felt suddenly self-conscious. She glanced at the counter and saw a folder stuffed with spreadsheets.

"What's this?" she asked, quickly, hoping for a distraction.

"Willis's spreadsheets. I'm trying to figure out if I have enough capital to expand the business."

"I could take a look at them, if you want. Just as a favor. I can let you know what I think."

Beck glanced at her. "That would be great, actually."

They stared at each other a beat. Allie didn't want to break the moment. She liked silence with Beck. It never really felt like silence, as she could almost hear the hum of their connectivity, the way being in a room with him alone just felt like all that she needed.

"So how much of a fool was I last night?" She

didn't want to hear the answer, but knew she'd have to face it eventually.

"Well, you kissed me at the bar."

"I…what?" Now Allie felt hot and cold all over. Allie furrowed her brow. She had no memory of kissing Liam Beck. "Was that all I did?" she asked, tentative. She sneaked a glance at his bare chest, feeling flaming heat in her cheeks.

Beck chuckled, a warm, low sound that traveled to her own middle. "No, that was definitely not all." He flipped the egg and crossed his fit arms across his chest. "You threw up in the bar bathroom, yes, and in the parking lot, and out the door of my truck, and then twice when we got back here."

Allie groaned. No wonder her stomach felt so empty and her head hurt so much.

"Beck, I'm sorry. Do I need to clean up? I…" She stood, a bit too fast, and a sharp pain stabbed her brain behind her eyes. The hangover wasn't going to tolerate any quick moves this morning.

"Sit. Eat. I'm just glad to see you human again." He slid the fried egg onto his own plate and then moved to sit next to her at the breakfast bar. She was reminded of the morning after their first night at the lodge, when he'd made her breakfast. He was good at it. She took another bite of her egg, the warm gooeyness melting on her tongue. The more she ate, the more she felt…closer to normal. She felt stupidly grateful he wasn't making too much of a big deal about it. He could've been lording it over her, teasing her relentlessly. She didn't have the energy to defend herself at the moment, but that was Beck. Beneath all his bluster and ego, he was amazingly kind. It always took her by surprise. When she expected him to be a jerk, he did something surprisingly nice. Thoughtful, even. It was almost as if he used the egomaniac, player persona to hide his real self, as if it were just a hard shell to protect the big softie beneath.

He took a bite of his breakfast.

"But… I mean, did you…? Did we…?" She trailed off. She couldn't get the words out of her mouth. *Did we have sex?* God, she couldn't believe she even had to ask him this. How had she let herself get into this position in the first place? But then she glanced at his amused crystal-blue eyes and knew the answer to that. Because this was Beck, and he was pretty much irresistible.

"You want to know if we had a reunion of the carnal kind?" he asked between bites. Her eyes drifted down to his bare chest and she ordered them back up again.

She could only just nod her head but failed to look him in the eye. What would she do if the answer was yes? She had no idea.

"And if we did… What do you think of that?" He patted his mouth with a paper napkin.

"Beck, just tell me, already. Did we or didn't we?" Now the suspense was really killing her.

"You hoping we did? Or…didn't?" He was enjoying this so much. She actually wanted to give him a good shove and tell him to cut it out.

"Didn't," she said, but then she glanced up and saw his pec flex as he moved the piece of toast on his plate to sop up the runny egg yolk and had a sudden change of mind. She wished they did have sex. Somehow, it would be a relief of a sort. Since they'd kissed at the holiday party she'd been worried that sex might just be inevitable, that she'd slip up, like an addict sneaking in a binge. If she had slipped up, then she could start walking the straight and narrow again... Maybe.

Beck sent her a rueful smile. "You're in luck. We didn't."

Surprise tickled the back of her neck, and something more... Disappointment? "What about my... clothes, then?" She nodded down to his shirt. "Did you...? I mean..."

"You were in no place to consent, Al. I don't take advantage of anyone that way." He shrugged. "Your clothes are in the wash. During one of your trips to the bathroom, your sweater and jeans got hit. Well... splattered. That's all. I got you out of them, and into bed—on your stomach—and then I slept on the couch. You were in rough shape." He glanced at her, clear worry on his face. It was the concern that rattled her, even more than his bare skin. Did he still care about her?

"So we didn't..." Allie frowned. She wished she

could remember the night, but no matter how hard she tried, no memories came to mind.

"No, but…" Beck grinned, as he laughed a little. "But not for want of trying on your part."

"Oh, no." Allie covered her face with her hands. She was worried about that. She had a hard enough time fighting her attraction when she was a hundred percent sober and in control. She didn't want to hear what uninhibited Allie might be like.

"I mean, you were definitely…absolutely…trying to get me into bed with you." He threw down his napkin and leaned back on the kitchen stool, enjoying himself.

"No, no, no." Allie shook her head and then regretted it, as the headache thrummed in her temples.

"You might have been sick, but you were tenacious. I had to peel you off me. You tried to take off my pants…three times."

Mortification stung her. And she realized arguing was futile. She felt the truth of his words in her bones. She could imagine herself doing it. That was the worst part. Maybe it was all this Greenie nonsense. Was she trying to prove something to Beck? To herself? Or was she just hot and heavy for the man, and no amount of time or distance would ever cool her desire for him?

Beck flashed her a grin and then gave her shoulder a playful nudge. "Don't worry, Al. You weren't that bad."

That just made her think she was that bad…and worse.

"Well…" She swallowed, almost glad she didn't remember the scene she'd made. "Thanks for taking care of me."

"Of course." Beck acted as if he'd always be ready to be called up to protect her. Not as if he was the man who'd walked out of her life. Everything about him confused her.

"I'm surprised Mira let you take me home."

"She didn't…exactly." Beck shrugged. "I'd gotten you into my truck already, and she was there, asking you if you were sure, and…" Beck took a deep breath. "And you said you were never surer of anything in your life, and then, I think, you called me a sex god."

Allie was going to die of mortification. Right there. She was going to die on the spot. At least, she hoped she did.

"God!" she wailed and buried her face in her hands again. "Oh…no. Oh, no, no, nô."

"Mira said she knew it, and then she let you go with me. Is this what you call me to your friends? A sex god?" Even Beck couldn't quite keep a straight face. His ego was already out of control, and with this new feather in his cap, he'd be intolerable.

"I'm going to crawl under the bed and die," Allie murmured, more to herself.

"Do you think I'm a sex god? Is that right?" Beck flexed his arm muscles in a show of strength. "You never told me that."

"I'm literally going to die. Right now. I'm dead. Dying." Allie pushed away her plate and laid her face on Beck's breakfast nook. "Just leave me here to die of mortification."

"I'll just use my sex-god powers to revive you."

"You're never going to let me live this down, are you?"

"Of course not." Beck laughed. "This is too good."

Allie groaned and rubbed her face, as if trying to scrub this nightmare of the last twenty-four hours out of her head. Why had she had so much tequila? Why had she admitted so much? Now Beck held all the cards, and she had none. Again. Why did it feel like a game of poker she could never win?

"Al," Beck said, and he put both his big hands on her shoulders and gave her a gentle shake. "If it's any consolation, I think you're pretty much a sex goddess, too."

She lifted her head and squinted at him. "You're just trying to make me feel better."

"Nope. I'm not. You're sexy as hell, Miss Goddess." He grinned, mischief in his eyes. "And sex gods don't lie."

"Oh, is that in the Sex Gods' bible?" Allie teased. She was only vaguely starting to be okay with living.

"Sure it is. It's right in our holy book, the Kama Sutra."

Allie gave Beck a playful shove. "Okay, so if I'm so great, then why didn't you call…after? Why'd you ghost me?"

Beck sighed. Allie didn't even know why she'd asked. She didn't really want to know the answer.

"I didn't call because you need a steady guy. Not someone like me. I'm reckless. I run away. I'm not the solid relationship type. You deserve all that and more." He blinked twice and ran a hand through his thick shock of blond hair. He pushed his now-empty breakfast plate away and leaned back on the stool. "But now that you're flirting with other guys, I'm stupidly jealous. I can't stop myself, either. I know it's wrong. But there it is."

Allie's heart ticked up a beat. "You're jealous?"

"Yes. Any time a man lays a hand on you, I want to break it."

Allie laughed a little bit. "That might be the most honest thing you've ever said."

"Are you okay? Have you been eating?" he asked, blue eyes tinged with concern. "You look like you've lost weight."

"Why do you care so much?" She couldn't figure this out. Was it just guilt? Did he not like seeing his decisions had consequences?

"I never stopped caring about you." His eyes were so serious now that Allie couldn't look away from them. How could he truly care about her when he'd let her go?

"No, I haven't been eating all that well," she admitted, though she couldn't look him in the eye. "Or sleeping, actually." In fact, the night she'd spent passed out in Beck's bed was probably the first full night in many weeks. "It's stupid. It was only a weekend, and believe me, I know you. I never expected you to change. I knew what I was getting into. I just didn't expect…" She trailed off. She was about to say *didn't expect to fall in love with you*. And that would've been the dumbest thing she could've said.

Beck sucked in a breath. "This is all my fault."

"What's your fault?"

"That you're doing all this crazy stuff. These… dares?"

"No." *Yes, of course it is*, she wanted to shout. But that felt like giving him too much information. Too much power. And she'd already given him far too much of that.

"You're not trying to get my attention?" A look passed through Beck's eyes then. Something like hope? Though she told herself it was just smugness. On another man it would be ego, but with Beck, it was just fact. She and every straight woman in Aspen was interested.

"No, I'm not trying to get your attention," she said. "You're stalking *me*. I'm just trying to live my life. Without you."

He flinched slightly at the last two words.

"Look, I'm worried about you. That's all. Last night… You were a little out of control."

"And?" She raised her chin a little. She was her own woman who could do as she pleased. She didn't need a babysitter.

"What if I hadn't been there to take you home?"

"Mira would have." And Mira now knew the truth, if she hadn't already, that Allie was still hung up on Beck. So much for the brave face she'd put on for her friend.

"But what about Taylor? Or what if some other man had taken advantage?"

"You mean like you?" She took a swig of her cooled coffee, but wrapped both hands around the mug anyway, as if looking for a way to keep her hands busy. She felt fidgety suddenly, and vulnerable, all too aware that she was sitting on Beck's breakfast stool wearing just his shirt, her bare feet swinging above the ground.

"You know what I mean." Beck grasped her elbow and she turned to look at him. She saw genuine worry on his face. She slowly put the coffee mug down.

"I'm a big girl. You don't have to look after me, okay? I'm fine." She was glad her voice came out strong and convincing, at least to her ears. Besides, where was all this concern when she was curled up on her couch eating ice cream from the container and watching slasher films because that was the only way to get away from true love and big-screen kisses and everything else that might remind her of Beck?

"I think this is all about you regretting your decision to sleep with me."

She glanced up at him sharply, suddenly worried that her heart was written across her face in bold ink.

"I don't regret that decision." How could she? It

was the best sex of her life. It was like an out-of-body experience, only one that occurred deep within her body. An inner-body experience. The problem was the sex had been all she'd imagined and more. He *had* been a sex god, and she'd finally worshipped him like she wanted to, and it all made her feel stupid. She was a self-made woman. She made her own money, and took care of herself and didn't need a man to make her feel whole, and yet…and yet…with Beck, she worried that she did need him. Too much.

She studied her coffee mug, not quite able to look him in the eye. She didn't want him to see how much that weekend meant to her. "It was fun. We just took it too far."

She had a flash of his mouth on her breast, enveloping her nipple. She almost could feel the hungry heat on her skin.

"You're not acting like yourself, is all. Stop these silly dares. And wild partying at the bar and downing tequila shots and…"

"Wild? Maybe I like wild."

"Wild like almost going home with a married man?" Beck's attention was now fully on her, his blue eyes sharp.

"Okay, not my best moment, agreed. But I was never going home with him."

Beck slowly shook his head. He was now playing the part of the sage father type, but she thought he didn't do that. Hadn't he always railed against all things paternal? Yet he was lecturing her like a tired dad of a wayward teen. "You're going too far. You need to stop this. It isn't you."

"Maybe you don't know me." And now she was acting like a petulant teenager. She wasn't even sure why.

"I know you better than anyone." The way he said it made her feel a chill down the back of her legs. They stared at each other for a second and she remembered all the ways he had gotten to know her better than anyone, in his bed. She had to stop thinking about how his hands felt on her, but it was next to impossible with him sitting shirtless and barefoot next to her. Being the object of his full attention felt like being warmed, as if she were sitting by a roaring fire. She'd missed holding his attention, but also hated that she liked it so much. She'd never cared about the attention of other men. And now she'd gone and fallen for the one man everyone wanted. She was living a cliché and she didn't like it.

"I know that you like to play it safe, but you also like to flirt with danger *sometimes*. That underneath that good-girl, always-by-the-book, drive-the-speed-limit exterior, there beats the heart of someone who likes to take a risk now and again. You don't need to prove that to me. I *know* you."

"What makes you say that?"

"Because that's what made you fall into my bed in the first place. You *liked* the danger."

"No, I didn't." But the minute she denied it, she knew it was true. Hadn't she gone into Beck's bed knowing full well he'd do exactly what he did: make her come so often she almost forgot her own name and then disappear afterward? It was what he did to everyone else, so she couldn't expect anything different. She'd been beating herself up for being foolish, but maybe he was right. Maybe it was the danger that drew her to him in the first place. Maybe this had been what she wanted all along.

"Look, maybe I'm turning over a new leaf. Maybe this doesn't have anything to do with you." She wanted to say anything to keep him watching her, attentive. Why did she care about making herself sound interesting to the man who'd shown her how little he cared? She shouldn't, and yet keeping his focus felt like a perverse accomplishment. "I'm a *new* Allie, one you don't know so well."

Beck's lips quirked up in a patient, though patronizing, smile. "So, this new Allie Connor. Tell me about her."

"She takes risks. She's spontaneous," Allie began. "She doesn't need Liam Beck." She didn't need to know *everything about him*. She no longer felt the need to pry open all those secret boxes inside his heart and see what was inside.

He chuckled, a sound she felt low in her belly. God, she loved making this man laugh. She wanted to do it again, make him throw back his head and belly laugh.

"Or any man. And she's not boring."

"I never thought you were boring."

"Is that why you spread those rumors about me, then? Called me Greenie?" She looked at him sharply.

"What are you talking about?" Now Beck looked thoroughly confused.

"I heard that you'd been spreading rumors about me, about how dull I was. Like a green ski run."

"I have no idea what the hell you're talking about." Beck shook his head. "I never spread rumors about you. I swear to you, I've never said anything bad about you. Because there's nothing bad to say. You're damn near perfect, Allie Connor."

This shut her up completely. She felt stunned, down to her toes. The connection she felt between them thrummed, and she vibrated, like he'd pulled a guitar string that ran straight to the center of her.

"But you ran. You didn't even want to be friends afterward. I just thought… I was dumb, I guess, but I thought we'd at least be friends." Tears glistened on her lashes. She batted them away, frustrated. Why did she care so much? She knew she shouldn't care.

"I'm sorry, Al. I really am." She could almost feel him pulling away from her. She needed to stop all this heaviness. Beck didn't do heavy emotions. He liked to play in the shallow end of the pool. The more she lingered here, the more he'd want to run away again. "What were we supposed to do? We'd had some wine, and we were snowed in for thirty hours alone in a lodge."

Beck had offered to show her his ski lodge that he was thinking about selling. He wanted to ask her opinion about updating the bathrooms in the place, which slept twelve, and as his friend, she was happy to oblige. Hell, to be honest, anywhere Beck asked her to go, she would've gone. She knew that. She'd been secretly thrilled when she learned the lodge was accessible only by snowcat or helicopter. How she'd *wished* the snowstorm would move in earlier, and then it had. As if she'd willed it there.

He had plenty of provisions, and tons of wood to keep his stove and fireplace stoked and the lodge warm. They'd also dipped into his serious wine collection. It was a recipe for sex. It was what the place was made for. The sauna for two, the shower with the many, many hot jets of water pouring from the ceiling and the tiled walls, and, of course, Beck. She remembered how she'd wondered how many other women he'd taken there, how many other women had lain on his bearskin rug by the fireplace, how many others he'd taken into his massive bed made of pine and shown them what it was like to melt their bones. She hated that she'd so badly jumped into that queue, eager to take her turn.

"The weather forecasters were wrong. We were supposed to be long gone before that snow hit. And…" He sighed. "I knew I shouldn't cross that line with you, Al."

Line? What line? He hadn't crossed it at all. She'd pulled him over it with both hands. The thought that he seduced her was absolutely ridiculous. Beck glanced at her.

"You think you seduced me?" Allie couldn't believe her ears. "You thought you lured me into bed with you? That I didn't want to go?"

Beck glanced at her, momentarily puzzled. "Well, yeah. That's what happened."

"I was *hoping* for that snowstorm," Allie said. "I was hoping we'd get trapped there. Why do you think I asked to go later in the day? Why do you think I wore red lace lingerie?"

Beck blinked twice. "You were planning to sleep with me."

"Yes." She stared at him.

"You took advantage of *me*, then."

"Absolutely, yes." Allie stared at Beck, daring him to contradict her.

"You were going to risk our friendship?" Beck still seemed in disbelief.

Allie nodded.

"Even if I wasn't going to be your boyfriend or whatever normal people do when they date."

"I didn't care. I just wanted you."

"But you can't do casual, Allie. You're not built that way."

"I just want you, Beck. Any way I can have you."

Beck stared, and for a split second, Allie thought he might lean over and kiss her. Or maybe she just wished it, hoped for it. She'd laid herself bare, because she couldn't help it. Not around Beck.

"But I know you want something more."

That was the truth. She *knew* he refused to be seri-

ous in his relationships, yet part of her had hoped she
was wrong. Believed that he might care for her more
than he let on. But then, she chastised herself for believing that. Why did she think she'd be any different than any of the other women he took to his bed?
Why did she think she could change him? It was the
worst cliché of all time.

"I can handle it."

"You're not handling it." How could he do that?
Beck just had a way of making her feel *seen*. She
could never have any real secrets from him. It wasn't
fair. She had no choice now but to lie.

"I'm the new and improved Allie. I am not who
you think I am." And why did she care so much about
what he thought of her anyway? Why did she care to
prove to him that he hadn't hurt her?

"So, the new Allie will do what? Climb mountains?"

"Maybe. Ski more at least."

"Even backcountry trails?"

"Maybe."

Beck raised a blond eyebrow in surprise. Of course,
he would be surprised. How often had she cautioned
him about the dangers of skiing unmarked trails high
in avalanche country? Every time there'd been an accident with a skier she'd pointed it out to him. Tried
to convince him how dangerous his hobbies were.

"What else? Bungee jump?"

"Yes." She didn't flinch.

"And…?"

"And take anyone to bed I want." There, she'd said it.

"Anyone?" He quirked an eyebrow and Allie realized her mistake at once. She'd meant to tell him she planned to sleep with someone else, but the fact was, there wasn't anyone else she wanted to sleep with, and she felt like they both knew it.

"Dare me," she murmured, voice low. *Dare me to do anything.* To strip naked. To get on her knees and take all of him in her mouth. The worst part was that she wanted him to. Even after he'd run away, she still wanted him. She pressed her thighs together and felt a tingle there, the spark of want. She could almost imagine his hands on her, how they'd feel running up the softest skin of her thigh, his fingers exploring her. She realized that if he asked any of those things, she might just do it. She wanted to do it. Even after all that Beck had done, and all this time trying to recover, she still felt that magnetic pull to him, a force that seemed far out of her control.

"Okay." Beck was going to take his time asking for what he wanted. Allie's heart thudded in her chest and her breathing grew shallow. She could tell him she'd made a mistake, that she'd never take a dare from him. But deep in the pit of her stomach she knew she hadn't made any mistake at all. This was what she wanted. Ball in his court, see what he'd do with it. His face was so close to hers that she could almost feel him breathing. She was all too aware of her bare knees and his bare chest, and how little clothing they both wore, how quickly it could be shed.

"Yes?" She tried to keep her voice neutral, but it came out more as a hoarse whisper, something like a prayer.

"I dare you to tell me what you want."

CHAPTER SEVEN

SHE FELT SUDDENLY on the spot, as if he could sense the
changes in her body, the white-hot heat that flooded
her. Beck was asking her what she wanted. And it felt
like the doorway to so much more.

"What do you mean?" But the mood in the kitchen
had already shifted, grown more serious, more sensual.

"Tell me what you *want*." His blue eyes fixed her to
the spot, dazzling her with a menu of daring options.
But the fact was she wanted them all. Wanted him
to kiss her. Wanted him to explore her with his fingers, wanted him inside her, the deepest parts of her.
She wanted to lose herself in him, now and always.

"I—I…"

"I'm right here, Allie. You have my full attention
now. I'll give you whatever you want." He glanced at
her lips. "Just tell me."

Now, at last, there it was. The single shift of power.
He'd given her the reins now, and she clutched at them.
The heady, delirious power. What would she ask of
him? There were so many options, and she wanted
them all.

"I want you to touch me."

"Where?"

"Here." She spread her legs a little. He touched her inner thigh and she shivered. He took his time working upward, and then he met the soft lace of her underwear. He stroked the fabric.

"There?"

She nodded, and his fingers slipped beyond the fabric, finding her warm, wet center.

"Do you want anyone else to touch you here, Allie?" he asked, moving ever so slowly, building the heat within her. For the first time, she could see the real jealousy, the real hurt in him. He didn't want to share her, and that thrilled her.

She shook her head.

"No one else," she said. That was the truth.

"Good," he murmured and pressed his mouth against hers, as he slipped his fingers inside, finding the delicate ridges of her G-spot. She gasped in his mouth. Allie couldn't think with his hands in her, on her, his mouth devouring her. She wanted…everything. She wanted Beck to love her; she wanted Beck never to leave her; she wanted him…forever.

"Tell me, Al. Tell me," he pleaded, as if he, too, were swept up in the game, unable to stop himself. There was no dousing the flame she'd lit in her own belly. He was staring at her, blue eyes intent, and she was very much aware that they were both half-naked—her without pants, and him without a shirt.

"I want you to kiss me."

And then he reached up and gently took her glasses off. She blinked as he set them deliberately on the counter. Then his lips were on hers. And he tasted so damn good. She kissed him back, fervently, desperately, the last two months disappearing entirely. She might as well be back at the lodge, lying on that bearskin rug, Beck's delicious tongue in her mouth. Her brain switched off and her body took over. She wanted him, wanted him as much as she had then, as she had for the last seven years. She burned with need for him.

And yet was she ready for him to walk out of her life again? Was she ready for that to happen?

She broke the kiss, panting, and she saw the want in his eyes, a need that mirrored her own. He craved her, too.

"I thought you…didn't want…me." Her voice came out so low she herself barely heard it.

"I'll always want you, Allison Connor." He was so sincere, so serious, that something in her broke then. She'd thought she'd built up a wall of defense against Liam Beck, but now, with him so close, the wall she'd built crumbled, and she realized that it had only been made of paper this whole time. She almost laughed to herself to think that she'd thought she could keep him out of her heart.

They both knew it was wrong. They both knew they shouldn't go here. Not again. But she couldn't help it. And she had a growing feeling that neither could he. She kissed him then, softly at first. He didn't push her away. He wanted the kiss as much as she did. Her lips had a mind of their own as they returned his kiss, deepening it, as the hunger inside her for him grew. Her want was like a pilot light flicking on, igniting a flame that burned hot. Before she knew it, her hands slipped up his bare, muscled back, crawling up his amazingly smooth skin. She knew she should break away from him. She should stop this before it went further, before she wouldn't be able to stop herself from what came next. But her body screamed for this, for his hands on her, for every pleasure he could give her. She wanted him more than she'd ever wanted anyone in her life. No matter what she told herself, she'd always wanted Liam Beck.

He lifted her easily up off the stool and placed her gently on the breakfast bar. For once she was taller as he arched up to reach her lips. She wrapped her legs around his waist, pressing her hot center against his belly, nothing separating them but the thin, sheer fabric of her underwear. She needed to wake up from this dream. This would not change a thing between her and Beck—neither one of them had changed and hasty sex wasn't going to take away the last two months—but her body craved him, like an addict that needed a fix. And their bodies spoke a language that flowed so much better than words. Their bodies had an understanding their minds didn't. His hands were all over her, under her shirt, and the tee came off and she was there in nothing more than her sheer pink lace, bright against her pale skin. She didn't care as he cupped her breast gingerly over her bra.

Need exploded in her chest, white-hot and demanding, and her legs tightened their grip around his waist, her thighs burning with effort.

"God, Al," he murmured into her mouth. Their tongues lashed together in the most primal of dances, tasting each other, devouring each other. He pushed into her, and she knocked over his salt and pepper shakers, not that either of them took notice. All she could think about was the man's mouth and his expert hands and the way his muscled bare back felt against her calves. She wanted to squeeze him and never let him go. She wanted this forever.

She wasn't drunk now, had no excuse for the fever burning for him in her brain. This was just…Beck. All Beck. The way he was so strong, so built, yet touched her so gently, almost with reverence. He trailed a line of kisses down the delicate skin of her neck and she gasped, the heat building in her, pooling in slickness between her legs. She wanted him. She was ready for him. She needed him more than she'd needed anyone in her life. He pushed against her and an empty coffee cup rattled dangerously next to them.

Beck picked her up then as if she weighed nothing and carried her away from the crowded breakfast bar and over to the bare wall. He held her against it, her back pressed to the cool, flat surface. He held her there, pinned, his muscles working as he pushed against her warm center, his mouth on hers. She felt his need, hard and ready, straining against the thin mesh of his gym shorts. That was all that separated them now, bits of tiny fabric, all that stopped them from the reunion Allie had dreamed of so often, late at night in her bed, or in the hot stream of her shower. She'd be embarrassed by how often she'd thought of Beck, of him having her, just like this, again.

Her legs tightened around his waist as she held to his neck, and he moaned a little as he pressed himself, bulging and stiff, against her. Then he'd whirled her again, away from the wall and to the plush couch nearby. He laid her down easily, his blue eyes searching hers. He took one hand and pulled at the edge of her lacy underwear, tugging it down to her knees and then past her ankles.

Now was the time she should find the resolve to resist him. She should tell him no; she should tell him this was a mistake. What would sex do for them now? Show her all she'd been missing and break her heart all over again? But the distant thoughts felt far away, drowned out by the humming want in her body, all the nerve endings in her eagerly responding to Beck's touch. The cool air of his condo hit her bareness and she shivered, even as she watched Beck tug down his shorts. He was freed then, heavy and hard, and she remembered how often she'd enjoyed him in that lodge, how often she'd wrapped her hands around him and made him moan. She did that now, an instinct, her hands flying to him, finding him heavy and thick and ready. He bit his lower lip as she worked him just the way he liked, from the base of his shaft to the tip. She loved that feeling of power. *Yes,* she thought, *I know you. I know what you like. I know how to make you moan.*

She thought of how he must've had other women since her, perhaps just this way, on this couch. She knew that he'd have other women after her, too. She couldn't fool herself now. Beck was Beck. He wasn't going to change for her. But she didn't care. Not in this moment. Still, she hesitated.

"What's wrong?" Beck asked, and she wanted to say "everything" and "nothing" all at the same time. Everything was wrong because everything felt right. It didn't make sense, but then, nothing about them ever did.

"Do you want to stop?" he asked her, concerned.

"No," she murmured. She didn't want to stop and that was the problem. She wanted Beck deep inside her, possessing her in all ways, to hell with the consequences, with what any of it meant. For one small moment, she just wanted to be Beck's once more. When he was inside her, everything was perfect. And she desperately wanted to feel that perfection again.

"You sure?" he asked, but he had himself in his hands now, and he moved so that his bulging tip rubbed softly against her. She moaned at the contact, soft, delicate. Her hips moved to meet him, as he continued to tease her, rolling himself across her in a way that drove her wild with want. He kept working her even as he dipped down to kiss her, now the full length of him between the folds of her most delicate skin. His tongue found hers as he began to move against her. The torture was delicious. She wanted him inside her, yet he seemed happy to keep her wanting. It drove her mad as the pleasure began to build. She realized even this little bit of him against her was enough. This bare contact would take her over the edge.

She clutched at his bare back, the power of what was coming too big to control. She spread her thighs wider beneath him, a prayer for him to take her, to plunge deeper, but he refrained, as he skimmed her in a steady rhythm, stroking her clit, and before she knew it her body went rigid, and she was coming as she couldn't remember coming before. Pure pleasure exploded in her veins, running from the roots of her hair to the tips of her toes. She squeezed her eyes shut and cried out, unable to keep quiet as the tsunami of her climax washed over her. She opened her eyes to see Beck studying her, a look of admiration and awe on his face.

"You're so beautiful when you come," he said, voice low. "No one comes like you."

And that was when the words bubbled up in her throat. *I love you.* They almost tumbled out of her mouth, almost jumped straight out in the air, but she caught them in time, swallowing them back, realizing in horror that she'd almost done the unthinkable: admitted the hold he had on her. Then, suddenly, logic switched on again. What the hell was she doing? Letting Beck make her come, make her forget the last

two months? Beck had been close to negating all of
what she'd worked so hard to heal. He'd broken her
heart, and if she let him inside her, let him come, part
of her knew her heart would break all over again.
What would happen after? When he'd had his fill,
scratched his itch and realized he still needed the
comfort of other women? She might not be able to recover this time. The thought of tumbling to rock bottom, climbing her way out of heartbreak once more,
sickened her. Yet, looking at his intense blue eyes,
she was willing to risk all of that and more. What she
wanted was to give him the best climax of his life.
She wanted to show him what he'd given up.

"Al…" he breathed, and she felt his hardness against
her thigh, his want. "God, Al, I want to be inside you."

"How bad do you want me?"

"Bad."

She reached down and felt the thickness of his shaft,
understanding all too well he was telling the truth.

"What did you do the other night? When I left
you like this." She felt him heavy in her hands as she
worked him, clutching him so tight he moaned for
more.

"I finished it myself later," he admitted. "I…thought
of you. I…always think of you."

She felt giddy with power then. Good. *Want me.
Need me. Like I need you.* She shifted herself, and
he moved, so that he was half sitting, half lying on
the couch. She slipped off the side and found herself kneeling beside him, hands still working him.

All she wanted to do was put her mouth on his big, throbbing self, make him groan with every lash of her tongue, make him remember just how very good she was at driving him wild. She had never felt like this with any other man, felt the need to worship him with her tongue.

"Do you like this?" she asked, as she licked him, from base to tip. He shuddered at the contact.

"Yes," he groaned, as he lay back farther in the couch. She put her mouth around the head of his cock, flicking it with her tongue. He moaned again, closing his eyes. She released him once more.

"Want more?" she asked him, and he nodded, once. "Good," she said, feeling the vixen as she took him once more in her mouth. She worked him, with her tongue and her hands, the long, fast strokes that she knew he liked. His whole body stiffened and she relished the power she had over him. Now he would know what she felt like, when she was at his mercy, at the mercy to her own clawing want.

"Don't stop," he pleaded with her, his hands in her hair. "Please, don't stop."

But then she did stop. She pulled away, teasing him, relishing in bringing him to the brink of the ultimate pleasure, before backing away.

"You're torturing me," Beck moaned.

"You deserve it," she said and grinned, wickedly. She laughed, feeling heady with power. She straddled him then, grinding slowly against him, making him grow even more.

"You regret not calling me now?"

"I've always regretted it," he admitted, voice solemn.

She paused then, a whirl of emotions floating inside her. "So, what is this we're doing?" She rubbed against him, slowly, and he sucked in a breath. She could feel him grow stiff between her legs, this desire growing with his cock.

"I don't know," he admitted.

"Do you want me?" she asked, grinding against him, but not letting him in. Not yet.

"Yes," he said.

"Are you going to let me in? For real this time?" She needed to know. What this was. She needed a label put on it. She needed to know. She was tired of him running hot and cold.

Beck glanced away. "I don't know, Al. I want to, but..."

"But...?" She dug in, moving her hips, making him groan.

Beck said nothing, but his eyes met hers, full of want. "Is this all we are, then?" She slid her hand between their stomachs and grabbed his cock. "Is it just sex?" She rubbed him harder. "I told you, I've changed. Maybe Allie 2.0 just wants this. Wants sex and nothing else."

CHAPTER EIGHT

BECK REALIZED THAT the gorgeous woman on top of him, wrapping her hand around his throbbing cock, was giving him an offer no sane man would ever refuse. Sex with her? No commitment, nothing but the beauty of their bodies pressed together in the way nature intended, finding ways to please each other that had nothing to do with emotion, and everything to do with pure sexual chemistry. They'd always had chemistry, he and Al, and that didn't stop no matter how much reality got in the way. Any man would be crazy to turn down her offer, except that Beck wasn't just any man. He didn't want just her body; he also wanted her mind and soul.

"No, this isn't all we are." He managed to say the words out loud. He almost wished it was. Just sex would be infinitely easier. Infinitely less terrifying.

"Are you sure?" She laid a trail of delicate kisses down the side of his throat and he could feel the pulse there, thudding. There was no such thing as casual sex with Allie Connor. He already loved her. He'd forever love her. She was asking him to ignore every single beat of his heart.

"Yes," he murmured. "I'm sure. I've slept with other women. But I've never wanted to care for them like I care for you."

She dipped down and kissed him, long and hard. Then she pulled away.

"Condom?" she asked, and he involuntarily glanced over at the small drawer in the unvarnished end table beyond her. She slipped open the drawer and pulled out a thin package.

"I know how to help myself," she said, and then she ripped the package open. He should've stopped her, told her that he couldn't do what she asked: sex without emotion, and he doubted she could, either. He knew she was already as invested as he was, already in too deep. She slipped the latex sleeve on him, rolling it down slowly, so slowly that he thought he'd die from anticipation. He wanted her so badly. He'd been without her for so long. She moved him with her hand, guiding him between her legs, and then, before he could react, she'd moved him inside her. He felt the walls of muscle inside her constrict around him and he nearly came right there. They were the perfect fit, he and Al, made for each other.

She gasped, too, her beautiful green eyes widening with surprise, as she took him inch by delicious inch. He wanted to move faster, but he waited, letting her ease him inside, little by little. She bit her lip, and suddenly, he wanted to do the same, feel the delicate skin of her bottom lip held gently between his teeth. He wanted to feel all of her, all at once.

She began moving, ever so slowly on top of him, rocking forward, taking him ever deeper. He held on to her hips as she whipped off her T-shirt, revealing her delicate lace bra. She was spilling out of it, her shell-pink nipples straining against the sheer fabric. She looked like a sex goddess, that was all he could think, a woman who knew exactly what she wanted and how to get it. That was what made Allie a woman and not a girl, he thought. She was a force to be reckoned with. She never broke eye contact as she reached behind her and unhooked her bra. It fell forward and she tossed it gently aside, but his eyes were focused on her heavy breasts, now free, her pale pink nipples erect against her creamy skin.

He reached up for them, finding them too big for his hands, and he loved that, feeling as if there were just more of Allie than he could possibly handle. Defying logic, he grew even bigger, even harder inside her, his body pushed to its limits by his want for her. He felt like a man starved of sex, and it was because he'd been without Allie for far, far too long. She watched him, green eyes never leaving his, as she rode him slowly at first, and steadily faster. She dipped down and he reached up, taking one delicious nipple in his mouth. He gently grazed the tip with his teeth and she moaned. God, he loved all the little sounds she made. They were guideposts for him, signal lights as clear as any he'd ever seen on the street. He read the language of her body as if he'd been born knowing it.

He licked the other nipple now and she shuddered, squeezing him even tighter. She pulled away from him then, eyes on his, and then she moved faster, her need growing. He met her thrust for thrust. When she came, she cried out, but never closed her eyes. She kept her eyes intently on his, and he saw an amazing explosion of pleasure in them, of awe, and he thought he'd never seen a woman more beautiful in all his life, more raw or more authentic, than Allie.

And then, seeing the pure joy on her face, he came, too, feeling the deepest, most secret part of him come a little loose then, and threaten to bob to the surface. He cried out, but he worried that it was all too late, that he'd never fully recover.

She was looking down at him now, as she ran a finger down the side of his cheek.

"Why don't we spend Christmas Eve together," she said.

The offer came out of the blue. Christmas? His stomach tightened at the thought. The perfection of the climax fading quickly. He had a ritual at Christmas.

"Christmas Eve, I ski," he said. It was his tradition. He always hit the mountain, no matter how bad the weather, trying to outrun his memories.

"And Christmas Day?" Something in her voice felt like a warning. He knew he should heed it, but he didn't. Christmas Day, he'd wake sore in his bed, and treat it steadfastly just like every other day. That was how he coped with the holiday.

"Al…"

Allie rolled off him. He felt the loss of her warmth like a blow. She was unnervingly quiet. He didn't like it. What was going on in that head of hers?

"Why do you hate Christmas?" she asked him, voice low.

"Come back to here." He didn't want to talk about Christmas. Or his family. He wanted to hold Allie in his arms and forget all about everything else.

"If we're going to do this, then you have to let me in. A little." He knew by the rigid set of her back she was serious. "Maybe you should see a counselor. Maybe that would help."

"A counselor? No." Beck shook his head. The idea was preposterous. He'd seen what counseling had done with his father, when he'd gone to sessions for addiction, and it hadn't helped him, so why would it help Beck?

Allie blinked. "Counselors help a lot. My parents went to marriage counseling when they were having trouble a few years ago. It helped them."

Beck shook his head. "No," he said, determined. Going to a counselor felt like admitting defeat, admitting he was broken. He thought, with a little time, he could simply fix himself.

"Well, if you don't go see someone, then at least *talk* to me."

He sighed, feeling like he had no choice. "When I was eight, my dad was arrested Christmas morning. He'd been dealing and doing drugs. Opioids." Beck glanced at her, blue eyes steely. "It was the first of many Christmases I spent at Child Services."

"Beck, God, I'm sorry." She turned back to him, rubbing his chest with her hand.

"This is why I don't tell this story," Beck said. "I don't want pity."

"You're not going to get it from me. I'm Allie 2.0."

He laughed at that.

"How did he get addicted?" Allie asked, but Beck just wanted to close off this memory, wall it off and never think about it again, even as Allie seemed determined to drag it into the light and inspect all its ugly imperfections.

"I don't want to talk about it anymore," Beck said. "Come on, let's do something else." He ran a finger up the side of her leg. He knew it was meant to distract her, to divert. But she wiggled away.

"Did he get treatment?"

He stayed mute. Allie let out a frustrated sigh.

"I think I should go." She stood.

Beck realized she was serious. She was going to walk if he didn't share something. "It doesn't matter about the treatment. He quit that like he quit everything."

She sat on the bed then, near him. But he wanted her closer, wanted her in his arms where she was meant to be. "You know you're not him, right?" she said.

"Most people who think they aren't going to turn into their parents are just naive. It happens to all of us, eventually." Beck grabbed her hand and squeezed it. "We either turn into them, or we spend our lives fighting to be the opposite. Either way, they drive us. Whether we want them to or not."

"And you think you're going to be your dad or…"

"Whatever the opposite of him is."

"Well, that would be a good thing, wouldn't it? That would mean a sober family man."

Beck threw back his head and laughed. "No way that's where I'm headed. I've got too much of Dad's wildness in me."

Allie studied Beck. "I like the wild in you. That's my problem." She stroked his cheek. She looked suddenly sad, and Beck wasn't sure why.

"Come here." He spread open his arms, hoping she'd walk into them. He'd never wanted anything more in his life than for Allie to stop being so serious and to just get onto this couch with him. Once their skin was touching, he was sure he could convince her all was right. Their bodies shared a better language than their brains, anyway.

Allie sighed, though, and stood. "I think I'm going to go." She grabbed her clothes from the floor.

"Why? You could sleep here," he offered.

She smiled, faintly. "I think we'd better take it slow."

Beck didn't understand. He'd given her what he thought she wanted, but she was leaving anyway. "Why?"

"Because if I sleep here with you, then I'll think it's this whole thing that it might not be."

"Maybe it *is* this thing. Maybe it will be if you let it." Beck reached out for her.

"Or maybe I'll just grill you incessantly about your childhood and you'll flip out, and not talk to me again."

"I won't flip out," Beck promised.

She studied him, eyes growing cloudy. He didn't like that look on her face, that studious one. She was overthinking things again. "I think you only want me when I'm leaving," she said.

"What? That's not true. Al, you know it's not."

"When I'm all in, you run for the door." She considered this, nibbling on her bottom lip. "But when I leave, then you're all after me. It's all about the chase for you."

"That doesn't mean you need to leave." The thought of her leaving disturbed him greatly. He wanted to sleep with her in his arms, wanted to re-create that magical night in the lodge when they stayed together, bundled up, naked, for hours. Why didn't she want that, too?

She grabbed her bra and wiggled back into it, and then found her underwear on the floor and stepped into those. She walked to the already-open door of his utility closet and pulled her now-dry and clean clothes from the dryer. She dragged on her jeans and sweater from the night before.

He badly wanted to peel those clothes right off her. He wanted to hold her in his arms, whisper promises in her ear, but most of all, he just wanted her here. With her in his arms. Her leaving felt like an icicle in his abdomen.

"You don't have to go." This much was true.

"I know," she said. She tugged on one sock and then the other and twirled around until she found her boots near his front door. "But I'm going anyway. The old Allie, she would have stayed. I told you I was the new and improved Allie. This is Allie 2.0," she said.

She grabbed her phone and small cross-body bag off his console table, grabbed the folder of Excel spreadsheets she'd promised to audit and flipped her auburn hair back and gave him a vixen's grin.

He got up, but she held up a hand to stop him even as she reached out for the knob of his front door.

"I'll call you when I've looked at these," she said. "I'll see you around, Beck."

See him around? That sounded like something he'd say.

And then she'd swung open the door and disappeared into the cold December air. Well, hell.

Beck sat literally with his now-spent cock in his hands, feeling like he'd been hit by a tornado. What the hell had happened? But then again, he knew. Allie 2.0 had happened. He could feel himself slick with Allie's juices, the smell of her on his stomach, in his hair, seemingly everywhere. The ache for her burned in his belly. Would he ever stop wanting her? Ever tire of her?

The sex they'd just had didn't even scratch the

surface of his craving for her. He'd thought that two months away from her might break the spell she'd woven through his life, but two months without her had made him want her more. He should run after her, call her back, but... For what? Was she right? Did he care about her only when she was running away from him? Was he just a simple predator? Was she the gazelle to his lion? But, no, he didn't think that was true. It wasn't just a game of big cat and his prey. Not to him.

He wanted more than just sex. He wanted all of Allie Connor. He wanted to breathe her in every morning and pull her into his arms every night. He needed her. Sure, he'd take as much as he could get it, but he wanted her sharp mind, her quick wit, the way she always kept him accountable and on his toes.

She'd blown apart every last thing he thought he knew about his life, every assumption he'd ever made about how he wanted to live it. And then she'd just sauntered out.

Now what?

Allie kept his mind spinning. Just when he thought he had her figured out, she pivoted, changed tack and slipped from his grasp. The woman dazzled him, confounded him. All he wanted now was that fiery redhead in his bed all night. Hell, he wanted her in his bed for the rest of his life.

Could he break free from his father's ghost long enough to make this work? He didn't even know how to start. How did he even start thinking about his future now? How could he settle down? He ran extreme adventure tours. Taking on one big risk after another. That was not what family men did: put their lives at risk every day to make a buck. That was what he did, though, to remind himself he still was alive. What would he do if he couldn't do that anymore? He couldn't let go of the idea he'd had for his life to live fast and not worry about tomorrow. Yet he couldn't shake the feeling that Allie was meant to be his next chapter or, truly, his every chapter after this one.

Beck shut his eyes, remembering how quickly Allie had come for him, how she'd held nothing back. She never did, which was one of the reasons she was so damn hard to quit. Beck never quite shared everything. He always kept something in reserve. Living with an addict had taught him to be careful and hide his feelings. He'd never gotten out of the habit. Allie wore her heart on her sleeve, and he could see in her eyes how much she missed him even if she'd rather die than admit it.

But the real problem was that he missed her, too. She had gotten under his skin and made a home there, and no matter what he did, he couldn't shake her loose. Worse, he didn't want to. And he had no idea what to do about it.

Maybe he did need to think about seeing a counselor. Maybe he'd do it, too, if it meant winning Allie back. Convincing her he was worth her time. But maybe, it was really himself he needed to convince.

His mind was spinning. He needed to see her again. He also knew he was playing with fire, because the more Allie insisted she could handle a casual relationship, the more he knew she simply couldn't. But was casual even what he wanted anymore? His head felt like it was going to explode. And this was all Allie's fault.

What he did know was that a woman hadn't ever tried harder to get his attention all while insisting that wasn't what she was doing. And he'd never met a woman so insistent that she'd changed, when he knew she was exactly the same Allie she'd always been, and that Allie was pretty damn wonderful.

He pulled out his phone and scrolled through it, deliberately ignoring the many messages he'd received over the last day. Channing had texted. Willis, too. Everyone wanted a piece of him. He scrolled through his social media accounts, and there, in his feed, was a picture of the perfect necklace for Allie. Rose gold, two initials, which he could envision already—*Al*. It would make a perfect Christmas present.

And then he stopped himself. He was buying *Christmas* presents now? He didn't do Christmas. He hated Christmas.

Yet he could imagine that delicate rose gold necklace, the color of the blush in her cheeks when she came, hanging around her neck, the charm nestled in the hollow at her throat. He thought how surprised she'd be to get it. He wanted to see her face when she opened it. He wanted to be with her Christmas morning—and every morning. God, he was in love with her. It was so obvious that he didn't want to admit it even to himself. But it was the truth.

Liam Beck had fallen deeply, irrevocably, in love.

CHAPTER NINE

ALLIE HAD SPENT the next week battling wild mood swings as she fluctuated from relishing Beck's astonished look when she'd left his apartment to feeling hopeless that she could ever, truly, get through the emotional barriers he'd set like barbed wire across his heart. Beck had called and texted a few times over the next few days, but Allie was the one who went radio silent this time. She was still dealing with the realization that Beck seemed to be interested in her only when *she* was doing the leaving, when she left him wanting, and how was a decent relationship supposed to flourish like that?

Beck wanted her only when he had to chase after her, when she was grabbing his attention by kissing strangers at a bar, but what happened when it was just the two of them, when there was no chase? Beck was right. He wasn't the settling-down type, so why was Allie desperately trying to squeeze him into that mold? It was almost as if she were trying to trick him, trying to get him to chase her straight into monogamy. It seemed a foolhardy plan.

Her heart ached at the realization that Beck would always be Beck. What had she expected? *She* couldn't change Beck. Only Beck could change Beck, and he seemed not to want to or not to know how. Either way, she was silly to think they could really make it work. Besides, when she imagined them together, what did she think? That she'd be enough to satisfy his deep restlessness?

And if he truly wasn't interested in something long-term, was she really willing to sacrifice her wants, her needs, just to sleep with him sometimes? The fact was, she was actually considering it. She shook herself. When did this happen? When had the confident, take-charge Allie been replaced by a love-sick girl willing to betray her own heart just to keep Beck around?

But they weren't compatible if she really sat down and thought about it. He was a risk taker and she was an accountant. He flew by the seat of his pants and never planned anything and she had every bit of her financial future mapped out down to the monthly contribution to her 401(k). He was wild, and it was the very wildness that she loved that also repelled her. How could she love the core of a man and then ask him to change it at the same time? She couldn't.

So, she was ignoring his calls. She was tired of pushing so hard, trying to make him something he wasn't. But at least this time she knew she hadn't been imagining the incredible chemistry between them. Now she knew he felt it, too. It wasn't all in her head. *And that's all it is, or ever will be*, she told herself.

Allie stood in her office, staring out the window of her small tax accounting firm that she'd proudly started herself. She had a shop just off the main streets of downtown Aspen, in an old office that used to be a telegraph office, back when this was an old mining town. Silver had brought people here back in the late 1800s, but now it was the white-capped mountains that lured in tourists looking to spend cash on ski lessons and fine dining. The short wooden buildings were brightly painted, but she could still imagine them as they were back in the Old West, when the streets would've been made of frozen mud and snow. At the end of her street, she could see the Rocky Mountains jutting up, covered in snow and evergreens, a view that never ceased to take her breath away.

She lived in a small condo she rented above the office, so didn't even have to step outside for her commute. She took another sip of her quickly cooling tea and watched as a flutter of snowflakes taken by the wind swirled along the street. The view couldn't be more Christmassy if it tried: a dusting of fresh white snow on the cars, small shops and restaurants outlined in white lights, almost everything wreathed in evergreen and red ribbon. The afternoon sun shone on the snow, making it sparkle.

"Allie? Did you hear me?" came the familiar voice of her assistant, Maggie. Maggie was about her mother's age, midsixties, and helped Allie answer phones, pay bills and do simple accounting for her less complicated clients.

"Sorry, Maggie," she said, dragging her attention away from the window. "What did you say?"

"Well, you just agreed to give me a hundred-percent raise, so woo-hoo for me!" Maggie grinned, her silver hair catching the light.

"You'd deserve it," Allie said. "Wish I could afford it."

Maggie shook her head. "It's all that tax software's fault." Maggie made a disapproving noise in the back of her throat. She hated the tax software that seemed to be everywhere and was cutting into their business. Some people still preferred the old-fashioned way of doing taxes, but Allie wondered how long that would last. "Have you thought more about that job offer?"

Allie glanced at her assistant. A college friend had offered a job in Denver not long ago, to be an accountant at a big firm there. It would give her a twenty-percent raise, and cover the cost of her relocation.

"I don't know."

"Well, don't worry about me. I'm retiring in January, no matter what." She grinned. She had two grandkids living with her son and daughter-in-law in Florida, and she planned to move there to help them.

"I know and I'm going to miss you." This was the truth.

"You got a place to go this Christmas?" Maggie sent her a sympathetic look. Maggie had adopted her as her own, since her family lived so far away.

"Not sure yet," Allie said. The mention of Christmas sent a bolt of sadness through her heart. All she wanted to do was spend it with Beck, but he'd shut her out—again. He'd tried to stuff her down into her Allie box once more. But she wasn't going to stay there.

"Well, you know you always have a seat at my table." Maggie was the sweetest. "Maybe I'll invite Beck, too."

Maggie had been trying to get Beck and Allie together for years. She didn't know about the weekend in the lodge or the reunion the Saturday before, and Allie would like to keep it that way.

"He won't come if I'm there." It was the sad truth.

Maggie glanced at her a bit. "He will. He likes you."

Allie shook her head. Maggie was working from a point of what-ifs and what-would-bes, but Allie knew the truth. Allie saw a flash of memory from last Saturday, his magnificently naked body above hers. She pushed the memory away. Now was not the time for that. She needed to put Beck behind her, for her own sanity. She was tired of crashing herself against the wall he'd built around his heart.

"He called today."

Allie turned, surprised. "Did he leave a message?"

"He wanted to know if you'd looked over some papers."

Allie glanced down at Beck's open file on her desk, frowning a little. She'd gone through the paperwork and everything seemed all right, except something was bothering her. The payroll was off. It was too high for the number of employees she thought they had, but then maybe Beck had hired more help, or contracted out some of the tours. She'd have to check with Beck about it. She calculated that, based on last year's numbers, the payroll had gone up thirty percent, even though she didn't find any new recipients of the pay. Maybe Beck had been overly generous that year and given out bonuses. She'd have to go over the numbers again, sometime when she wasn't distracted by thoughts of Beck himself.

Maggie wasn't finished. "And…" Maggie paused, dramatically. "And he mentioned something about bungee jumping? He said you guys had a date?" Maggie's eyes lit up with excitement.

"Oh, no. No, no, no. We don't have a date." Allie shook her head fiercely.

"You might want to tell him that." Maggie nodded toward the glass door and Allie glanced up and saw Beck there, wearing a fleece-lined bomber jacket, a familiar knit skull cap covering his blond hair. His breath came out in foggy puffs against her glass door. He raised a hand in a wave and a question.

Her heart thumped in her chest, and her brain ping-ponged from sheer shock to immense relief. But what did the appearance mean? She tried to calm the fluttering hope in her chest that this meant something, that he was here to tell her something important like he'd decided she was the only woman in the world for him, and that her life was about to turn into a climactic scene from one of her favorite rom-coms. Except that this wasn't a rom-com, this was her life, and that was Beck, and she needed to calm the heck down.

Allie strode forward and pulled the door open.

"Hi?" she offered tentatively.

"Hi," he said, his blue eyes lighting up when they saw her. Or was that just her imagination? She'd imagined so much when it came to Beck, she needed to remind herself this was about her dignity. About not letting him see he'd hurt her. And that she was still, on some level, supposed to be peeved with him. Even though she'd forgotten why as he stood before her in all his Beck glory.

"Gonna invite me in?" He flashed a white grin that made her stomach twist. Feeling like she was over Beck was much easier when he wasn't standing right in front of her, when she wasn't imagining his big strong hands on her hips. Allie watched as he took in her outfit; her skinny jeans, hiking boots and thin wool sweater. She thought she saw the glint of approval in his eyes, the heat of desire. She felt heat rush to her inner thighs, and she knew if he peeled her jeans off her, he'd find her wet and ready. She hated that her body responded instantly to him—there was that frequency again, the one tuned straight to him.

"Oh, Allie, don't let the poor boy freeze to death out there," Maggie chided as she welcomed him in. Allie doubted Beck could freeze. He spent his days outdoors heli-skiing on some of the highest and coldest peaks around. Cold never bothered the man. Beck sauntered in and hugged Maggie, who had to stretch up on her tiptoes to fold her arms around the back of his neck.

"Beck! So good to see you," she said, grinning, and seeming to work hard to make up for Allie's lack of enthusiasm. Allie couldn't help but feel the two were in league against her.

"What do you want?" Allie asked, and then instantly wanted to slap her forehead. Why did she say that? She was trying to sound professional and cool, but she saw by the look on his face that he took it as an invitation to a menu of sex acts.

"You'd know if you ever answered my calls," Beck said dryly. "If I didn't know better, I'd say you were ignoring me on purpose. To get me here. Didn't you say I only loved the chase?"

"Beck." Allie let out a frustrated sound and rolled her eyes. "Seriously. I have work to do. So…?"

Beck's face broke into a devious grin. "Well, I had some clients cancel on me and I thought you might want to bungee."

"Oh, let me look at my calendar…" Allie pretended to thumb through an imaginary calendar in the air. "Uh, nope. I'm busy."

"Come on."

"I've got to work."

"I can watch the office," Maggie chimed in, grinning. "You go. Have fun. While you're young."

"Uh…" Why did Maggie do that? She sent her a glance to show she didn't appreciate it, but Maggie stubbornly refused to make eye contact. The woman was determined to get them together. She'd have to have a word with her assistant later.

"Well, sounds like your afternoon just freed up." Beck swiped Allie's coat off the rack and held it up. "So, let's go."

"No." Allie crossed her arms across her chest. Beck put her coat over her shoulders like a cape. "You can make plans, like a normal person. I need some notice."

"Well, I *would've* made plans, if you'd returned my calls or texts. But you didn't. So, now, here we are."

Allie shook her head. "Still not going," she said, firmly.

"Okay, then. So you admit Allie 2.0 isn't real."

"Oh, she's real." Allie 2.0 was about to smack Beck, that was what Allie 2.0 was going to do.

"Okay, then. What's the problem?" Beck leaned in and Allie was acutely aware of the man's massive size. She craned her neck to meet his blue gaze, something she never had to do with anyone else. She was used to being among the tallest in a room. Allie tried not to feel off balance, but Beck always seemed to mess with her equilibrium.

"You're the problem." Allie glared. Beck just stared back, as if he already knew he'd won.

"Well, I've got a whole afternoon and evening planned for you. Allie 2.0 will love it."

This made Allie hesitate. Beck never planned anything. "A plan? You? I don't believe it. You don't even believe in dinner reservations."

Beck laughed a little. "Well, maybe this is Beck 2.0."

"You can't copy me and my 2.0."

"As long as you're pretending to be me, I can pretend to be you. Fair's fair."

"Go on, you two, argue on the way. You're wasting sunlight," Maggie chimed in. Allie glanced at Maggie, who shooed her with both hands. Maggie would like nothing better than for her to spend the afternoon with Beck. The worst part was that Allie would like nothing better, either.

"Fine," she ground out between clenched teeth. She was too tired to argue with both of them, and if she was honest with herself, she wanted to see what Beck had planned. He grinned, and somewhere, deep inside, Allie knew she was going to be in trouble.

CHAPTER TEN

ALLIE WALKED BY Beck's side in the freshly fallen snow, the late afternoon sun glinting on the crystals. She was a little tongue-tied. What was she doing letting him convince her a date was a good idea? The main street with the wreaths and red ribbons all felt so very festive…and romantic. Ahead of them, the Rocky Mountains jutted up, a tall, snowcapped peak in the distance against the bright blue sky. She sucked in a breath, feeling lucky to be living in such a beautiful place.

She glanced up at Beck's profile, wondering if he felt the beauty of the place, too. Normally, he hated the town. He preferred the pristine peaks far above the reach of ski lifts and amateur skiers. She wondered if he was thinking of those right now.

"Do you want to tell me why you've been ignoring me all week?" Beck asked. "I've been calling."

"I know."

"And texting."

"I just… Maybe you're right about us."

Beck shook his head. "Allie, I know you're trying to *be* me, but this is ridiculous. I'm the only one that gets to ghost people." The way he said it made Allie laugh.

"I'm not ghosting you."

"You're not?"

"I'm just *taking things slow*."

"By ignoring me."

"Mmm-hmm."

Beck stopped near a light pole decorated with a green laurel and glanced at the motorcycle parked in the snowy space. "Here we are," he declared.

"What's this?"

"My new ride," he said. "Truck's in the shop getting new tires, so…"

She glanced at the motorcycle, which already had a dusting of snow on its black seat. It was all chrome and black leather, a mean machine that looked like it spit out danger from its impressive tailpipe. The motorcycle suited Beck. It was a little bit wild, just like he was. She almost felt drawn to it, wanting to touch the black leather seat. But she held her gloved hands back. Was she really considering riding a motorcycle in snow?

"Oh, no." Allie held up her hands and backed away from Beck and the two-wheeled death machine. "No way am I getting on that. It's *winter*. In Aspen. You'd have to be crazy to ride one of those now. We'll slip on ice and die."

"Well, maybe the snow will break our fall." Beck shrugged.

"No. *No.* I'm not getting on that thing." Allie had always been taught to fear motorcycles a little. Her uncle had been an orthopedic surgeon and had often said that motorcycle accidents and trampolines made up the bulk of his business.

"I thought you were Allie 2.0," Beck challenged, as he straddled the motorcycle. The cycle was big, but Beck was bigger and made it look small. "I thought you took risks and did things the old Allie wouldn't do."

"Yeah, but…"

"Yeah, but what?" He patted the seat behind him.

"You did this on purpose," she said, suspicious. "Is your truck really in the shop?"

"It is. But, yes, I did this on purpose." He laughed. "So? Come on, Allie 2.0. Part of you is curious."

To ride a motorcycle, no, she thought, but to sit behind Beck? Wrap her arms around his waist and snuggle against his broad back? Maybe. Feel the wild wind whipping over their bodies? Possibly. But to go hurtling down the ice-slick highway on one? Uh, no.

"I've got a helmet for you," he said, offering her one. "Even this date has some *safety* requirements."

Her fingers tingled a little at the word *date*. What was his game?

"I'll freeze to death." She realized she was just coming up with excuses now. Part of her wanted to jump right behind him, and she squished that part down, feeling at war with herself.

Beck laughed a little. "I'll keep you warm. And

it's a short ride, anyway." He patted the seat again. "What? Are you scared?"

"No." Maybe. A little. She sucked in a breath. Not that she'd ever let him know that. "Oh, hell. Why not?" Her reckless half won, as she grabbed the helmet and stuffed it on, and then took her place behind Beck. His shoulders were so broad she could barely see over or around them. It was a wall of Beck in front of her.

"You might want to hold on," he cautioned her. She reached around and wrapped her arms around his middle. Then the motorcycle roared to life, pure power between her legs as Beck backed up into the street and then hit the gas. The jolt startled her and she pressed her face into the back of his bomber jacket. The hum of the wheels against the newly plowed street made her worry that they would somehow slip, but Beck, as usual, controlled the machine with rigid precision. He was a man who could bend machines and snowboards to his will, so it shouldn't surprise her that he could maneuver a motorcycle with ease. The roads had been thoroughly plowed and salted by trucks after the last snowfall, so they were mostly clear. She found herself actually enjoying the ride, as he wound through the narrow streets of Aspen, past the adorable shops decorated for the holidays. Soon, she loosened her grip a tad, feeling every small shift of weight Beck made, and then she copied it, their bodies melded together in perfect harmony.

The smell of wood-burning fireplaces hung in the

night air and she inhaled the scent and tightened her grip on Beck's waist, thankful for the gloves on her hands as the cold December wind whipped across them. The sun, however, warmed her dark coat as they sped down the small two-lane highway, winding around the mountain. Up above, the snow clung to ridges, and the mountains stretched up into the sky. Allie was amazed by how much she could feel every last vibration, that she felt as much a part of Beck as she did a part of the bike beneath her. He kicked up the speed another notch and Allie sucked in her breath, nerves humming in her temples. But then she found herself loving the speed, the wind against the mask of her helmet as they passed a slow-moving truck and sped down the highway. There was freedom in the open road, behind Beck. She wanted to drink it in, savor it. She loved how his body talked to hers, telling it when to shift weight, when to hold on tighter.

The ride was over way too soon as he pulled off the road near a long metal walking bridge across a huge ravine. Far below, at least twenty stories down, the rush of the not-quite-frozen river flooded over boulders that were coated in snow. She recognized the spot. It was where Beck took clients who wanted to bungee jump.

"Oh, no," she murmured, but her helmet echoed the sound back to her own ears. "You were serious about this?"

"Well, that's what we've been talking about all this time. You said you'd bungee jump." Well, in theory she had, but now that she was here, she didn't much like the idea of leaping off a bridge tied to a rubber band. She hopped off the bike, her legs still vibrating from the engine. She tugged off the helmet and immediately felt the static electricity run through her hair as she shook it loose.

"I thought you were kidding."

"When do I ever kid about *bungee*?" He set the kickstand to the ground and left the bike and helmet near the steps leading up to the bridge. In minutes, he'd unlocked the storage unit attached to the foot-bridge and dragged out a harness and the gear she'd need to free-fall.

Allie felt a little weakness at the back of her knees.

"Am I?" she asked, peeking over the edge of the metal bridge and feeling her stomach shrink as she calculated the sheer drop down. She didn't do well with heights.

"Having second thoughts? If so, you can just admit that we're great together and stop running away from me."

"Says the man who ran away from me first." Allie crossed her arms across her chest and frowned. "You cannot take the high road on this."

"Well, I've grown. Matured. Seen the errors of my ways." Beck flashed a grin and she felt her insides melt a little. Felt the pull to him, the powerful tug. All he had to do was crook his finger in her direction and she'd do just about anything he said. The depth of that power made her dizzy.

"I don't believe you've matured." She shook her head.

"Well, then, seen the errors of my ways." He cocked his head to one side. "So…are you going to jump? Or admit you want me? That what you'd rather be doing right now is be naked in bed with me."

Maybe now would be a good time to call this whole thing off, and let Beck know she'd only been kidding about Allie 2.0, that he was one hundred percent right. It was just a ploy to try to prove that, what? She wasn't boring? That she wasn't a Greenie. Or that, above all else, she wanted Beck to notice her. And keep on noticing her.

"No," she lied. She glanced at the harness. It had a lot of buckles and loops, and while it seemed to be made of seat belts, she wondered if it would truly hold her weight. Oh, Lord. What happened if she ended up losing all control of her bladder? If her accountant parents ever found out about this, they'd have a fit.

"Come here." Beck motioned her over and her stomach clenched. She didn't know if it was because she was moving closer to Beck, or because he planned to hurl her off the edge of a bridge. She swallowed, hard.

"Do I have to?"

He nodded, and his blue eyes focused on her with an intensity she would've liked under different circumstances.

"Okay, Allie 2.0." He busied his hands slipping the harness over her legs, and she was achingly aware of how close he was. For a second, she completely

forgot she was standing on a bridge a hundred or so
feet in the air about to plummet headfirst. She could
stop this at any time, she told herself. She didn't have
to play Beck's game. But the problem was, a part of
her wanted to. Beck fastened the harness securely at
waist level and then he started to work around her
ankles, lashing them together. He tugged at the nylon
to make sure it was all secure and double-checked the
hook to the winch that would pull her back up once
she'd taken her dive.

She glanced at the massive amount of bright blue
bungee rope on the platform.

"You ready to plunge headfirst?" he asked her.

"You bet I am," she lied, but was glad her voice
sounded relatively calm. With her ankles together,
she had a hard time moving, but she leaned on Beck.
Beck swept her into his arms and she squealed, legs
still lashed to the bungee cord. She grasped his neck,
as he held her easily in his arms.

"You don't have to do this," Beck said. They were
nearly nose to nose now, and she watched his lips as
they moved. Remembering how they felt on hers.
"You could kiss me instead." His blond brow crooked
upward, and she felt the challenge.

"You'd like that, wouldn't you?"

"More than you know." Beck's lips were so close,
she could feel the warmth of his breath on her. She
wanted to taste him suddenly. She wanted his tongue
in her mouth. He nuzzled her nose ever so slightly,
and then just when she thought he might cover her lips

with his, he put her down on the hard platform right near the edge. She felt oddly off balance with her legs lashed together. "Say the word, and I'll untie you."

"And then what?"

"And then you admit you'd rather get into bed with me than jump off this bridge."

For a half second, Allie imagined Beck naked, his amazing athlete's body in all kinds of interesting positions. Allie couldn't help it—she laughed. "You're an egomaniac."

"And you're in love with me."

Allie froze, feeling suddenly on the spot, vulnerable, exposed. Did he know? Could he know that? Panic and denial rose in her throat.

"I am not." Allie's heartbeat thumped louder in her own ears. Suddenly, she almost wanted to jump so she could avoid Beck's very serious and very intense stare. She couldn't admit that she loved him. That would be giving him everything. Yet the way he was looking at her now told her he already knew everything. Everything she was feeling, everything she was thinking, everything she wanted to do to him in her bed tonight.

"Now who's being cagey?" he asked her.

The icy wind whipped across the small metal platform bridge and it swayed a bit. She reached out and grabbed the railings.

"Is it supposed to do that?" *Yes, let's talk about the bridge. About me hurtling off it. Anything but how I really feel about you.* Admitting she had fallen in love with Beck was the scariest thing she could think of. Even if she knew it was true. Admitting she loved Beck would be the same as losing him forever. She knew him well enough to know that much. If she could keep it light, remind them of their friendship, then maybe she could keep him. As a friend. As a casual lover. As something. And as pathetic and silly as that sounded, she'd rather have something than nothing. And she'd rather have it and her dignity all at the same time.

"Yes," Beck said and dropped his length of bungee cord. She was inches from the edge. All she had to do was fall forward, and she'd be doing it: jumping into the ravine. "You look a little pale. You sure you want to do this? Or do you want to talk about your feelings about me some more?"

"I don't have feelings for you." Her voice shook a little, but she told herself it was the icy wind and the fact that she was at the edge of a thin metal platform about to free-fall. Her legs shaking had nothing to do with her feelings for Beck.

"You sure?" His gaze told her he knew she was lying. But she had to cling to the thin lie anyway. It was the only protection she truly had against him. She needed her dignity.

"Stop playing around, Beck." It was almost a plea. If he kept at her, she just might admit what she'd sworn never to tell him, ever. "Am I going to jump or are we going to gossip about our feelings some more like girls at a tea party?"

Beck threw his head back and laughed then. "Suit yourself." He tugged on her ropes, checking the safety harness once more. "You know, you really don't have to do this. But I also know, if you do it, you're going to love it."

He grinned. And in that smile, she trusted him, even though she *was* terrified. Every cell in her body, every survival instinct she had, told her that jumping would be suicide, no matter how secure the ropes might be around her feet. Still, she needed to do this. She glanced up at Beck.

"I am, but I want to do it."

"Or you could just skip this part and get into bed with me?"

She wanted to do that, too.

"So you can brag about being right? No way. I'm jumping."

"Okay, if you're really going to do this, then make sure to just dive off, like you're jumping in a pool. Try not to pinwheel your arms. It's best to keep them straight out by your sides. The bungee will catch you, but it shouldn't be too rough. And when you stop bouncing, then I'll reel you back in." Beck tapped the winch next to her head. "Are you ready?"

Allie nodded. She scooted to the edge of the platform and glanced down. Good grief, that was a long way down. A cold sweat broke out on her lower back as she stood near the edge. What was she doing? Her conservative accountant parents would literally have a heart attack if they knew. Yet part of her felt the urge to just take the leap. Feel the wind on her face. Feel the free fall and, for a delicious second, all that chaos that could clear her mind entirely of everything but that single moment.

"You sure you don't want to change your mind?"

Allie wasn't sure at all. But then she spread her arms and jumped.

Beck had never found a woman sexier in all his life. She dived off that platform like a pro, arms out, legs pressed together, a beautiful, lithe bird, diving straight into the ravine below. For a woman who claimed to like to play it safe, she sure took to danger. The bungee caught her and she let out a delighted squeal, a sound that Beck felt in his entire body. Her auburn hair had come loose from its tie. Beautiful waves of gold and red caught the sunlight as she bounced once and then twice, before she came to a stop at the end of the bungee. She stretched her arms out and shouted with joy, her voice ricocheting off the rocks below and bouncing up around them. He had to laugh at the purity of her celebration and felt himself a little envious. He remembered the rush of his first jump, and how it had made him feel invincible. There was truly nothing like staring down death to make you feel truly alive. Not that there was any real danger here, but try telling the body that. It doesn't know or care about safety harnesses. All it feels is the free fall and the pure lick of adrenaline.

"That was amazing!" she screamed, her face absolute joy, as he activated the winch and pulled her up. In seconds, she was in his arms and on the platform. He set her down, and she threw her arms around his neck and kissed him. Surprised, he stumbled back a bit, but then caught himself, the fierceness of her lips demanding his full attention. Her hands were in his hair and her tongue in his mouth before he knew what was happening. Not that he was complaining. He kissed her back, right there on that platform, feeling his body come to life, summoned up to do whatever she commanded. She pulled away, her green eyes bright.

"You never told me that would be so amazing. Is this what skiing unmarked trails is like? Or any of the other crazy things you do?"

"Even better," he said. It was true. That was what cheating death felt like. Addictive and wonderful.

"So this is why you do it. Pure thrill. God, my heart is beating so fast." Beck knelt to take off her harness, freeing her feet. She ran her hands through her hair. "It's just amazing. I've never felt so…"

"Alive?"

She nodded.

"Now, isn't this better than taking married men home for a one-night stand?"

Allie laughed. "Marginally better." She grinned. Allie glanced at the harness in his hand. "Wait. Can I put that back on? Can I do it again?"

Right there, with Allie standing in the sunlight, beaming from head to toe, her green eyes shining like emeralds, Beck knew he loved this woman. He didn't know how he'd do it, but he'd find a way to convince her they belonged together.

Something shifted after the bungee jump, Allie could feel it, though she couldn't say what. She rode with her arms around his back as he took her to dinner. It was the day before Christmas Eve and all the restaurants were packed with out-of-towners, tourists who'd flown in for the holidays. Allie never thought most people would opt to go away from home for Christmas, but Aspen was always full to bursting with those who did. After searching and failing to find a restaurant that didn't have an hour's wait, they ended up back at Allie's condo with pizza and a bottle of red wine.

Sitting in front of her blazing wood fireplace, with Beck lounging casually on her leather armchair, and Allie's stomach full of thin-crust spinach-and-sausage pizza, she felt strangely content. Maybe she could just be fine with this, whatever *this* was. Beck glanced at her small Christmas tree, the one she'd set near her window overlooking the street. It was lit with white lights and she'd filled it with all-silver ornaments. Allie knew how Beck felt about Christmas, and suddenly wished the tree wasn't there.

"It's pretty," Beck said, nodding at the tree. "Where did you find that star?"

"My father made it," Allie said. "He likes to repurpose odd pieces of metal. It's a hobby. He makes them for the church fair, and he sent me one. Of course, now he and Mom have a tradition of traveling on a church trip every Christmas. I think they're building homes in Puerto Rico right now."

"Your father is much different than mine," Beck said, shaking his head. "My dad didn't even know when or where he was half the time."

"Are you up for talking about him?"

Beck glanced at her, wary. "Maybe."

"How did he become an addict?" Allie asked.

"Does it really matter?" Beck shrugged, and for a second she thought he'd do what he usually did when questions turned to his personal life and deflect. But then he met her gaze and seemed to reconsider. "My dad was a trick skier, before that was even a thing," Beck said, staring at the flames in the fireplace as he seemed to sink into those distant memories. "He never medaled, since back in his prime they didn't have medals for the things he did. Twists and flips down the mountain. He was my hero. I idolized that fool. It was no accident that I'm good at going fast." Beck laughed at this a little. Shook his head. Allie heard real love in his voice. "But one day, he was just doing his normal thing. Jumping. Spinning. But he landed a trick wrong, that was all. A freak accident. He broke two vertebrae in his back. Several back surgeries and many prescriptions later, and he was suddenly selling off everything we owned to get his fix."

"That's awful." Allie tried to imagine Beck as a little boy, struggling to understand what was happening.

"He cheated, too, on my mother. Slept around. Ran with women who had a supply of oxy, or who knew someone who did. He used his good looks and his charm there, too. He didn't care much about my mother and me at home." Beck frowned at the fire. "Mom eventually had enough of that and had an affair with someone she met at the grocery store, of all places. She divorced Dad, married this other guy and moved to Florida."

"Why didn't she take you with her?"

Beck glanced sharply at her, and Allie suddenly wished she hadn't asked that question. She feared he'd clam up now, just when she was starting to truly understand him. Or at least have some understanding of what made him tick. "I was fourteen then and didn't get along so well with the stepdad. I thought they were abandoning Dad, and I wasn't going to do that to him."

"You were loyal. That's admirable, Beck."

"Loyalty didn't get me anything but a lot of headaches." Beck shook his head. "I thought I could take care of Dad, but he was a mess."

"And you were basically just a kid yourself," Allie pointed out. "It shouldn't have fallen to you."

"There was no one else." Beck made it sound like the thing he had to do. "I went out to visit Mom once in Tampa on Christmas." He stared at the tree a beat, and Allie wondered if he were reliving the time. "It wasn't a great visit. I hadn't seen her in months, and I had a lot of anger."

"I don't blame you. You were taking care of your dad and trying to be a kid all at the same time, and your mom left, so, I get it. You felt abandoned."

"Maybe I did. I didn't think about it much." Beck glanced at her. She wanted to lean over and hug away all the sadness in his life. "Still, I said some pretty rotten things to her. She didn't deserve them." Beck ran a hand over the blond stubble coating his chin. "When she told me I was too much like my dad, I couldn't argue. And after that, I didn't get Christmas invites to Tampa anymore."

Allie felt the heavy weight of that sadness, of a kid stuck between two parents who weren't really parents at all.

"No wonder you hate Christmas," Allie said.

Beck chuckled a little.

"It just reminds me of the family I didn't have. Won't have."

"What makes you so sure you're going to be like your father?"

"My mother was right about me and him. There's something unpredictable in him…and me. That's what makes us able to do dangerous stunts on the mountain. You can't put that away and settle down, really. It always burns there. My way of dealing with it is…not dealing with it." Beck shrugged. "Plus, I know that with how fast I live, it's really only a matter of time before I have a serious injury."

"You could quit all the extreme stuff."

Beck laughed. "I can't quit. It's in my blood."

Allie considered this. "Or you could see someone. A counselor."

"Nah." Beck shook his head. "I don't like to talk to *you*. Why would I be more comfortable with a stranger?"

"We all have issues."

"Even you, raised by perfect accountants?" Firelight danced on his face.

"Even me," Allie said and laughed. "Hey, I had the opposite problem. I had helicopter parents who would wrap me in bubble wrap if they could."

"Probably explains why you can't get enough of me," Beck said. "I'm the bad boy you could never have." Beck pushed himself away from his chair and joined her on the floor by the fireplace. His knee touched hers as he sat down beside her. He reached over and tickled her a little.

She shrieked. "Hey! Stop it!"

"I'm bad! I can't stop it…"

Allie fought his fingers as she dissolved in giggles. He tickled her mercilessly until she begged him to stop.

"Fine, I'll let you go," Beck said, his strong fingers finally relenting. Her side hurt from laughing as she gulped in air. Being with Beck felt like the ground was always shifting—serious, white-hot sex, laughter, all in a flash. She liked it, the unpredictability. She was beginning to think she truly wasn't the conservative, by-the-book woman she'd always thought she was.

"Wait… I'm not done." Beck lunged once more and Allie squealed as he tickled her again. She tried valiantly to fight him off, but he was too big and too strong, and soon he was right on top of her, chest to chest.

"Beck! Stop!" She moved to defend herself, but he grabbed her wrist.

"I will. I'm sorry."

"You should be." Now they were eye to eye. Breathing heavy, their bodies pressed together. She fought the urge to kiss him. She glanced at his lips.

"I'm sorry, Allie." She realized that he wasn't talking about the tickling anymore. He'd grown serious. Too serious. "I'm so sorry for being a jerk this last month. I…I owe you so many apologies. This time of year, starting with Thanksgiving on…just messes with my head. I make bad decisions, and… I'm sorry."

"Do you think sleeping with me was a bad decision? Be honest." Allie steeled herself for his answer, fearing the worst.

"No." He rolled off her then. The cool air hit her chest, and she sat up, blinking. "No, I don't regret that."

"Good. I don't regret it, either." The truth floating between them felt stark, but real. Steady. Grounded.

"Look, I don't know what's happening here. Between us." He looked at her, a long, steady gaze. "But I know it's turned my world upside down."

Allie almost wanted to hold her breath. She put her hand on his shoulder. He grabbed that hand and held it.

"I want to be with you. I want to laugh with you. I want to take care of you." Beck's blue eyes clouded. "Even though you make that really hard sometimes."

Allie laughed. She did, she knew she did.

"I don't know what any of this means, but I think about you all the time. I think about you when I wake up, and when I'm skiing or giving tours to clients, or when I'm in the shower or when I go to sleep. You're in my brain all the time like a fever, Allie, and no matter what I do, I can't shake it. I don't even want to shake it."

Allie could feel her pulse in her wrist and wondered if Beck could feel it, too.

"I've been running scared since the lodge, Allie. I know that. I thought I was saving you somehow from me, but if I'm honest with you, I was just scared."

"Scared of what?" Allie felt confusion whirl in her brain as she tried to process everything Beck was saying.

"Scared of losing you. Scared of hurting you. Scared of what I was going to become." Beck ran a hand through his blond hair and sighed.

"I was scared I'd already lost you," she said. "When you didn't call."

She saw pain cross his face and knew then that he'd known how much he hurt her. And that he regretted it.

"I know. I've been a fool. Can you forgive me?" He searched her face for the answer she already felt in her heart.

She nodded, suddenly unsure of her voice. Allie leaned in then and kissed Beck. Kissed him as if her life depended on it, because in some ways she thought it did. It felt terrifying to tell him the truth. Terrifying to lay herself bare like that. And then he kissed her back, kissed her hard, his tongue in her mouth, his lips on hers. His hand wrapped around the back of her neck, and she forgot about anything she might want to say next, or anything she might want to hear him say. In that moment, they didn't need words. Their bodies spoke for them, as her lips parted and welcomed his tongue. The mere taste of him made her want more, it always did, but today, she felt a fearsome desire for him, a black hole of need that she finally acknowledged to herself.

Beck leaned her down and the next thing she felt was the softness of her plush shag rug against her back and Beck's delicious weight on top of her. His mouth was on hers, devouring her, and she consumed him right back. Her leg kicked out, and she hit the table with the small Christmas tree. An ornament flew off, hitting the ground with a plink. Beck pulled away to inspect the damage, but Allie put her hands on his face and pulled him back down to her mouth. She didn't care about any ornament, didn't care about the whole tree.

All she wanted was Beck. Only Beck. All of him. He managed to pull away once more, his breath coming fast, his pupils so big his eyes looked dark with desire.

"Al…" It was a question, so much uncertainty conveyed in a single word. But Allie didn't want to think about what would come after. All she wanted was to climb into his skin, lose herself entirely in his body. She wanted him to fill her in every way possible, and she didn't want to think about what it might mean later. She wanted to taste him again. Close her eyes and pretend everything was as it should be. She wanted to heal his scars, reach back into his past and show him that boy was loved. She wanted to make it all better. It was that simple, and the only way she knew how to do that was with her mouth and her hands and the rest of her body. He eased backward, and she sat up, whipping off her shirt. His eyes widened as they took in the black lace beneath. If she'd known Beck would be here tonight, she would've worn the garters he always loved so much. But the quirk of an appreciative smile on his face told her he liked the black lace she was wearing just fine. He dipped down and laid a trail of kisses down the round slope of her breast. She groaned, as he flicked the thin lacy fabric down and freed her nipple. He licked it, softly, playfully as she arched her back, wanting more of his mouth, and she could feel the heat of the fire on her bare skin. Her body felt as if it had turned into a molten river of lava, and the heat pooled between her legs. Beck expertly worked the clasp behind her bra, and then both breasts came free. He licked one pink nipple and then the other, as they rose to meet his command, his eyes never leaving her face.

"You're beautiful," he murmured into her chest, and she groaned in response. "I want you. All of you." She wanted him, too, more than she'd ever dare admit to him or herself. His mouth on her body felt so right, as if it was meant for her, had been all along. He dipped downward, tickling her belly with his nose as he moved ever south. He clasped the delicate lace of her waistband with his teeth and tugged downward, driving her near wild with anticipation. He moved slowly, deliberately, as if he meant to take his time, savor her, inch by inch. His hands pushed the soft fabric away, sliding it down her bottom and her legs, and then she was bare, completely vulnerable beneath him. He expertly spread her legs, and they quivered beneath his touch, his strong fingers pressed into her thighs. "I'm going to make you come," he promised.

It was a vow that she knew he'd keep, as he put his mouth on her, his warm, wet mouth finding all the nerve endings at her most delicate center. She came alive then, every pleasure circuit in her brain lighting up, like holiday lights on a tree. She squirmed, her legs spreading wider for him, her pelvis rising up to meet him, lick for lick, moving to his rhythm. He'd remembered everything she liked, the tempo, the pressure, the perfect places. He played her with his mouth, as if she were an instrument that responded instantly to his touch. She clutched the thick carpet beneath her hands and held on for dear life. The desire built in her, a flame he tended with his tongue that grew hotter with each stroke.

"Beck," she murmured, running her hands through his thick shock of blond hair, not quite believing he was between her knees, worshipping her. She wanted it to last forever, but her body had a different idea. "God, Beck." She wouldn't be able to stop what happened next if she tried. She was tumbling toward the cliff, unable to stop. And then she climaxed, everything falling away but Beck and his expert tongue. Her body went rigid, every muscle taut as the white-hot molten lava of pleasure ran through her whole body. She let out a shout, something guttural and primal that she couldn't contain if she tried. Her muscles relaxed once more as she sank backward, her body feeling like it had lost all its bones. Her breath came hard, and her heart thumped in her chest.

Beck kissed the inside of her thigh.

"I love it when you come. You're so beautiful," he said. She had needed that. In fact, the last time she'd come like that…she'd been on Beck's couch. She wondered if any man could make her come like Beck did: hard and fast, with the sudden, earth-shattering shock she felt through her whole body, the after tremors coming in waves. Beck was on the move, slinking up beside her on the floor as she lay, spent, wondering how she could ever want sex again after a climax like that. She rolled over to face him and then they were kissing as she snaked a hand behind his head and threw a leg over his side. She could taste herself on his tongue, and soon the desire began to rise again in her belly. She forgot how easily Beck could make her want more, how she seemed never to get enough of the man. He was all muscle and talented hands.

She tugged at the waistband of his jeans, blinded with the need for more, and as he fell heavy and hard against her stomach, her white-hot want grew. He tossed his jeans aside, along with his wallet and his phone, not that he seemed to care.

"Condom?" she asked, but he was already reaching for his wallet. He pulled a single condom out and in seconds had rolled it down his shaft, the firelight behind him as the wood cracked and popped in the hearth. Then she pushed him back down, his back on the rug now, and took control. She straddled him and slowly, ever so slowly, began to move, each millimeter a delight of new sensation, as he filled her in the way she'd longed to be filled these last two months. Firelight danced on his bare skin as he grabbed her hips and moved her himself, a little faster, a little deeper. Sweat trickled down the back of her neck, the heat of the fire warm, as she lifted her hair to cool herself, both hands in her hair, her eyes on Beck. His gaze never left hers. He moved his hands up her torso and then cupped her breasts, and she arched into his hands, eyes fluttering shut. Pleasure, building, beautiful pleasure, rolled through her body as she picked up the pace. He groaned and she opened her eyes once more, eager to see his need grow on his face. She missed that, the want in his eyes for her.

"God, Al," he groaned, his thrusts deeper now, more urgent.

"Do you want me?" she asked, as she took him harder, her hips moving faster, grinding against his. She wanted to hear him beg, she realized. She wanted him to need her as much as she needed him.

"Yes," he admitted.

"How bad do you want me?" She suddenly broke contact, lifting her hips away from him, and he slipped free. He groaned, clutching at her, seemingly desperate to be inside her once more.

"Bad, Al. I want you so bad." She could see the need in his eyes, see the want. It fueled her, drove her. This was what she needed, his want. His need for her. She took her hand and wrapped it around him, working him with furious, long strokes. He threw his head back on the rug. "I want to be in you."

"Do you?" She teased him more with her hand, working him from root to tip.

"Al…" His voice was a warning, as he suddenly flipped her over on the floor, and she lost her grip on him. He was inside her then, making her gasp with surprise, the shock of him, fully taking her, delicious. He wouldn't be denied as he raked his chest against hers.

"God, I love this body. You're amazing."

Her whole body shivered with the compliment, its pulse purring in her veins. She loved Beck's attention. She couldn't apologize for it, either. She loved making him hot, making him lose control. She loved how even now his eyes burned with pure want. She felt heady with that power, and for once, it didn't feel like she was the one so powerless after all.

She lifted her hands and tangled her fingers in his soft blond hair, as her legs wrapped around his waist as she invited him in deeper, ever deeper. He groaned as she squeezed him. He pushed himself up on his elbows, and then the palms of his hands, and he gazed at her as he slowed the rhythm. His amazing chest muscles worked, and she traced them with her fingertips, awed by the simple beauty of his body in motion. This body he'd taken and pushed to limits other men didn't dream of, and now it was here in front of her and she was exploring it in ways she could never imagine tiring of. She stroked his body as if it belonged to her, because for this moment, this one moment, it did. She met his stare and for a second was fixed by it.

"I want to feel you in every way possible," Beck said, and he withdrew, rolling her over on her belly. It was primal, rabid, raw, as he pushed himself against her, entering her from behind. She gasped as he pushed between her legs, again and again and again, her chest against the carpet, his mouth on her ear. She felt primal, base, driven by pure animal instinct. No rules. No words. Just what the bodies did best.

"I think you need to be teased," he said, as he withdrew himself from her.

"No," she murmured. She wanted him in her, more than she wanted to breathe.

He moved his fingers between her legs, stroking her, making her pant with heat and need. "God, you're so wet. So very, very wet."

"I'm wet for you," she managed, voice hoarse.

He grabbed her by the waist and raised her up. He wanted her on all fours, and she wanted to be there. She loved and hated that he had all the control. But there was something delicious about giving in, giving up to her desire for him. He grabbed her by the hips and entered her fast, hard, the way she wanted it. He worked her hard, and the muscles in her arms strained as she struggled to keep herself upright. She loved the sound of him against her, how it felt being on all fours for him. She was surprised by how much she liked it, by how she wanted more. By how she felt like a dog in heat, run by pure animal need. This was what she was made to do. This was what her body needed. He reached around then, finding her most tender spot, and began rubbing it, ever so softly.

"You're going to come like this," he promised her, and she believed him. And then it was all him: his hands, his very hard self, and she knew she'd come again. She was already at the edge, and all it took was a gentle flick of the pad of his finger against her clit, and then she was toppling over the edge, plummeting into the great abyss. She clenched him, hard, crying out in a voice she hardly recognized. Pure animal. Pure release.

He pumped again and again, and then drove even deeper still, until he let out a guttural shout, and then, he, too, came at a deep, hard thrust, which he held fast against her. She took it, loved taking it, and when he collapsed on her back, sweaty and spent, she felt a glowing sense of pure accomplishment. That was sex worthy of any god. They fell together on the floor, needs temporarily satiated, and Beck spooned her protectively from behind. She felt so warm, so safe, so happy. It was the happiest she'd been in two months. The persistent ache in her chest was gone for the first time in a long time. Words bubbled up in her throat, like fizzy champagne, unable to be contained. She felt them coming, felt them take flight, and this time, there was no stopping them.

"I love you."

CHAPTER ELEVEN

BECK FROZE, HIS ARMS around Allie. The L-word landed loud and heavy in the room, and as much as he wanted to say *I love you, too*, the words dried up on his tongue, the familiar fear dragging them downward, keeping them deep inside him. He hated the L-word, hated how people threw it around so carelessly, so effortlessly. He'd never been able to say it all that easily. Hadn't been raised in a family where they said it routinely, by rote. He told himself that was because when he said it, he meant it. Except that what ended up happening was that he never said it at all. Not to his mother. Not even to his father, who died of an overdose at the hospital days before Beck's eighteenth birthday.

He knew in his heart he felt more for Allie than he'd ever felt for anyone. Was that love? It could be. So why couldn't he say it? Why was he such a coward that the words couldn't come out of his mouth? So he hugged her tighter to his chest, because he knew, without a doubt, that he was about to ruin this moment, about to possibly lose the only thing that mattered to him. It was as if that inky blackness in him, his father's legacy, had taken control of his vocal cords. But he knew that was a cop-out. He glanced past Allie to the Christmas tree near her window and felt like one of its bright silver balls was lodged in his throat. "I...need you."

That was horrible. He knew it was horrible, but it was the best he could do. He could admit he needed her, so why couldn't he say out loud he loved her? Meanwhile, Allie was pulling away from him, moving out of his arms. He could feel the distance growing between them, and he knew he put it there. He'd made this happen. And he felt lousy about it. But wasn't this what Beck men did? Pushed away the people who loved them?

Allie was silent for a minute, and he could feel all the wheels whirling in her head. He knew she'd be poring over this conversation in her mind, worrying over each word, and he hated that he'd done that to her. Something shifted between them. A wall had gone up between them in the space of a few seconds, made of something even harder than concrete and steel. He knew it was all his fault. He'd do anything he could to make her happy again, except that he knew the one thing that he couldn't give. Something in him was broken. He'd known it for a long time. And now Allie did, too.

Allie felt like a fool. She'd thought maybe Beck *might* say "I love you, too." Honestly, she was kicking herself for even saying it in the first place. She might as well just open the door so he could run out as fast as he could. What was she thinking? She hadn't been thinking, and that was the whole damn problem. She'd let the moment sweep her away, delirious with the aftershocks of Beck's hands and his tongue. Anytime she thought of the long pause after she'd said those awful three little words, she felt herself inwardly cringe. Yet he'd said he *needed* her. Was that good enough?

Her heart told her no.

Her heart told her that wasn't good enough, not by a long shot, and that needing wasn't the same as loving. Part of her felt confident Beck would come around, maybe, but another part of her felt tired of waiting. He'd slept over, but he might as well have been a million miles away. He managed to fall asleep, but Allie had lain there most of the night with her eyes wide open, trying to figure out what she was going to do next. She decided in the dark of the night that there really was only one solution to her problem with Beck. Only one thing she could do.

She must've fallen asleep in the wee hours of the morning, because she woke to find Beck tugging up his jeans.

"Leaving?" she asked him, sitting up and rubbing the sleep from her eyes. A dull ache of a headache thudded in her temples, a clear sign of lack of sleep. Sunlight shone weakly through her window, so it must yet be early morning.

"Gonna hit the slopes," he said as he zipped up. "My Christmas Eve run down Pete's Peak." Allie suddenly had a vision of her life with Beck: of eternally chipping away at the emotional wall he'd built, of waiting, constantly waiting, for him to give her what she needed, but not quite meeting that want. While he wanted her, did he want to change himself? Did he want to heal himself? As much as she wanted to do it, she knew she couldn't. Only he could do that. She sat silently, waiting for...what? An invitation to go along? He wouldn't invite her. This was Christmas. The time he ran away from everyone he cared about, when he cocooned himself in bad memories. She realized she had to make a change. She needed to do it. For herself, and probably for Beck, too.

"I'm moving to Denver." The words came out easily, but they landed heavily in the room. She'd decided this overnight when it seemed the only answer.

Beck froze as he pulled his shirt over his head. Then he quickly pulled it down and turned, eyeing her.

"Why?"

"I've got a job offer. For an accounting firm. Pays better."

"I thought you loved being your own boss." Beck moved closer and sat on the bed. His weight bounced her a little as she tried to read his face. Why wasn't he talking about *them*? But then, she knew why. There was no them.

Was he disappointed? Did she even want him to be? Wouldn't it be easier if this was just a clean break?

"I think it's better this way, if I go." Because she knew she would always be holding on to him if she stayed in the same town; she'd always be hoping he'd change. She realized she'd been waiting for him to change for years, waiting for him to want to change, and she couldn't wait any longer. She'd waited first for him to be more than a friend, and that had taken years, and now, when they were so close to being more, he didn't seem to want to move, to bend, to change at all. Worse, Beck wasn't arguing with her. He wasn't saying anything at all. She was about to walk out of his life forever, but he kept silent. Maybe he wasn't even into the chase after all. Or maybe she'd finally figured out how to run far enough.

"When did you decide this?"

"I've been thinking about it awhile." She shifted and turned, propping herself on one elbow.

"But what about...us?" Beck looked crestfallen and she could feel his pain, a thin cut of a very sharp knife. A surprisingly deep wound.

"What are we doing? I know you're not going to give me what I want, and I won't be able to give you what you want." She sighed. "I can't stay away from you. And you're right. I can't do casual."

"Al." Beck's voice sounded heavy, sad.

"Whatever it is we're doing isn't working," she said. "And I'm not going to ask you to change who you are."

"Ask me, Al. Just ask me." There was desperation in his voice. But how could she ask him? He had to want to do it himself. She couldn't just ask him to love her. He needed to do that all on his own.

"I can't do that." She shook her head.

"This is about last night, isn't it. About me not saying…"

Allie almost laughed. He couldn't even say *I love you* now. In some ways, it just underscored the chasm between them, a gap that might never be bridged.

"Al, I just need time. Please." Beck took her hand in his. "Please, just give me a little time."

His pleading tugged at her heartstrings. She wanted to give him this and so much more. She wanted to wait forever. But she couldn't.

"I just want to be loved, Beck. That's all. Completely and fully," she said. "I don't think you're ready to do that. You might never be ready."

Beck didn't argue the point. "When are you leaving?"

"Don't know yet. Most likely the first or second week of January."

"Can I change your mind?" Beck asked.

"I don't know."

Beck fell silent a moment. "Will you come with me? Today?"

"I thought you always skied solo on Christmas Eve."

"I want you to come with me."

Allie thought for a moment.

"Okay," she said after a beat. Her time with Beck

was running out and she didn't have the heart to deny herself what time she had left.

Few skiers were on the mountain, which surprised Allie. But then, a storm was supposed to move in around lunchtime, and so most skiers had opted to stay in their condos. They were the smart ones, Allie thought, as the air had already dropped ten degrees by the time they'd made it to the ski lift, which would take them to one of Beck's favorite black-diamond runs. The backcountry he normal skied was closed for the weekend, due to avalanche alerts, and Allie was just fine with that. The idea of skiing unmarked trails was still a little terrifying. Allie shivered, even though she was wearing an extra layer, and the clouds seemed to hang low in the sky. It felt colder than any of the weather reports predicted. Her fingers tingled in her gloves and she gripped her ski poles a little tighter.

As they got on the ski lift, empty of all but them in line, the snow flurries started to fall.

"Are we going to have time to make this run before the storm comes?" she asked him.

"We should," he said, looking up at the sky and then at his phone. "Weather says the worst shouldn't hit until after two."

"That weather app has been wrong before." Allie remembered their time at the lodge and then felt a little heartsick about it. If they'd never gotten stuck there, would Allie be leaving for Denver? Probably not. She'd probably still be pining for Beck, waiting in the shadows of his friendship, hoping he'd take notice. Denver would be better than that, too, she thought. Denver offered the possibility of a fresh start.

They rode the ski lift to the top, the view breathtaking from the suspended metal bench. She wore her downhill skis and poles, a traditional skier, and Beck sat loosely, one foot out of his snowboard as it dangled. Beneath them, it was a long way down to the snowy ground, and up here, Allie felt like she could reach out and touch the treetops.

"I don't want you to go to Denver." Beck wouldn't look at her, as they both stared out into the cloud-covered mountain above them.

"I know. But I think I have to do it." She just didn't see a way forward where she and Beck worked, and she wasn't always running after him and he wasn't always running away, or vice versa.

"I told you I was trouble," Beck said. "I told you that you'd be better off without me. But now I'm in deep with you. I don't know how to let you go."

"That's why I need to leave. You've got things you need to deal with...your past..."

"Let's talk about something else," Beck said, his mood abruptly turning black.

For once, Allie obliged him. She had to, or she'd start crying on this damn lift, and that was not what she wanted to do. "So, no adventure tours today?"

"Gave my staff the rest of the week off," Beck said. "Willis, Gwen and Zach deserve it. We don't need to chase the holiday dollars. We've gotten a lot of good trips already this year."

Allie nodded, but then remembered something that had stuck out to her on the spreadsheets. "You just have three employees and yourself? No more?"

Beck nodded. "That's right. Why?"

"I have to go back and check the paperwork, but it seemed like you had much more in payroll this year. Did you hire more staff?" *Focus on the mundane, focus on the business*, Allie thought, as she watched his snowboard swing beneath the seat. She was pressed against him in the two-person lift, their shoulders square.

"Not that I know of. And I approve every hiring decision."

"You didn't hire contractors, maybe? Temp workers?" She rubbed her own skis together and watched the snow fall, mingling with the snowflakes already in the air, headed to the ground far below.

"No. Gwen handles the front office, and Zach helps Willis and me with the tours. I run a pretty lean operation."

"Did you give raises to Gwen or Zach or Willis? Or bonuses?" The wheels in Allie's mind were already turning. This was what bothered her about Willis's books. It seemed like he was paying *too* many people. But maybe he was just paying himself.

"No bonuses, and just the normal three-percent raise I give every year," Beck said.

"You're sure."

"Positive."

"Then I think there's something wrong with Willis's reports." She tried to tread carefully. She didn't want to throw around allegations, but she suspected he could be embezzling.

"Like what?" Beck frowned.

"I don't know. I went over the books. Payroll went up by thirty percent over last year. I thought you must've hired new people. Or given raises. Or both." Allie glanced at Beck's profile as he stared out into the cloud-covered mountain. "But if you didn't, then Willis's reports are off."

"Willis does payroll," Beck said, voice low. "I never wanted to mess with it. And whenever I suggested you could do it for us, he balked."

Allie felt a growing unease in her stomach. Willis was embezzling—she was becoming more and more sure of it by the second.

"Could he be stealing from you?" Allie almost hated to bring it up.

Beck seemed to shut down then. "No," he said. "He wouldn't do that to me. There's got to be another answer."

Allie knew she was right. She hated that Beck doubted her, but she also understood that his friendship with Willis went back years, longer than she'd known him. But it still irked that he wasn't taking her claims seriously. It just underlined the fact that Beck didn't really trust her, wasn't really letting her in his life. It couldn't be more crystal clear to her: moving to Denver was the right decision.

The ski lift spit them out at the top of the mountain, just as the wind kicked up and suddenly the snow started falling harder. Allie put down her goggles, protecting her eyes from the icy onslaught, and glanced down the mogul monstrosity before her, the double-black-diamond run that Beck had picked. She was a confident skier, but even her confidence was challenged by the icy drop. And the increasingly poor visibility on the mountain.

They seemed to be the only two skiers crazy enough to take on this mountain today. Allie was beginning to regret her decision to come out. She feared that in the back of her mind she'd somehow wanted to believe that the magic of Christmas on Christmas Eve would fix everything. Beck would say he loved her and they'd live happily ever after.

"Visibility sucks," Beck said. "This isn't going to be easy." He glanced at the sky. "We could try to wait it out a bit, or we could call ski patrol and take a ride down. They could take us down in the snowcat or by snowmobile."

"Since when do you let the ski patrol babysit you?" Allie shook her head. "There's no way Liam Beck would let a little snow get in the way of a good run."

"Yeah, but…" He paused, looking at her. He didn't think *she* could make it. That was what this was all about.

"I can do it," she said, lifting her chin and adjusting her goggles.

"You don't have to, though. The storm is worse than predicted and coming in faster than we thought." Beck's warnings felt like a challenge.

"The fastest way is down. Isn't that what you always say?" she said, and she pushed off with her poles. There was really just one way down, and the faster she got to the base of the mountain, the faster this day would be done. She cut small turns around the moguls, the bumps hitting her knees as the force of gravity pulled her ever faster down the slope. She was fast, but Beck, of course, was faster. In seconds he'd caught up with her, zigzagging down the slope in front of her, cutting a winding S in the snow with the edges of his snowboard. It took her a minute to realize he was leading the way, his bright yellow jacket visible in the growing fog of snow. She was reassured by seeing him, as the trees on each side of the trail became harder and harder to see as the wind kicked up, flinging pellets of hard, icy snow against her goggles' lens.

The snow was nothing but ice, too, and her skis kept slipping as she willed them together with all the strength she had in her knees. At some point, Allie started to realize that she could barely see Beck. He was still just about twenty feet in front of her, but the snow was closing in, blurring his brightly colored jacket. She'd need to go faster, need to catch up with him. She drilled down, turning less and focusing on getting down that mountain even faster. Her skis felt only barely in her control on the icy incline, as if one small slip would send her crashing. She hit a bump and sailed into the air, flinging her arms out, and then landed hard, but managed by some miracle to stay on her skis.

Beck came into view once more. He moved like liquid—languid, easy, and yet she knew the effort it took to make taking this run look effortless. Then he disappeared again in the whiteout. Without Beck's yellow jacket it was quickly becoming a white blizzard of snow and she could barely see the tip of her own skis as they dived in and out of the newly fallen snow. Allie caught up to Beck once more. She watched as he took a wide turn, hit a ramp of ice and flew into the air, grabbing his snowboard's edge. Magnificent, really, she thought. He was an amazing athlete, so graceful, it was like watching a kind of dance.

He flew over a snow-covered boulder. He soared high in the air, but beneath him, Allie saw a dart of green. What the hell was that? It looked like another snowboarder, who'd come from seemingly nowhere. Allie thought they were alone on this mountain, but she'd been wrong. The green-jacket skier seemed out of control and flailing, and Beck, midair, contorted himself to narrowly avoid hitting the man in the green jacket. But in the process, he caught his edge on an icy patch on landing and went flying. Head over feet, toppling into the snow in a massive wipeout. Allie's

heart leaped in her chest. It looked horrible: he'd pin-
wheeled, and now he was facedown in the snow. She
skied to him and slid to a stop.

"Are you okay? Beck?" she cried, throwing down
her poles and kneeling to unbuckle her skis.

"I'm fine," he groaned, as he got to his feet. He
knocked the helmet he wore. "That's why I wear this,"
he said. "Damn that guy. Did you see him? Out of
control."

Allie nodded. She stepped out in the snow. "Come
on, then. I can help you."

He took her hand and got up on his feet, but then
groaned in pain and toppled over. "Ah, dammit." He
looked down at his ankle in the snow.

"I think I twisted it."

"Bad?"

Beck tried to put weight on it and nearly crumpled.
He would have except he'd caught Allie's shoulder for
support. She held him upright.

"Bad," Beck said. "Can't put weight on it." He
pulled his phone from his pocket. "No service," he
muttered. "Not on this side of the mountain." Allie
checked her phone as well, but found the same problem.

"What are we going to do?" Allie's mind darted in
a dozen different directions. The storm was coming.
Pretty soon it would be impossible to find Beck at all,
even if she did ski all the way down to the base of the
ski lift so they could dial in for help. How would the
snow patrol find him in the middle of this black dia-

mond when visibility was next to zero? They'd have to wait for the storm to pass, and who knew when that would be.

"We need to get to one of the towers of the ski lift. It might have a direct line to the ski patrol, or we might get better cell reception there."

Allie took off her skis and stuck them in the ground in the shape of an X.

"Lean on me," she said, offering her arm. "We can both get over there. I don't want to leave you here."

She already felt the cold start to seep into her bones as the icy snow pelted her face. The temperature around them was dropping steadily. She needed to get him to help as soon as possible, and in this whiteout, she doubted she'd be able to find him again if she left him here in the middle of the slope. Even the trees at the edges were hard to see in the now nearly horizontal snow. The angle of the slope was about forty degrees, so walking across it would be tricky in the best of conditions, and these were far from those, but she was willing to try.

Beck leaned on her and they made it, limping, across the slope. "Are you sure the lift is this direction?" she asked him.

"Better be," he said. It wasn't like they could see more than ten feet in front of them.

Eventually, though, Allie thought she could make out something in the distance. A lift chair moving across the sky, the cables mostly obscured by the blowing snow.

"There," she said, as the two hobbled toward it.
Beck's weight was heavy on her shoulder, his arm
around her as he leaned, but she wasn't about to leave
him in the blizzard. About halfway to one of the ski
lift markers, she pulled out her phone and saw she
had one bar. She hit the emergency call button on the
screen and the phone connected with the ski patrol.
In minutes, she'd told them their location, and a unit
was dispatched to pick them up.

"You saved us," Beck said, gratitude lighting up
his face. "What would I do without you?"

Beck was a horrible patient. He barely had the pa-
tience to lie still for the X-rays in the emergency room
where he'd landed, after a quick trip to the first aid
station at the ski patrol outpost proved that his injury
was more serious than a sprain. It turned out he had
an ankle broken in three places, and he'd be grounded
from all outdoor sports for about six to nine weeks.
Worse, he'd been admitted for surgery on the damn
thing. He needed pins to stabilize it, and the sooner
the better, so he'd be in the operating room first thing
in the morning.

The doctors argued among themselves, too, about
whether or not this injury would affect his snowboarding. One thought he'd recover with no issue,
but another thought his ankle might very well never
be the same. The news should've sent him into a tail-
spin. It should've made him fear he was finally following the path of his father: risky sport, injury and

then his ultimate demise. But he didn't fear that. He didn't even really care so much about the ankle, about the worry of recovery. All he cared about was Allie. All he worried about was that she might leave for Denver and he'd never see her again.

Right now, she'd left the hospital and gone home to shower and change. She promised to come back with food, but he was kicking himself for letting her go without apologizing. For everything. For not saying "I love you," for insisting they ski on Christmas Eve instead of doing Christmassy things, for messing up her life so much that she felt the need to move hundreds of miles away to Denver.

Beck could not let Allie go to Denver. Especially when he knew she was moving *to get away from him*. If it was a job she couldn't refuse, that would be one thing, but he knew Allie better than anyone, and he knew she loved being her own boss, loved owning her own shop. It was one of the many things he admired about her. He was the same way. He loved owning his own business. He couldn't imagine working for someone else, and he didn't see Allie doing it, either.

Who would look after Allie in Denver? Hell, who would look after him? If the day on the mountain had shown him anything, it had shown him that she looked after him as much as he looked after her. That was what real partnership was all about. He had to think. He had to figure out how to keep Allie here, how to keep her in his life. He knew it wasn't fair to ask her to wait for him to battle his old demons, to finally and at long last grow up. Every adult thought about the future, but Beck realized he'd been using his past as a get-out-of-adulthood card, and that all needed to end and it needed to end now.

Maybe she was right. Maybe he wasn't his father. Maybe he could live a life free of his parents' mistakes. He would apologize and then he'd give her the Christmas present burning a hole in the pocket of his ski jacket. He planned to give her the gift…and ask her to stay. Permanently. And he just wanted to get it over with, because nerves were beginning to build in his stomach, and he wasn't used to feeling jittery. Very little made him nervous. He wasn't used to the feeling and he didn't like it.

But he was worried his request would be too little too late.

"Dude!" Beck looked up to see Willis standing at his door. "I heard the ski patrol took you down the mountain. You okay?"

"You sure you care about that, Willis?"

"Course I do, man." Willis stroked his long beard and edged into the room. He looked like he always did: worn jeans, hoodie sporting the logo of some craft beer Beck had never heard of. But he might as well have been a stranger.

"Why don't you want Allie to take over our payroll? Really." As he'd had a couple of hours lying around in this bed with his foot in traction, Beck had a little bit of time to think about everything Allie had said on the lift. And he'd used his cell phone to double-check all the payroll numbers in the business bank account, and he'd found that Allie had been absolutely right. Willis had been paying "overtime" to employees that never actually went to them, but had been diverted directly to his own account.

"She's all in your head, man. I don't think you see clearly when it comes to her. Don't know what you see in Greenie."

"What did you say?"

"You heard me."

Beck frowned. "Did you start those rumors about Allie? Give her that nickname?"

"Damn straight, I did." Willis almost seemed perversely proud of that accomplishment. As if tarnishing someone's reputation was a skill to be admired. "It was for your own good, Beck. She's too tame for you."

"Had nothing to do with you trying to break us up so you could save your own skin." Beck felt sick inside. He'd trusted Willis, and the betrayal ran deep. Insulting Allie was just salt in the wound.

He glanced up, eyes sharp. "What do you mean?"

"You want to explain the overtime? The overtime that went directly to your account?"

Willis shifted on his feet and stuffed his hands into the pocket of his hoodie. "I don't know what you mean, man."

"Yes, you do. I trusted you. And you betrayed me."

"Beck, please. I can explain."

Beck waited.

"I needed the money. I've been in trouble for a while."

"What kind of trouble?"

"Debt. Lots of it. I spend too much, got over my head with that house I bought last year and the new Jeep." Willis glanced away from Beck, ashamed.

"Why didn't you just come to me, then? I would've given you a loan."

Willis shook his head. "I didn't think you'd miss the money. You didn't care about it. You never really cared about it. You never once looked at the books. And, frankly, you haven't really given a shit about me, either. When was the last time we even *talked*, man? We used to grab beers all the time, but it's been months since we went out."

"So you steal from me?"

"I didn't know what else to do."

Beck shook his head. He wasn't going to take the blame for Willis's decisions. "I want you out of my sight. This partnership is dissolved."

"Beck, man. Please."

"No, Willis. How can I trust you now?"

A soft knock on the door took both men's attention. Allie stood there with a carryout bag filled with hamburgers and fries. "Come in, Al. Willis was just leaving."

Allie glanced uneasily at Willis, but he just brushed past her, muttering.

"Did you confront him?" Allie asked, when he'd gone.

"Yeah. You were right. He was stealing from me. I

can't really believe it." Beck shook his head. "I trusted him with everything." He glanced at Allie as she set down the bag of food at his bedside table. She looked beautiful in her skinny jeans and oversized sweater that showed both bare shoulders. She wore her auburn hair loose, and the fiery highlights shone even beneath the bright hospital fluorescent bulbs. He felt gratitude bloom in his chest. Allie had saved him on that mountain, showing the kind of resolve and courage that few people had. She deserved at least the same amount of courage from him. "I've got something for you."

Allie stopped unpacking food and glanced over her shoulder. "What?"

"Look in the right pocket of my ski jacket." She glanced at the jacket slung over a chair near the bed. She dug her hand in and pulled out the white box with the red ribbon.

"What's this?" Allie asked, surprise lighting her features.

"Merry Christmas," Beck said.

Allie looked shocked. "But…but I didn't get you anything."

"Open it."

She opened the box. A beautiful, delicate rose gold necklace shone there, with the simple word, *Al*.

"Beck." Her eyes filled with emotion. He saw tears in her lashes.

"Do you like it?"

"Like it?" She looked like pure joy. "I love it."

"Put it on."

Allie took it out of the wrapping and hung it around her neck. She latched the clasp and then it fell, right where he knew it would, in the small hollow of her neck. It gleamed in the light and looked perfect against her skin.

"It looks beautiful on you," he said. "Al. Come here." He reached out his hand and she took it. The contact felt so right.

"I love you."

"Beck." Emotion choked her voice. If she was going to cry, he would cry, too, he realized.

"I was an idiot for not saying it before. I love you. I've loved you since probably the first moment I met you. But I've been scared of what that means. All this time, I've been an idiot. I've been telling myself I'm protecting you, but I've just been protecting myself." He squeezed her hand and she squeezed it back. "But then, on the mountain, I broke my ankle and I thought…this is it. The injury that ends it all. I knew the injury would come one day and I used to think it would be the end of the world. I'd be like my dad. Lost, you know? But I wasn't. Because I had you. And I realized that if I have you, nothing else matters."

Allie seemed frozen to the spot, her eyes bright with emotion. He had to get the words out. He had to tell her how he felt. It was his only chance at making things right.

"Allie, I love you." The words flew out of his mouth, as if they were always intended for her. "I want whatever *this* is between us to be real. I'll do whatever it takes." He meant this, too. From the depths of his heart. "Allie, I don't want you to go to Denver. I know I have no right to ask you to stay, but I'm asking. I'll see a counselor. I'll get better. For you. Because I want to be the man you deserve. And if you decide to move to Denver anyway, then I'm going to open up an adventure company *there* and move right next door to you."

He held her hand tightly. Now the ball was in her court. She could still reject him. He prayed she wouldn't. Allie laughed a little as she swiped a tear from her eye. "So you are stalking me."

"I want to stalk you for the rest of your life, if you'll let me," Beck said. Allie leaned forward then and kissed him. "I never want to let you go again, Allie Connor."

"Is that a dare?" she asked him.

"One that I plan to keep," he said.

"Good," she said and took a deep breath. "Then I plan to stay and see that you do."

His heart filled with pure joy in that moment. Then he pulled her down to him and kissed her, tenderly, sweetly, with the promise of many more kisses to come.

EPILOGUE

One year later

THE SNOW JUST kept coming. Allie looked out the
window of Beck's lodge, the one that had changed
their lives forever, and watched as the snow poured
down outside, falling in the crevices near the windows, coating the big pines outside, and the deep
tread tracks left by the snowcat that dropped them
here. The only way in was by snowcat or helicopter, but that was just fine by Allie. A cozy, no-fuss
Christmas by the fire with Beck was exactly what
she wanted.

"I guess we can always count on a blizzard when
we come here," Beck said, laying a kiss on her bare
shoulder as he came up behind her. She was barefoot, wearing only an oversized sweater, nothing underneath. Since they'd arrived, they'd taken off their
clothes and had hardly put them back on. While not
a traditional Christmas, it was surely the kind of celebration that Allie could quickly grow to love.

"I guess so. I'm glad you didn't sell it, though."

Beck nuzzled her neck and Allie leaned back into his touch.

"Me, too," he said. "We've christened every possible inch of this place, I think. We should call it the Sex Lodge."

Allie laughed. "I like it," she said. "Is this where we spend every Christmas?"

"I hope so."

Beck hit a button on the universal remote and the speaker system in the place turned on, playing a familiar Christmas song. Allie turned, eyes bright.

"I thought you hated Christmas carols."

"I do, but you love them. And anything for the love of my life." Beck grinned and Allie threw her arms around his neck. "You've changed my mind about Christmas, anyway. It might not be so bad, especially if we spend every year celebrating naked."

She broke the hug and then stood on her tiptoes to kiss him. She meant it as a quick peck, but with Beck there wasn't any such thing as he tightened his arms around her lower back and deepened the kiss. Allie wondered if the man would always leave her breathless like this, make her heart pound like she'd just run a sprint. It had been a year, and she still couldn't keep her hands off the man, still thought she was the luckiest woman in Aspen. No…the world. The last year had brought all kinds of amazing surprises, but most of all, the fact that Beck had mastered a complete one-eighty. Once he put his mind to something, it happened, and overnight, the partying and the playing around stopped. She had worried she'd be jealous, of all the women who came before and of all that flirted with him now, but in reality, he showed her every day that he picked her above them all, and made sure she felt that choice all the time. She'd been worried he'd grow bored, but as the days passed, he seemed to fall only deeper in love with her. He was a partner in the truest sense, and she was so, so very glad she hadn't moved to Denver.

He'd been seeing a counselor, too, to work through his childhood a bit, and the changes had been extraordinary. A year ago, Allie would've thought Beck would've never opened up to a stranger, a clinician, but the counselor had helped him work through some of his issues with his father and mother, and he'd been processing his anger toward them and his deep-seated fear of rejection that he carried from his childhood. She'd shown him that locking away emotions hurt him and Allie. Honestly, she was so proud of how far they'd come, and she was bursting with hope for the future.

"You've got a surprise under the tree," Beck said, nodding at the small real fir he'd brought into his house. The Christmas decorations were just a little sign of all the progress he'd made.

Allie glanced at the large bright box, wrapped in a bow.

"And so do you," she said. "I'm prepared this time." She fetched the silver bag from beneath the tree.

Beck raised his eyebrows in appreciation. "What's

this?" he asked, taking the bag and pretending to weigh it in his hands and then shake it.

"Well, if I tell you, that would spoil the surprise."

He dug into the bag and pulled out a silver ID bracelet with longitude and latitude measurements. "What's this?" he asked again.

"It's the location of this place," she said. "This place changed everything."

Beck took the bracelet out and immediately put it on. "It's beautiful. I love it." He looked at her and nodded. "Now...you."

Allie opened up the large box, trying to guess what it could be. The box was light, and she wondered if it might be that cashmere sweater she'd been eyeing in the boutique she loved on Main Street. Except when she opened the box, she found another wrapped one inside. And then another one inside of that, and then she pulled out a box about two inches square. She opened it, too, but inside, she found a brilliant diamond ring, a flat emerald cut, which looked almost completely clear, like glass. Her mouth fell open. And when she looked up, she saw Beck, kneeling before her.

"I love you, Allie. You've made me a better person, a better man, and I want to spend the rest of my life with you. Will you do me the honor of being my wife?"

"You're proposing?" A million thoughts invaded Allie's mind at once. Beck—the eternal commitment-phobe, the sex god, the man who'd vowed never to settle down—was settling down? Part of her was surprised, but, even more shocking, part of her wasn't. She realized, all this time that she'd been so sure of Beck's love, so sure of his commitment, that the proposal felt…completely natural. The next inevitable step in their relationship.

"Are you going to say yes?" Beck was starting to look nervous. And that was when Allie realized she'd just been staring, mouth open, at the beautiful ring. "Do I have to *dare* you to marry me? Is that it?"

Allie just laughed and jumped into his arms, wrapping her arms around his neck and letting out a monstrous squeal. Allie couldn't believe this. In no way had she seen this coming. But her heart filled with joy. She wanted nothing more than to live the rest of her days by Beck's side.

"Is that a yes?"

"Yes, yes, a thousand times, yes!" She kissed him, and he kissed her back, and Allie felt the whole world grow a little bit brighter. The frequency that ran between them seemed to grow stronger then, louder, and she loved it.

Beck plucked the ring from the box and slipped it over her finger. "Well, that was the most stressful game of double dare you I've ever played," he said, putting his hand over his heart and pretending to be winded.

"What are you? Scared of a little game? Scared of a dare?"

"I'll dare you to do something, all right. Come over here," he growled and pulled her into his arms.

"I dare you to love me," Allie said, looking up at him.

"I dare *you* to love me forever."

"Double dare?" Allie asked.

"Double dare you," he said and grabbed her by the waist, pulled her into his arms and kissed the life out of her. Allie knew in that moment in Beck's arms, she was exactly where she was meant to be.

* * * * *

COMING SOON!

We really hope you enjoyed reading this book. If you're looking for more romance, be sure to head to the shops when new books are available on

Thursday 28th November

To see which titles are coming soon, please visit **millsandboon.co.uk/nextmonth**